BLEEDING EDGE

BLEEDING EDGE

THOMAS PYNCHON

Jonathan Cape
London

Published by Jonathan Cape 2013

2 4 6 8 10 9 7 5 3 1

First published in Great Britain in 2013 by
Jonathan Cape
Random House, 20 Vauxhall Bridge Road,
London SW1V 2SA

www.vintage-books.co.uk

Addresses for companies within The Random House Group Limited can be found at:
www.randomhouse.co.uk/offices.htm

The Random House Group Limited Reg. No. 954009

A CIP catalogue record for this book is
available from the British Library

ISBN 9780224099028 (cased edition)
ISBN 9780224099103 (trade paperback edition)

The Random House Group Limited supports the Forest Stewardship Council®
(FSC®), the leading international forest-certification organisation. Our books
carrying the FSC label are printed on FSC®-certified paper. FSC is the only forest-
certification scheme supported by the leading environmental organisations,
including Greenpeace. Our paper procurement policy can be found at:
www.randomhouse.co.uk/environment

Printed and bound in Great Britain by Clays Ltd, St Ives PLC

New York as a character in a mystery would not be the detective, would not be the murderer. It would be the enigmatic suspect who knows the real story but isn't going to tell it.

—DONALD E. WESTLAKE

BLEEDING EDGE

I

t's the first day of spring 2001, and Maxine Tarnow, though some still
have her in their system as Loeffler, is walking her boys to school. Yes
maybe they're past the age where they need an escort, maybe Maxine
doesn't want to let go just yet, it's only a couple blocks, it's on her way to
work, she enjoys it, so?

This morning, all up and down the streets, what looks like every Cal-
lery Pear tree on the Upper West Side has popped overnight into clusters
of white pear blossoms. As Maxine watches, sunlight finds its way past
rooflines and water tanks to the end of the block and into one particular
tree, which all at once is filled with light.

"Mom?" Ziggy in the usual hurry. "Yo."

"Guys, check it out, that tree?"

Otis takes a minute to look. "Awesome, Mom."

"Doesn't suck," Zig agrees. The boys keep going, Maxine regards
the tree half a minute more before catching up. At the corner, by reflex,
she drifts into a pick so as to stay between them and any driver whose
idea of sport is to come around the corner and run you over.

Sunlight reflected from east-facing apartment windows has begun
to show up in blurry patterns on the fronts of buildings across the

street. Two-part buses, new on the routes, creep the crosstown blocks like giant insects. Steel shutters are being rolled up, early trucks are double-parking, guys are out with hoses cleaning off their piece of sidewalk. Unsheltered people sleep in doorways, scavengers with huge plastic sacks full of empty beer and soda cans head for the markets to cash them in, work crews wait in front of buildings for the super to show up. Runners are bouncing up and down at the curb waiting for lights to change. Cops are in coffee shops dealing with bagel deficiencies. Kids, parents, and nannies wheeled and afoot are heading in all different directions for schools in the neighborhood. Half the kids seem to be on new Razor scooters, so to the list of things to keep alert for add ambush by rolling aluminum.

The Otto Kugelblitz School occupies three adjoining brownstones between Amsterdam and Columbus, on a cross street *Law & Order* has so far managed not to film on. The school is named for an early psycho-analyst who was expelled from Freud's inner circle because of a recapitu-lation theory he'd worked out. It seemed to him obvious that the human life span runs through the varieties of mental disorder as understood in his day—the solipsism of infancy, the sexual hysterias of adolescence and entry-level adulthood, the paranoia of middle age, the dementia of late life . . . all working up to death, which at last turns out to be "sanity."

"Great time to be finding *that* out!" Freud flicking cigar ash at Kugel-blitz and ordering him out the door of Berggasse 19, never to return. Kugelblitz shrugged, emigrated to the U.S., settled on the Upper West Side, and built up a practice, soon accumulating a network of high-and-mighty who in some moment of pain or crisis had sought his help. During the fancy-schmancy social occasions he found himself at increasingly, whenever he introduced them to one another as "friends" of his, each would recognize another repaired spirit.

Whatever Kugelblitzian analysis was doing for their brains, some of these patients were getting through the Depression nicely enough to kick in start-up money after a while to found the school, and to duke

Kugelblitz in on the profits, plus creation of a curriculum in which each grade level would be regarded as a different kind of mental condition and managed accordingly. A loony bin with homework, basically.

This morning as always Maxine finds the oversize stoop aswarm with pupils, teachers on wrangler duty, parents and sitters, and younger siblings in strollers. The principal, Bruce Winterslow, acknowledging the equinox in a white suit and panama hat, is working the crowd, all of whom he knows by name and thumbnail bio, patting shoulders, genially attentive, schmoozing or threatening as the need arises.

"Maxi, hi?" Vyrva McElmo, gliding across the porch through the crowd, taking much longer than she has to, a West Coast thing, it seems to Maxine. Vyrva is a sweetheart but not nearly time-obsessed enough. People been known to get their Upper West Side Mom cards pulled for far less than she gets away with.

"I'm like in another scheduling nightmare this afternoon?" she calls from a few strollers away, "nothing too major, well not yet anyway, but at the same time . . ."

"No prob," just to speed things up a little, "I'll bring Fiona back to our place, you can come get her whenever."

"Thanks, really. I'll try not to be too late."

"She can always sleep over."

Before they got to know each other, Maxine would bring out herbal tea, after putting on a pot of coffee for herself, till Vyrva inquired, pleasantly enough, "Like I'm wearing California plates on my butt, or what?" This morning Maxine notes a change from the normal weekday throw-together, what Barbie used to call an Executive Lunch Suit instead of denim overalls, for one thing, hair up instead of in the usual blond braids, and the plastic monarch butterfly earrings replaced by what, diamond studs, zircons? Some appointment later in the day, business matters no doubt, job hunting, maybe another financing expedition?

Vyrva has a degree from Pomona but no day job. She and Justin are transplants, Silicon Valley to Silicon Alley. Justin and a friend from Stanford have a little start-up that somehow managed to glide through the dotcom disaster last year, though not with what you'd call irrational exuberance. So far they've been coming up OK with the tuition at Kugelblitz, not to mention rent for the basement and parlor floors of a brownstone off Riverside, which the first time Maxine saw she had a real-estate envy attack. "Magnificent residence," she pretended to kvell, "maybe I'm in the wrong business?"

"Talk to Bill Gates here," Vyrva nonchalant, "I'm just hangin out, waitin for my stock options to vest? Right, honey?"

California sunshine, snorkel-deep waters, most of the time anyway. Once in a while, though . . . Maxine hasn't been in the business she's in for this long without growing antennas for the unspoken. "Good luck with it, Vyrva," thinking, Whatever it is, and noting a slow California double take as she exits the stoop, kissing her kids on top of their heads on the way past, and resumes the morning commute.

Maxine runs a small fraud-investigating agency down the street, called Tail 'Em and Nail 'Em—she once briefly considered adding "and Jail 'Em," but grasped soon enough how wishful, if not delusional, this would be—in an old bank building, entered by way of a lobby whose ceiling is so high that back before smoking was outlawed sometimes you couldn't even see it. Opened as a temple of finance shortly before the Crash of 1929, in a blind delirium not unlike the recent dotcom bubble, it's been configured and reconfigured over the years since into a drywall palimpsest accommodating wayward schoolkids, hash-pipe dreamers, talent agents, chiropractors, illegal piecework mills, mini-warehouses for who knows what varieties of contraband, and these days, on Maxine's floor, a dating service called Yenta Expresso, the In 'n' Out Travel Agency, the fragrant suite of acupuncturist and herb specialist Dr. Ying, and down the hall at the very end the Vacancy, formerly Packages Unlimited, seldom visited even when it was occupied. Current tenants remember the days when those now chained and padlocked doors were flanked by Uzi-packing gorillas in uniform, who signed for mysterious shipments and deliveries. The chance that automatic-weapons fire might break out at any minute put a sort of motivational edge on the day, but now the Vacancy just sits there, waiting.

The minute she steps out of the elevator, Maxine can hear Daytona Lorrain down the hall and through the door, set to high-dramatic option, abusing the office phone again. She tiptoes in about the time Daytona screams, "I'll sign them muthafuckin papers then I'm outta here, you wanna be a dad, you take care of that whole shit," and slams the phone down.

"Morning," Maxine chirps in a descending third, sharping the second note maybe a little.

"Last call for his ass."

Some days it seems like every lowlife in town has Tail 'Em and Nail 'Em on their grease-stained Rolodex. A number of phone messages have piled up on the answering machine, breathers, telemarketers, even a few calls to do with tickets currently active. After some triage on the playback, Maxine returns an anxious call from a whistle-blower at a snack-food company over in Jersey which has been secretly negotiating with ex-employees of Krispy Kreme for the illegal purchase of top-secret temperature and humidity settings on the donut purveyor's "proof box," along with equally classified photos of the donut extruder, which however now seem to be Polaroids of auto parts taken years ago in Queens, Photoshopped and whimsically at that. "I'm beginning to think something's funny about this deal," her contact's voice trembling a little, "maybe not even legit."

"Maybe, Trevor, because it's a criminal act under Title 18?"

"It's an FBI sting operation!" Trevor screams.

"Why would the FBI—"

"Duh-uh? Krispy Kreme? On behalf of their brothers in law enforcement at all levels?"

"All right. I'll talk to them at the Bergen County DA, maybe they've heard something—"

"Wait, wait, somebody's coming, now they saw me, oh! maybe I better—" The line goes dead. Always happens.

She now finds herself reluctantly staring at the latest of she's lost count how many episodes of inventory fraud involving gizmo retailer Dwayne Z. ("Dizzy") Cubitts, known throughout the Tri-State Area for his "Uncle Dizzy" TV commercials, delivered as he is spun around at high speed on some kind of a turntable, like a little kid trying to get high ("Uncle Dizzy! Turns prices around!") schlepping closet organizers, kiwi peelers, laser-assisted wine-bottle openers, pocket rangefinders that scan the lines at the checkout and calculate which is likely to be shortest, audible alarms that attach to your TV remote so you'll never lose it, unless you lose the remote for the alarm also. None of them for sale in stores yet, but they can be seen in action any late night on TV.

Though he has approached the gates of Danbury more than once, Dizzy remains gripped in a fatality for sublegal choices, putting Maxine herself on moral pathways that would make a Grand Canyon burro think twice. The problem being Dizzy's charm, at least a just-off-the-turntable naïveté that Maxine can't quite believe is fake. For the ordinary fraudster, family disruption, public shame, some time in the joint are enough to get them to seek legal if not honest employment. But even among the low-stakes hustlers she is doomed to deal with, Dizzy's learning curve is permanently flatlined.

Since yesterday an Uncle Dizzy's branch manager out on Long Island, some stop on the Ronkonkoma line, has been leaving increasingly disoriented messages. A warehouse situation, inventory irregularities, something a little different, fucking Dizzy, please. When will Maxine be allowed to kick back, become Angela Lansbury, dealing only with class tickets, instead of exiled out here among the dim and overextended?

On her last Uncle Dizzy field visit out there, Maxine came around the corner of a towering stack of cartons and actually collided with whom but Dizzy himself, wearing a Crazy Eddie T-shirt in eye-catching yellow, creeping around behind some auditing team, average age of twelve, their firm being notorious for hiring solvent abusers, videogame addicts, diagnosed cases of impaired critical thinking, and assigning them immediately to asset inventory.

"Dizzy, what."

"Oops, I did it again, as Britney always sez."

"Look at this," stomping up and down the aisles taking and lifting sealed cartons at random. A number of these, to somebody's surprise maybe, not Maxine's, seemed, though sealed, to have nothing inside. Gee. "Either I'm Wonder Woman here, or we're experiencing a little inventory inflation? . . . You don't want to stack these dummy cartons up too high, Dizzy, one look at the bottom layer and how it *isn't* buckling under all the weight on top? usually a pretty good tipoff, and, and this kid auditing team, you should really at least let them clear the building *before* you bring the truck up to the loading dock to shift the same set of cartons over to the next fucking *branch store,* see what I'm saying . . ."

"But," eyes wide as fairground lollipops, "it worked for Crazy Eddie."

"Crazy Eddie went to jail, Diz. You're headed for another indictment to add to your collection."

"Hey, no worries, it's New York, grand juries here will indict a salami."

"So . . . right now, what do we do? I should be calling in the SWAT team?"

Dizzy smiled and shrugged. They stood in the cardboard-and-plastic-smelling shadows, and Maxine, whistling "Help Me Rhonda" through her teeth, resisted the urge to run him down with a forklift.

She glares now at Dizzy's file for as long as she can without opening it. Spiritual exercise. The intercom buzzes. "There's some Reg somebody here don't have an appointment?"

Saved. She puts aside the folder, which like a good koan will have failed to make sense anyway. "Well, Reg. Do get your ass on in here. Long time."

2

Couple years in fact. Reg Despard looks considerably hammered at by the interval. He's a documentary guy who began as a movie pirate back in the nineties, going into matinees with a borrowed camcorder to tape first-run features off the screen, from which he then duped cassettes that he sold on the street for a dollar, two sometimes if he thought he could get it, often turning a profit before the movie was through its opening weekend. Professional quality tended to suffer around the edges, noisy filmgoers bringing their lunch in loud paper bags or getting up in the middle of the movie to block the view, often for minutes of running time. Reg's grip on the camcorder not always being that steady, the screen would also wander around in the frame, some-times slow and dreamy though other times with stunning abruptness. When Reg discovered the zoom feature on his camcorder, there was a lot of zooming in and out for what you'd have to call its own sake, details of human anatomy, extras in crowd scenes, hip-looking cars in the back-ground traffic, so forth. One fateful day in Washington Square, Reg happened to sell one of his cassettes to a professor at NYU who taught film, who next day came running down the street after Reg to ask, out of breath, if Reg knew how far ahead of the leading edge of this post-postmodern art form he was working, "with your neo-Brechtian subversion of the diegesis."

Because this somehow sounded like a pitch for a Christian weight-loss program, Reg's attention began to drift, but the eager academic persisted, and soon Reg was showing his tapes to doctoral seminars, from which it was only a step to shooting his own pictures. Industrials, music videos for unsigned bands, late-night infomercials for all Maxi knows. Work is work.

"Looks like I'm catching you at a busy time."

"Seasonal. Passover, Easter week, NCAA playoffs, St. Patrick's on a Saturday, da yoozh, not a problem, Reg—so what have we got here, a matrimonial?" Some call this brusque, and it has lost Maxine some business. On the other hand, it weeds out the day-trippers.

A wistful head angle, "Not an issue since '98 . . . wait, '99?"

"Ah. Down the hall, Yenta Expresso, check it out, coffee dates are their specialty, first latte grosso's free if you remember to ask Edith for the coupon— OK, Reg, so if it's nothing domestic . . ."

"It's this company I've been shooting a documentary about? I keep running into . . ." One of those funny looks Maxine by now knows better than to ignore.

"Attitude."

"Access issues. Too much I'm not being told."

"And are we talking recent here, or will this mean going back into history, unreadable legacy software, statutes about to run?"

"Nah, this is one of the dotcoms that *didn't* go under last year in the tech crash. No old software," half a decibel too quiet, "and maybe no statute of limitations either."

Uh-oh. "'Cause see, if all you want's an asset search, you don't need a forensic person really, just go on the Internet, LexisNexis, HotBot, AltaVista, if you can keep a trade secret, don't rule out the Yellow Pages—"

"What I'm really looking for," solemn more than impatient, "probably won't be anyplace any search engine can get to."

"Because . . . what you're looking for . . ."

"Just normal company records—daybooks, ledgers, logs, tax sheets. But try to have a look, and that's when it gets weird, everything stashed away far far beyond the reach of LexisNexis."

"How's that?"

"Deep Web? No way for surface crawlers to get there, not to mention the encryption and the strange redirects—"

Oh. "Maybe you need more of an IT type to look at this? 'cause I'm not really—"

"Already have one on the case. Eric Outfield, Stuyvesant genius, certified badass, popped at a tender age for computer tampering, trust him totally."

"Who are these people, then?"

"A computer-security firm downtown called hashslingrz."

"Heard of them around, yes doing quite well indeed, p/e ratio approaching the science-fictional, hiring all over the place."

"Which is the angle I want to take. Survive and prosper. Upbeat, right?"

"But . . . wait . . . a movie about hashslingrz? Footage of what, nerds staring at screens?"

"Original script had a lot of car chases, explosions, but somehow the budget . . . I have this tiny advance the company's kicking in, plus I'm allowed total access, or so I thought till yesterday, which is when I figured I'd better see you."

"Something in the accounting."

"Just like to know who I'm working for. I haven't sold my soul yet—well, maybe a couple bars of rhythm and blues here and there, but I figured I'd better have Eric do some looking around. You know anything about their CEO, Gabriel Ice?"

"Dimly." Cover stories in the trades. One of the boy billionaires who walked away in one piece when the dotcom fever broke. She can recall photos, off-white Armani suit, tailor-made beaver fedora, not actually bestowing papal blessings right and left but prepared to should the need arise . . . permission note from his parents instead of a pocket square. "I read as far as I could, I'm not, like, gripped. He makes Bill Gates look charismatic."

"That's only his party mask. He has deep resources."

"You're suggesting what, mob, covert ops?"

"According to Eric, a purpose on earth written in code none of us can read. Except maybe for 666, which tends to recur. Reminds me, you still have that concealed-carry permit?"

"Licensed to pack, ready to roll, uh-huh . . . why?"

A little evasive, "These people are not . . . what you usually find in the tech world."

"Like . . ."

"Nowhere near geeky enough, for one thing."

"That's . . . it? Reg, in my vast experience, embezzlers don't need shooting at very often. Some public humiliation usually does the trick."

"Yeah," almost apologetic, "but suppose this isn't embezzlement. Or not only. Suppose there's something else."

"Deep. Sinister. And they're all in on it together."

"Too paranoid for you?"

"Not me, paranoia's the garlic in life's kitchen, right, you can never have too much."

"So then there shouldn't be any problem . . ."

"I hate when people say that. But sure, I'll have a look and let you know."

"Ah-right! Makes a man feel like Erin Brockovich!"

"Hm. Well, we do come to an awkward question. I guess you aren't here to hire me or anything, right? Not that I mind working on spec, it's just that there are ethical angles here, such as ambulance chasing?"

"Don't you people have an oath? Like if you see fraud in progress—?"

"That was *Fraudbusters*, they had to cancel it, gave people too many ideas. Rachel Weisz wasn't bad, though."

"Just sayin that 'cause you're lookalikes." Smiling, hands and thumbs up as if framing a shot.

"Why, Reg."

This was a point you always got to with Reg. First time they met was on a cruise, if you think of "cruise" in maybe more of a specialized way. In the wake of her separation, back in what still isn't quite The Day, from her then husband, Horst Loeffler, after too many hours indoors with the blinds drawn listening on endless repeat to Stevie Nicks singing "Land-slide" on a compilation tape she ignored the rest of, drinking horrible Crown Royal Shirley Temples and chasing them with more grenadine directly from the bottle and going through a bushel per day of Kleenex, Maxine finally allowed her friend Heidi to convince her that a Caribbean cruise would somehow upgrade her mental prognosis. One day she went sniffling down the hall from her office and into the In 'n' Out Travel Agency, where she found undusted surfaces, beat-up furniture, a disheveled model of an ocean liner that shared a number of design elements with RMS *Titanic*.

"You're in luck. We've just had a . . ." Long pause, no eye contact.

"Cancellation," suggested Maxine.

"You could say." The price was irresistible. To anyone in their right mind, too much so.

Her parents were more than happy to look after the boys. Maxine, still runny-nosed, found herself in a taxi with Heidi, who'd come along to see her off, headed for a terminal in Newark or possibly Elizabeth, which seemed to handle mostly freighters, in fact Maxine's "cruise" ship turned out to be the Hungarian tramp container vessel M/V *Aristide Olt*, sailing under a Marshallese flag of convenience. It wasn't till her first night out at sea that she learned she'd actually been booked into "AMBO-PEDIA Frolix '98," a yearly gathering of the American Borderline Personality Disorder Association. Great fun, who would have dreamt of canceling? Unless . . . aahhh! She gazed back at Heidi on the pier, possibly having some schadenfreude, diminishing into the industrial shoreline, which by now was too far away to swim to.

At the first seating for dinner that evening, she found a crowd in the mood to party, gathered beneath a banner reading WELCOME BORDER-LINES! The captain appeared nervous and kept finding excuses to spend time under the tablecloth of his table. About every minute and a half, a deejay cued up the semiofficial AMBOPEDIA anthem, Madonna's "Borderline" (1984), with everybody joining in on the part that goes "O-ver the bor-derlinnne!!!" with a peculiar emphasis on the final *n* sound. Some sort of tradition, Maxine imagined.

Later in the evening, she noticed a calmly drifting presence, eyeball stuck to a viewfinder, taping lensworthy targets of opportunity with a Sony VX2000, moving from guest to guest, allowing them to talk or not talk, whatever, and this turned out to be Reg Despard.

Thinking it might be a way out of this possibly horrible mistake she'd made, she tried to follow him on his pathway among the merrymakers. "Hey," after a while, "a stalker, I'm finally in the big time."

"Didn't mean to—"

"No, actually you could help me distract them a little, not feel so self-conscious."

"Wouldn't want to compromise your cred, I'm weeks overdue at the colorist, this whole puttogether here ran me under a hundred bucks at Filene's Basement—"

"Don't think that's what they'll be checkin out."

Well. When was the last time anybody suggested even this obliquely that she qualified as . . . maybe not arm candy, but arm popcorn maybe? Should she be offended? How little?

Tracking from one group of attendees to another, locating presently a normal-enough-looking citizen with an interest in migratory-bird hunting and conservation stamps, known to collectors as duck stamps, and his perhaps-less-involved wife, Gladys—

" . . . and my dream is to become the Bill Gross of duck stamps." Not only federal duck stamps, mind you, but every state issue as well—having wandered with the years into the seductive wetlands of philatelic zealotry, this by-now-shameless completist must have them all, hunters' and collectors' versions, artist-signed, remarques, varieties, freaks and errors, governors' editions . . . "New Mexico! New Mexico issued duck stamps only from 1991 through 1994, ending with the crown jewel of all duck stamps, Robert Steiner's supernaturally beautiful Green-Winged Teals in flight, of which I happen to own a plate block . . ."

"Which someday," Gladys announces chirpily, "I am going to take out of its archival plastic, compromise the gum on the back with my slobbering tongue, and use to send in the gas bill."

"Not valid for postage, honeybunch."

"You staring at my ring?" A woman in a beige eighties power suit entering the shot.

"Attractive piece. Something . . . familiar . . ."

"I don't know if you're a *Dynasty* person, but that time Krystle had to pawn her ring? this is a cubic zirconia knockoff, $560, retail of course, Irwin always pays retail, being the 301 point 83 in the relationship, I'm just the supportive partner. He drags me to these things every year, and I end up pigging my way into a mid-two-figures dress size 'cause there's never anybody to talk to."

"Don't listen to her, she's the one who has all two hundred–whatever episodes on Betamax. Focused? you have no idea—sometime in the mid-eighties, she actually changed her *name* to Krystle. A less understanding husband might call this unnatural."

Reg and Maxine find their way eventually to the onboard casino, where people in ill-fitting tuxedos and gowns are playing roulette and baccarat, chain-smoking, leering back and forth, and grimly waving fistfuls of make-believe money. "Jujubes," they're informed, "Generic Undiagnosed James Bond Syndrome, whole different support group. Hasn't made it into the *DSM* yet, but they're lobbying, maybe the fifth edition . . .

always welcome here at convention time mostly for the stability, see what I'm saying." Actually, Maxine didn't, but bought a "five-dollar" chip and walked away from the table with enough, had it been real money, for a short trip to Saks if and when she was lucky enough to get back off of this.

At some point a face rosy with drink, fatefully belonging to one Joel Wiener, appears in the viewfinder. "Yeah, I get it, you recognize me from the news coverage, and now I'm just camera fodder, right? even though I was acquitted, in fact for the third time, on charges of that nature." Proceeding to unstopper a lengthy epic of injustice, somehow related to Manhattan real estate, that Maxine has trouble following in all of its nuances. Maybe she should have, it could've saved her some trouble down the line.

Borderlines by the boatload. Eventually Maxine and Reg find a quiet few minutes out on deck watching the Caribbean glide by. Cargo containers tower everywhere, stacked up four or five high. Like being in certain parts of Queens. Not yet mentally all the way on board this cruise, she finds herself wondering how many of the containers are dummies and what the chances might be for some seagoing inventory fraud in progress here.

She notices Reg hasn't made any attempt to get her on videotape. "I didn't have you figured for a borper. Thought you might be staff, like a social director or something." Surprised that it's been, oh, maybe an hour or more since she last thought about the Horst situation, Maxine understands that if she gets so much as a toenail's worth into that subject, Reg's camera will come on again.

The long-standing practice at these AMBOPEDIA get-togethers is to visit literal geographical borderlines, a different one every year. Shopping tours at Mexican *maquiladora* outlets. Gambling-addiction indulgence at the casinos of Stateline, California. Pennsylvania Dutch pig-outs along the Mason-Dixon Line. This year the destination borderline is between Haiti and the Dominican Republic, uneasy with melancholy karma dating back to the days of the Perejil Massacre, little of which has found its way into the brochure. As the *Aristide Olt* sails into picturesque Manzanillo Bay, things rapidly grow unfocused. No sooner has the ship tied up to the pier at Pepillo Salcedo than passengers preoccupied with large fish are excitedly chartering boats to go out after tarpon. Others, like Joel Wiener, whom real estate has driven from curiosity into obsession, are soon cruising local agencies and being dragged into the fantasies of those from whose motives greed, not to mention fuck-the-yanqui, must not be ruled out.

Folks ashore talk a combination of Kreyòl and Cibaeño. At the end of the pier, souvenir stands have quickly materialized, snack vendors selling yaniqueques and chimichurros, practitioners of voodoo and Santería with spells for sale, purveyors of mamajuana, a Dominican specialty which comes in gigantic glass jars in each of which what looks like a piece of a tree has been marinating in red wine and rum. For a cross-borderline cherry on the sundae, there's also been an authentic *Haitian voodoo love spell* laid on each jar of Dominican mamajuana. "Now you're talking!" cries Reg. He and Maxine join a small group who have begun drinking the stuff and passing jars around, presently finding themselves a few miles out of town at El Sueño Tropical, a half-built and for the moment abandoned luxury hotel, screaming through the corridors, swinging across the courtyard on jungle vines, which have found a purchase overhead, chasing lizards and flamingos not to mention one another, and misbehaving on the moldering king-size beds.

Love, exciting and new, as they used to sing on *The Love Boat,* Heidi was right on the money, this was Just the Ticket all right, though later Maxine would not be so sure of the details.

Picking up memory's remote now, she hits PAUSE, then STOP, then POWER OFF, smiling without visible effort. "Peculiar cruise, Reg."

"You ever hear from any of those folks again?"

"An e-mail now and then, and every holiday season of course

AMBOPEDIA's after me for a donation." She peers at him over the rim of her coffee cup. "Reg, did we ever, um . . ."

"I don't think so, I was mostly with that Leptandra from Indianapolis, and you kept disappearing with the real-estate obsessive."

"Joel Wiener," Maxine's eyeballs, in semi-horrified embarrassment, scanning the ceiling.

"I wasn't gonna bring that up, sorry."

"You heard about them pulling my license. That was indirectly Joel. Who, without meaning to, did me such a mitzvah. Like when I was a CFE I was cute, but a defrocked CFE? I'm irresistible. To a certain type. You can imagine what comes in the door, nothing personal."

The big selling point about a Certified Fraud Examiner gone rogue, she guessed, is a halo of faded morality, a reliable readiness to step outside the law and share the trade secrets of auditors and tax men. Having run into cultists who'd been expelled from their cults, Maxine was afraid for a while it would be that kind of social badlands. But word had gotten around, and soon Tail 'Em and Nail 'Em had more business than ever, more than she could handle. New clients were not of course always as reputable as they'd been in her licensed days. Darkside wannabes oozing out of the damn wallpaper, among them Joel Wiener, for whom she found herself cutting what turned out to be way too much slack.

Regrettably, Joel had somehow forgotten to include in his long recitals of real-estate injustice certain crucial details, such as his habit of committing serial co-op board membership, the beefs resulting over sums entrusted to him, typically, as co-op treasurer, plus the civil RICO indictment in Brooklyn, the wife with a real-estate agenda of her own, "It goes on. Not easy to explain," wiggling all her fingers above her head, "Antennas. I felt comfortable enough about Joel to share a few tricks of the trade. For me, no worse than an IRS guy moonlighting as a tax preparer."

But running her gravely afoul of the ACFE Code of Conduct, which

Maxine in fact had been skating up to and all along the posted edges of for years. This time the ice, without creak or visible darkening, had given beneath her. Enough of the review committee saw conflict of interest, not only once but a pattern, where for Maxine it was, still is for that matter, a no-brainer of a choice between friendship and super-picky guideline adherence.

"Friendship?" Reg is puzzled. "You didn't even like him."

"A technical term."

The stationery the decertification letter came on was pretty fancy, worth more than the message, which was basically fuck you, plus canceling all her privileges at The Eighth Circle, an exclusive CFEs' club over on Park, with a reminder to return her member's card and settle her bar tab, which showed a balance. There did seem to be a P.S. at the bottom, however, about filing an appeal. They included forms. This was interesting. This would not go into Accounts Shreddable, not just yet. Alarmingly, what Maxine noticed for the first time was the Association seal, which showed a torch burning violently in front of and slightly above an opened book. What's this? any minute the pages of this book, maybe allegorically The Law, are about to be set on fire by this burning torch, possibly the Light of Truth? Is somebody trying to say something, the Law in flames here, the terrible inflexible price of Truth . . . That's it! Secret anarchist code messages!

"Interesting thought, Maxine," Reg trying to talk her down. "So you filed the appeal?"

Actually, no—as days passed, there were always reasons not to, she couldn't afford the legal fees, the appeals process could all be just for show, and the fact remained that colleagues she respected had thrown her out on her ear, and did she really want back into that kind of vindictive surroundings. Sort of thing.

"A little oversensitive, these guys," seems to Reg.

"Can't blame them. They want us to be the one incorruptible still point in the whole jittery mess, the atomic clock everybody trusts."

"You said 'us.'"

"The certificate's put away in storage, but still hanging on the office wall of my soul."

"Some rogue."

"*Bad Accountant*, it's a series I'm developing, here, I got a script for the pilot, you wanna read it?"

3

The past, hey no shit, it's an open invitation to wine abuse. Soon as she hears the elevator doors close behind Reg, Maxine heads for the refrigerator. Where, in this chilled chaos, is the Pinot E-Grigio? "Daytona, we're out of wine again?"

"Ain't me drinkin that shit up."

"Course not, you're more of a Night Train person."

"Ooh. Do I really need wine-ism today?"

"Hey, you're off it so I'm just kidding, right?"

"Therapism!"

"Beg pardon?"

"You think twelve-step people's a lower class than you, always did, you on some spa program, lay around with the seaweed all on your face and shit, you don't even know what it's like—well, and I am telling you . . ." Pausing dramatically.

"You are not going," Maxine prompts.

"I am telling you, it is work, girl."

"Oh, Daytona. Whatever this is, I'm sorry."

So it all comes plotzing forth, the usual emotional cash-flow statement, full of uncollected receivables and bad debts. Bottom line, "Do not, ever, associate with nobody from Jamaica the island, he thinks joint custody means who brought the ganja."

"I was lucky with Horst," Maxine reflects. "Weed never had any effect on him at all."

"Figures, it's that white food y'all eat, white bread and that," paraphrasing Jimi Hendrix, "mayonnaise! All in your brain—every one of y'all, *terminally* honky." The phone has been blinking patiently. Daytona gets back to work, leaving Maxine to wonder why Rasta drug preferences should have anything to do with Horst. Unless Horst is somehow on her mind, which she can't say he has been, not that much, not for a while.

Horst. A fourth-generation product of the U.S. Midwest, emotional as a grain elevator, fatally alluring as a Harley knucklehead, indispensable (God help her) as an authentic Maid-Rite when hunger sets in, Horst Loeffler to this day has enjoyed a nearly error-free history of knowing how certain commodities around the world will behave, long enough before they themselves do to have already made a pile by the time Maxine came into the picture, and to watch it keep growing higher while struggling to remain true to some oath he apparently took at thirty, to spend it as fast as it comes in and keep partying for as long as he can hold out.

"So . . . the alimony's good?" inquired Daytona, her second day on the job.

"Isn't any."

"What?" having a good long stare at Maxine.

"Anything I can help you with?"

"That is the craziest crazy-white-chick story I have heard yet."

"Get out more," Maxine shrugged.

"You got some problem with a man partying?"

"Of course not, life is a party isn't it Daytona, yes and Horst was fine with that, but as he happened to think marriage is a party also, well, that's where we found we had different thoughts."

"Her name was Jennifer and shit, right?"

"Muriel. Actually."

By which point—part of the Certified Fraud Examiner skill set being a tendency to look for hidden patterns—Maxine began to wonder . . . might Horst actually have a preference for women named after inexpensive cigars, was there perhaps a Philippa "Philly" Blunt stashed in London he's playing FTSE with, some alluring Asian arbitrix named Roi-Tan in a cheongsam and one of those little haircuts . . . "But don't let's dwell, because Horst is history."

"Uh-huh."

"I got the apartment, of course he got the '59 Impala in cherry condition, but there I go, whining again."

"Oh, I thought it was this fridge."

Daytona is an angel of understanding, of course, next to Maxine's friend Heidi. The first time they really got to sit down and chat about it, after Maxine had gone on at a length that embarrassed even her.

"He called me up," Heidi pretended to blurt.

Right. "What, Horst? Called . . ."

"He wanted a date?" eyes too wide for total innocence.

"What'd you tell him?"

A perfect beat and a half, then, "Oh, my God, Maxi . . . I'm so sorry?"

"You? and Horst?" It seemed odd, but not much more than that, which Maxine took as a hopeful sign.

But Heidi seemed upset. "God forgive me! All he did was talk about you."

"Uh-huh. But?"

"He seemed distant."

"The three-month LIBOR, no doubt."

Though this discussion did go on, for a school night, quite late, Heidi's escapade doesn't rank as high as some offenses Maxine in fact still finds herself brooding about from back in high school—clothes borrowed but never returned, invitations to nonexistent parties, Heidi-arranged hookups with guys Heidi knew were clinically psychopathic.

Sort of thing. By the time they adjourned for exhaustion, it may have disappointed Heidi a little that her mad fling had somehow only found its natural place among other episodes of a continuing domestic series, begun long ago in Chicago, which is where Horst and Maxine originally met.

Maxine, in on some overnight CFE chore, found herself at the bar in the Board of Trade building, the Ceres Cafe, where the physical size of the drinks had long been part of the folklore. It was happy hour. Happy? My goodness. Irish, which for some says it all. You ordered a "mixed drink," you got this gigantic glass filled up to the brim with, say, whiskey, maybe one or two tiny ice cubes floating in it, then a separate twelve-ounce can of soda, and then a *second glass* to mix it all in. Maxine somehow got in an argument with a local bozo about Deloitte and Touche, which the bozo, who turned out to be Horst, insisted on calling Louche & De Toilet, and by the time they had this sorted, Maxine wasn't sure she could even stand up let alone find her way back to the hotel, so Horst kindly saw her into a taxi and apparently slipped her his card also. Before she had a chance to deal with her hangover, he was on the phone snake-oiling her into the first of what would be many ill-fated fraud cases.

"Sister in distress, nobody to turn to," and so forth, Maxine went for the pitch, as she would continue to, took the case, pretty straightforward asset search, routine depositions, almost forgotten till one day there it was in the *Post*, S-S-S-PLOTZVILLE! SERIAL GOLD DIGGER STRIKES AGAIN, HUBBY DUMBFOUNDED.

"Says here it's the sixth time she's cashed in this way," Maxine thoughtfully.

"Six that we know of," Horst nodded. "That's not a problem for you, is it?"

"She marries them and—"

"Marriage agrees with some people. It has to be good for something."

Oooh.

And why, really, go into the list? From check kiters and French-roundoff artists to get-even dramas that have pinned her revenge detector way over in the blind, forget-but-never-forgive, sooner-or-later-felonious end of the scale, still she kept going for it, every time. Because it was Horst. Fuckin Horst.

"Got another one for you here, you're Jewish, right?"

"And you're not."

"Me? Lutheran. Not sure what kind anymore 'cause it keeps changing."

"And my own religious background comes up because . . ."

Kashruth fraud in Brooklyn. Seems a goon squad of fake *mashgichim* or kosher supervisors have been making their way around the neighborhoods pulling surprise "inspections" on different shops and restaurants, selling them fancy-looking certificates to put in the window while rooting through their inventory stamping jive-ass *hechshers* or kosher logos on everything. Mad dogs. "Sounds like more of a shakedown racket," to Maxine. "I just look at books."

"Thought you might have a rapport."

"Try Meyer Lansky—no wait, he's dead."

So . . . some kind of Lutheran, huh. Way too early for any *shaygetz*-dating issues to arise of course, still, there it was, the outside-your-faith thing. Later on, deep in the first romantic onset, Maxine was to hear a certain amount of wild—for Horst—talk about converting to Judaism. How ironic that "Jew" also rhymes with "clue." Eventually Horst became aware of prerequisites such as learning Hebrew and getting circumcised, which triggered the sort of rethink you'd expect. Cool with Maxine. If it's a truth universally acknowledged that Jews don't proselytize, Horst certainly was and remains a prime argument for why not.

At some point he offered her a consultancy contract. "I could really use you."

"Hey, anytime," a piece of lighthearted industry repartee which this time, however, would prove fateful. Later on, post-nup, she grew much more careful with the blurting, reaching, in fact, along toward the windup there, almost to the point of silence, while Horst sat grimly pecking at a spreadsheet application he'd found in some Software Etc bargain bin, called Luvbux 6.9, totaling up sums in the range Hefty to Whopping he had spent for the sole purpose of getting Maxine to fall silent. To torture himself further, he then opened a feature that would calculate what it had been costing him per minute of silence actually obtained. Aaahh! bummer!

"Once I realized," as Maxine presented it to Heidi, "that if I complained enough, he'd give me whatever I wanted? just to shut me up? well, the romance, I don't know, somehow went out of it for me."

"As a natural kvetch, it got too easy for you, I understand," Heidi cooed. "Horst is such a pushover. The big alexithymic lug. You never saw that about him. Or rather, you—"

"—saw it too late," Maxine joined in on the chorus of. "Yes, Heidi, and yet despite it all sometimes I would almost welcome somebody that accommodating in my life again."

"You, ah, want his number? Horst?"

"You have it?"

"No, uh-uh, I was going to ask you."

They shake their heads at each other. Without needing a mirror, Maxine knows they look like a couple of depraved grandmas. An untypical adjustment to have to make, their roles being usually a little more glamorous. At some point early in their relationship, which has been forever, Maxine understood that she was not the Princess here. Heidi wasn't either, of course, but Heidi didn't know that, in fact she *thought she was* the Princess and furthermore has come over the years to believe that Maxine is the Princess's slightly less attractive *wacky sidekick*. Whatever the story of the moment happens to be, Princess Heidrophobia is always the lead babe while Lady Maxipad is the fastmouthed soubrette, the heavy lifter, the practical elf who comes while the Princess is sleeping or, more typically, distracted, and gets the real work of the princessipality done.

It probably helped that they both had East European roots, for even in those days you could still find on the Upper West Side certain long-lived intra-Jewish distinctions being drawn, least enjoyable maybe the one between Hochdeutsch and Ashkenazi. Mothers were known to shanghai their recently eloped children down to Mexico for quickie divorces from young men with promising careers in brokerage or medicine, or from ravishing tomatoes with more brains than the guy they thought they were marrying, whose fatal handicap was a name from the wrong corner of the Diaspora. Something like this happened in fact to Heidi, whose surname, Czornak, set off all kinds of alarms, though the matter didn't get quite as far as the airplane. On that caper it was the Practical Elf who acted as agent and presently bagperson, holding up the Strubels for a sum nicely in excess of what they had initially offered to buy Heidi, the little Polish snip, off. "Galician, actually," Heidi remarked. It was not for her the issue of conscience Maxine had been afraid of, for Evan Strubel turned out to be a feckless putz who lived in reflexive fear of his mother, Helvetia, whose timely entrance that day in a St. John suit and a snappish mood prevented Evan from putting further moves on Maxine herself, is how serious he was about Heidi to begin with. Not that Maxine shared details of young Strubel's perfidy with the Princess, settling for "I think he sees you mostly as a way to get out of the house." Heidi was far, further than Maxine expected, from desolated. They sat at her vast kitchen table counting the Strubels' money, eating ice-cream sandwiches and cackling. Now and then down the line, under the influence of assorted substances, Heidi would relapse into blubbering, "He was the love of my life, that evil bigoted woman destroyed us," for which the Wacky Sidekick would always be there with a witty remark like "Face it, babe, her tits are bigger."

Certain lobes of Heidi's spirit may have been compromised—because Mrs. Strubel had perhaps only casually threatened Mexican divorce, for example, Heidi presently found herself in a struggle with the Spanish tongue rivaling that of Bob Barker at a Miss Universe pageant. The language question in turn spilled over into other areas. Heidi's idea of the echt Latina seemed to be Natalie Wood in *West Side Story* (1961). It did no good to point out, as Maxine has done again and again with dwindling patience, that Natalie Wood, born Natalia Nikolaevna Zakharenko, came from a somewhat Russian background and her accent in the picture is possibly closer to Russian than to *boricua*.

Putzboy went on into a Wall Street apprenticeship, and has probably been through several more wives by now. Heidi, relieved to be single, pursued a career in academia, having recently been given tenure at City College in the pop-culture department.

"You totally pulled my meatloaf out of the microwave on that one," Heidi airily, "don't think I'm not eternally grateful."

"What choice did I have, you always thought you were Grace Kelly."

"Well, I was. Am."

"Not career Grace Kelly," Maxine points out. "Only, specifically, *Rear Window* Grace Kelly. Back when we used to surveil the windows across the street."

"You sure about that? You know what that makes you."

"Thelma Ritter, yeah, but maybe not. I thought I was Wendell Corey."

Teen mischief. If there can be haunted houses, there can also be karmically challenged apartment buildings, and the one they liked to spy on, The Deseret, has always made The Dakota look like a Holiday Inn. The place has obsessed Maxine for as long as she can remember. She grew up across the street from where it still looms over the neighborhood, trying to pass as just another stolid example of Upper West Side apartment house, twelve stories and a full square block of sinister clutter—helical fire escapes at each corner, turrets, balconies, gargoyles, scaled and serpentine and fanged creatures in cast iron over the entrances and coiled around the windows. In the central courtyard stands an elaborate fountain, surrounded by a circular driveway big enough to allow a couple of stretch limos to sit there and idle, with room left over for a Rolls-Royce or two. Film crews come here to shoot features, commercials, series, blasting huge volumes of light into the unappeasable maw of the entranceway, keeping everybody for blocks around up all night. Though Ziggy claims to have a classmate who lives there, it's far from Maxine's social circle, key money even for a studio in The Deseret said to run $300,000 and up.

At some point back in high school, Maxine and Heidi bought cheap binoculars down on Canal and took to lurking in Maxine's bedroom, sometimes into the early A.M., staring over at the lighted windows across the way, waiting for something to happen. Any appearance of a human figure was a major event. At first Maxine found it romantic, all the mutually disconnected lives going on in parallel—later she came to take more of a what you'd call gothic approach. Other buildings might be haunted, but this one seemed itself the undead thing, the stone zombie, rising only when night fell, stalking unseen through the city to work out its secret compulsions.

The girls kept hatching schemes to sneak in, swanning, or possibly pigeoning, their way up to the gate carrying street Chanel bags and disguised in designer dresses from East Side consignment shops, but never got further than a long, leering vertical scan from an Irish doorman, a glance at a clipboard. "No instructions," shrugging elaborately. "Till I see it on here, you understand what I'm saying," bidding them a peevish good day, the gate clanging shut. When Irish eyes are *not* smiling, you should have a better story or a good pair of running shoes.

This went on until the fitness craze of the eighties, when it dawned on The Deseret management that the pool on the top floor could serve as the focus of a health club, open to visitors, and be good for some nice extra revenue, which is how Maxine was finally allowed upstairs—though, as an outsider or "club member," she still has to go around to the back entrance and take the freight elevator. Heidi has declined to have anything more to do with the place.

"It's cursed. You notice how early the pool closes, nobody wants to be there at night."

"Maybe the management don't want to pay overtime."

"I heard it's run by the mob."

"Which mob exactly, Heidi? And what difference does it make?"

Plenty, as it would turn out.

4

Later that afternoon Maxine has an appointment with her emotherapist, who happens to share with Horst an appreciation of silence as one of the world's unpriceable commodities, though maybe not in the same way. Shawn works out of a walk-up near the Holland Tunnel approach. The bio on his Web site refers vaguely to Himalayan wanderings and political exile, but despite claims to an ancient wisdom beyond earthly limits, a five-minute investigation reveals Shawn's only known journey to the East to've been by Greyhound, from his native Southern California, to New York, and not that many years ago. A Leuzinger High School dropout and compulsive surfer, who has taken a certain amount of board-inflicted head trauma while setting records at several beaches for wipeouts in a season, Shawn has in fact never been closer to Tibet than television broadcasts of Martin Scorsese's *Kundun* (1997). That he continues to pay an exorbitant rent on this place and its closetful of twelve identical black Armani suits, speaks less to spiritual authenticity than to a gullibility, otherwise seldom observed, among New Yorkers able to afford his fees.

For a couple of weeks now, Maxine has been showing up for sessions to find her youthful guru increasingly bent out of shape by the news from Afghanistan. Despite impassioned appeals from around the world, two colossal statues of the Buddha, the tallest standing statues of him in the world, carved in the fifth century from a sandstone cliffside near Bamiyan, have been for a month now dynamited and repeatedly shelled by the Taliban government, till finally being reduced to rubble.

"Fuckin rugriders," as Shawn expresses it, "'offensive to Islam' so blow it up, that's their solution to everything."

"Isn't there something," Maxine gently recalls, "about if the Buddha's in your way on the path to enlightenment it's OK to kill him?"

"Sure, if you're a Buddhist. These are Wahhabists. They're pretending it's spiritual, but it's political, like they can't deal with having any competition around."

"Shawn, I'm sorry. But aren't you supposed to be above this?"

"Whoa, overattached me. Think about it—all it takes is, like, a idle thumb on a space bar to turn 'Islam' into 'I slam.'"

"Thought-provoking, Shawn."

A glance at the TAG Heuer on his wrist, "Hope you don't mind if we run a little short today, *Brady Bunch* marathon, you understand . . . ?" Shawn's devotion to reruns of the well-known seventies sitcom have drawn comment all up and down his client list. He can footnote certain episodes as other teachers might the sutras, with the three-part family trip to Hawaii seeming to be a particular favorite—the bad-luck tiki, Greg's near-fatal wipeout, Vincent Price's cameo as an unstable archaeologist . . .

"I've always been more of a Jan-gets-a-wig person myself," Maxine was once careless enough to admit.

"Interesting, Maxine. You want to, like, talk about it?" Beaming at her with that vacant, perhaps only Californian, the-Universe-is-a-joke-but-you-don't-get-it smile which so often drives her to un-Buddhist daydreams seething with rage. Maxine doesn't want to say "airhead" exactly, though she guesses if somebody put a tire gauge in his ear it might read a couple psi below spec.

Later at Kugelblitz, Ziggy gone off to krav maga with Nigel and his sitter, Maxine picks up Otis and Fiona, who are soon in front of the living-room Tube about to watch *The Aggro Hour,* featuring both of Otis's currently favorite superheroes—Disrespect, notable for his size and attitude, which could be called proactive, and The Contaminator, in civilian life a kid who's obsessively neat about always making his bed and picking up his room but who, when out on duty as TC, becomes a lonely fighter for justice who goes around strewing garbage through disagreeable government agencies, greedy corporations, even entire countries nobody likes much, rerouting waste lines, burying his antagonists beneath mountains of toxic grossness. Trying for poetic justice. Or, as it seems to Maxine, making a big mess.

Fiona is in that valley between powerhouse kid and unpredictable adolescent, having found, long may it wave, an equilibrium that nearly has Maxine wiping her nose here, as she considers on what short notice such calm can be disrupted.

"You're sure," Otis in full being-a-gent mode, "this won't be too violent for you."

Fiona, whose parents actually should consider heartbreaker insurance, bats eyelashes possibly enhanced by a raid on her mom's makeup supplies. "You can tell me not to look."

Maxine, recognizing that girlhood technique of pretending anybody can tell you anything, slides a bowl of health-food Cheetos in front of them, along with two cans of sugar-free soda, and waving *Enjoy,* quits the room.

"'Suckers beginnin to get me upset," murmurs Disrespect, as armed personnel carriers and helicopters converge on his person.

ZIGGY COMES IN from krav maga in his usual haze of early-adolescent sex angst. He has a big crush on his instructor, Emma Levin, who's rumored to be ex-Mossad. On the first day of class, his friend Nigel, overinformed and unreflective as always, blurted, "So Ms. Levin, you were what, one of those kidon lady assassins?"

"I could say yes, but then I'd have to kill you," her voice low, mocking, erogenous. A number of mouths had dropped open. "Nah, guys, sorry to disappoint, just an analyst, worked in an office, when Shabtai Shavit left in '96, so did I."

"She's a looker, huh?" Maxine couldn't help inquiring.

"Mom, she's . . ."

After thirty long seconds, "Words fail you."

There's also Naftali, the ex-Mossad b.f., who will kill anybody even looks at her sideways, unless maybe it's a kid who can't help having some preadolescent longing.

Vyrva calls to say she won't be there till after supper. Fortunately, you cannot call Fiona a picky child, in fact there's nothing she won't eat.

Maxine finishes up the dishes and puts her head in the boys' room, where she finds them with Fiona intensely attending to a screen on which is unfolding a first-person shooter, with a generous range of weaponry in a cityscape that looks a lot like New York.

"You guys? What have I been saying about violence?"

"We disabled the splatter options, Mom. It's all good, watch." Tapping some keys.

A store something like Fairway, with fresh produce displayed out in front. "OK, now keep an eye on this lady here." Coming down the sidewalk, middle class, respectably turned out, "Enough money to buy groceries, right?"

"Wrong. Check it out." The woman pauses in front of the grapes, so far in this dewy morning light unmolested, and without the least sign of guilt begins poking around, picking grapes off stems and eating them. She moves on to the plums and nectarines, fondles a number of these, eats some, stashes a couple more in her purse for later, continues early lunch at the berry section, opening up the packaging and stealing strawberries, blueberries and raspberries, scarfing it all down totally without shame. Reaching for a banana.

"What do you say, Mom, good for a hundred points easy, right?"

"She is quite the fresser. But I don't think—"

33

Too late—from the shooter's edge of the screen now emerges the front end of a Heckler & Koch UMP45, which swivels to point at the human pest, and, accompanied by bass-boosted machine-pistol sound effects, blows her away. Clean. She just disappears, not even a stain on the sidewalk. "See? No blood, virtually nonviolent."

"But stealing fruit, this isn't a capital offense. And what if a homeless person—"

"No homeless people on the target list," Fiona assures her. "No kids, babies, dogs, old people—never. We're out after yup, basically."

"What Giuliani would call quality-of-life issues," adds Ziggy.

"I had no idea grouchy old people designed video games."

"My dad's partner Lucas designed it," sez Fiona. "He calls it his valentine to the Big Apple."

"We're beta-testing it for him," Ziggy explains.

"Bearing eight o'clock," Otis sez, "dig it."

Adult male in a suit, carrying a briefcase, standing in the middle of the sidewalk traffic screaming at his kid, who looks to be about four or five. The volume level grows abusive, "And if you don't—" the grown-up raising his hand ominously, "there'll be *a consequence*."

"Uh-uh, not today." Out comes the full auto option again, and presently the screamer is no more, the kid is looking around bewildered, tears still on his little face. The point total in the corner of the screen increments by 500.

"So now he's all alone in the street, big favor you did him."

"All we have to do—" Fiona clicking on the kid and dragging him to a window labeled Safe Pickup Zone. "Trustworthy family members," she explains, "come and pick them up and buy them pizza and bring them home, and their lives from then on are worry-free."

"Come on," sez Otis, "let's just cruise around." Off they go on a tour of the inexhaustible galleries of New York annoyance, zapping loudmouths on cellular phones, morally self-elevated bicycle riders, moms wheeling twins old enough to walk lounging in twin strollers, "One behind the other, we let them off with a warning, but not this one, look, side by side so nobody can get past? forget it." Pow! Pow! The twins go flying, all smiles, above New York and into the Kiddy Bin. Passersby are largely oblivious to the sudden disappearances except for Christers, who think it's the Rapture. "Guys," Maxine astonished, "I had no idea— Wait, what's this?" She has spotted a line jumper at a bus stop. Nobody paying attention. H&Kwoman to the rescue! "All right, how do I do this?" Otis is happy to instruct, and before you can say "Be more considerate," the pushy bitch has been despatched and her children dragged to safety.

"Way to go Mom, that's a thousand points."

"Actually, sort of fun." Scanning the screen for her next target. "Wait, I didn't say that." Trying later to put a positive spin on it, Maxine figures maybe it's a virtual and kid-scale way of getting into the antifraud business . . .

"Hi, Vyrva, come on in."

"Didn't think I'd be this late." Vyrva goes and puts her head in Otis and Ziggy's room. "Hi, sweetie?" The girl looks up and murmurs hi, Mom, and gets back to yuppicide.

"Oh, look, they're blowing away New Yorkers, how cute? I mean, nothing personal?"

"You're good with this—Fiona, virtual murder sort of thing?"

"Oh, it's bloodless, like Lucas didn't even write in a splatter option? They think they're disabling it, but it's not even there?"

"So," shrugging away any scold signifiers in face and voice, "a mom-approved first-person shooter."

"That's exactly the slogan we're gonna use in the ads."

"You're advertising where, on the Internet?"

"The Deep Web. Down there advertising is like still in its infancy? And the price is what Bob Barker might call 'right'?" Air quotes, Vyrva's hair, back in braids, bouncing to and fro.

Maxine reaches a bag of some Fairway coffee blend out of the freezer and pours beans in the grinder. "Watch your ears a minute." She grinds the coffee, pours it into a filter in the electric drip unit, hits the power switch.

"So Justin and Lucas are branching into games now."

"It isn't really business the way I learned it in college," Vyrva confides, "at this point life should be serious? The guys are still having too much fun for their age."

"Oh—male anxiety, yes that's much better."

"The game is just a promotional freebie," Vyrva frowning cute-apologetic. "Our product is still totally DeepArcher?"

"Which is . . ."

"Like 'departure,' only you pronounce it DeepArcher?"

"Zen thing," Maxine guesses.

"Weed thing. Just lately everybody's been after the source code—the feds, game companies, fuckin Microsoft? all have offers on the table? It's the security design—like nothing any of these people've ever seen, and it's makin them all crazy."

"So, today you were out scouting your next round? Who's the lucky VC this time?"

"Can you keep a secret?"

"What I do. Professionally D and D."

"Maybe," Vyrva considers, "we should pinkie-swear?"

Maxine patiently holding out her pinkie, hooking it with Vyrva's and obtaining eye contact, "Then again—"

"Hey, if you can't trust another Kugelblitz mom?"

So, with the usual caveats, Maxine keeps her other hand in her pocket with fingers crossed as she solemnly pinkie-swears. "I think we got a preempt today? Even back at the height of the tech bubble, this would be awesome money? And it's not a VC, it's another tech company? Big deal this year down in the Alley, hashslingrz?"

Whoopwhoopwhoop. "Yeah . . . think I've . . . heard that name. That's where you were today?"

"All day down there. I'm still, like, vibrateen? He's a bundle of energy, that guy."

"Gabriel Ice. He's made you a big offer to buy, what, this source code?"

Ear to shoulder, one of those long West Coast shrugs, "He sure came up with a impressive piece of change from someplace? Enough to rethink the IPO? We already put the red herring on indefinite hold?"

"Wait a minute, what's with acquisition fever down the Alley, didn't all that go belly-up last year with the crash?"

"Not for the managed-security people, they're making out fiercely at the moment. When everybody's nervous, all corporate suits can think about is protecting what they've got."

"So you guys've been out schmoozing with Gabriel Ice. Can I have your autograph?"

"We went to an afternoon soiree over at his mansion on the East Side? Him and his wife, Tallis, she's the comptroller at hashslingrz, sits on the board too, I think?"

"And this is an outright buy?"

"All they want is, there's a part about getting somewhere without leaving a trail. The content, they could care less. It isn't about the destination or even the trip, really, not for these jokers."

Maxine is much too familiar by now, even God forbid intimate, with this cover-your-tracks attitude. Next it morphs from innocent greed into some recognizable form of fraud. She wonders if anybody's ever run a Beneish model on hashslingrz, just to see how ritually slaughtered the public numbers are. Note to self—find the time. "This DeepArcher, Vyrva, it's what—a place?"

"It's a journey. Next time you're over, the boys'll give you a demo."

"Good, haven't seen that Lucas for a while."

"He hasn't been around a lot. There's been, like, issues? He and Justin find any excuse to get into a fight. whether to even sell the source code in the first place. Same old classic dotcom dilemma, be rich forever or make a tarball out of it and post it around for free, and keep their cred and maybe self-esteem as geeks but stay more or less middle income."

"Sell it or give it away," some scrutiny, "tough call, Vyrva. Which one wants to do what?"

"Both want to do both," she sighs.

"Figures. How about you?"

"Oh? Torn? You'll think it's just hippyeen around, but I'm not that cool with a whole shitload of money crashing into our life right now? That can be so destructive, we know of one or two people back in Palo Alto, it gets ugly and sad so fast, and I'd rather see the guys keepin on with their work, maybe start up something new." A tilted grin. "Hard for a New York person to understand, sorry."

"Seen it forever, Vyrva. Direction of flow, in or out, don't matter, above a critical amount, it's all bad."

"Not that I'm living through my husband, OK? I just hate it when the guys argue. They're in love, for goodness sakes. They put on all this who-are-you-again-dude, but in fact it's like a couple of skateboarders together? Should I be jealous?"

"What for?"

"You know this kind of old-school movie where there's these two kids are best friends and one grows up to be a priest and the other turns out to be a mobster, well, that's Lucas and Justin. Only don't ask which is which."

"But say Justin is the priest . . ."

"Well, the one who . . . doesn't get into a shoot-out at the end."

"Then Lucas . . ."

Vyrva looks off into the distance, trying for Surf Bunny Gazes at the Sea but revealing instead a look Maxine has seen maybe more of than she wants to. Don't—don't put in, she advises herself, despite the all-but-irresistible question arising, Has Vyrva been shtupping, excuse me, "seeing" her husband's partner on the sly?

"Vyrva, you're not . . ."

"Not what?"

"Never mind." Both women then beam elaborately and shrug, one fast, the other slow.

Another unexplored corner here, of which there are already enough. Maxine has only recently for example found out about Vyrva and Beanie Babies. Seems Vyrva's been out running some arbitrage hustle with the trendy stuffed-toy/beanbag hybrids. Soon after their first play date, "Fiona has every Beanie Baby," Otis nodding for emphasis, "in the world." He thought a minute. "Well, every *kind* of Beanie Baby. Every one in the world, that'd be . . . like warehouses and stuff."

As happened off and on with the boys, Maxine was reminded of Horst, this time of his blockhead literalism, and she had to restrain herself from grabbing Otis, slobbering kisses and squashing him like a tube of toothpaste, and so forth.

"Fiona has . . . the Princess Diana Beanie Baby?" she asked instead.

"'The'? Good luck, Mom. She's got all the variations, even the BBC Interview Anniversary Edition. Under the bed, all in the closets, they're pushing her out of her room."

"You're saying Fiona's . . . a Beanie Baby person."

"Not her so much," Otis sez, "it's her mom who's totally the obsessive in the house."

Maxine has noticed that at least once a week, as soon as she has Fiona safely delivered at Kugelblitz, Vyrva is off on the 86th Street crosstown bus headed for yet another Beanie Baby transaction. She has compiled a list of retailers on the East Side who get the critters shipped all but directly in from China by way of certain shadowy warehouses adjoining JFK. 'Suckers don't just fall off the truck, they parachute out of the airplane. Vyrva buys them up dirt cheap on the East Side, then rushes back to various West Side toy and variety stores whose delivery schedules she has carefully recorded, sells them for a price somewhat lower than what the stores will pay when their own truck shows up, and everybody pockets the difference. Meantime Fiona, though not much of a collector, gets to keep on accumulating Beanie Babies.

"And that's just short-term," Vyrva has explained, quite, it seems to Maxine, enthusiastically. "Ten, twelve years down the line, college looming, you know what these are gonna be worth to collectors?"

"Lots?" Maxine guesses.

"Uncomputable."

Ziggy's not so sure. "Except for one or two special editions," he points out, "there's no packaging on Beanie Babies, which is important to collectors, and also means that 99–plus percent are out there loose in the environment, getting trampled, chewed apart and drooled on, lost under the radiator, eaten by mice, in ten years there won't be one in collectible condition, unless Mrs. McElmo is stashing them in archival plastic someplace besides Fiona's room. Like dark and temperature-controlled would be nice. But that'll never occur to her, because it makes too much sense."

"You're saying . . ."

"She's crazy, Mom."

5

As a paid-up member of the Yentas With Attitude local, Maxine has been snooping diligently into hashslingrz, before long finding herself wondering what Reg has gotten himself into and, worse, what he's dragging her uncomfortably toward. The first thing that jumps out of the bushes, waggling its dick so to speak, is a Benford's Law anomaly in some of the expenses.

Though it's been around in some form for a century and more, Benford's Law as a fraud examiner's tool is only beginning to surface in the literature. The idea is, somebody wants to phony up a list of numbers but gets too cute about randomizing it. They assume that the first digits, 1 through 9, are all going to be evenly distributed, so that each one will turn up 11% of the time. Eleven and change. But in fact, for most lists of numbers, the distribution of first digits is not linear but logarithmic. About 30% of the time, the first digit actually turns out to be a 1—then 17.5% it'll be a 2, so forth, dropping off in a curve to only 4.6% when you get to 9.

So when Maxine goes through these disbursement numbers from hashslingrz, counting up how often each first digit appears, guess what.

Nowhere near the Benford curve. What in the business one refers to as False Lunchmeat.

Soon enough, drilling down, she begins to pick up other tells. Consecutive invoice numbers. Hash totals that don't add up. Credit-card numbers failing their Luhn checks. It becomes dismayingly clear that somebody's taking money out of hashslingrz and starbursting it out again all over the place to different mysterious contractors, some of whom are almost certainly ghosts, running at a rough total to maybe as high as the high sixes, even lower sevens.

The most recent of these problematical payees is a little operation downtown calling itself hwgaahwgh.com, an acronym for Hey, We've Got Awesome And Hip Web Graphix, Here. Do they? Somehow, doubtful. Hashslingrz has been sending them regular payments, always within a week of each almost certainly dummy invoice, till all of a sudden the little company goes belly-up, and here are all these huge fuckin payments *still going* to the operating account, which somebody at hashslingrz has naturally been taking steps to conceal.

She hates it when paranoia like Reg's gets real-world. Probably worth a look, though.

MAXINE APPROACHES the address from the other side of the street, and as soon as she catches sight of it, her heart, if it does not sink exactly, at least cringes more tightly into the one-person submarine necessary for cruising the sinister and labyrinthine sewers of greed that run beneath all real-estate dealings in this town. Thing is, is it's such a nice building, terra-cotta facing, not as ornate as commercial real estate could get a century ago when this unit was going up, but tidy and strangely welcoming, as if the architects had actually given some thought to the people who'd be working there every day. But it's too nice, a sitting duck, asking to get torn down someday soon and the period detailing recycled into the decor of some yup's overpriced loft.

The directory in the lobby lists hwgaahwgh.com up on the fifth floor. Maxine knows old-school fraud investigators who'll admit to walking away at this point, satisfied enough, only to regret it later. Others have advised her to keep going no matter what, until she can actually stand in the haunted space and try to summon the ghost vendor out of its nimbus of crafted silence.

On the way up, she watches floors flash by out the porthole in the elevator door—folks in workout gear gathered by a row of snack machines, artificial bamboo trees framing a reception desk of wood blonder than the blonde stationed behind it, kids in school jackets and ties sitting blank-faced in the waiting area of some SAT tutor or therapist or combination thereof.

She finds the door wide open and the place empty, another failed dotcom joining the officescape of the time—tarnished metallic surfaces, shaggy gray soundproofing, Steelcase screens and Herman Miller workpods—already beginning to decompose, littered, dust gathering . . .

Well, almost empty. From some distant cubicle comes a tinny electronic melody Maxine recognizes as "Korobushka," the anthem of nineties workplace fecklessness, playing faster and faster and accompanied by screams of anxiety. Ghost vendor indeed. Has she entered some supernatural timewarp where the shades of office layabouts continue to waste uncountable person-hours playing Tetris? Between that and Solitaire for Windows, no wonder the tech sector tanked.

She creeps toward the plaintive folk tune, reaching it just as an ingenue voice goes "Shit," and silence follows. Seated in a half-lotus on the scuffed and dusty floor of a cubicle is a young woman in nerd glasses holding a portable game console and glaring at it. Beside her is a laptop, lit up, plugged into a phone jack on a wire emerging from the carpeting.

"Hi," sez Maxine.

The young woman looks up. "Hi, and what am I doing here, well, just downloading some shit, 56K's a awesome speed, but this still takes some time so I'm working on my Tetris skills while the ol' unit's crankin

along. If you're lookin for a live terminal, I think there's still a few scattered a round these other cubes. Maybe a couple pieces of hardware ain't
been looted yet, RS232 shit, connectors, chargers, cables, and whatever."

"I was hoping to find somebody who works here. Or who used to
work here's more like it I guess."

"I did do some temping here off and on back in the day."

"Rude surprise, huh?" gesturing around at the emptiness.

"Nah, it was obvious from the jump they were spending way over
their head tryin to buy traffic, the classic dotcommer delusion, before
you know it here's another liquidation event and one more bunch of
yups goes blubberin down the toilet."

"Do I hear sympathy? Concern?"

"Fuck 'em, they're all crazy."

"Depends what tropical beach they're lounging around on as we
continue to work our ass off."

"Aha! another victim, I bet."

"My boss thinks they might've been double-billing us," Maxine im-
provises, "we did stop the last check, but somebody thought we should
introduce a personal note. I happened to be in screaming distance."

The girl's gaze keeps flicking to the screen of her little computer.
"Too bad, everybody's split, only scavengers now. You ever see that
movie *Zorba the Greek* (1964)? the minute this old lady dies, the villagers
all go rushing in to grab her stuff? Well, this here's Zorba the Geek."

"No easy-open wall safes here, or . . ."

"All emptied out, the minute the pink slips showed up. How about
your company? Did they at least get your Web site up and running for
you OK?"

"Without meaning to offend . . ."

"Oh, tell me, tag soup, right, lame-ass banners all over the place random as the stall walls in a high-school toilet? All jammed together? finding anything, after a while it hurts your eyes? Pop-ups! Don't get me
started, 'window.open,' most pernicious piece of Javascript ever written,

pop-ups are the li'l goombas of Web design, need to be stomped back down to where they came from, boring duty but somebody's got to."

"Strange idea of 'awesome and hip web graphics' anyway."

"Kind of puzzling. I mean I did what I could, but somehow it felt like that their heart just wasn't in it?"

"That maybe Web design wasn't really their main business?"

The girl nods, consciously, as if somebody might be monitoring.

"Listen, when you're done here—I'm Maxi by the way—"

"Driscoll, hi—"

"Let me buy you a cup of coffee or something."

"Better yet there's a bar right down the street's still got Zima on tap."

Maxine gives her a look.

"Where's your nostalgia, man, Zima's the bitch drink of the nineties, come on, I'm buyin the first round."

Fabian's Bit Bucket dates from the early days of the dotcom boom. The girl behind the bar waves at Driscoll when she and Maxine come in and reaches for the Zima tap. They are soon settled into a booth behind a couple oversize schooners of the once wildly popular novelty beverage. At the moment nothing much is happening, though happy hour looms, and with it the onset of another impromptu pink-slip party, for which the Bucket has begun to get a reputation.

Driscoll Padgett is a freelance Web-page designer, "making it up as I go along, just like everybody else," also temping as a code writer, for $30 an hour—she's fast and conscientious, and the word has got around, so she's more or less steadily in demand, though now and then there's a gap in the rent cycle where she's had to resort to the Winnie list, or index cards stuck up next to dumpsters, and so forth. Loft parties sometimes, though that's usually for the cheap drinks.

Driscoll was over at hwgaahwgh.com today looking for Photoshop filter plug-ins, having like many of her generation acquired a Jones which has led them off on scavenger hunts after ever-more-exotic varieties.

"Should be custom-designin plug-ins of my own, been tryin to teach my-self Filter Factory language, not that hard, almost like C, but looting's easier, today I actually downloaded something off of the people who Photoshopped Dr. Zizmor."

"What, the babyface dermatologist in the subway?"

"Otherworldly, right? First-rate work, the clarity, the glow?"

"And . . . the legal situation here . . ."

"Is if you can get in, snatch and grab it. Never had that happen?"

"All the time."

"Where do you work?"

OK, Maxine figures, let's see what happens. "Hashslingrz."

"Oboy." Such a look. "Done a few quick in and outs over there too. Don't think I could ever handle it full-time. Sooner lick the remains of a banana cream pie off of Bill Gates's face, they make fuckin Microsoft look like Greenpeace. Guess I never saw you around."

"Oh, I'm only temping there myself. Go in once a week and do the accounts receivable."

"If you're a devoted fan of Gabriel Ice, just ignore me, but— even in a business where arrogant pricks are the norm? anybody inside a mile radius of ol' Gabe ought to be wearin a hazmat suit."

"I think I got to see him once. Maybe. At a distance? All kinds of entourage in my sight line sort of thing?"

"Not doin too bad, for somebody just got in under the wire."

"How's that."

"Street cred. Anybody who got in before '97 is considered OK—from '97 to 2000 it can go either way, maybe they're not always cool, but usu-ally they're not quite the kind of full-service dickhead you're seeing in the business now."

"He's considered cool?"

"No, he's a dickhead, but one of the early ones. A pioneer dickhead. Ever get to any of those legendary hashslingrz parties?

"Nope. You?"

"Once or twice. That time they had all the naked chicks out in the freight elevator covered with Krispy Kreme donuts? and the one where Britney Spears showed up disguised as Jay-Z? Only it turned out to be a Britney Spears look-alike?"

"Gee, the stuff I keep missing out on. Knew I shouldn't've had all those kids . . ."

"Those days's all history now anyway," Driscoll shrugs. "Echoes in the past. Even if hashslingrz is hirin like it's 1999."

Hmm . . . "Thought I noticed a lot of new payroll around. What's going on?"

"Same old satanic pact, only more of it. They've always liked to trawl for amateur hackers—now they've set up this, well it's more than just a firewall with a dummy computer, it's a virtual corporation, totally bogus, sittin out there as bait for the script kiddies, who they can then keep a eye on, wait till they're just about to crack all the way into core, then bust them and threaten legal action. Offer them a choice between pullin a single over on Rikers or an opportunity to take the next step toward becoming a 'real hacker.' Is how they put it."

"You know somebody this happened to?"

"A few. Some took the deal, some split town. They enroll you in a course out in Queens where you learn Arabic and how to write Arabic Leet."

"That's . . ." taking a guess, "using a qwerty keyboard to make characters that look like Arabic? So hashslingrz is, what, expanding into a new Mideast market area?"

"One theory. Except that every day civilians walk around, no clue, even when it's filling up screens right next to them at Starbucks, cyberspace warfare without mercy, 24/7, hacker on hacker, DOS attacks, Trojan horses, viruses, worms . . ."

"Didn't I see something in the paper about Russia?"

"They're serious enough about cyberwar, training people, spending budget, but even Russia you don't have to worry about so much as"—pretending to smoke air hookah—"our Muslim brothers. They're the true global force, all the money they need, all the time. Time is what the

Stones call on their side, yes it is. Trouble ahead. Word around the cubes is there's 'ese huge U.S. government contracts, everybody's after em, big deal comin up in the Middle East, some people in the community sayin Gulf War Two. Figures Bush would want to do his daddy one better."

Toggling Maxine immediately into Anxious Mom mode, thinking about her boys, who might be too young to draft at the moment, but ten years from now, given the way U.S. wars tend to drag out, will be fish in a barrel, more than likely the kind of barrel that holds 42 gallons and is going currently for about 20, 25 bucks . . .

"You OK, Maxi?"

"Thinking. Sounds like Ice wants to be the next Evil Empire."

"Sad thing is, is 'ere's enough code monkeys around who'll just go jumpin in blind, fodder for the machine."

"They're not any smarter than that? What happened to revenge of the nerds?"

Driscoll snorts. "*Is* no revenge of the nerds, you know what, last year when everything collapsed, all it meant was the nerds lost out once again and the jocks won. Same as always."

"What about all these nerd billionaires in the trades?"

"Window dressing. The tech sector tanks, a few companies happen to survive, awesome. But a lot more didn't, and the biggest winners were men blessed with that ol' Wall Street stupidity, which in the end is unbeatable."

"C'mon, everybody on Wall Street can't be stupid."

"Some of the quants are smart, but quants come, quants go, they're just nerds for hire with a different fashion sense. The jocks may not know a stochastic crossover if it bites them on the ass, but they have that drive to thrive, they're synced in to them deep market rhythms, and that'll always beat out nerditude no matter how smart it gets."

As happy hour begins and the price of well drinks goes down to $2.50, Driscoll switches to Zimartinis, which are basically Zima and vodka. Maxine, humming the working-mom blues, stays with Zima.

"Really like your hair, Driscoll."

"I was doing it like everybody else, you know, seriously black, with those short bangs? but all the time I secretly wanted to look like Rachel on *Friends*, so I started collecting these Jennifer Aniston images? off of Web sites and tabloids and shit?"

Finding herself soon enough with a purseful of photo clips and screen grabs, going from one hair salon to another, increasingly desperate, trying to get her own do exactly the way it looked on JA—something that might, it finally began to dawn on her, be easier to get wrong than right, because even with the hours of obsessive hair-by-hair color blending and strange custom-styling equipment out of geek-movie lab sets, the results never came in better than close-but-no-cigar.

"Maybe," Maxine gently, "you aren't really supposed to, like, what's the word, *be* . . . ?"

"No, no! that's just it! I love Jennifer Aniston! Jennifer Aniston is my role model! on Hallowe'en? I've always been Rachel!"

"Yes, but this . . . wouldn't have anything to do with Brad Pitt, or . . ."

"Oh, that, that'll never last, Jen is way too good for him."

"Too . . . 'good' . . . for Brad Pitt."

"Wait and see."

"OK, Driscoll, this is against my better judgment, but you might want to go try Murray 'N' Morris, over in the Flower District?" Rooting through her purse to find one of their cards, or, well, more like a 10%-off introductory coupon. These two demented yet somehow board-certified trichologists have recently spotted an opportunity in the Jennifer Aniston wannabe boom, and are investing heavily in Sahag curlers and forever going off to Caribbean resorts for intensive tutorial workshops in color weaving. Their remorseless urges toward innovation extend to other salon services as well.

"Our Meat Facial today, Ms. Loeffler?"

"Uhm, how's that."

"You didn't get our offer in the mail? on special all this week, works miracles for the complexion—freshly killed, of course, before those enzymes've had a chance to break down, how about it?"

"Well, I don't . . ."

"Wonderful! Morris, kill . . . the chicken!"

From the back room comes horrible panicked squawking, then silence. Maxine meantime is tilted back, eyelids aflutter, when— "Now we'll just apply some of this," wham! ". . . *meat* here, directly onto this lovely yet depleted face . . ."

"Mmff . . ."

"Pardon? (Easy, Morris!)"

"Why is it . . . uh, moving around like that? Wait! is that a— are you guys putting a real dead chicken in my— aaahhh!"

"Not quite dead yet!" Morris jovially informs the thrashing Maxine as blood and feathers fly everywhere.

Each time she comes in here, it is something like this. Each time she exits the salon swearing it's for the last time. Still, she can't help noticing the crowds of Jennifer Aniston more-or-less look-alikes competing for dryer time lately, as if downtown is Las Vegas and Jennifer Aniston the next Elvis.

"This is expensive?" Driscoll wonders, "what they do?"

"It's still what you guys would call in beta, so I think they should offer you a price."

The crowd has begun to sort into a mix of hackers and hacker grrrlz and corporate suits repackaged in somebody's idea of barhopping gear, out looking for romance or cheap labor, whichever way the night develops.

"The one element there ain't so much of anymore," Driscoll points out, "is the gold diggers of both sexes who thought there was all these nerd billionaires just about to come step out of the toilet and fiercely into their lives. Never was better than delusional back then, but these days even a hardcore techno-adventuress has to admit, it's mighty slim pickings."

Maxine has noticed a pair of men at the bar who seem to be eyeball-ing her, or Driscoll, or both of them, with uncommon intensity. Though it's hard to say what normal is around here, they don't look too normal to Maxine, and it ain't just the Zima talking.

Driscoll follows her gaze. "You know those guys over there?"

"No, uh-uh. Thought it was somebody you knew."

"It's their first time in here," Driscoll is pretty sure, "and they look like cops. Should this be freaking me out?"

"Just remembered it's my curfew," snickers Maxine, "so I'm outta here. You stay. See which one of us they're tailing."

"Let's make a big deal about writing down our e-mail and phone numbers and shit, that way we don't look so much like longtime associates."

Turns out it's Maxine who's their Person of Interest. Good news, bad news, Driscoll seems like a nice kid and doesn't need these idiots, on the other hand it's Maxine, now inside a lemon-lime alcopop haze, who has to try and shake them. She gets in a taxi headed down- instead of uptown, pretends to change her mind much to the driver's annoyance, and ends up in Times Square, which for a few years now she has made a conscious effort not to go near if she can help it. The sleazy old Deuce she remembers from her less responsible youth is so no more, Giuliani and his developer friends and the forces of suburban righteousness have swept the place Disneyfied and sterile—the melancholy bars, the choles-terol and fat dispensaries and porno theaters have been torn down or renovated, the unkempt and unhoused and unspoken-for have been pushed out, no more dope dealers, no more pimps or three-card monte artists, not even kids playing hooky at the old pinball arcades—all gone. Maxine can't avoid feeling nauseous at the possibility of some stupefied consensus about what life is to be, taking over this whole city without mercy, a tightening Noose of Horror, multiplexes and malls and big-box stores it only makes sense to shop at if you have a car and a driveway and a garage next to a house out in the burbs. Aaahh! They have landed, they are among us, and it helps them no end that the mayor, with roots in the outer boroughs and beyond, is one of them.

And here they all are tonight, converged into this born-again imitation of their own American heartland, here in the bad Big Apple. Blending with this for as long as she can, Maxine finally seeks refuge in the subway, takes the Number 1 to 59th, changes to the C train, gets off at The Dakota, threads in and out of a busload of Japanese visitors snapping photos of the John Lennon assassination site, and next time she looks back, she can't see anybody following her, though if they've had her on their radar since before she walked into the Bucket, then they probably also know where she lives.

6

P izza for supper. What else is new?

"Mom, this really crazy lady showed up at school today."

"And so . . . somebody, what, called the cops?"

"No, we had assembly and she was the guest speaker. She graduated from Kugelblitz sometime back in the olden days."

"Mom, did you know that the Bush family does business with Saudi Arabian terrorists?"

"Oil business, you mean."

"I think that's what she meant, but . . ."

"What"

"Like there was something else. Something she wanted to say but not in front of a kid audience."

"Sorry I missed it."

"Come to the upper-school commencement. She's gonna be guest speaker again."

Ziggy hands over a flyer with an ad for a Web site called Tabloid of the Damned, and "March Kelleher" autographed on it.

"Hey, so you saw March. Well. In fact, well well." The hashslingrz legend continues, here. March Kelleher happens to be Gabriel Ice's mother-in-law, her daughter Tallis and Ice having been college sweethearts, Carnegie Mellon maybe. A subsequent coolness, pari passu with the dotcom billionaire's revenue growth no doubt, is said to've developed. None of Maxine's business of course, though she knows that March herself is divorced and that there are two other kids besides Tallis, boys, one is some kind of IT functionary out in California and another went off to Katmandu and has been postcard-nomadic ever since.

March and Maxine go back to the co-opping frenzy of ten or fifteen years ago, when landlords were reverting to type and using Gestapo techniques to get sitting tenants to move. The money they offered was contemptuously little, but some renters went for it. Those who didn't got a different treatment. Apartment doors removed for "routine maintenance," garbage uncollected, attack dogs, hired goons, eighties pop played really loud. Maxine noticed March on a picket line of neighborhood gadflies, old lefties, tenants'-rights organizers and so forth, in front of a building over on Columbus, waiting for the union's giant inflatable rat to show up. Picket-sign slogans included RATS WELCOME—LANDLORD'S FAMILY and CO-OP—CRUEL OFFENSIVE OUTRAGEOUS PRACTICES. Undocumented Colombians carried furniture and household possessions out to the sidewalk, trying to ignore the emotional uproar. March had the anglo crew boss cornered against a truck and was giving him an earful. She was slender, with shoulder-length red hair parted in the middle and then pulled back into a snood, as it turned out one of a wardrobe of these retro hair accessories, which had become her trademark around the neighborhood. On that particular day in late winter, the snood was scarlet, and March's face seemed to Maxine silvery at the edges, like some antique photograph.

Maxine was looking for a chance to get into a conversation with her when the landlord showed up, one Dr. Samuel Kriechman, a retired plastic surgeon, along with a small posse of heirs and assigns. "Why you miserable, greedy old bastard," March cheerfully greeted him. "You dare to show your face around here."

"Ugly cunt," replied the genial patriarch, "nobody in my profession would even touch a face like yours, who is this bitch, get her the fuck out of here." A great-grandson or two stepped forward, eager to obey.

March produced from her purse a 24-ounce aerosol can of Easy-Off oven cleaner and began to shake it. "Ask the eminent physician what lye can do for your face, kids."

"Call the cops," ordered Dr. Kriechman. Elements of the picket line came over and began to discuss matters with Kriechman's entourage. There was some, well, argumentative gesturing, extending to casual contact which the *Post* may have amplified slightly in the story it ran. Cops showed up. As light faded and deadlines approached, the crowd thinned out. "We don't picket at night," March told Maxine, "hate to step off the line personally, but then again I could use a drink about now."

The nearest bar was the Old Sod, technically Irish, though an aging gay Brit or two may have wandered infrequently in. The drink March had in mind was a Papa Doble, which Hector the bartender, previously only seen drawing beers and pouring shots, assembled for March as if he'd been doing it all week. Maxine had one too, just to keep her company.

They discovered they'd been living only blocks from each other all this time, March since the late fifties when the Puerto Rican gangs were terrorizing the Anglos in the neighborhood, and you didn't go east of Broadway after sunset. She hated Lincoln Center, for which an entire neighborhood was destroyed and 7,000 *boricua* families uprooted, just because Anglos who didn't really give a shit about High Culture were afraid of these people's children.

"Leonard Bernstein wrote a musical about it, not *West Side Story,* the other one, where Robert Moses sings,

Throw those Puerto
Ricans out in the

street— It's just a
slum, Tear it all
d-o-o-own!"

In a shrill Broadway tenor plausible enough to curdle the drink in Maxine's stomach. "They even had the chutzpah to actually film *West Side* fuckin *Story* in the same neighborhood they were destroying. Culture, I'm sorry, Hermann Göring was right, every time you hear the word, check your sidearm. Culture attracts the worst impulses of the moneyed, it has no honor, it begs to be suburbanized and corrupted."

"You should meet my parents sometime. No love for Lincoln Center, but you can't keep em away from the Met."

"You kidding, Elaine, Ernie? we go back, we used to show up at the same demonstrations."

"My mother demonstrated? What for, a discount someplace?"

"Nicaragua," unamused, "Salvador. Ronald Raygun and his little pals."

This was when Maxine was living at home, getting her degree, sneaking out into weekend club-drug mindlessness, and only noticing at the time that Elaine and Ernie seemed a little distracted. It wasn't till years later that they felt comfortable about sharing their memories of plastic handcuffs, pepper spray, unmarked vans, the Finest doing what cops do best.

"Making me the Insensitive Daughter once again. They must've picked up some some tell, some shortfall in my character."

"Maybe they were only trying to keep you clear of trouble," March said.

"They could have invited me along, I could have had their backs for them."

"Never too late to start, there's enough to do God knows, you think anything's changed? dream on. The fucking fascists who call the shots haven't stopped needing races to hate each other, it's how they keep wages down, and rents high, and all the power over on the East Side, and everything ugly and brain-dead just the way they like it."

"I do remember," Maxine tells the boys now, "March was always sort of . . . political?"

She sticks a Post-it on her calendar to go to graduation and see what the old snood-wearing mad dog is up to these days.

REG REPORTS IN. He's been to see his IT maven Eric Outfield, who's been down in the Deep Web looking into hashslingrz's secrets. "Tell me something, what's an Altman-Z?"

"A formula they use to predict if a company will go bankrupt in, say the next two years. You plug numbers into it and look for a score below maybe 2.7."

"Eric found a whole folder of Altman-Z workups that Ice has been running on different small dotcoms."

"With a view to . . . what, acquiring?"

Evasive eyeballs. "Hey, I'm just the whistle-blower."

"Did this kid show you any of these?"

"We haven't been meeting much online, he's so paranoid," yeah, Reg, "he only likes to meet face-to-face on the subway."

Today an insane white Christer at one end of the car was competing with a black a cappella group at the other. Perfect conditions. "Brought you something." Reg handing over a disc. "I'm supposed to tell you it's been personally blessed by Linus himself, with penguin piss."

"This is to make me have guilt now, right?"

"Sure, that'd help."

"I'm on it, Reg. Just not too comfortable."

"Better you than me, frankly I wouldn't have the cojones." It has turned out to be a cannonball dive into strange depths. Eric is using the computer at the place he's been temping, a large corporation with no IT chops to speak of, in the middle of a crisis nobody saw coming. Something a little different. Each time he surfaces from the Deep Web he's a little more freaked, or so it seems to those in neighboring cubes, though so many of these spend their hours down in the mainframe room snorting Halon out of the fire extinguishers that they may lack some perspective.

The situation is not as straightforward as Eric might have been hoping. The encryption is challenging, if not mad serious. Whereas Reg has been entertaining fantasies of a quick in and out, Eric has found the clerks at this 7-Eleven are packing assault rifles on full auto.

"I keep running into this dark archive, all locked down tight, no telling what's stashed there till I crack in."

"Limited access, you're saying."

"Idea is to have a failsafe in case of a disaster, natural or man-made, you can hide your archive on redundant servers out in remote locations, hoping at least one'll survive anything short of the end of the world."

"As we know it."

"If you want to be chirpy about it, I guess."

"Ice is expecting a disaster?"

"More likely just wants to keep stuff away from inquiring minds." Eric's original tactic was to pretend to be a script kiddie out for a joyride, seeing if he could get in with Back Orifice and then install a NetBus server. A message came up immediately written in Leet characters along the lines of "Congratulations noob you think you made it in but all you're really in now is a world of deep shit." Something in the style of this response caught Eric's attention. Why should their security be going to the trouble to make it so personal? Why not just brief and bureaucratic, like "Access Denied"? Something, maybe only its amused vehemence, reminded him of older hackers from the nineties.

Are they playing with him? What sort of playmates are they likely to be? Eric figured if he was supposed to be just some packet monkey nosing around, he'd have to pretend he doesn't know how heavy-duty, or even who, these guys are. So at first he goes after the password as if it might be something old-school like the Microsoft LM hash, which even retards can crack. To which Security replies, again in Leet, "Noob do you really know who you're fucking with?"

Reg and Eric were out in the middle of Brooklyn by this point, the doo-wop and Bible recitation long out the exits and Eric poised for flight. "You're in and out of there all the time, Reg, you ever happen to run into any of their security people?"

"Rumor I hear is that Gabriel Ice runs the department himself. There's supposed to be some history. Somebody had a live terminal in a desk drawer and forgot to tell him."

"Forgot."

"Next thing anybody knew, there was all kinds of proprietary code out there for free. Took months to fix, cost them a big contract with the navy."

"And the careless employee?"

"Disappeared. All this is company folklore, understand."

"That's reassuring."

No more dangerous than a chess game, it seems to Reg. Defense, retreat, deception. Unless it's a pickup game in the park where your opponent turns violently psychopathic without warning, of course.

"Paranoia, whatever, Eric's still intrigued," Reg reports to Maxine. "It's dawning on him that this could be a kind of entrance exam. If it's the Ice Man himself on the other end of this, if Eric's good enough, maybe they'll let him in. Maybe I should be telling him to run like hell."

"I heard it's a recruiting tactic over there, you might want to point that out. Meantime, Reg, you sound a lot less enthusiastic about your project."

"Actually, it's a coastal thing you're hearing, I don't even know what I'm doing on this one anymore."

Uh-oh. Intuition alert. None of Maxine's business, of course, but, "The ex."

"Same ol' blues line, nothin important. Except now her and hubby, they're making noises about moving out to Seattle. I don't know, he's some kind of corporate hotshot. Vice President in Charge of Rectal Discomfort."

"Ah, Reg. Sorry. In the old soap operas, 'transferred to Seattle' was code for written out of the script. I used to think Amazon, Microsoft, and them were started up by fictional soap-opera rejects."

"Keep waiting for the other shoe to drop, cute li'l announcement card from Gracie, 'Hooray! we're pregnant!' Should be happening about now, right? So end the suspense already."

"You'd be OK with that?"

"Better than some creep thinking my kids are his. Which gives me nightmares. Literally. Like he could be a fuckin abuser."

"C'mon, Reg."

"What. These things happen."

"Too much family television, bad for your brain, watch the after-midnight cartoons instead."

"Come on, how'm I supposed to deal with that?"

"Not the sort of thing you can just let go, I guess."

"Actually, I had a li'l more proactive approach in mind?"

"Oh no, Reg. You're not . . ."

"Packing? Bust a cap in the muthafucker's ass, lovely fantasy ain't it . . . but then Gracie I suppose would never talk to me again. The girls either."

"Hmm, maybe not."

"Also thought about a snatch-and-grab, can't afford even that. Sooner or later I'd have to go to work, Social Security number and they've got me again, and it's lawyers dealt into what's left of my life. And ol' Pointy-Hair gets the girls back anyway, and I'm forbidden ever to see them again. So my latest thinkin is, is maybe I should go out there and make nice instead."

"Uh huh and . . . they're expecting you?"

"Maybe I'll find a job first, then surprise everybody. Just don't want you thinkin too badly of me. I know it looks like I'm running away from something, but New York is really where I've been running away, and now there's about to be a whole continent between me and my kids. Too far."

IT IS MAXINE'S practice when checking into little start-ups like hwgaah wgh.com to also have a look at any investors in the picture. If somebody stands to lose money, there's always a chance, emergency-vehicle exhaust-fume issues or whatever, they'll want to hire Maxine. The name that keeps popping up in connection with hwgaahwgh is a VC down in SoHo, doing business as Streetlight People. As in "Don't Stop Believing," Maxine imagines. Among whose listed clients—coincidence, no doubt— also happens to be hashslingrz.

Streetlight People is located in a cast-iron-front ex-factory space somewhat off the major shopping routes around SoHo. Karmic echoes of the sweatshop era long smoothed away by portable soundbreaks, screens and carpeting, passed into a neutral, unhaunted hush. Buddy Nightingale seating in a spectrum of hesitant aquas, daffodils, and fuchsias, brushed-nickel workstations custom-designed by Zooey Chu, punctuated now and then with black leather bosses' chairs by Otto Zapf.

If asked, Rockwell "Rocky" Slagiatt would explain that losing the vowel at the end of his name was the price of smoothness and rhythm in doing business, like lyrics in an opera. Actually he thought it would sound more Anglo, though for special visitors, of whom Maxine today seems to be one, he is known to suddenly flip polarity and become disingenuously ethnic again.

"Hey! You want sum'na eat? Peppuhvr-n-egg sangwidge."

"Thanks, but I just—"

"My *mothuh's* peppuhvr-n-egg sangwidge."

"Well, Mr. Slagiatt, that depends. Do you mean it's your mother's recipe? or, it's, like, her personal pepper-and-egg sandwich, that for some reason she keeps in that credenza there instead of a fridge where it should be?" From her studies with Shawn, Maxine is trained in the exotic

Asian technique known as "False Eating," so if it comes to it, she'll only have to *make believe* eat the pepper-and-egg sandwich, which despite its authentic appearance could be poisoned with almost anything.

"'t's alright!" grabbing back the object, now seen actually to have an unnatural wobble to it. "It's plastic!" throwing it in a desk drawer.

"Little hard to chew."

"You're a sport, Maxi, it's OK I call you that, Maxi?"

"Sure. OK if I don't call you Rocky?"

"Your choice, no rush," suddenly, for a moment, Cary Grant. What? Somewhere on Maxine's perimeter, long-disused antennas quiver and begin to track.

He picks up the phone. "Hold my calls, OK? What? Talk to me . . . Nah. Nah, the drag-along is set in cement. The full ratchet, maybe doable, but see Spud on that." Ringing off, summoning a file onto his screen. "OK. This is about the recently belly-up hwgaahwgh dotcom."

"For whom you are, or should I say were, their VC."

"Yeah, we did their Series A. Since then we been tryin to evolve to more of a mezz posture here, early stages are way too easy, the real challenge," busy tapping keys, "comes in structuring the tranches . . . valuing the company, where you get the Wayne Gretzky Principle of where the puck is gonna be instead of where it is now, see what I'm saying."

"How about where it was?"

Squinting at the screen, "Part of the doo-doo diligence is, is we keep these daily logs, it all gets archived, impressions, hopes and fears . . . Looks like . . . even back puttin together the term sheet, these guys were being way too picky about liquidation preferences. Took days more than it should. We ended up with a 1-X multiple on only a little tiny position, so . . . without wishing to pry, why you come zoomin in on us about this?"

"Are you upset by unwelcome attention, Mr. Slagiatt?"

"Ain't like we're loan sharks here. Look up on that shelf."

She looks. "You . . . have a company bowling team."

"Industry awards, Max. Since that thing with the Wells notice in '98?

our wake-up call," earnest as a victim on a talk show, "we all went up to Lake George on retreat, shared our feelings totally, took a vote, cleaned up our act, those days are behind us now."

"Congratulations. Always a plus to find a moral dimension. Maybe it'll help you appreciate some funny numbers I found."

She fills him in on the Benford-curve and other discrepancies at hashslingrz. "Prominent among payees of these fishy expenditures is hwgaahwgh.com. What's strange is that after the company is liquidated, the amounts paid to it grow dramatically even more lavish and it all seems to be disappearing someplace offshore."

"Fuckin Gabriel Ice."

"Beg your pardon?"

"The book on this guy is he takes a position, typically less than five percent, in each of a whole portfolio of start-ups he knows from running Altman-Z's on them are gonna fail within a short-term horizon. Uses them as shells for funds he wants to move around inconspicuously. Hwgaahwgh seems to be one of these. Where to and what for, ya got to wonder, huh?"

"Working on that."

"Mind if I ask, who got you onto this?"

"Somebody who'd rather not be involved. Meantime, I see from your client list you also do some business with Gabriel Ice."

"Not me directly, not for a while."

"No schmoozing with Ice in any social way? you and maybe even . . ." head-gesturing at a framed photo on Rocky's desk.

"That would be Cornelia," nods Rocky.

Maxine waves at the picture. "How do you do, I'm sure."

"Not only a looker as you can see, but a elegant hostess from the old school. Equal to any social challenge."

"Gabriel Ice, he's . . . challenging?"

"OK, we been out to dinner, once. Twice maybe. Places on the East Side a guy comes by with a grater and a truffle, grates it all over your food till you say stop? Vintage dates on the Champagne, so forth—with ol' Gabe it's always about the price . . . Ain't seen either of them since maybe last summer out in the Hamptons."

"The Hamptons. It figures." Glittering rat hole and summertime home to America's rich, famous, and a vast seasonal inflow of yup wannabes. Half Maxine's business sooner or later tracks back to somebody's need for the diseased Hamptons fantasy, which is way past its sell-by date by now, in case nobody's noticed.

"More like Montauk. Not even on the beach, back in the woods."

"So your paths . . ."

"Cross now and then, sure, couple times in the IGA, enchiladas at the Blue Parrot, but the Ices are running in way different circles these days."

"Had them figured for Further Lane at least."

Shrug. "Even out on the South Fork, my wife tells me, there's still resistance to money like Ice's. One thing to build a house with its foundation in the sand, right, somethin else to pay for it with money not everybody believes is real."

"I Ching talk."

"She noticed." The semimischievous look again.

Uh, huh, "A boat, how about a boat, they own a boat?"

"Lease one maybe."

"Oceangoing?"

"What am I, Moby Dick? You're that curious, go out there and see."

"Yeah, right, who springs for the jitney, where's the per diem, see what I'm saying."

"What. You doin this on spec?"

"So far it's a buck and a half for the subway down here, that I can probably absorb. Beyond that . . ."

"Shouldn't be a problem." Picking up the phone, "Yes Lupita *mi amor,* could you cut us a check, please, for . . . uh," raising his eyebrows at Maxine, who shrugs and holds up five fingers, "five thousand U.S., payable to—"

"Hundred," sighs Maxine, "Five hundred, jeez all right I'm impressed, but it's only enough so I can start a ticket. Next invoice you can be Donald Trump or whatever, OK?"

"Just tryin to help, not my fault I'm a giving generous type of guy, is it? Lemme at least buy yiz lunch?"

She risks a look at his face, and sure enough—the Cary Grant beam, the Interested Smile. Aahh! What would Ingrid Bergman do, Grace Kelly? "I don't know . . ." Actually, she does know, because she has this built-in fast-forward feature in her brain that can locate herself, a day or two from now, glaring into the mirror going, "What, in the fuck, were you thinking?" and right at the moment it's coming up No Signal. Hmm. Maybe it's just that she can do with some lunch.

They go around the corner to Enrico's Italian Kitchen, which she recalls getting raves in Zagat, and find a table. Maxine heads for the ladies' toilet, and on the way back, in fact while she's still in there, she can hear Rocky and the waiter arguing. "No," Rocky with a sort of evil glee Maxine has noticed also in certain children, "not 'pas-ta e fa-gio-li,' I think what I said was pastafazool."

"Sir, if you'll look on the menu, it's clearly spelled," pointing helpfully at each word, "'pasta, e, fagioli'?"

Rocky gazes at the waiter's finger, deciding on how best to remove it from its hand. "But ain't I a reasonable person? of course I am, so let's go to the classical source here, tell me, kid, does Dean Martin sing 'When the stars make-a you droli / Just-a like-a pasta e fagioli'? no. No, what he sings is—"

Maxine sits quietly, attending to her eyeblink rate, as Rocky, far from sotto voce but on pitch, makes with his Dean Martin impression. Marco the owner sticks his head out of the kitchen. "Oh, it's you. *Che si dice?*"

"Would you explain to the new guy?"

"He bothering you? five minutes, he's in the dumpster with the scungilli shells."

"Maybe just change the spelling on the menu for him?"

"You sure? Got to go in the computer for that. Be easier to just whack him."

The waiter, whose credits include a couple of *Sopranos* episodes, recognizing this for what it is, stands by, trying not to roll his eyes too much.

Maxine ends up having the homemade strozzapreti with chicken livers, and Rocky goes for the osso buco. "Hey, what kinda wine?"

"How about a '71 Tignanello?— but then again with all the wiseguy dialogue, maybe just, uh, li'1 Nero d'Avola? small glass?"

"Readin my mind." Not exactly doing a double take at the pricey supertuscan, but a certain gleam has entered his eye, which is what she may have been looking to provoke. And why would that be, again?

Rocky's mobile phone goes off, Maxine recognizing the ringtone as "Una furtiva lagrima." "Listen my darling, here's the situation— Wait . . . *Un gazz*, I'm talkin to a robot here, right? Again. So! uh-huh! how you doing? how long you been a robot . . . You wouldn't be Jewish, by any chance? Yeah, like when you were thirteen, did your parents give you a bot mitzvah?"

Maxine scrolls the ceiling, "Mr. Slagiatt. Mind if I ask you something? Just professional interest—the seed money for hashslingrz, do you happen to know who put it up originally?"

"Speculation at the time was lively," Rocky remembers, "usual suspects, Greylock, Flatiron, Union Square, but nobody really knew. Big dark secret. Could've been anybody with the resources to keep it quiet. Even one of the banks. Why?"

"Trying to narrow it down. Angel money, some eccentric right-winger out in a Sunbelt mansion with central air? Or a more institutional type of evil?"

"Wait—what are you attempting to imply, as my wife might say?"

"What with you folks," Maxine deadpan, "and your longtime GOP connections . . ."

"Us folks, ancient stuff, Lucky Luciano, the OSS, please. Forget it."

"No ethnic slurs intended of course."

"Should I bring up Longy Zwillman? Welcome to Streetlight People," raising his glass and tapping hers lightly.

She can hear from inside her purse the as-yet-undeposited check laughing at her, as if she has been the butt of a great practical joke.

The Nero d'Avola on the other hand is not bad at all. Maxine nods amiably. "Let's wait till my invoice."

7

Maxine finally gets over to Vyrva's one evening to have a look at the widely coveted yet ill-defined DeepArcher application, bringing along Otis, who disappears immediately with Fiona into her room, where along with the Beanie Baby overpop she keeps a Melanie's Mall, with which Otis has become strangely intrigued. Melanie herself is a half-scale Barbie with a gold credit card she uses for clothes, makeup, hairstyling, and other necessities, though the secret identity Otis and Fiona have given her is a bit darker and requires some quick costume changes. The Mall has a water fountain, a pizza parlor, an ATM, and most important an escalator, which comes in handy for shoot-out scenarios, Otis having introduced into the suburban girl idyll a number of four-and-a-half-inch action figures, many from the cartoon show *Dragonball Z,* including Prince Vegeta, Goku and Gohan, Zarbon, and others. Scenarios tend to center on violent assault, terrorist shoplifting sprees, and yup discombobulation, each of which ends in the widespread destruction of the Mall, principally at the hands of Fiona's alter ego the eponymous Melanie, in cape and ammo belts, herself. Among fiercely imagined smoke and wreckage, with generic plastic bodies horizontal and disassembled everywhere, Otis and Fiona kiss off each episode by high-fiving and singing the tag from the Melanie's Mall commercial, "It's cool at the Mall."

Justin's partner Lucas, who lives down in Tribeca, shows up a little late this evening, having been chasing his dealer through half of Brooklyn in search of some currently notorious weed known as Train Wreck, wearing a green glow-in-the-dark T-shirt reading UTSL, which Maxine at first takes for an anagram of LUST or possibly SLUT but later learns is Unix for "Use The Source, Luke."

"We don't know what Vyrva's told you about DeepArcher," sez Justin, "it's still in beta, so don't be surprised at some awkwardness now and then."

"Should warn you, I'm not too good at these things, drives my kids crazy, we play Super Mario and the little goombas jump up and stomp on me."

"It's not a game," Lucas instructs her.

"Though it does have forerunners in the gaming area," footnotes Justin, "like the MUD clones that started to come online back in the eighties, which were mostly text. Lucas and I came of age into VRML, realized we could have the graphics we wanted, so that's what we did, or Lucas did."

"Only the framing material," Lucas demurely, "obvious influences, Neo-Tokyo from Akira, Ghost in the Shell, Metal Gear Solid by Hideo Kojima, or as he's known around my crib, God."

"The further in you go, as you get passed along one node to the next, the visuals you think you're seeing are being contributed by users all over the world. All for free. Hacker ethic. Each one doing their piece of it, then just vanishing uncredited. Adding to the veils of illusion. You know what an avatar is, right?"

"Sure, had a prescription once, but they always made me a little, I don't know, nauseous?"

"In virtual reality," Lucas begins to explain, "it's a 3-D image you use to represent yourself—"

"Yeah, actually, gamers in the house forever, but somebody told me also that in the Hindu religion avatar means an incarnation. So I keep wondering—when you pass from this side of the screen over into virtual reality, is that like dying and being reincarnated, see what I'm saying?"

"It's code," Justin a little bewildered, maybe, "just keep the thought, couple geeks up all night on cold pizza and warm Jolt wrote this, not exactly in VRML but something hypermutated out of it, 's all it is."

"They don't do metaphysical," Vyrva flashing Maxine a smile falling noticeably short of fond amusement. She must see a lot of this.

Justin and Lucas met at Stanford. Kept running into each other within a tight radius of Margaret Jacks Hall, which in that day housed the Computer Science department and was affectionately known as Marginal Hacks. They primal-screamed their way together through one finals week after another, and by the time they graduated, they'd already put in weeks of pilgrimage up and down Sand Hill Road, pitching to the venture-capital firms which lined that soon-to-be legendary thorough-fare, arguing recreationally, trembling in performance anxiety, or, re-solved to be Zenlike, just sitting in the traffic jams typical of that era, admiring the vegetation. One day they took a wrong turn and wound up caught in the annual Sand Hill soapbox derby. The roadside was lined with bales of hay and spectators who numbered up in the low five fig-ures, watching a streetful of homemade racers barreling downhill at top speed toward the Stanford tower in the distance, allegedly powered by nothing but the earth's gravity.

"That kid over there who just spun out in the fifties spaceship rig," Justin said.

"That's no kid," said Lucas.

"Yeah I know, isn't it that Ian Longspoon dude? The VC we had lunch with last week? drinks Fernet-Brancas with ginger-ale chasers?" Another of their regrettable lunch dates. Most likely at Il Fornaio in the Garden Court Hotel in Palo Alto, though neither could remember now, everybody got kind of hammered. Toward the end of it, Longspoon had actually begun to make out a check but seemed unable to stop writing zeros, which soon ran off the edge of the document and continued onto the tablecloth, on which presently the VC's head came to rest with a thump.

Lucas reached stealthily for the checkbook and saw Justin making for the exit. "Wait, hey, maybe somebody'll cash this, where you going?"

"You know what'll happen when he wakes up. We're not gonna get stuck paying for another lunch we can't afford."

It wasn't their most dignified moment. Waiters began hollering urgently into little lapel mikes. Beach-tanned technocuties at distant tables who'd scanned them with interest when they came in now turned away scowling. Truculent busboys splashed uneaten soup on them as they sped past. Chuchu in the parking lot, briefly having considered keying Justin's ride, settled for spitting on it.

"Guess it could have been worse," Lucas remarked once they were safely out on 280 again.

"Old Ian sure ain't gonna be happy."

Well, here he was now at the soapbox race, a perfect opportunity for them to find out how he did feel, and somehow the partners only kept slouching further down behind the dashboard instead. They thought they knew from intimidation, but at this point they hadn't yet run into any of the finance providers in New York.

Maxine can imagine. Silicon Alley in the nineties provided more than enough work for fraud investigators. The money in play, especially after about 1995, was staggering, and you couldn't expect elements of the fraudster community not to go after some of it, especially HR executives, for whom the invention of the computerized payroll was often confused with a license to steal. If this generation of con artists came up short now and then in IT skills, they made up for it in the area of social engineering, and many entreprenerds, being trusting souls, got taken. But sometimes distinctions between hustling and being hustled broke down. It didn't escape Maxine's notice that, given stock valuations on some start-ups of interest chiefly to the insane, there might not much difference. How is a business plan that depends on faith in "network effects" kicking in someday different from the celestial pastry exercise known as a Ponzi scheme? Venture capitalists feared industrywide for their rapacity were observed to surface from pitch sessions with open wallets and leaking eyeballs, having been subjected to nerd-produced videos with subliminal messages and sound tracks featuring oldie mixes that pushed more buttons than a speed freak with a Nintendo 64. Who was less innocent here?

Scanning Justin and Lucas for spiritual malware, Maxine, whose acquaintance with geekspace, since the tech boom, had grown extensive though nowhere near complete, discovered that even by the relaxed definitions of the time, the partners checked out as legit, maybe even innocent. It could've just been California, where the real nerds are supposed to come from, while all you ever see on this coast is people in suits monitoring what works and what doesn't and trying to copy the last hot idea. But anybody adventurous enough to want to move their business from out there to New York ought to be warned—it would be unprofessional of Maxine, wouldn't it, not to share what she knows of the spectrum of hometown larceny. So she kept finding herself, with these guys, slipping back and forth between Helpful Native and its more sinister variant, the kvetchy, spoon-waving source of free advice she lives in terror of turning into, known locally as a Jewish Mother.

Well, as it turns out, no worries—Lucas and Justin in reality are smarter cookies than the Girl Scout type Maxine was imagining. Somewhere back in the Valley, among those orange groves casually replaced with industrial campuses, they came to a joint epiphany about California vis-à-vis New York—Vyrva thinks maybe more joint than epiphany—something to do with too much sunshine, self-delusion, slack. They'd heard this rumor that back east content was king, not just something to be stolen and developed into a movie script. They thought what they needed was a grim unforgiving workplace where the summer actually ended once in a while and discipline was a given daily condition. By the time they found out the truth, that the Alley was as much of a nut ward as the Valley, it was too late to go back.

Having managed to score not only seed and angel money but also a series-A round from the venerable Sand Hill Road firm of Voorhees, Krueger, the boys, like American greenhorns of a century ago venturing into the history-haunted Old World, lost no time back east in paying the necessary calls, setting up shop around early '97 in a couple of rooms sublet from a Website developer who welcomed the cash, down in the then still enchanted country between the Flatiron Building and the East Village. If content was still king, they got nonetheless a crash course in patriarchal subtext, cutthroat jostling among nerd princes, dark dynastic histories. Before long they were showing up in trade journals, on gossip sites, at Courtney Pulitzer's downtown soirees, finding themselves at four in the morning drinking kalimotxos in bars carpentered into ghost stops on abandoned subway lines, flirting with girls whose fashion thinking included undead signifiers such as custom fangs installed out in the outer boroughs by cut-rate Lithuanian orthodontists.

"So . . ." some presentable young lady spreading her upturned palms, "warm and friendly here, right?"

"And after the stories we heard," Lucas nodding, gazing amiably at her tits.

"I was in California once, I gotta say, you go out there expecting all those howdy-there vibes, it comes as a shock—talk about entitled? suspicious? Nobody here in the Alley's about to snoot you the way you get snooted by those folks in Marin. Oh, I'm sorry, you're not Well people, are you?"

"Hell no," cackles Lucas, "we're as sick as they come."

By the time the tech market began its toiletward descent, Justin and Vyrva had enough squirreled away for a down payment on a house and some acreage back in Santa Cruz County, plus a little more in the mattress. Lucas, who'd been putting his money in places a bit less domestic, flipping IPOs, buying into strange instruments understood only by sociopathic quants, got hit way harder when tech-stock enthusiasm collapsed. Soon people were coming around inquiring, often impolitely, after his whereabouts, and Vyrva and Justin found themselves overditzing to deflect the unwelcome attention.

"Come on." Leading Maxine up a set of spiral stairs to Justin's work-room, an obsessive clutter of monitors, keyboards, loose discs, printers, cables, Zip drives, modems, routers, the only books visible being a CRC manual and a Camel Book and some comics. There's custom wallpa-per designed to look like a hex dump, in which Maxine out of habit searches for repeating cells but can't find any, and some Carmen Electra posters, mostly from her *Baywatch* period, and a gigantic Isomac steam-punk espresso machine in the corner, which Vyrva keeps calling the Insomniac.

"DeepArcher Central," Lucas with one of those may-I-introduce armwaves.

Originally the guys, you have to wonder how presciently, had it in mind to create a virtual sanctuary to escape to from the many varie-ties of real-world discomfort. A grand-scale motel for the afflicted, a des-tination reachable by virtual midnight express from anyplace with a keyboard. Creative Differences arose, to be sure, but went strangely un-acknowledged. Justin wanted to go back in time, to a California that had never existed, safe, sunny all the time, where in fact the sun never set unless somebody wanted to see a romantic sunset. Lucas was searching for someplace, you could say, a little darker, where it rains a lot and great silences sweep like wind, holding inside them forces of destruction. What came out as synthesis was DeepArcher.

"Whoa, Cinerama here."

"Cute, huh?" Vyrva switching on a gigantic 17-inch LCD monitor, "Brand new, retails for about a thousand, but we got a price."

"You're assimilating." Maxine meantime reminding herself that she has never had a clear idea of how these guys make their money.

Justin goes to a worktable, sits at a keyboard and begins tapping at it while Lucas rolls a couple of joints. Presently remotely linked window blinds close their slats against the secular city, and the lights go down and the screens light up. "You can get on that other keyboard over there too if you want," Vyrva sez.

A splash screen comes on, in shadow-modulated 256-color daylight, no titles, no music. A tall figure, dressed in black, could be either sex, long hair pulled back with a silver clip, The Archer, has journeyed to the edge of a great abyss. Down the road behind, in forced perspective, recede the sunlit distances of the surface world, wild country, farmland, suburbs, expressways, misted city towers. The rest of the screen is claimed by the abyss—far from an absence, it is a darkness pulsing with whatever light was before light was invented. The Archer is poised at its edge, bow fully drawn, aiming steeply down into the immeasurable uncreated, waiting. What can be seen of the face from behind, partly turned away, is attentive and unattached. A light wind is blowing in the grass and brush. "Looks like we cheaped out and didn't bother to animate much," Justin comments, "but look close and you can see the hair rippling too, I think the eyes blink once, but you have to be watching for it. We wanted stillness but not paralysis." When the program is loaded, there is no main page, no music score, only a sound ambience, growing slowly louder, that Maxine recognizes from a thousand train and bus stations and airports, and the smoothly cross-dawning image of an interior whose detail, for a moment breathtakingly, is far in advance of anything she's seen on the gaming platforms Ziggy and his friends tend to use, flaring beyond the basic videogame brown of the time into the full color spectrum of very early morning, polygons finely smoothed to all but continuous curves, the rendering, modeling, and shadows, blending and blur, handled elegantly, even with . . . could you call it genius? Making Final Fantasy X, anyway, look like an Etch A Sketch. A framed lucid dream, it approaches, and wraps Maxine, and strangely without panic she submits.

The signs say DEEPARCHER LOUNGE. Passengers waiting here have been given real faces, some at first glance faces Maxine thinks she knows, or ought to.

"Nice to meet you, Maxine. Going to be with us for a while?"

"Don't know. Who told you my name?"

"Go ahead, explore around, use the cursor, click anywhere you like."

If it's a travel connection that Maxine's supposed to be making, she keeps missing it. "Departure" keeps being indefinitely postponed. She gathers that you're supposed to get on what looks like a shuttle vehicle of some kind. At first she doesn't even know it's ready to leave till it's gone. Later she can't even find her way to the right platform. From the sumptuously provisioned bar upstairs, there's a striking view of rolling stock antiquated and postmodern at the same time vastly coming and going, far down the line over the curve of the world. "It's all right," dialogue boxes assure her, "it's part of the experience, part of getting constructively lost."

Before long, Maxine finds herself wandering around clicking on everything, faces, litter on the floor, labels on bottles behind the bar, after a while interested not so much in where she might get to than the texture of the search itself. According to Justin, Lucas is the creative partner in this. Justin's the one who translated it into code, but the visual and sound design, the echoing dense commotion of the terminal, the profusion of hexadecimal color shades, the choreography of thousands of extras, each differently drawn and detailed, each intent on a separate mission or sometimes only hanging out, the nonrobotic voices with so much attention to regional origins, all are due to Lucas.

Maxine locates at last a master directory of train schedules, and when she clicks on "Midnight Cannonball"—bingo. On she is crossfaded, up and down stairways, through dark pedestrian tunnels, emerging into soaring meta-Victorian glass- and iron-modulated light, through turnstiles whose guardians morph as she approaches from looming humorless robots into curvaceous smiling hula girls with orchid leis, up to a train whose kindly engineer leans beaming from the cab and calls out, "Take your time, young lady, we're holdin her for you . . ."

The instant she steps on board, however, the train accelerates insanely, zero to warp speed in a tenth of a second, and they're off to DeepArcher. The detail of the 3-D countryside barreling past the windows on both sides is surely on a much finer scale than it has to be, no loss of resolution no matter how closely she tries to focus in. Train hostesses out of Lucas and Justin's beach-babe fantasies keep coming by with carts full of junk food, drinks with Pacific subtexts like Tequila Sunrises and mai tais, dope of varying degrees of illegality . . .

Who can afford bandwidth like this? She mouses her way to the back of the car, expecting grand vistas of trackscape receding, only to find, instead, emptiness, absence of color, the entropic dwindling into Netscape gray of the other brighter world. As if any idea here of escaping to refuge would have to include no way back.

Though she's on board the train now, Maxine sees no reason to stop clicking—she clicks on the hostesses' toe rings, on the chili-glazed rice crackers in the Oriental Party Mix they bring, on the festively colored toothpicks which impale the chunks of tropical fruit on the drinks, you never know, it could be the next click—

Which eventually it is. The screen begins to shimmer and she is abruptly, you could say roughly, taken into a region of permanent dusk, outer-urban somehow, no longer aboard the train, no more jolly engineer or bodacious waitstaff, underpopulated streets increasingly unlit, as if public lamps are being allowed to burn out one by one and the realm of night to be restored by attrition. Above these somber streets, impossibly fractal towers feel their way like forest growth toward light that reaches this level only indirectly . . .

She's lost. There is no map. It isn't like being lost in any of the romantic tourist destinations back in meatspace. Serendipities here are unlikely to be in the cards, only a feeling she recognizes from dreams, a sense of something not necessarily pleasant just about to happen.

She senses dope smoke in the air and Vyrva at her shoulder with coffee in a mug that reads I BELIEVE YOU HAVE MY STAPLER. "Holy shit. What time is it?"

"Not that late," Justin sez, "but I think we should log off pretty soon, no telling who's monitoring."

Just as she was getting comfortable.

"This isn't encrypted? Firewalled?"

"Oh, heavily," sez Lucas, "but if somebody wants in, they'll get in. Deep Web or whatever."

"That's where this is?"

"Way down. Part of the concept. Trying to stay clear of the bots and spiders. A robots.txt protocol is OK for the surface Web, and well-behaved bots, but then there's rogue bots who aren't just ill-mannered, they're mighty fuckin evil, the instant they see any disallow code, they home right in."

"So better to stay deep," Vyrva sez. "After a while it can get to be an addiction. There's a hacker saying—once you've gone Deep, never get back to sleep."

They have reconvened downstairs at the kitchen table. The more loaded the partners get and the more smoke in the air, the more comfortable they seem to grow talking about DeepArcher, though it's hacker stuff Maxine has trouble following.

"What's known as bleeding-edge technology," sez Lucas. "No proven use, high risk, something only early-adoption addicts feel comfortable with."

"The crazy shit VCs used to go for," as Justin recalls. "Back then, '98, '99, some of the places they were putting their money? You'd have to be a lot weirder than DeepArcher to even get them to raise their eyebrows."

"We were almost too vanilla for them," Lucas agrees. "Our design precedents happened to be pretty solid, for one thing"

According to Justin, DeepArcher's roots reach back to an anonymous remailer, developed from Finnish technology from the penet.fi days and looking forward to various onion-type forwarding procedures nascent at the time. "What remailers do is pass data packets on from one node to the next with only enough information to tell each link in the chain where the next one is, no more. DeepArcher goes a step further and forgets where it's been, immediately, forever."

"Kind of like a Markov chain, where the transition matrix keeps resetting itself."

"At random."

"At pseudorandom."

To which the guys have also added designer linkrot to camouflage healthy pathways nobody wants revealed. "It's really just another maze, only invisible. You're dowsing for transparent links, each measuring one pixel by one, each link vanishing and relocating as soon as it's clicked on . . . an invisible self-recoding pathway, no chance of retracing it."

"But if the route in is erased behind you, how do you get back out?"

"Click your heels three times," Lucas sez, "and . . . no wait, that's something else . . ."

8

eg's paranoia has the side effect of warping his judgment about
places to eat. Maxine finds him in the strange crowded neighborhood around the Queensboro Bridge, sitting by the street window
of something called Bagel Quest, eyeballing the foot traffic for undue
interest in himself, behind him a dark, perhaps vast, interior from which
no sound or light seems to emerge, and waitstaff rarely.

"So," Maxine sez.

There's a look on his face. "I'm being followed."

"You're sure?"

"Worse, they've been in my apartment too. Maybe on my computer."
Scrutinizing, as if for evidence of occupancy, a cheese danish he has impulsively bought.

"You could just let this go."

"I could." Beat. "You think I'm crazy."

"I know you're crazy," sez Maxine, "which doesn't mean you're
wrong about this. Somebody's been showing some interest in me too."

"Let's see. I start looking under the surface at Ice's company, next
thing I know, I'm being followed, now they're following you? You want

to tell me there's no connection? I shouldn't be freaking out in fear of my life or anything." With a suspended chord also, about to resolve.

"There's something else," she noodges. "Any of my business?"

A rhetorical question Reg ignores. "You know what a *hawala* is?"

"Sure . . . yeah, uh, in the movie *Picnic* (1956), right, Kim Novak comes floating down the river, all these local people put their hands up in the air and go—"

"No, no, Maxi please, it's . . . they tell me it's a way to move money around the world without SWIFT numbers or bank fees or any of the hassle you'd get from Chase and them. A hundred percent reliable, eight hours max. No paper trail, no regulation, no surveillance."

"How is this possible?"

"Mysteries of the Third World. Family-type operations usually. All depending on trust and personal honor."

"Gee, I wonder why I never ran across this in New York."

"*Hawaladars* around here tend to be in import-export, they take their fees in the form of discounts on prices and stuff. They're like good bookies, keep it all in their heads, something Westerners can't seem to do, so at hashslingrz somebody has been hiding a lot of major transaction history down behind multiple passwords and unlinked directories and so forth."

"You heard about this from Eric?"

"He has a tap in a back office at hashslingrz."

"Somebody's in there wearing a wire?"

"It's, actually it's a Furby."

"Excuse me, a—"

"Seems there's a voice-recognition chip inside that Eric was modifying—"

"Wait, the cute fuzzy little critter every child in town including my own had to have a couple of Christmases back, that Furby? this genius of yours *hacks Furbys*?"

"Common practice in his subculture, seems to be a low tolerance there for cuteness. At first Eric was only looking for ways to annoy the yups—you know, teach it some street language, emotional-outburst chops, so forth. Then he noticed how many Furbys were showing up in the cubicles of code grinders over where he works. So we took the Furby he was messing with, upgraded the memory, put in a wireless link, I brought it in to hashslingrz, sat it on a shelf, now when I want I can stroll by with a pickup inside my Nagra 4 and download all kinds of confidential stuff."

"Such as this *hawala* that hashslingrz is using to get money out of the country."

"Over to the Gulf, it turns out. This particular *hawala* is head-quartered in Dubai. Plus Eric's been finding that to even get to where hashslingrz's books are stashed, they put you through elaborate routines written in this, like, strange Arabic what he calls Leet? It's all turning into a desert movie."

This is true. An offshore angle, with more dimensions than angles are supposed to have, has not escaped Maxine's attention. She has found herself consulting current updates of the always useful Bribe Payers Index and its companion list the Corrupt Perceptions Index, which rank countries around the world for their likelihood of bent behavior, and hashslingrz seems to have dodgy linkages all over the map, particularly in the Mideast. Lately she's been picking up certain tells for the well-known Islamic allergy to anything interest-bearing. Bond activity is rare to nonexistent. Instead of selling short, there is a tendency to go to elab-orate sharia-compliant workarounds like arboon auctions. Why the con-cern for Muslim phobias about charging interest, unless . . . ?

Unless Ice stands to make a bundle in the region, what else?

Convection currents in Maxine's coffee keep bringing something to the surface just long enough for her to mutter "Hey, wait . . ." before submerging again too quickly to ID it. She isn't about to put her finger in and explore. "Reg, say your guy cracks all the encryption. What are you planning to do with what you find?"

"Something's up," impatient, also anxious. "Maybe even something that's got to be stopped."

"Which you think is more serious than simple fraud. What could be that big of a deal?"

"You're the expert, Maxine. If it was a classic fraud haven, Grand Cayman or whatever, it'd be one thing. But this is the Mideast, and somebody's going to way too much trouble to keep secrets, as if Ice or somebody in his shop ain't just squirreling it away but bankrolling something, something big and invisible—"

"And . . . funneling sums over to the Emirates in the Hefty Smurf range can't be for some totally innocent reason, because . . . ?"

"Because I keep trying to come up with innocent reasons and can't. Can you?"

"I don't do international intrigue, remember? Well, maybe Nigerian e-mails, but usually I'm down here with the bent baristas and the pigeon-drop artists."

They sit there for a minute while unknown forms of life pursue recreational activities in their food.

"Keepin that Tomcat in your purse there, I hope."

"Oh, Reg. Maybe it's you that should be carrying."

"Maybe I should be finalizing travel plans, like, far, far away. Eric needless to say keeps getting more spooked the further into this he goes. Insists now on rendezvousing down in the Deep Web instead of in the subway, and frankly I'm a little reluctant."

"What's to be reluctant about?"

"Were you ever down there?"

"Not long ago. Seems like a nice secure place to meet."

"You're so comfortable with it, maybe you should be the one to go down there and talk to Eric. Cut out the middleman here."

"Maybe, long as you don't mind." Is she thinking about *hawalas,* hashslingrz, even Reg's personal safety, actually no, it's that deco-derivative shuttle terminal of Lucas and Justin's that might or might not get her access to DeepArcher. Whatever that turns out to be. She isn't quite ready to admit it, but she's already entertaining the first draft of a fantasy in which Eric, sherpa of the Deep Web, faithful and maybe even cute, helps her find her way through the maze. Nancy fuckin Drew, here. "Maybe if I made a realworld approach first. Face-to-face. See how much we trust each other."

"Good luck. You think I'm paranoid? These days you even go near this guy, he freaks."

"I can make it an accidental meeting. Pretty standard maneuver. Can you give me a list of his hangouts?"

"I'll e-mail something to you." And soon Reg, taking a quick gander around at the street, has gone sidling off in the direction of downtown, miles away in the springtime shimmer.

AMONG MAXINE'S MORE USEFUL SENSORS is her bladder. When she's out of range of information she needs, she can go whole days without any particular interest in pissing, but when phone numbers, koans, or stock tips from which she's likely to profit are close by, the gotta-go alarm has reliably steered her to enough significant restroom walls that she's learned to pay attention.

This time she's down in the Flatiron District when the alarm goes off. Against her better judgment, she steps into the dimly lit grease- and cigarette-smoke interior of Wall of Silence, once a tech-bubble hot spot, since fallen into greasyspoondom. The way to the restrooms is not as clearly marked as it could be. She finds herself wandering among customers at tables, who seem to be either unhappy couples or single men, possibly help-line candidates. One of whom, actually, now seems to be calling her name, with some urgency. Well, there's urgency and there's urgency. She squints through the gloom.

"Lucas?" Yep, and signs of seedy personal disarray even in this light. "You happen to know where they keep the toilet around here?"

"Hi, Maxi, listen, while you're in there could you do me a favor—"

"You just broke up with somebody," this being the kind of place you'd naturally choose for that, "and want to know how she's doing. Sure. What's her name?"

"Cassidy, but how did you—"

"And where is it?"

Back through the kitchen, down some stairs, around a couple of corners. Lit no more brightly than upstairs, and some would call this being considerate. There is a smell of cannabis purposefully alight. Maxine scans the short row of stalls. No blood coming from under the doors, no sounds of uncontrollable sobbing, good, good . . . "Yo Cassidy?"

"Who's that?" from inside one of the stalls. "The bitch he's dumping me for, no doubt."

"Nah, thanks for the guess, but I'm in enough trouble already. Just gonna go in here for a minute," stepping into the stall next to Cassidy's.

"I should have known what was up the minute I saw this place," Cassidy sez. "Better if we'd handled everything out in the street."

"Lucas is having a little guilt, wants to know if you're OK."

"Not a problem, I came in here to piss, not open a vein. Lucas who?"

"Oh."

"Figures, these fuckin clubs I keep ending up in. He told me Kyle."

They sit there side by side, mutually invisible, the partition between inscribed in marker pen, eye pencil, lipstick later rubbed at and smeared by way of commentary, gusting across the wall in failing red shadows, phone numbers with antiquated prefixes, cars for sale, announcements of love lost, found, or wished for, racial grievances, unreadable remarks in Cyrillic, Arabic, Chinese, a web of symbols, a travel brochure for night voyages Maxine has not yet thought about making. Meantime Cassidy is outlining some unsold pilot about dysfunctional dating south of 14th Street in which Lucas, near as Maxine can tell, only gets a walk-on. That's until, inexplicably though only so for a moment, Cassidy is on to the topic of DeepArcher.

"Yeah, that splash screen," Maxine kvells, "it's awesome."

"I designed it. Like that chick who did the tarot deck. Awesome and don't forget hip," half, but only half, ironic.

"Wait, awesome and hip, where have I heard that."

Yep, turns out when she first met Lucas, Cassidy was working for hwgaahwgh.com.

"Did you have any kind of a contract with Lucas, Kyle, whatever?"

"No and I wasn't doing it out of love, either. Hard to explain. It was all just coming from somewhere, for about a day and a half I felt I was duked in on forces outside my normal perimeter, you know? Not scared, just wanted to get it over with, wrote the file, did the Java, didn't look at it again. Next thing I remember is one of them saying holy shit it's the edge of the world, but frankly I can't see a way they're going to build any traffic. If I was a new user, coming to it cold, I'd be like, Public Void Close in a real hurry and try to forget about it. Better if they go for the single customer, Gabriel Ice or somebody."

Presently, through strange toilet ESP, the ladies emerge at the same moment from their stalls and have a look at each other. Maxine is not too surprised to find tats, piercings, hair of an orchid shade not on any map of the human genome, an age somewhat south of legal for anything. The way Cassidy's looking back meanwhile makes Maxine feel like Hillary Clinton or something.

"Can you check upstairs and see if he's still there?"

"Happy to." She ascends into the murky bummersphere again. Yes he's still there.

"Startin to get worried about both of you."

"Lucas, she's twelve. And you better start paying her royalties."

9

Now and then a taxing entity like the NYC Finance Department will hire an outside examiner, especially when there's a Republican mayor, given that party's curious belief that private sector always equals good and public bad. Maxine gets back to the office in time for a call from Axel Quigley down at John Street, with the latest on another heartrendingly sad case of sales-tax evasion, taking it personally as always, even though it's been going on for a while. Axel's whistle-blowers tend to be disgruntled employees, he and Maxine in fact met at a Disgruntled Employee Workshop led by Professor Lavoof, generally acknowledged godfather of Disgruntlement Theory and developer of the influential Disgruntled Employee Simulation Program for Audit Information and Review, aka DESPAIR.

According to Axel, somebody at a restaurant chain called Muffins and Unicorns has been using phantomware to falsify cash-register receipts. Sales-suppression devices are either factory-installed in the cash registers themselves or being run off of a custom application known as a zapper, kept externally on a CD. Evidence points to a high-level manager, maybe owner. Axel's most likely suspect is Phipps Epperdew, better known as Vip because he always looks like he's just emerged from a Lounge or flashed a Discount Card with that acronym on it.

The interesting thing for Maxine about zapper fraud is the face-to-face element. You don't learn it from a manual, because there's nothing in print. Features written into the software that you don't find in the manual are meant instead to be passed on in person, orally, from cash-register vendor to user. The way certain kinds of magical lore go from rogue rabbis to apprentices in kabbalah. If the manual is scripture, phantomware tutorials are the secret knowledge. And the geeks who promote it—except for one or two little details, like the righteousness, the higher spiritual powers—they're the rabbis. All strictly personal and in a warped way even romantic.

Vip is known to be doing business with shadowy elements in Quebec, where the zapper industry is flourishing at the moment. Back in the dead of last winter, Maxine got added to a city budget line, on the QT as always, and flown to Montreal to *chercher le geek*. Manifested into Dorval, checked in to the Courtyard Marriott on Sherbrooke, and went schlepping around the city, one fool's errand after another, down into random gray buildings where many levels below the street and down the corridors you'd hear cafeteria sounds, round a corner and here'd be *le tout Montréal* having lunch in a lengthy series of eating rooms, strung in an archipelago across the underground city, which in those days seemed to be expanding so rapidly that nobody knew of a reliable map for it all. Plus shopping enough to challenge Maxine's nausea threshold, back ends of Metro stations, bars with live jazz, crepe emporia and poutine outlets, vistas of sparkling new corridor just about to be tenanted by even more shops, all without any need to venture up into the snowbound subzero streets. Finally, at a phone number obtained off a toilet wall at a bar in Mile End, she located one Felix Boïngueaux, who'd been working out of a basement apartment, what they call a *garçonnière*, off of Saint-Denis, for whom Vip's name didn't just ring a bell but threatened to kick the door in, since there were apparently some late-payment issues. They arranged to meet at an Internet-enabled laundromat called NetNet, soon to be a legend on the Plateau. Felix looked almost old enough to drive.

Once they were past *enchantée,* like everybody else in town Felix had no problem shifting clutchlessly into English. "So you and Mr. Epperdew, you're colleagues?"

"Neighbors, actually, in Westchester." Pretending to be another bent businessperson interested in the "hidden delete options" for her point-of-sale network, only out of technical curiosity, of course.

"I might be down your way soon, looking for financing."

"I think in the States there might be a legal problem?"

"No, actually it'd be for starting up a PCM project."

"Some, ah, recreational drug?"

"Phantomware countermeasures."

"Wait, you're supposed to be pro-phantomware, what's with this 'counter'?"

"We build it, we disable it. You're frowning. We're beyond good and evil here, the technology, it's neutral, eh?"

Back to Felix's basement pad in time for the evening movie on the Aboriginal Peoples' Television Network, whose film library contained every Keanu Reeves movie ever made, including, that night, Felix's personal favorite, *Johnny Mnemonic* (1995). They smoked weed, ordered in Montreal pizza topped with little-known forms of sausage, grew absorbed in the movie, and Nothing, as Heidi would put it, Happened, except that a couple days later Maxine flew back to New York with a file on Vip Epperdew chunkier by far than what she'd flown off with, and the tax office figured their money was well spent.

Then, for months, silence from them, till now suddenly here's Axel again. "Just wannit to let you know, Vip's ass is grass and the Finance lawn mower's about to make its pass."

"Thanks for the bulletin, I've been losing sleep."

"The DA's office is initiating the paperwork as we speak. All we still need to have is a couple of details. Like where is he. You wouldn't happen to know."

"Vip and I don't exactly schmooze, Axel. Gee. A girl smiles even once at a material witness and everybody starts getting ideas."

TONIGHT'S DESCENT INTO SLEEP is helical and slow. As insomniacs revisit certain melodies and lyrics of their youth, so Maxine keeps circling back to Reg Despard, back on board the *Aristide Olt*, that thin twinkling kid, so resolutely smiling through the miserable day-to-day of the underconnected indie moviemaker. To hope that this hashslingrz project of his will not turn too horrible on him is to wallow in a warm tub of denial. Something else is up, Reg knew exactly who to bring this ticket to, he read Maxine correctly, knew she could feel something like his own alarm at the perimeters of ordinary greed overstepped, the engines of night and contrived oblivion, out on the tracks, cranking up to speed . . .

At which point, just before the transition to REM, the phone rings and it's Reg himself.

"It ain't a movie anymore, Maxi."

"How early tomorrow you planning to be up, Reg?" Or to put it another way, it's the middle of the fucking night here.

"Not going to sleep tonight."

Meaning Maxine's not likely to either. So they meet for very early breakfast at a 24-hour Ukrainian joint in the East Village. Reg is over in a corner in back, picking away at his PowerBook. It's summertime, not too humid or horrible yet, but he's sweating.

"You look like shit, Reg, what happened?"

"Technically," moving his hands away from the keyboard, "I'm supposed to have free run of hashslingrz, right? Except I always knew I didn't. And, well, yesterday, finally, I walked through the wrong door."

"You're sure you didn't find it locked and jimmy it?"

"Well, it shouldn't've been locked, sign on the door said 'Toilet.'"

"So you entered illegally . . ."

"Whatever. Here's this room, no porcelain in sight, looks like a lab, test benches, equipment and shit, cables, plugs, parts and labor for some job order I quickly realize I don't want to know nothin about. Plus then's when I notice there's all these jabberin A-rabs around, who the minute I come through the door they all dummy up."

"How do you know it's Arabs, they're wearing outfits, there's camels?"

"Sounded like that's what they were talking, they weren't Anglos, or Chinese, and when I waved at them like 'Yo my sand niggas, what up—'"

"Reg."

"Well, more like *Ayn al-hammam,* where's the toilet, and one of them comes right over, cold, polite, 'You are looking for toilet, sir?' There is some muttering, but nobody shoots at me."

"Did they see the camera?"

"Hard to say. Five minutes later I'm summoned to the office of the Big Ice Pick himself, first thing he wants to know is did I get any footage of the room or the guys in it. I tell him no. I'm lying of course.

"And he's like, 'Cause if you did get footage, you would need to give that to me.' It was that 'need,' I think, like when the cops tell you you 'need' to step away from the car. That's when I started to get scared. Second thoughts about the whole fuckin project, frankly."

"What were these guys doing? Assembling a bomb?"

"I hope not. Way too many circuit cards layin around. Any bomb with that much logic attached to it? Trouble down the line."

"Can I look at the footage?"

"I'll put it on a disc for you."

"Has Eric seen it?"

"Not yet, he's been out on patrol, as we speak someplace in the Brooklyn-Queens border country, pretending to be a doper looking for qat. But really looking for Ice's *hawaldar.*"

"How'd he get so motivated all of a sudden?"

"Think it's about scoring, but I try not to ask."

. . .

SHE'S IN THE SHOWER trying to get lucid when somebody sticks their head around the curtain and begins making with the shrill ee-ee-ee shower-scene effects from *Psycho* (1960). Time was she would have screamed, had some kind of episode, but now, recognizing the idea of merriment here, she only mutters, "Evening, honeybunch," for it is who but the of course nowhere-near-history Horst Loeffler, showing up, like Basil St. John in the life of Brenda Starr, unannounced, another year's worth of lines deepening on his face, poised already for departure, while in the reverse shot the little polarized tear flashes, right on cue, appear along the edges of Brenda Starr's eyelids.

"Hey! I'm a day early, you surprised?"

"No and also try to quit leering, Horst? I'll be out of here in a minute." Is that a hardon? She has retreated into the shower too quick to tell.

She arrives in the kitchen, steam-rosy and damp, hair twisted up in a towel, wearing a terry-cloth robe stolen from a spa in Colorado where they once passed a couple of weeks, back when the world was romantic, to find Horst humming, for some reason she will never ask about, the *Mister Rogers* theme, "It's a beautiful day in this neighborhood," while rooting around in the freezer. Commenting on different pieces of frost-covered history. Slim pickings on the airplane, no doubt.

"Here it is." Horst, with a dowser's gift specific to Ben & Jerry's ice cream, brings out a semicrystallized quart of Chunky Monkey, sits down, takes an oversize spoon in each hand, and digs in. "So," after a while, "where are the boys?"

The extra spoon, she has learned, is for mooshing it up. "Otis is having supper at Fiona's, Ziggy's over at school, rehearsing. They're putting on *Guys and Dolls* Saturday night, so you're just in time, Ziggy's gonna be Nathan Detroit. Got some on your nose there."

"Missed you guys." Something peculiar in his tone suggests, not for the first time, that if Maxine chooses to, she might concede that, far from demanding a self-obsessed chase around the world after black-orchid serum, in fact and scarcely known to Horst himself, what his immune system is really not handling too well these days is the dreaded Ex-Husband Blues.

"We're probably ordering in, soon as Ziggy gets back, if you're interested."

Which is about when Ziggy comes strolling in. "Mom, who's the sleazebag, lemme guess, another blind date?"

"What," Horst with the once-over, "you again."

Embracing, it seems to Maxine out the corner of her eye, a little longer than you'd expect.

"How's 'at Jewish asskicking?"

"Oh, comin along. Killed an instructor last week."

"Awesome."

Maxine pretending to look through a pile of take-out menus, "What do you guys want to eat? Besides something that's still alive."

"Long 's it ain't none that macro wacko hippie food."

"Ah, come on, Dad—Sprout Loaf? Organic Beet Fritters? mmm-mmm!"

"Gets a man droolin just thinkin about it!"

They are presently joined by Otis, the really picky one, still hungry because Vyrva's recipes tend toward the experimental, so even more take-out menus are added to the pile and negotiations threaten to run well into the night, further complicated by Horst's Rules of Life, such as avoid restaurants with logos where the food has a face or wears a whimsical outfit. They end up as always ordering in from Comprehensive Pizza, whose menu of toppings, crusts, and formatting options runs to about the thickness of a Hammacher Schlemmer catalog at holiday time and whose delivery area arguably does not even include this apartment, requiring the usual Talmudic telephone discussion over whether they will bring food to begin with.

"Long as I'm tubeside by nine," Horst being a devoted viewer of the BPX cable channel, which airs film biographies exclusively, "U.S. Open coming up, golfer biopics all this week, Owen Wilson as Jack Nicklaus, Hugh Grant in *The Phil Mickelson Story . . .*"

"I was planning to watch a Tori Spelling marathon on Lifetime, but I can always use the other TV, please, make yourself right at home here."

"Mighty accommodating of you, my lit-tle everything bagel."

The boys are rolling their eyes, more or less in sync. The pizzas arrive, everybody starts grabbing, turns out this trip Horst plans on staying in New York for a while. "I took a sublet on some office space down at the World Trade Center. Or should I say up, it's the hundred-and-something floor."

"Not exactly soybean country," Maxine remarks.

"Oh, it don't matter where we are anymore. The open-outcry era's coming to an end, everybody's switching over to this Globex thing on the Internet, I'm just taking longer to adjust than most, trading don't work out, I can always be an extra in dinosaur movies."

Very late, managing to detach herself from the complexities of the hashslingrz ticket, Maxine is drawn to the spare bedroom by a voice from the TV set there, speaking with a graceful derangement of emphasis, almost familiar—"I respect your . . . experience and intimacy with the course but . . . I think for this hole a . . . five-iron would be . . . inappropriate . . ." and sure enough, here's Christopher Walken, starring in *The Chi Chi Rodriguez Story.* And Ziggy and Otis and their father all on the bed snoozing in front of it.

Well, they love him. What's she supposed to do about that? She wants to lie down next to them, is what, and watch the rest of the movie, but they've taken up all available space. She goes in the living room and puts it on there, and falls asleep on the couch, though not before Chi Chi wins the 1964 Western Open by a stroke, over Gene Hackman in a cameo as Arnold Palmer.

If you were really as bitter as everybody—well, Heidi—thinks you should be about this, she tells herself just before nodding off, you'd get a restraining order and send them to camp in the Catskills . . .

Next day Horst takes Otis and Ziggy down to his new office at the

World Trade Center, and they eat lunch at Windows on the World, which has a dress code, so the boys wear jackets and ties. "Like going to Collegiate," Ziggy mutters. There happens to be a more-than-moderate wind blowing that day, making the tower sway back and forth in five-, what feel like ten-foot excursions. On days of storm, according to Horst's co-tenant Jake Pimento, it's like being in the crow's nest of a very tall ship, allowing you to look down at helicopters and private planes and neighboring high-rises. "Seems kind of flimsy up here," to Ziggy.

"Nah," sez Jake, "built like a battleship."

10

Saturday night at Kugelblitz, despite the lighting crew getting stoned and confusing or forgetting cues and the kids playing Sky and Sarah, who have been going steady in real life, breaking up loudly and publicly at the dress rehearsal, *Guys and Dolls* is a roaring success, which will look even better on the DVD Mr. Stonechat, the director, is shooting of it, given the many sight-line issues at the Scott and Nutella Vontz Auditorium, whose architect owing to some sort of mental condition kept changing his mind about such nuances of design as getting rows of seats to actually face the stage and so forth.

The grandparents holler bravos and take snapshots. "Come back to the apartment," Elaine giving Horst the usual *shviger* evil eye, "we'll have coffee."

"I'll walk you all to the corner," sez Horst, "but then I have to go see about some business."

"We hear you're taking the boys out west?" sez Ernie.

"Midwest, where I grew up."

"And you're just going to hang around in the video arcades all day," Elaine being as nice as pie.

"Nostalgia," Horst tries to explain. "When I was a kid, it was the golden age of arcades then, and now I guess I can't bring myself to admit it's over. All this home-computer gaming, Nintendo 64, PlayStation, now this Xbox thing, maybe I just want the boys to see what blowing aliens away was like in the olden days."

"But . . . isn't it technically kidnapping? Across state lines and whatever?"

"Ma," Maxine surprising herself here, "he's . . . their dad?"

"My gallbladder, Elaine, please," advises Ernie.

The corner, mercifully. Horst waves. "See you guys later."

"Call if you're gonna be too late?" Maxine trying to remember what normal and married sounds like. Eye contact with Horst would be nice also, but no soap.

"This time of night?" Elaine wonders after Horst is out of earshot. "What kind of 'business' can that be, again?"

"If he came with us, you'd be complaining about that," Maxine wondering why suddenly now she's defending Horst. "Maybe he's trying to be polite, you've heard of that?"

"Well, we bought enough pastry to feed an army, maybe I should just call—"

"No," Maxine growls, "nobody else. No litigation lawyers, no drop-by ob-gyns in Harvard running shorts, none of that. Please."

"She will never let that go," sez Elaine, "one time. So paranoid, I swear."

"Who does she get it from," Ernie doesn't exactly ask. Being a passage from a duet Maxine may possibly have heard once or twice in her life. Tonight, beginning as a temperate discussion of Frank Loesser as an operatic composer, the conversation soon unfocuses into general opera talk, including a spirited exchange about who sings the greatest "Nessun Dorma." Ernie thinks it's Jussi Björling, Elaine thinks it's Deanna Durbin in *His Butler's Sister* (1943), which was on television the other night. "That English lyric?" Ernie making a face, "sub–Tin Pan Alley. Awful. And she's a lovely girl, but she's got no squillo."

"She's a soprano, Ernie. And Björling, he should have his union card revoked, that Swedish lilt he puts on '*Tramontate, stelle,*' unacceptable."

And so forth. When Maxine was a kid, they kept trying to drag her along to the Met, but it never took, she never made the transition to Opera Person, for years she thought Jussi Björling was a campus in California. Not even dumbed-down kiddy matinees featuring TV celebs with horns out the sides of their helmet could get her interested. Fortunately it only skipped a generation, and both Ziggy and Otis now have turned into reliable opera dates for their grandparents, Ziggy partial to Verdi, Otis to Puccini, neither caring that much for Wagner.

"Actually, Grandma, Grandpa, all due respect," it occurs to Otis now, "it's Aretha Franklin, the time she filled in for Pavarotti at the Grammys back in '98."

"'Back in '98.' Long, long ago. Come here, you little bargain," Elaine reaching to pinch his cheek, which he manages to slide away from.

Ernie and Elaine live in a rent-controlled prewar classic seven with ceilings comparable in height to a domed sports arena. Needless to say within easy walking distance of the Met.

Elaine waves a wand, and coffee and pastries materialize.

"Not enough!" Each kid holding a plate piled unhealthily high with danishes, cheesecake, strudel.

"You, I'll give you such a frosk . . ." as the boys run into the next room to watch *Space Ghost Coast to Coast*, all of whose episodes their grandfather has thoughtfully taped. "And no crumbs in there!"

By reflex Maxine has a look into the bedrooms she and her sister, Brooke, used to occupy. In Brooke's there now seems to be all new furniture, drapes, wallpaper also. "What's this."

"For Brooke and Avi when they get back."

"Which is when?"

"What," Ernie with an impish glint, "you missed the press conference? Latest word is sometime before Labor Day, though he probably calls it Likud Day."

"Now, Ernie."

"I said something? She wants to marry a zealot, her business, life is full of these nice surprises."

"Avram is a decent husband," Elaine shaking her head, "and I've got to say, he isn't very political."

"Software to annihilate Arabs, I'm sorry, that's not political?"

"Trying to drink some coffee here," Maxine puts in melodiously.

"It's all right," Ernie with his palms raised to heaven, "always the mother's heart that falls out of the shoe box in the snow, nobody ever asks about a father, no, fathers don't have hearts."

"Oh, Ernie. He's a computer nerd like everybody else his generation, he's harmless, so cut him some slack."

"He's so harmless, why is the FBI always coming around to ask about him?"

"The what?" As a gong from a hitherto-unreleased Fu Manchu movie goes off, abrupt and strident, in some not-too-obscure brain lobe, Maxine, though long diagnosed with Chronic Chocolate Deficiency, sits now with her fork in midair arrest, still staring at a three-chocolate mousse cake from Soutine, but with a sudden redirection of interest.

"So maybe it's the CIA," Ernie shrugging, "the NSA, the KKK, who knows, 'Just a few more details for our files,' is how they like to put it. And then hours of these really embarrassing questions."

"When did this start?"

"Just after Avi and Brooke went off to Israel," Elaine is pretty sure.

"What kinds of questions?"

"Associates, employment former and current, family, and yes, since you're about to ask, your name did come up, oh and," Ernie now with a crafty look she knows well, "if you didn't want that piece of cake there—"

"Long as you explain over at Lenox Hill about the fork wounds."

"Here, one guy left you his card," Ernie handing it over, "wants you to call him, no rush, just when you get a minute."

She looks at the card. Nicholas Windust, Special Case Officer, and a phone number with a 202 area code, which is D.C., fine but nothing else on the card, no agency or bureau name, not even a logo of one.

"He dressed very nicely," Elaine recalls, "not like they usually do. Very nice shoes. No wedding ring."

"I don't believe this, she's trying to pimp me onto a fed? What am I saying, of course I believe it."

"He was asking about you a lot," continues Elaine.

"Rrrrr . . ."

"On the other hand," tranquilly, "maybe you're right, nobody should ever date a government agent, at least not till they've seen *Tosca* at least once. Which we had tickets for, but you made other plans that night."

"Ma, that was 1985."

"Plácido Domingo and Hildegard Behrens," Ernie beaming. "Legendary. You're not in trouble, are you?"

"Oh, Pop. I have maybe a dozen cases going at any one time, and there's always a federal angle—a government contract, a bank regulation, a RICO beef, just extra paperwork and then it goes away till there's something else." Trying not to sound too much like she's addressing anybody's anxieties here.

"He looked . . ." Ernie squinting, "he didn't look like a paper pusher. More like a field guy. But maybe my reflexes are off. He showed me my own dossier, did I mention that?"

"He what? Establishing trust with the interviewee, no doubt."

"This is me?" Ernie said when he saw the photo. "I look like Sam Jaffe."

"A friend of yours, Mr. Tarnow?"

"A movie actor." Explaining to Efrem Zimbalist Jr. here how in *The Day the Earth Stood Still* (1951) Sam Jaffe, playing Professor Barnhardt, the smartest man in the world, Einstein only different, after writing some advanced equations all over a blackboard in his study, steps out for a minute. The extraterrestrial Klaatu shows up looking for him and finds this boardful of symbols, like the worst algebra class you were ever in, notices what seems to be a mistake down in the middle of it, erases something and writes something else in, then leaves. When the Professor comes back, he immediately spots the change to his equations and stands there kind of beaming at the blackboard. It was some such expression that had crossed Ernie's face just as the covert federal shutter fell.

"I've heard of that movie," recalled this Windust party, "pacifist propaganda in the depths of the Cold War, I believe it was flagged as potentially Communist-inspired."

"Yeah, you people blacklisted Sam Jaffe too. He wasn't a Communist, but he refused to testify. For years no studio would hire him. He made a living teaching math in high school. Strangely enough."

"He taught high school? Who would've been disloyal enough to hire him?"

"This is 2001, Maxeleh," Ernie now shaking his head back and forth, "the Cold War is supposed to be over, how can these people not have changed or moved on, where is such a terrible inertia coming from?"

"You always used to say their time hasn't passed, it's yet to come."

At bedtime Ernie used to tell his daughters scary blacklist stories. Some kids had the Seven Dwarfs, Maxine and Brooke had the Hollywood Ten. The trolls and wicked sorcerers and so forth were usually Republicans of the 1950s, toxic with hate, stuck back around 1925 in almost bodily revulsion from anything leftward of "capitalism," by which they usually meant keeping an increasing pile of money safe from the depredations of the IRS. Growing up on the Upper West Side, it was impossible not to hear about people like this. Maxine often wonders if it didn't help steer her toward fraud investigation, as much as maybe it's steered Brooke toward Avi and his techie version of politics.

"So you'll call him back?"

"You sound like what's-her-name in there. No, Pop, I have no plans to do that."

IT DOESN'T SEEM to be up to Maxine, however. Next day, evening rush hour, it's just starting to rain . . . sometimes she can't resist, she needs to be out in the street. What might only be a simple point on the workday cycle, a reconvergence of what the day scattered as Sappho said some-place back in some college course, Maxine forgets, becomes a million pedestrian dramas, each one charged with mystery, more intense than high-barometer daylight can ever allow. Everything changes. There's that clean, rained-on smell. The traffic noise gets liquefied. Reflections from the street into the windows of city buses fill the bus interiors with un-readable 3-D images, as surface unaccountably transforms to volume. Average pushy Manhattan schmucks crowding the sidewalks also pick up some depth, some purpose—they smile, they slow down, even with a cellular phone stuck in their ear they are more apt to be singing to some-body than yakking. Some are observed taking houseplants for walks in the rain. Even the lightest umbrella-to-umbrella contact can be erotic.

"If it's the right umbrella, you're saying," Heidi once sought to clarify.

"Picky Heidi, any umbrella, what would it matter?"

"Airhead Maxi, it could be Ted Bundy."

Which this evening turns out to be something like that, actually. Maxine's under some scaffolding waiting out a brief intensity in the downpour when she becomes aware of some kind of male presence. Umbrellas touch. Strangers in the night, exchanging— No wait, that's something else.

"Evening, Ms. Tarnow." He's holding out a business card, which she recognizes as a copy of the same one Ernie passed on to her last night. This one she doesn't take. "It's OK, no GPS chip or anything."

Oboy. The fucking voice, sonorous, overcoached, phony as a cold call on an answering machine. She flicks a sidelong glance. Fiftyish, midnight-brown shoes, Elaine's idea of nice, trench coat with a high polyester content, ever since grade school exactly the kind of person everybody including herself has warned her to stay away from. So of course she starts in with the blurting.

"Already have one of these. This is you in person, Nicholas Windust, I don't suppose you carry a federal ID, warrant or something? just being a careful citizen, understand, trying to do my part to fight crime?" When will she learn to dummy up? No wonder the Borderline Personality folks keep after her, their seasonal noodges are in fact paranoia-calibration updates and she ignores them at her peril. So what's wrong with me, she wonders, am I some kind of a make-nice compulsive? Am I as desperate as Heidi always tells me I am?

He has flipped open meanwhile some pocket-size item of leather goods, flipped it shut again, it could be a Costco membership card, anything. "Look, you can really help us. If you wouldn't mind coming down to the Federal Building, it shouldn't take—"

"Are you fuckin insane?"

"OK, then how about La Cibaeña over on Amsterdam? I mean, you could still get drugged and abducted, but the coffee's got to be better than it is downtown."

"Five minutes," she mutters. "Think of it as speed interrogating." Why is she even allowing him that much? Need for parental approval, thirty, forty years down the line? Swell. Of course Ernie still believes the Rosenbergs were innocent and loathes the FBI and all clones thereof, while Elaine suffers from undiagnosed OY, or Obsessive Yenta syndrome. Besides which, something about him, relentless as a car alarm, is screaming Not Acceptable. James Bond has it easy, Brits can always fall back on accents, where you got your tux, a multivolume set of class signifiers. In New York all you have really is shoes.

At which point in her analysis the rain has let up a little and they've reached La Cibaeña Chinese-Dominican Café. This is my neighborhood, it belatedly occurs to her, what if somebody sees me here with this creep?

"You might want to try the General Tso's catibias, they're highly spoken of."

"Pork, I'm Jewish, something in Leviticus, don't ask." Maxine is in fact hungry but orders only coffee. Windust wants a morir soñando and has a nice chat about this in Dominican dialect with the waitress.

"Fantastic morir soñando here," he informs Maxine, "old Cibao recipe, handed down through the family for generations."

Maxine happens to know it's the owner going in the back and throwing Creamsicles in the blender. She considers letting Windust in on this and is instantly annoyed at how reflexively wiseassed it will sound. "So. This was about my brother-in-law? He'll be back in a couple weeks, you can talk to him yourself."

Windust exhales audibly through his nose, more in regret than annoyance. "You want to know what's been getting the security community all nervous lately, Ms. Tarnow? It's a piece of software called Promis, originally designed for federal prosecutors, to share data among the district courts. It works regardless of what language your files are written in, even what operating system you're using. The Russian mob have been selling it to the rugriders, and more to the point, Mossad have been generously traveling all over the world helping local agencies install it, sometimes throwing in a krav maga course as a sales incentive."

"And sometimes rugelach from the bakery, do I begin to detect a Jewphobic note here?" Something a little lopsided about his face, she notices, not sure what exactly, looks like it could have been in a couple of fights. A line or two, some nonnegotiable tension, the beginnings of that pitted texture men get sometimes. An unexpectedly precise mouth. The lips held together when he isn't talking. No openmouthed expectancy around this one. His hair is still wet from the rain, cut short and plastered down, part on the right, going gray . . . Eyes that may have seen too much and should really be covered by shades . . .

"Hello?"

Not a good idea right now, Maxine, this drifting into thought. OK, "And because I'm Jewish, you figure I'll want to hear about Jewish software? Some people-skills seminar they make you go to every review cycle perhaps."

"No offense," his smirk indicating otherwise, "but what's disturbing about this Promis software is that there's always a backdoor built in, so anytime it gets installed on a government computer anywhere in the world—law enforcement, intelligence, special ops—anybody who happens to know about this backdoor can just slip in through it and make themselves at home—wherever—and all manner of secrets get compromised. Not to mention there's a couple of Israeli chips, highly sophisticated, which Mossad have been known to install at the same time, without necessarily informing the client. What these chips do is scavenge information even while the computer's turned off, hold it till the Ofeq satellite comes over, then transmit everything out to it in a single data burst."

"Oh, devious, these Jews."

"Israel doesn't spy on us? Remember the Pollard case back in 1985? Even left-wing papers like the *New York Times* carried that story, Ms. Tarnow."

How right-wing, Maxine wonders, does a person have to be to think of the *New York Times* as a left-wing newspaper? "So Avram has been working on what then, the chips, the software?"

"We think he's Mossad. Maybe not a graduate of Hertzliya but at least one of their civilian sleepers, what they call *sayanim*. Holding down a day job out here in the Diaspora, waiting for a call."

Maxine looks at her watch, gathers her purse, and rises. "Not about to shop my sister's husband. Think of it as a personal quirk. Oh and your five minutes were up a while ago." She feels rather than hears his silence. "What. Such a face."

"One more thing, all right? People at my shop have learned of your interest, we assume professional, in the finances of hashslingrz.com."

"These are all public, the sites I use, nothing illegal, how do you know what I'm researching anyway?"

"Child's play," sez Windust, "we like to think of it as 'No keystroke left behind.'"

"So let me guess, you people want me to back off of hashslingerz."

"No, actually, if there's a fraud issue, we'd like to know about it. Sometime."

"You want to hire me? For money? Or were you planning to rely on charm?"

He finds a pair of tortoiseshell Wayfarer clones in his coat pocket and covers his eyes. Finally. Smiles, with that precision mouth. "Am I that much of a bad guy?"

"Oh. Now I'm supposed to help him with his self-esteem, Dr. Maxine here. Listen, a suggestion, you're from D.C., try the self-help section at Politics & Prose—empathy, we're all out of that today, the truck didn't show up."

He nods, rises, heads for the door. "Hope I see you again sometime." With the shades on, of course there is no telling what if anything this means. And he has stuck her, the cheapskate, with the check.

Well. Should've been it for Agent Windust. So it doesn't help that that very night, or actually next morning just before dawn, she has a vivid, all-but-lucid dream about him, in which they are not exactly fucking, but fucking around, definitely. The details ooze away as dawn light and the sounds of garbage trucks and jackhammers grow in the room, till she's left with a single image unwilling to fade, this federal penis, fierce red, predatory, and Maxine alone its prey. She has sought to escape but not sincerely enough for the penis, which is wearing some strange headgear, possibly a Harvard football helmet. It can read her thoughts. "Look at me, Maxine. Don't look away. Look at me." A talking penis. That same jive-ass radio-announcer voice.

She checks the clock. Too late to go back to sleep, though who would want to, necessarily? What she needs is to go in to the office and work on something nice and normal for a while. Just as she's about to head out with the boys to school, the doorbell rings its usual Big Ben theme which somebody a hundred years ago figured would be appropriate to the grandiosity of the building. Maxine squints through the peephole and here's Marvin the kozmonaut, dreads pushed up under his bike helmet, orange jacket and blue cargo pants, and over his shoulder an orange messenger bag with the running-man logo of the recently failed kozmo.com.

"Marvin. You're up early. What's with the outfit, you guys folded weeks ago."

"Don't mean I have to stop ridin. My legs are still pumpin, no mechanical issues with the bike, I can ride forever, I'm the Flyin Dutchmahn."

"Strange, I'm not expecting anything, you must have me mixed up with some other lowlife again." Except Marvin has an uncanny history of always showing up with items Maxine knows she didn't order but which prove each time to be exactly what she needs.

This is the first time she's ever seen him in the daylight hours. His shift used to begin at nightfall, and from then till dawn he'd be out on his orange fixed-gear track bike delivering donuts, ice cream, and videotapes, guaranteed to arrive within the hour, to the all-night community of dopers, hackers, instant-gratification cases who thought the dotcom balloon would ascend forever.

"It was all these ritzy neighborhoods up here," is Marvin's theory, "I knew the minute we started deliverin north of 14th Street it was the beginnin of the end."

According to folklore, Mayor Giuliani, who hates all bike delivery people, is said to have declared a vendetta against Marvin personally, which along with his Trinidadian origins and single-digit employee number at kozmo have brought him iconic status in the track-rider community.

"Missed you, Marvin."

"Lotta work. These days I'm all over the place, like Duane Reade. Don't give me that banknote you're wavin all around, it's way too much and way too sentimental, oh and here, this is for you as well."

Producing some kind of high-tech gizmo in beige plastic about four inches long by an inch wide, which seems to have a USB connector on one end.

"Marvin, what is it?"

"Ah, Mizziz L, always makin with those jokes. I just deliver em my dear."

Time to seek the advice of an expert. "Ziggy, what is this thing?"

"Looks like one of those little eight-megabyte flash drives. Like a memory card, only different? IBM makes one, but this is some Asian knockoff."

"So there could be files or something stored on this?"

"Anything, most likely text."

"What do I do, just plug it in my computer?"

"Yaahh! No! Mom! you don't know what's on it. I know some kids at Bronx Science—let them check it out in the computer lab up there."

"Sound like your grandma, Zig."

Next day, "That thumb drive? it's OK, safe to copy, just a lot of text, looks semiofficial."

"And now your friends have seen it before I have."

"They . . . uh, they don't read that much, Mom. Nothing personal. A generational thing." Turns out to be a piece of Nicholas Windust's own dossier, downloaded from some Deep Web directory for spooks called Facemask, and displaying the kind of merciless humor also to be found in high-school yearbooks.

Windust does not after all seem to be FBI. Something worse, if possible. If there is a brother- or God forbid sisterhood of neoliberal terrorists, Windust has been in there from the jump, a field operative whose first recorded job, as an entry-level gofer, was in Santiago, Chile, on 11 September 1973, spotting for the planes that bombed the presidential palace and killed Salvador Allende.

Beginning with low-level bagman activities, graduating to undercover surveillance and corporate espionage, Windust's list of credits at some point turned sinister, perhaps as early as his move across the Andes to Argentina. Job responsibilities began to include "interrogation enhancement" and "noncompliant-subject relocation." Even with her light grasp of Argentine history during those years, Maxine can translate this well enough. Around 1990, as part of a cadre of old Argentina hands, U.S. veterans of the Dirty War who then stayed on to advise the IMF stooges that rose to power in its aftermath, Windust was one of the founders of a D.C. think tank known as Toward America's New Global Opportunities (TANGO). He has a thirty-year history of visiting-lecturer gigs, including at the infamous School of the Americas. Is surrounded by the usual posse of younger protégés, though he seems to be against cults of personality on principle.

"Too Maoist for him, maybe," is one of the less bitchy comments, and indeed colleagues seem to have struggled at length with doubts about Windust. Considering the money to be made off of troubled economies worldwide, his unexpected reluctance to grab a piece of the proceeds for himself soon aroused suspicions. Duked in, he'd've been a safely co-enabling partner in crime. To be motivated only by raw ideology—besides greed, what else could it be?—made him weird, almost dangerous.

So, over time, Windust got pushed into a peculiar compromise. Whenever a government at the behest of the IMF sold off an asset, he agreed either to go in for a percentage or, later on, with more leverage, to buy it outright—but he never, the hippie nutcase, cashed anything in. A power plant goes private for pennies on the dollar, Windust becomes a silent partner. Wells that supply regional water systems, easements across tribal lands for power lines, clinics dedicated to tropical ailments unheard of in the developed world—Windust takes a modest position. If one day, untypically idle, he should pull out his portfolio to see what he's got he'd find himself with controlling interests in an oil field, a refinery, an educational system, an airline, a power grid, each in a different newly privatized part of the world. "None of them especially grand in scale," concludes one confidential report, "but considering the assembled set all together, by Zermelo's Axiom of Choice, subject at times has effectively found himself in control of an entire economy."

By the same kind of thinking, it occurs to Maxine, Windust has acquired a portfolio of pain and damage applied to various human body parts that might have added up to hundreds—who knows, maybe thousands—of deaths on his karmic ticket. Should she tell somebody? Ernie? Elaine, who's been trying to fix her up? They would so plotz.

This is fucking appalling. How does it happen, how does somebody get from entry-level foot soldier to the battered specimen who accosted

her the other night? This is a text file, no pictures, but Maxine can somehow see Windust back then, a clean-looking kid, short hair, chinos and
button-down shirts, only has to shave once a week, one of a globetrot-
ting gang of young smart-asses, piling into cities and towns all over the
Third World, filling ancient colonial spaces with office copiers and coffee machines, pulling all-nighters, running off neatly bound plans for
the total obliteration of target countries and their replacement by free-
market fantasies. "Need one of these on everybody's desk by nine A.M.,
¡ándale, ándale!" Comical Speedy Gonzales dialogue would've been standard among these generally eastern-seaboard snotnoses.

Back in that more innocent day, the damage Windust caused, if any,
all stayed safely on paper. But then, at some point, somewhere she thinks
of as down in the middle of a vast and unforgiving flatland, he took a
step. Hardly measurable in that immensity and yet, like finding and clicking on an invisible link on a screen, transported in the act over into his
next life.

Generally, all-male narratives, unless it's the NBA, challenge Maxine's
patience. Now and then Ziggy or Otis will hustle her into watching an
action movie, but if there aren't that many women in the opening credits, she'll tend to drift away. Something like this has been happening as
she scans through Windust's karmic rap sheet here, that's until she gets
to 1982–83, when he was stationed in Guatemala, ostensibly as part of an
agricultural mission, in coffee-growing country. Helpful Farmer Windust. Here, as it turned out, he met, courted, and married—as his nameless biographers put it, "deployed into a spousal scenario with"—a very
young local girl named Xiomara. For a minute Maxine imagines a wedding sequence out in the jungle, with pyramids, native Mayan rituals,
psychedelics. But no, instead it was in the sacristy at the local Catholic
church, everyone there already or about to become strangers . . .

If government agencies were in-laws, Xiomara would've been less
than acceptable on a number of counts. Politically her family was trouble waiting to happen, from old-school arevalista "spiritual socialists" on
leftward, through activists with a history of nonnegotiable hatred for

United Fruit, hardcore anarcho-Marxist aunts and cousins who ran safe houses and talked Kanjobal with the folks out in the country, plus assorted gun runners and dope dealers who just wanted to be left alone but were invariably described as Suspected Guerrilla Sympathizers, which seemed to mean everybody who lived in the region.

So . . . what do we have here, true love, imperialist rape, a cover story to get in good with the indigenous? The record is less than forthcoming. No further mention of Xiomara or for that matter Windust in Guatemala. A few months later he surfaces in Costa Rica, but without the missus.

Maxine scrolls onward but is now focusing more on why did Marvin bring her this in the first place, and what's she supposed to do with it? All right, all right, maybe Marvin is some kind of otherworldly messenger, an angel even, but whatever unseen forces may be employing him at the moment, she's obliged to ask professional questions, such as how in secular space might the data-storage gizmo have found its way to Marvin? Somebody wants her to see it. Gabriel Ice? Elements in the CIA or whoever? Windust himself?

11

A week or so later, Maxine's in Vontz Auditorium again for eighth-grade graduation. After the usual interfaith parade of clergy, each wearing some appropriate outfit, which always reminds her of the setup to a joke, the Kugelblitz Bebop Ensemble plays "Billie's Bounce," Bruce Winterslow sets some kind of Guinness Book record for most polysyllabic words in a sentence, and then on comes the guest speaker, March Kelleher. Maxine is a little shocked at the effects of only a couple years—wait, she wonders with a sudden pulse of panic, how many years exactly? March now has gray not just coming in but putting its feet up and making itself at home, and she's wearing oversize shades today that suggest a temporary loss of faith in eye makeup. She's wearing desert-camo fatigues and her signature snood, today a sort of electric green. Her commencement speech turns out to be a parable nobody is supposed to get.

"Once upon a time, there was a city with a powerful ruler who liked to creep around town in disguise, doing his work in secret. Now and then someone recognized him, but they were always willing to accept a small handful of silver or gold to forget all about it. 'You have been exposed for a moment to a highly toxic form of energy,' is his usual formula. 'Here is a sum I trust will compensate you for any damage done. Soon you will begin to forget, and then you'll feel better.'

"At the time, out and about in the night, there was also an older lady, probably didn't look too different from your grandmother, who carried a huge sack full of dirty rags, scraps of paper and plastic, broken appliances, leftover food, and other rubbish she collected off the street. She went everywhere, she had lived out in the city longer than anyone there, unprotected and in the open regardless of the weather, and she knew everything. She was the guardian of whatever the city threw away.

"On the day she and the ruler of the city finally crossed paths, he got a rude surprise—when he offered his well-meant handful of coins, she angrily flung them back at him. They went scattering and ringing on the paving stones. 'Forget?' she screeched. 'I cannot and must not forget. Remembering is the essence of what I am. The price of my forgetting, great sir, is more than you can imagine, let alone pay.'

"Taken aback, somehow thinking he must not have offered enough, the ruler began to dig through his purse again, but when he looked up, the old woman had vanished. That day he returned from his secret tasks earlier than usual, in a queer state of nerves. He supposed now he'd have to find this old woman and render her harmless. How awkward.

"Though he was not by nature a violent person, he had learned a long time ago that nobody held on to a job like his unless they were willing to do whatever it took. For years he had sought new and creative methods short of violence, which usually came down to buying people off. Stalkers of imperial celebrities were hired as bodyguards, journalists with nasal-length issues were redesignated 'analysts' and installed at desks in the state intelligence office.

"By this logic the old woman with her sack of garbage should have become an environmental cabinet minister and someday get parks and recycle centers all across the realm named after her. But whenever anyone tried to approach her with job offers, she was never to be found. Her criticisms of the regime, however, had already entered the collective consciousness of the city and become impossible to delete.

"Well, kids, it's just a story. The kind of story you were likely to hear in Russia back in the days when Stalin was in power. People told each other these Aesop's fables and everybody knew what stood for what. But can we in the 21st-century U.S. say the same?

"Who is this old lady? What does she think she's been finding out all these years? Who is this 'ruler' shes's refusing to be bought off by? And what's this 'work' he was 'doing in secret'? Suppose 'the ruler' isn't a person at all but a soulless force so powerful that though it cannot ennoble, it does entitle, which, in the city-nation we speak of, is always more than enough? The answers are left to you, the Kugelblitz graduating class of 2001, as an exercise. Good luck. Think of it as a contest. Send your answers to my Weblog, tabloidofthedamned.com, first prize is a pizza with anything you want on it."

The address gets her some applause, more than it would've at the snob academies east and west of here, but not as much as you might've expected a Kugelblitz alum to get.

"It's my personality," she tells Maxine at the reception afterward. "The women don't like the way I turn myself out, the men don't like my attitude. Which is why I'm starting to cut back on the personal appearances and concentrate instead on my Weblog." Handing Maxine one of the flyers that Otis brought home.

"I'll visit it," Maxine promises.

Nodding across the patio, "Who's that you came in with, the Sterling Hayden look-alike?"

"The what? Oh, that's my ex. Well. Sort of ex."

"This is the same 'ex' as two years ago? It wasn't final then, it isn't final yet, what are you waiting for? Some Nazi name, if I remember right."

"Horst. Is this gonna be on the Internet now?"

"Not if you do me a big favor."

"Uh-oh."

"Seriously, you're a CFE, right?"

"They pulled my certificate, I'm freelance now."

"Whatever. I have to pick your brain about something."

"Should we have lunch someplace?"

"I don't do lunch. Corrupt artifact of late capitalism. Breakfast maybe?"

She's smiling, however. It occurs to Maxine that contrary to the speech she just gave, March isn't a crone, she's a dumpling. With the face and demeanor of somebody who you know within five minutes of meeting them will be telling you to eat something. Something specific, which she will have on a spoon already on its way to your mouth.

THE PIRAEUS DINER on Columbus is littered, dilapidated, full of cigarette smoke and cooking odors from the kitchen, a neighborhood institution. Mike the waiter drops a couple of very heavy menus bound in cracked brown plastic on the table and stalks off. "I can't believe this place is still here," March says. "Talk about living on borrowed time."

"Come on, this joint, it's eternal."

"What planet are you from again? Between the scumbag landlords and the scumbag developers, nothing in this city will ever stand at the same address for even five years, name me a building you love, someday soon it'll either be a stack of high-end chain stores or condos for yups with more money than brains. Any open space you think will breathe and survive in perpetuity? Sorry, but you can kiss its ass good-bye."

"Riverside Park?"

"Ha! Forget it. Central Park itself isn't safe, these men of vision, they dream about CPW to Fifth Avenue solid with gracious residences. Meantime the Newspaper of Record goes around in a little pleated skirt shaking pompoms, leaping in the air with an idiot grin if so much as a cement mixer passes by. The only way to live here is not to get attached."

Maxine is hearing similar advice from Shawn, though not necessarily in terms of real estate. "I checked out your Weblog last night, March, so now you're chasing dotcoms also?"

"Real estate, easy to hate, these techies it's a little different. You know what Susan Sontag always sez."

"'I like the streak, I'm keeping it'?"

"If there's a sensibility you really want to talk about, and not just exhibit it yourself, you need 'a deep sympathy modified by contempt.'"

"I get the contempt part, but remind me about the sympathy?"

"Their idealism," maybe a little reluctantly, "their youth . . . Maxi, I haven't seen anything like it since the sixties. These kids are out to change the world. 'Information has to be free'—they really mean it. At the same time, here's all these greedy fuckin dotcommers make real-estate developers look like Bambi and Thumper."

The coin-op washing machine of Intuition clangs on into a new cycle. "Let me guess. Your estranged son-in-law, Gabriel Ice."

"She's a magician. You do birthday parties?"

"Actually right at the moment, hashslingrz also happen to be causing a client of mine some agità. Sort of client."

"Yeah, yeah?" Eagerly, "Fraud maybe?"

"Nothing forensic that'd hold up in court, or not yet anyway."

"Maxi, there is something really, really weird going on over there."

Mike shows up with a smoldering cigar gripped in his teeth. "Ladies?"

"Not lately," March beams. "How about waffles, bacon, sausage, homefries, coffee."

"Special K," sez Maxine, "skim milk, some kind of fruit?"

"Today for you, a banana."

"Some coffee too. Please."

March is shaking her head slowly. "Early-stage food nazi here. So tell me, you and Gabriel Ice, what?"

"Just good friends, don't believe Page Six." Maxine gives her a quick rundown—the Benford Curve anomalies, the ghost vendors, the Gulf-ward flow of capital. "I've only got a surface picture so far. But there do seem to be a lot of government contracts."

March nods sourly. "Hashslingrz is as tight as it gets with the U.S. security apparatus, an arm of, if you like. Crypto work, countermeasures, heaven knows what-all. You know he's got a mansion out in Montauk, just a morning jog down the trail from the old air base." Funny look on her face, a strange mixture of amusement and doom.

"Why would that—"

"The Montauk Project."

"The . . . Oh, wait, Heidi's mentioned that . . . She teaches it, some kind of . . . urban legend?"

"You could say." Beat. "You could also say, the terminal truth about the U.S. government, worse than anything you can imagine."

Mike shows up with the food. Maxine sits peeling her banana, slicing it over the cereal, trying to keep her eyes wide and unjudging while March digs in to her high-cholesterol eats and is soon talking with her mouth full. "I see my share of conspiracy theories, some are patently bullshit, some I want to believe so much I have to be careful, others are inescapable even if I wanted to escape. The Montauk Project is every horrible suspicion you've ever had since World War II, all the paranoid production values, a vast underground facility, exotic weapons, space aliens, time travel, other dimensions, shall I go on? And who turns out to have a lively if not psychopathic interest in the subject but my own reptilian son-in-law, Gabriel Ice."

"As another kid billionaire with a wacko obsession, you mean, or . . . ?"

"Try 'power-hungry little CIA-groupie jerkoff.'"

"That's if it's real, this Montauk thing."

"Remember, back in '96, TWA Flight 800? Blown out of the sky over Long Island Sound, a government investigation which got so cute that everybody ended up thinking it was them that did it. Montaukies say it was particle-beam weapons being developed in a secret lab under Montauk Point. Some conspiracies, they're warm and comforting, we know the names of the bad guys, we want to see them get their comeuppance. Others you're not sure you want any of it to be true because it's so evil, so deep and comprehensive."

"What—time travel? Aliens?"

"If you were doing something in secret and didn't want the attention, what better way to have it ridiculed and dismissed than bring in a few Californian elements?"

"Ice doesn't strike me as an antigovernment crusader or a seeker after truth."

"Maybe he thinks it's all real and wants to be duked in. If he isn't already. He doesn't talk about it at all. Everybody knows that Larry Ellison races yachts, Bill Gross collects stamps. But this, what *Forbes* would probably call, 'passion' of Ice's, isn't too widely known. Yet."

"Sounds like something you want to post on your Weblog."

"Not till I find out more. Every day there's new evidence, too much Ice money going for hidden purposes in too many directions. Maybe all connected, maybe only part. These ghost payments you've been trying to follow, for example."

"Trying. They're getting smurfed out all over the world to pass-through accounts in Nigeria, Yugoslavia, Azerbaijan, all finally reassembled in a holding bank in the Emirates, some Special Purpose Vehicle registered in the Jebel Ali Free Zone. Like the Smurf Village, only cuter."

March sits blinking at the food on her fork, and you can almost see those old-lefty gears being double-clutched into engagement and starting to spin. "Now, *that* I might want to post."

"Maybe not. I wouldn't want to scare anybody off quite yet."

"What if it's Islamic terrorists or something? Time might be of the essence."

"Please. I just chase embezzlers, what do I look like, James Bond?"

"I don't know, give us a macho smirk here, let's see."

But something now in March's face, some obscure collapse, starts Maxine wondering who else is going to cut her any slack. "OK look, my whistle-blower has a source, some kid übergeek, he's been digging, trying to crack into some stuff that hashslingrz has encrypted. Whatever he finds, whenever that is, I could pass it on to you, OK?"

"Thanks, Maxi. I'd like to say I owe you one, though at the moment, technically, I don't. But if you'd really like me to . . ." She looks almost embarrassed, and Maxine's mom ESP, cranking into action now, tells her this will not be unconnected with Tallis, the child March is not shy about admitting she once literally prayed to have, the one she misses most of all, living over on the Upper East Side, just across the park but it might as well be Katmandu also, society lady, a kid of her own that March seldom if ever sees—lost Tallis, bought and sold into a world March will never give up her hatred of.

"Let me guess."

"I can't go over there. I can't, but maybe you could on a pretext, just to see how she's doing. Really, just a secondhand report's all I want. From what I can tell off the Internet, she's the company comptroller at hashslingrz, so maybe you could, I don't know . . ."

"Just call up, say 'Hi, Tallis, I think somebody at your company's playing Who Stole the Cookie from the Cookie Jar, maybe you need a decertified CFE?' Come on, March, it's ambulance chasing."

"So . . . they'll re-decertify you, what?"

Carefully, "When's the last time you saw her?"

"Carnegie Mellon when she got her M.B.A. Years now. I wasn't even invited, but I went anyhow. Even from where I was, way in the back, she was radiant. I lurked around the Fence there for a while hoping she'd come by. Kind of fuckin pathetic, looking back. That Barbara Stanwyck movie, without the bad fashion advice."

Provoking a reflex appraisal of March's turnout choices today. Maxine notices how the snood matches her handbag. Sort of a vivid turnip purple. "OK, look, I can probably use the occasion to do a little social engineering. Even if she won't take a meeting, even that'll tell me something, right?"

12

Tallis is briefly back from Montauk and able to make some space for Maxine before work. Very early in the morning, through queasy summer light, Maxine first heads downtown to a weekly appointment with Shawn, who looks like he's just pulled an all-nighter at a sensory-deprivation tank.

"Horst is back."

"Is that, like," air quotes, "'back'? Or just back?"

"I'm supposed to know?"

Tapping a temple as if hearing voices from far away, "Vegas? Church of Elvis? Horst 'n' Maxine take two?"

"Please, this is what I'd hear from my mother, if my mother didn't hate Horst so much."

"Too oedipal for me, but I can refer you to a really awesome Freudian, flexible rates, all that."

"Maybe not. What do you think Dōgen would do?"

"Sit."

After what seems like a good part of the hour has ticked away, "Um . . . sit, yes, and . . . ?"

"Just sit."

THE CABDRIVER ON THE WAY uptown has his radio tuned to a Christian call-in station, which he's listening to attentively. This does not bode well. He decides to get on Park and take it all the way up. The biblical text being discussed on the radio at the moment is from 2 Corinthians, "For you suffer fools gladly, seeing you yourselves are wise," which Maxine takes as a sign not to suggest alternate routes.

Park Avenue, despite attempts at someone's idea of beautification, has remained, for all but the chronically clue-free, the most boring street in the city. Built originally as a kind of genteel lid to cover up the train tracks running into Grand Central, what should it be, the Champs-Élysées? Sped through, at night, by stretch limo, let's say, on the way to Harlem, it might register as just bearable. In broad daylight, however, at an average speed of one block per hour, jammed with loud and toxic-smelling traffic, all in advanced states of disrepair, whose drivers suffer (or enjoy) a hostility level comparable to that of Maxine's driver here—not to mention police barricades, Form Single Lane signs, jackhammer crews, backhoes and front-end loaders, cement mixers, asphalt spreaders, and battered dump trucks unmarked by any contractor's name let alone phone number—it becomes an occasion for spiritual exercise, though maybe more of the Eastern type than anything connected with this radio station, now blasting some kind of Christian hip-hop. Christian what? No, she doesn't want to know.

Presently they are cut off by a Volvo with dealer plates, flaunting its polyhedral crush zones, secure in its exemption from accident.

"Fucking Jews," the driver glaring, "people drive like fucking animals."

"But . . . animals can't drive," soothes Maxine, "and actually . . . would Jesus talk like that?"

"Jesus would love it if every Jew got nuked," the driver explains.

"Oh. But," she somehow can't help pointing out, "wasn't . . . he Jew-ish himself?"

"Don't give me that shit, lady." He points to a full-color print of his Redeemer clipped to the sun visor. "That look like any Jew you ever saw? Check out his feet—sandals? right? Everybody knows Jews don't wear sandals, they wear loafers. Honey, you must be from way out of town."

You know, she almost replies, *I must be.*

"You're my last fare of the day." In a tone so strange now that Maxine's warning lights begin to blink. She glances at the time on the backseat video display. It is far from the end of any known shift.

"I've been that rough on you?" Hopefully playful.

"I have to begin the process. I keep putting it off, but I'm out of time, today's the day. We don't just get scooped up like fish in a net, we know it's coming, we have to prepare."

All thoughts of insult tips or end-of-ride lectures have evaporated. If she arrives safely, it's worth . . . what? Double the fare at least.

"Actually, I need to walk a couple blocks, why don't you let me off here?" He's more than happy to and before the door's fully shut has peeled away around a corner eastbound and on to some destiny she doesn't need to think about.

Maxine is no stranger to the Upper East Side, though it still makes her uncomfortable. As a kid she went to Julia Richman High—well, she could've been on the natch once or twice—over on East 67th, rode cross-town buses five days a week, never got used to it. Deep hairband coun-try. Visiting over here is always like stepping into a planned midgets' community, everything scaled down, blocks shorter, avenues less time to walk across, you expect any minute to be approached by a tiny official greeter going, "As mayor of the Munch-kin City . . ."

The Ice residence, on the other hand, is the sort of place about which real-estate agents tend to start cooing, "It's huge!" To put it another way, fucking enormous. Two whole floors, possibly three, it's unclear though Maxine understands she isn't about to qualify for a tour. She enters through a public area, used for parties, musicales, fundraisers &c. Central air-conditioning is set on high, which as the day is developing couldn't hurt. Further in, some respectable fraction of a mile, she glimpses an elevator to someplace undoubtedly more private.

The rooms she's allowed to pass through lack character. Celadon walls on which are hung assorted expensive works of art—she recognizes an early Matisse, fails to recognize a number of abstract expressionists, maybe there's a Cy Twombley or two—not coherently enough to suggest the passions of a collector, more like the need of an acquirer to exhibit them. The Musée Picasso, the Guggenheim in Venice, it ain't. There is a Bösendorfer Imperial in the corner, at which generations of hired piano players have provided hours of Kander & Ebb, Rodgers & Hammerstein, Andrew Lloyd Webber medleys while Gabe and Tallis and assorted henchfolks work the room, gently thinning the checkbooks of East Side aristos on behalf of various causes, many of them trivial by West Side standards.

"My office," announces Tallis. A vintage George Nelson desk but also one of his Omar the Owl wall clocks. Uh-oh. Cute Alert.

Tallis has perfected the soap-opera trick of managing through all the daylight hours to look turned out for evening activities. High-end makeup, hair in a tousled bob with every strand expensively disarranged, taking its time, whenever she gestures with her head, to slide back into its artful confusion. Black silk slacks and a matching top unbuttoned halfway down, which Maxine thinks she recognizes from the Narciso Rodríguez spring collection, Italian shoes that only once a year are found on sale at prices humans can afford—some humans—emerald earrings weighing in at a half carat each, Hermès watch, Art Deco ring of Golconda diamonds which every time she passes through the sunlight coming in the window flares into a nearly blinding white, like a superheroine's magical flashbang for discombobulating the bad guys.

Who, it will occur to Maxine more than once during their tête-à-tête, maybe includes herself.

A downstairs maid of some kind brings a pitcher of iced tea and a bowl of root-vegetable chips of different colors including indigo.

"I love him forever, but Gabe is a weird guy, I've known it since we first started dating," Tallis in one of these small, sub-Chipmunk voices fatally charming to certain kinds of men. "He had all these, not creepy, but to me, unusual expectations? We were only kids, but I could see the potential, I told myself, honey, get with the program, this could be the perfect wave, and it's been . . . the worst it's been is educational?"

Me, I want a hula hoop.

Tallis and Gabriel met at Carnegie Mellon back in the golden age of the computer-science department there. Gabe's roommate Dieter was majoring in bagpipes, which CMU happened to offer a degree in, and even though the kid was allowed only a practice chanter in the dorms, the sound was enough to drive Gabe out to the computer cluster, which still wasn't far enough. Soon he was out gazing at student-lounge television screens or using the facilities at other dorms, including Tallis's, where he quickly slipped into a tubelit clustergeek existence, often unsure if he was awake or dreaming in REM, which might have accounted for his early conversations with Tallis, which she remembers nowadays as "unusual." She was his dream girl, literally. Her image became conflated with those of Heather Locklear, Linda Evans, and Morgan Fairchild, among others. She went around anxious about what might happen if he ever got a good night's sleep and saw her, the real Tallis, without the tubal overlay.

"So?" with a look.

"So what am I complaining about, I know, exactly what my mother used to say. When we were talking."

One concept of raising a topic, Maxine supposes. "Your mom and me, we're neighbors, it turns out."

"Are you a follower?"

"Not too much, in high school they even thought I had leadership potential."

"I meant a follower of my mother's Weblog? Tabloid of the Damned? Not a day passes without her flaming us, Gabe and me, our company, hashslingrz, she's been on our case forever. Obvious mother-in-law trip. Lately she's throwing around these wild accusations, massive diversions, a covert U.S. foreign-policy scam, of money overseas bigger than Iran/contra back in the eighties. According to my mother."

"I take it she and your husband don't get along."

"No more than she and I do. We basically hate each other, it's no secret."

The estrangement from March and her father Sid apparently began Tallis's junior year. "Spring break they wanted us off on some horror vacation to witness them screaming, which there was enough of already at home, so Gabe and I went to Miami instead, and apparently there was some footage of me topless that found its way on to MTV, tastefully pixelated and all, but it just got worse from there. And they got so busy fucking with each other's brain, by the time that was sorted out, Gabe and I were married and it was all too late."

Maxine keeps wanting to mention that she doesn't put into family dynamics, even if this is what March has her over here doing. But miles across the parquetry between them, some inertia of resentment is carrying Tallis along. "Anything bad she can find to say about hashslingrz, she'll post it."

But wait. Did Maxine just hear one of those implicit "buts"? She waits. "But," Tallis adds (no, no, is she going to—Aahhh! yes look she's actually putting her fingernail in her mouth here, ooh, ooh), "it doesn't mean she's wrong. About the money."

"Who does your auditing, Mrs. Ice?"

"Tallis, please. That's part of . . . the problem? We use D. S. Mills down on Pearl Street. Like, they actually do wear white shoes and stuff? But do I trust them? mmmh . . . ?"

"Far as I know, Tallis, they're kosher. Or whatever WASPs have for that. The book on these guys is the SEC loves them, maybe not enough to be the mother of its children, but enough. I can't see what problem they could be giving you."

"Suppose something's going on that they're not catching?"

Suppressing the urge to scream "Al-vinnn?" Maxine gently inquires, "Which . . . would be . . . ?"

"Ooh, I dunno . . . something weird about the disbursements after the last round? Considering the prime directive in this business is always be nice to your VCs?"

"And somebody at your company is being . . . mean to its?"

"The money is supposed to be earmarked for infrastructure, which since all that . . . second-quarter trouble last year has been going dirt cheap . . . Servers, miles of dark fiber, bandwidth there for the grabbing." Seeming to ditz over the technical stuff. Or is it something else? Just a skip, like you get from a blemish on a disc, nothing you'd ordinarily notice. "I'm supposed to be the comptroller, but when I bring any of it up with Gabe, he gets evasive. I'm beginning to feel like the babe in the window." Out with the lower lip.

"But . . . how do I put this tactfully . . . you and your husband have certainly had a grown-up chat, maybe even two, on this subject?"

A mischievous look, a hair toss. Shirley Temple should take notes. "Maybe. Would it be a problem if we didn't?" Did she say "pwobwem"? "I mean . . ." An interesting half a beat. "Until I know something for sure, I figure why bother him?"

"Unless he's in it up to his eyeballs himself, of course."

A quick inhale, as if just occurring to her, "Well . . . suppose you, or a colleague you might recommend, could look into it?"

Aha. "I hate matrimonials. Tallis. Sooner or later a firearm comes out. And this here, I can smell it, could turn matrimonial faster than you can say, 'But Ricky, it's only a hat.'"

"I'd be very appreciative."

"Uh huh, I'd still have to bring in your auditors."

"Couldn't you—" With the fingernail.

"It's a professional thing." Feeling all at once, in this obscenely overpriced interior, like so totally a sucker. Is Maxine slowing down? OK, maybe she can invoice this virtual bimbo any fee she wants to, the price of a high-ticket vacation far, far away, but not till later, deep in the winter months, as she relaxes on a tropical beach, will the rum concoction in her tall frosted glass suddenly curdle in her hand, as crashing in on her, too late, there arrives a freak wave of understanding.

Nothing in this fateful moment is what it seems. This woman here, despite her M.B.A., ordinarily a sure sign of idiocy, is playing you, smart-ass, and you need to be out of this place as quick as possible. A theatrically stressed glance at her G-shock Mini, "Whoa, lunch with a client, Smith & Wollensky, meat intake for the month, call you soon. If I see your mom, should I say hi?"

"'Drop dead' might be better."

Not too graceful a retreat. Given Maxine's lack of success, and the likelihood that Tallis's coolness will continue, she is stuck with telling March the unedited truth. That's assuming she can get a word in, because March, now under the impression that Maxine is some kind of guru in these matters, has begun another commencement speech, this time about Tallis.

A few years back, one bleak winter afternoon, on the way home from the Pioneer Market on Columbus, some faceless yuppie shoved past March saying "Excuse me," which in New York translates to "Get the fuck outta my way," and which turned out finally to be once too often. March dropped the bags she was carrying in the filthy slush on the street, gave them a good kick, and screamed as loud as she could, "I hate this miserable shithole of a city!" Nobody seemed to take notice, though the bags and their strewn contents were gone in seconds. The only reaction was from a passerby who paused to remark, "So? you don't like it, why don't you go live someplace else?"

"Interesting question," she recalls to Maxine now, "though how long did I really need to think about it? Because Tallis is here, is why, there it begins and ends and what else is new."

"With the two boys," Maxine nods, "it's different, but sometimes I'll sit and fantasize, what it would've been like, a girl."

"So? go have one, you're still just a kid."

"Yeah, problem is, so is Horst and everybody I've dated since."

"Oh, you should have seen my ex. Sidney. Disturbed adolescents from around the country would show up on pilgrimages just to inhale his secondhand smoke and stay calibrated."

"He's still . . ."

"Still kicking. He ever passes, it's gonna be such a rude surprise for him."

"You're in touch?"

"More than I would like, he lives out on the Canarsie line with some 12-year-old named Sequin."

"He gets to sees Tallis?"

"I think there's a restraining order dating back a couple years from when Sid started hanging around in the street under their window with a tenor sax and playing this old rock 'n' roll she used to like, and of course Ice put the kibosh on that quick enough."

"One tries not to wish anyone ill, but this Ice person, really . . ."

"She goes along with it. You never want to see kids repeat your own mistakes. So what happens, Tallis goes ahead just like me and marries the wrong promising entrepreneur. The worst you can say for Sid is he couldn't handle the stress of being around me all the time. Ice on the other hand appreciates stress, the more the better, so naturally Tallis, my perverse child, goes out of her way *not* to give him any. And he pretends he loves it. He's evil."

"So," carefully, "job title at hashslingrz and so forth aside, how duked in would you say she is?"

"On what? Company secrets? She's not whistle-blower material, if that's what you're hoping."

"Not disgruntled enough, you mean."

"She could be going around in a fit of rage 24/7, what difference would it make? Their prenup has more riders on it than the subway. Ice fucking owns her."

"I was only there for maybe an hour, but I got this feeling. Like an agenda she may not be sharing with the wunderkind."

"Like what?" A hopeful gleam. "A person."

"We were only talking fraud . . . but . . . you think there could be a BF in the picture also?"

"Certain chapters of history would suggest. Tell you, frankly, it wouldn't break her mother's heart."

"Wish I had better news for you."

"So I'll go on taking what I can get, my grandson Kennedy, I've got a graft in with the baby-sitter, Ofelia, she finds us a minute or two alone now and then. What else can I do but keep an eye on him, make sure they don't fuck him up too bad." Looks at her watch. "You got a minute?"

They proceed to the corner of 78th and Broadway. "Please don't tell anybody."

"We're waiting for your dealer, what?"

"For Kennedy. They're sending him to Collegiate. Where fuckin else. They want him seamlessly programmed on into Harvard, law school, Wall Street, the usual Manhattan death march. Well. Not if his grandma can help it."

"I bet he's crazy about you. Supposed to be the second-strongest human bond there is."

"Sure, 'cause you both hate the same people."

"Ooh."

"OK, maybe exaggerating, I do hate Tallis of course, but I also love her now and then."

Down the block in front of the ruling-class polytechnic, small boys in shirts and ties have begun to mill around. Maxine spots Kennedy right away, you don't have to be clairvoyant. Blond, curly-headed, an apprentice heartbreaker, he backs gracefully away from a knot of boys, waves, turns and comes at a dead run up the block and into March's embrace.

"Hey, kid. Tough day?"

"They're making me crazy, Grandma."

"Course they are, semester break's almost here, they're just getting in a couple more late hits."

"Somebody up the block waving at you," Maxine sez.

"Damn, it's Ofelia already? The car must be early. Well, my good lad, it's been short but meaningful. Oh and here, I almost forgot." Handing over two or three Pokémon cards.

"Gengar! Japanese Psyduck?"

"These I'm told you can only get out of machines in selected arcades in Tokyo. I may have a connection, stay tuned."

"Awesome, Grandma, thank you." Another hug and he's off. Watching him run to where Ofelia is now waiting, March goes a little telephoto with her gaze. "That happy Ice couple, I'm tellin ya, either they're still not on to me or they're doin a great impression of stupid. Either way somebody's told Gunther to get here sooner."

"Nice kid, there, for a Pokémaniac."

"I can only pray Tallis didn't get any neat-freak DNA from Sid's mother. Sid is still brooding about all his baseball cards that she threw out forty years ago."

"Horst's mother too. What was with that generation?"

"Never happen today, not with the handle these yups have on the collectibles market. Still, I buy two of everything, just to be safe."

"You're gonna get Grandma of the Year, you don't watch out."

"Hey," March determined to be a tough guy, "Pokémon, what do I know? some West Indian proctologist, right?"

HORST CAN'T FIND the ice-cream flavor he really needs today and is showing signs of gathering impatience, alarming in one usually so stolid.

"Chocolate Peanut-Butter Cookie Dough? Hasn't been any of that around for years, Horst." Aware that she sounds exactly like the acid-tongued spoiler she has labored all these years not to be, at least not sound like.

"I can't explain it. It's like Chinese medicine. Yang deficiency. Yin? One of them."

"Meaning . . ."

"I would not want to freak out in front of the boys."

"Oh, but in front of me, no problem."

"How do I begin with someone at your level of food education? Aaahhh! *Chocolate Peanut Butter Cookie Dough.* See what I'm saying?"

Maxine takes the cordless phone and uses it for half of a time-out sign. "Just going to dial 911 here, OK sweetie? Except of course, that, given all your priors . . ."

How serious a domestic incident this is shaping up to be no one will ever know, because just then Rigoberto buzzes up from the lobby. "Marvin's here?"

Before she can hang up the intercom, he's at the door. Ganjaportation, no doubt. "Again, Marvin."

"Day and night out there bringin the people what they need." From the soon-to-be-vintage kozmo bag he produces two quarts of Ben & Jerry's Chocolate Peanut Butter Cookie Dough ice cream.

"They discontinued this back in '97," Maxine less in wonder than annoyance.

"That's only the business page talkin, Mahxine. This is desire."

Horst, already gobbling ice cream with spoons in both hands, nods enthusiastically.

"Oh and this too, this is for you." Handing over a videocassette in a box.

"*Scream, Blacula, Scream?* We already have a good depth of copy in the house, including the director's cut."

"Dahlin, I only deliver em."

"You have a number I can call you at in case I want to forward this on someplace else?"

"Not how it works. I come to you."

Off he glides into the summer evening.

13

One early hour, all too soon, the boys and Horst are up and into a roomy black Lincoln to JFK. The plan for the summer is to fly to Chicago, take in the town, rent a car, drive to Iowa, visit with the grandparents there, then go off on a grand tour of what Maxine thinks of as the Midol West, because whenever she's there it feels like her period. She rides along out to the airport, like not being clingy or anything, just could do with a nice breeze, through the window of the Town Car, OK?

Flight attendants walk in pairs, hands devotionally in front of them, nuns of the sky. Long lines of people in shorts and towering backpacks shuffle slowly along in check-in lines. Kids mess with the spring-loaded tapes on the queue-control stanchions. Maxine finds herself analyzing the traffic flow to see which line is moving fastest. It's only a habit, but it makes Horst uneasy because she's always right.

She stays till the flight is called, embracing everybody, even Horst, watches them down the Jetway, and only Otis looks back.

On the way out as she's passing another departure gate, she hears her name called. Squealed, actually. It's Vyrva, decked out in sandals, big floppy straw hat, microlength sundress in a number of vibrant colors banned by statute in New York. "Headed for California, are we?"

"Couple weeks there with the folks, then we're coming back by way of Vegas."

"Defcon," Justin, in Hawaiian-print surfer's board shorts, parrots and so forth, explains, which is an annual hackers' convention, where geeks of all persuasions, on all sides of the law, not to mention cops at various levels who think they're working undercover, converge, conspire, and carouse.

Fiona's been off at some kind of anime camp in New Jersey—Quake movie and machinima workshops, Japanese staff who claim not to know a word of English beyond "awesome" and "sucks," which for a vast range of human endeavor, actually, is more than enough . . .

"And how's everything down in DeepArcher?" Only trying to be sociable, understand . . .

Justin looks uncomfortable. "One way or another, big changes on the way. Whoever's in there better be enjoying it while they can. While it's still relatively unhackable."

"It isn't going to be?"

"Not for long. Too many people after it. Vegas is gonna be like speed-pitching at the fuckin zoo."

"Don't look at me," sez Vyrva, "I just roll the joints and bring out the junk food."

A voice comes on the PA, making an announcement in English, though Maxine is suddenly unable to understand a word. The sort of resonant voice in which events are solemnly foretold, not at all a voice she would ever want to be summoned by.

"Our flight," Justin picking up his carry-on.

"My best to Siegfried and Roy."

Vyrva blows kisses over her shoulder all the way to the gate.

. . .

AT THE OFFICE, when Maxine checks back in, here's Daytona with a tiny TV set she keeps in her desk drawer, glued to an afternoon movie on the Afro-American Romance Channel (ARCH) called *Love's Nickel Defense,* in which Hakeem, a pro defensive linebacker, on the set of a beer commercial he's doing, meets and falls in love with Serendypiti, a model in the same commercial, who immediately gets this Hakeem revved up to where before long he is dealing with running backs the way in-laws deal with hors d'oeuvres. Sparked by his example, the offense begins to develop its own winning ways. What has up to now been the lackluster year of a team that never wins even coin tosses is turned around. Win after win—a wildcard! the playoffs! the Super Bowl!

Halftime at the Super Bowl, the team is down by ten points. Plenty of time to turn this around. Serendypiti comes storming through several layers of security and into the locker room. "Honey, we got to talk." Break for commercial.

"Whoo!" Daytona shaking her head. "Oh, you back? Listen, some muthafucker with white attitude called about ten minutes ago." She fishes around on her desk and finds a note to call Gabriel Ice and what looks like a cellular number.

"I'll do this in the other room. Your movie's back on."

"You be careful around this one, child."

Bearing in mind the ancient CFE distinction between being complicit and merely attending to phone calls that should probably be answered, she is presently on to Gabriel Ice.

No hello, how you doing, "Are you on a secure line?" is what the digital tycoon would like to know.

"I use it all the time for shopping, tell people my credit-card numbers and stuff, nothing bad's happened yet."

"I guess we could get into definitions of 'bad,' but—"

"We could drift seriously off topic, yes fatal to a busy, important life . . . So . . ."

"I think you know my mother-in-law, March Kelleher. Have you seen her Web site?"

"I click into it now and then."

"You may have read some harsh comments, like every day, about my company. Any idea why she's doing this?"

"She seems to distrust you, Mr. Ice. Deeply. She must believe that behind the dazzling saga of boy-billionaire excess we all find so entertaining, there lies a darker narrative."

"We're in the security business. What do you want, transparent?"

No, I prefer opaque, encrypted, sneaky-assed. "Too political for me."

"How about financial? The *shviger*—how much do you think it would cost me to get her to lay off? Just a ballpark estimate."

"Somehow, like, I get this dim feeling, March doesn't have a price."

"Yeah, yeah, maybe you could ask anyway? I'd be really, really grateful."

"She's got you that worried? Come on, it's only a Weblog, how many people even read it?"

"One is too many, if it's the wrong one."

Bringing them to a standoff, ethnicity of your choice. Her comeback should be, "With all your high-powered connections, who in the wide civilian world is ever going to hold you accountable for anything?" But that would be admitting she knows more than she's supposed to. "Tell you what, next time I see March, I'll ask her why she isn't speaking more highly of your company, and then when she spits in my face and calls me your bitch and a corporate sellout and so forth, I'll be able to ignore it 'cause down deep I'll know I'm doing a big favor for a swell guy."

"You despise me, right?"

She pretends to think about this. "People like you have a license to despise—mine got pulled, so I have to settle for being pissed off, and it doesn't last."

"Good to know. It might help you in future to stay away from my wife too, by the way."

"Wait a minute, li'l buddy," what a nasty piece of work this guy is, "you got me all wrong, like she's cute as a bug's ear and all but—"

"Just try to keep some distance. Be professional. Make sure you know who it is you're working for, OK?"

"Talk slower, I'm trying to write this down."

Ice, as intended, hangs up in a snit.

ROCKY SLAGGIATT CHECKS IN. As usual bringing no luggage. "Hey. Maxi, I got to come up to your neighborhood and intimidate, no wait what'd I say, I mean 'impress,' some customers. Need to discuss somethin witchyiz, in person."

"Important, right?"

"Maybe. You know the Omega Diner on 72nd?"

"Near Columbus, sure. Ten minutes?"

Rocky is sitting in a booth in the back, in the deep underlit recesses of the Omega, with a smooth business type in a bespoke suit, pale-rimmed glasses, medium height, yuppie demeanor.

"Sorry to pull yiz away from work and shit. Say hello to Igor Dashkov, nice guy to have on your Rolodex."

Igor kisses Maxine's hand and nods to Rocky. "She is not wearing wire, I hope."

"I'm wire-intolerant," Maxine pretends to explain, "I memorize everything instead, then later when they debrief me I can dump it all word for word on the feds. Or whoever it is you're so afraid of."

Igor smiles, angles his head like, charmed I'm sure.

"So far," Rocky murmurs, "the cop has not been invented who could get these guys any more than maybe faintly annoyed."

In the booth adjoining, Maxine notices two young torpedoes of a certain dimension, busy with handheld game consoles. "Doom," Igor waving a thumb, "just came out for Game Boy. Post–late capitalism run amok, 'United Aerospace Corporation,' moons of Mars, gateways to hell, zombies and demons, including I think these two. Misha and Grisha. Say hello, *padonki*."

Silence and button activity.

"How nice to make your acquaintance, Misha and Grisha." Whatever your real names may be, hi, I'm Marie of Roumania.

"Actually," one of them looking up, baring a lineup of stainless-steel jailhouse choppers, "we prefer Deimos and Phobos."

"Too much time with video games. Just out of zona, distant relatives, now not so distant. Brighton Beach, it's heaven for them. I bring them over to Manhattan so they can have look at hell. Also to meet my pal Rocco. VC business is treating you well, old amigo?"

"A little slow," Rocky shrugging, "*mi gratto la pancia*, you know, just scratcha da stomach."

"We say *khuem grushi okolachivat*," beaming at Maxine, "knocking pears out of pear tree with dick."

"Sounds complicated," Maxine smiling back.

"But fun."

Even if this guy looks like he still gets carded at clubs, apparently somewhere inside the smooth suburban packaging, nested *matrioshka*-deep, is a hulking battle-scarred ex-Spetsnaz toughguy eager to tell war stories from ten years ago. Next thing anybody knows, Igor is flashing back to a clandestine HALO jump over the northern Caucasus.

"Falling through night sky, over mountains, freezing my ass off, I begin to meditate—what is it I really want out of life? Kill more Chechens? Find true love and raise family, someplace warm, like Goa maybe? Almost forget to deploy my parachute. Down on ground again, everything is clear. Totally. Make lots of money."

Rocky cackles. "Hey, I figured that one out, didn't have to jump out of no airplane."

"Maybe if you jump, you decide to give all your money away."

"You know anybody ever did that?" sez Maxine.

"Strange things happen to men in Spetsnaz," replies Igor. "Not to mention upper altitudes."

"Ask her," Rocky leaning in toward Igor's ear. "Go ahead, she's OK."

"Ask me what?"

"Know anything about these people?" Igor slides a folder in front of her.

"Madoff Securities. Hmm, maybe some industry scuttlebutt. Bernie Madoff, a legend on the street. Said to do quite well, I recall."

"One to two percent per month."

"Nice average return, so what's the problem?"

"Not average. Same every month."

"Uh-oh." She flips pages, has a look at the graph. "What the fuck. It's a perfect straight line, slanting up forever?"

"Seem a little abnormal to you?"

"In this economy? Look at this—even last year, when the tech market went belly-up? No, it's got to be a Ponzi scheme, and from the scale of these investments he could be front-running also. You have any money with him?"

"Friends of mine. They've become concerned."

"And . . . these are grown-up persons who can deal with unwelcome news?"

"In their special way. But they warmly appreciate wise advice."

"Well, that's me, and my advice today is proceed quickly, unemotionally if possible, to the nearest exit strategy. Time is of the essence. Last month would have been good."

"Rocky says you have gift."

"Any idiot, nothing personal, could see this. Why isn't the SEC taking action here? The DA, somebody."

A shrug, eloquent eyebrows, thumb rubbing fingers.

"Well yes, that's certainly a thought."

For a while Maxine has been aware of peripheral armwaving and hand jive, not to mention quiet declamation and deejay sound effects, from the direction of Misha and Grisha, who turn out to be great fans of the semiunderground Russian hip-hop scene, in particular a pint-size Russian Rastafarian rap star named Detsl—having committed to memory his first two albums, Misha doing the music and beatboxing, Grisha the lyric, unless she has them switched around . . .

Igor pointedly consulting a white-gold Rolex Cellini, "Do you think hip-hop is good for them? You have children? What about them, do they . . ."

"The stuff I was listening to at that age, I'm in no position—but this number they're doing now, it's kinda catchy."

"'Vetcherinka U Detsla,'" Grisha sez.

"'Party at Detsl's,'" explains Misha.

"Wait, wait, let's do 'Ulitchnyi Boyets' for her."

"Next time," Igor rising to leave, "promise." He shakes hands with Maxine, kissing her on both cheeks, left-right-left. "I'll pass your advice on to my friends. We'll let you know what happens." Tunefully away and out the door.

"Those two gorillas," Rocky announces, "just ate two whole chocolate cream pies. Each. And I get stuck with the check."

"So it was Igor who wanted to see me, not you?"

"Ya disappointed?"

"Nah, my kinda fella. He's mob, or what?"

"Still tryinna figure it out. People he hangs with in Brighton Beach, some of them were in Yaponchik's circle before the li'l Jap got popped, definitely a old-school crowd. But just doing a quick eyeball scan, no visible tats, 15 and a half collar size, ehh," wobbling his hand, "it's doubtful. He seems to me more like a fixer."

ONE DAY, headed for The Deseret pool, Maxine finds the service elevator is tied up, perhaps till further notice—more yuppie scum moving in, no doubt. She goes looking for another elevator and eventually finds herself downstairs in the labyrinthine basement about to step, much against her better judgment, into the infamous Back Elevator, a legacy from earlier days, rumored to possess a mind of its own. In fact, Maxine has come to believe it is haunted, that Something Happened in it years ago that never got resolved, and so now whenever it sees a chance to, it tries to steer occupants in directions that might help it find some karmic relief. This time instead of going all the way up to the pool, whose button she has pressed, it takes her to a floor she doesn't recognize right away, which turns out to be . . .

"Maxi, hey."

She squints into the somehow greasy dimness. "Reg?"

"It's like being in some Asian horror movie," Reg whispers. "Oxide Pang probably. Can you kind of slide over here alongside the wall so we stay clear of that security camera?"

"And why are we keeping out of camera range, again?"

"They don't want me in the building. By now there's got to be at least a restraining order."

"You're what, you . . . stalk buildings now?"

"That fake toilet at hashslingrz? Just now out in the street, happened to spot one of the guys from there, had enough blank tape with me, so I started following and taping. Zigzagging all over the neighborhood, after a while he picks up a couple-three others I recognize, and next thing I knew, they're all going into The Deseret here, getting star treatment at the gate. It occurs to me that since Gabriel Ice is one of the owners of this place—"

"Wait a minute, Ice? Since when?"

"Thought you knew. Any case it's all academic now, we've been overtaken by events. Ice fired me off the movie yesterday. My apartment got broken into again, this time trashed, all my footage taken except what I hid."

Not a promising development. "You better come with me. There might be a service elevator free by now."

By way of which they manage to escape out the back and over to Riverside, where they just make it onto a bus heading downtown.

"I don't suppose you've mentioned this to the cops or anything."

"In case they need a good laugh to lighten up their otherwise grim workday, you mean. Sure, how about on my way out of town?"

"Seattle."

"It's time, Maxi. Ice did me a favor. I don't need a hashslingrz movie on my résumé, bad for my image, and you know what, hashslingrz is history. Whatever happens, it's fuckin doomed."

"Wouldn't say they're on the brink of Chapter Eleven exactly."

"If a dotcom had an immortal soul," Reg strangely distant, as if already calling back out the window of some westbound conveyance, "hashslingrz's'd be lost."

They get off at 8th Street, find a pizza joint, sit for a while at a side-walk table. Reg drifts into a patch of philosophical weather.

"Ain't like I was ever Alfred Hitchcock or somethin. You can watch my stuff till you're cross-eyed and there'll never be any deeper meaning. I see something interesting, I shoot it is all. Future of film if you want to know—someday, more bandwidth, more video files up on the Internet, everybody'll be shootin everything, way too much to look at, nothin will mean shit. Think of me as the prophet of that."

"You're fishing for compliments, Reg, what about that unscheduled redecoration on your apartment? Somebody must have thought highly of something you shot."

"Ice," he shrugs. "Tryin to repo what he thinks is his."

No, Maxine thinks with a sudden flulike ache in her fingers, Ice would be best-case. And if it's anybody else, Seattle might not be far enough. "Listen, if you need me to hold on to anything for you—"

"Don't worry, you're on my list."

"And you'll let me know when you leave town?"

"I'll try."

"Please. Oh, and Reg."

"Yeah, I know, I used to watch the old *Bionic Woman* myself. Sooner or later Oscar Goldman says, 'Jaime—be careful.'"

"He was a strong Jewish-mother role model for me. Just remember even Jaime Sommers needs to step cautious once in a while."

"Don't worry. I used to think that as long as I could see it through the viewfinder, it couldn't hurt me. So it took a while, but now I know different. You happy?" Disillusioned child written all over him.

"I guess I could take that as the good news."

14

Among the mystery vendors discovered by the resourceful Eric Outfield down in the encrypted files of hashslingrz is a fiber brokerage called Darklinear Solutions.

Who in their right mind, you wonder, would go into fiber these days, given the huge decline in new installation since last year? Well, back during the tech bubble, it seems so much cabling was put in that now miles of existing fiber are just sitting there what they call "dark," and the result is that outfits like Darklinear have come swooping down on the carcass of the business, scouting out overinstalled, unused fiber in otherwise "lit" buildings, mapping it, helping clients put together customized private networks.

What's puzzling Maxine is why hashslingrz's payments to Darklinear are being kept hidden when they don't have to be. Fiber's a legitimate company expense, bandwidth needs at hashslingrz more than justify it, even the IRS seems to be happy. And yet, just as with hwgaahwgh.com, the dollar amounts are way too big, and somebody's putting up password protection out of all proportion.

Sometimes, better than letting things fester, it is perverse fun to give in to annoyance. Maxine calls up Tallis Ice and gets lucky. Or doesn't get the machine, put it that way. "I had a call from your charming husband. Somehow he knew about our visit the other day."

"Not me—I swear, it's the building, they keep logs, there's video surveillance, well, maybe I did mention something about, you came by?"

"I'm sure he's a wonderful person regardless," replies Maxine. "While I've got you on the phone, can I pick your brain?"

"Sure?" Like, let's see, where'd I put it . . .

"You were talking about infrastructure the other day. I'm working for a client over in New Jersey with a capitalizing issue, and they're curious about a fiber broker in Manhattan called Darklinear Solutions. This is all out of my area—did you ever do business with them, or know anybody who has?"

"No." But there it is again, some peculiar hiccup in continuity that Maxine has learned means Look Closer. "Sorry?"

"Just trying to get educated on the cheap, thanks, Tallis."

DARKLINEAR SOLUTIONS IS a hip-looking chrome-and-neon establishment in the Flatiron District. In the E-rated video game of this, it sells echinacea smoothies and seaweed panini, instead of doped silica to feed depraved fatpipe fantasies that still may linger from the era recently ended.

Maxine is just about to alight from her cab when she sees a woman coming out the door in a tight leopard-print jumpsuit and Chanel Havana shades over her eyes instead of up on her head acting as a hairband, who, despite this effort, possibly conscious, at disguise, is obviously, well, well, Mrs. Tallis Kelleher Ice.

Maxine considers waving and hollering hi, but Tallis is acting too nervous here, she makes the average urban paranoid look like James Bond at the baccarat table. What's this? Fiber is suddenly so hush-hush?

No, actually it's the getup, which screams accommodation to somebody else's idea of provocative, and Maxine naturally finds herself wondering whose.

"You getting out, lady?"

"Maybe you should put the meter on again, while I just take a minute here."

Tallis makes her way up the block, glancing around anxiously. At the corner she pretends to stand gazing in the window of a toilet showroom, her feet in third ballet position, some Barnard girl in an art gallery here. A minute later the door of Darklinear Solutions swings open once again and out comes this compact party in a sales-floor blazer and slacks, carrying a shoulder-strap attaché and casing the street apprehensively also. He turns the other direction from Tallis but only goes as far as a Lincoln Navigator parked a few spaces away, gets in, heads back toward Tallis at a slow cruise. When he reaches the corner, the passenger door swings open and Tallis slides in.

"Quick," sez Maxine, "before the light changes."

"Your husband?"

"Somebody's, maybe. Let's see where they go."

"You a cop?"

"I'm Lennie on *Law & Order*, you didn't recognize me?" They follow the ponderous gas gobbler all the way over to the FDR and proceed uptown, exiting at 96th, continuing north on First Avenue into a fringe neighborhood no longer Upper East Side and not quite East Harlem, where you might once have gone to visit your drug dealer or arrange a compensated evening rendezvous, but which is now showing symptoms of gentrification.

The reconfigured heavy pickup pauses near a building newly converted, according to a sign tastefully draped across its upper stories, to condos running a million or so per bedroom, and then takes about an hour to park.

"Time was," mutters the cabbie, "leavin somethin like that on the street up here? You'd have to be insane, man, now everybody's afraid to touch it 'cause it might belong to some badass who thinks with his Glock."

"There they go. Could you wait here for me, I just want to try something."

She gives Tallis and 'Gator Man a couple minutes to get in the elevator, then goes stomping up to the doorman. "Those people that just came in? those idiots with the big SUV they don't know how to park? They just fucking knocked my bumper off."

He's a nice enough kid, doesn't exactly cower but does sound apologetic. "I can't really let you go up there."

"It's OK, you don't have to let them come down here either, it'll only mean a lot of screaming in your lobby, the mood I'm in possibly bloodshed also, who needs that, right? Here," handing him the card of a tax lawyer and byword of nineties excess who far as she knows is still inside, up at Danbury, "this is my attorney, maybe you can pass this along next time you see Mr. and Ms. Road & Track, and oh better let me have their phone number too, e-mail, whatever, so the lawyers can get in touch."

At which point some doormen will get all technical and pissy, but this one here, like the building, is new on the block and just as happy to be rid of some crazy bitch with a parking beef. Maxine manages a quick scan over the records at the front desk and returns to the cab with everything on the BF but his credit-card numbers.

"This is fun," sez the cabbie. "Where next?"

She glances at her watch. Back to the shop, it looks like. "Upper Broadway, anyplace around Zabar's'd be good?"

"Zabar's, huh?" Some junior-sidekick note seems to have crept into his voice.

"Yeah, had some strange information about a lox, need to check that out." She pretends to examine the safety on her Beretta.

"Maybe I should give you the special rate for PIs."

"But I'm only a . . . never mind, I'll take it."

. . .

"MAXI. WHATCHYIZ DOIN TONIGHT."

Masturbating to a movie on the Lifetime channel, *Her Psychopathic Fiancé*, I believe, why, what's it to you? Actually what she sez is, "You're asking me out, Rocky?"

"Hey. She called me Rocky. Listen, it's all respectable, Cornelia's gonna be there, my partner Spud Loiterman, maybe a couple other people."

"You're kidding. A soiree. Where are we going?"

"Korean karaoke, there's a . . . they call it a *noraebang,* up in K-Town, the Lucky 18."

"Streetlight People, Don't Stop Believing, karaoke boilerplate, I should've figured."

"We all used to be regulars over at Iggy's on 2nd Avenue, but last year we got—not me so much—but—Spud got us . . ."

"Eighty-sixed."

"Spud, he . . ." Rocky a little embarrassed, "he's a genius, my partner, you ever have a problem with like Regulation D . . . but he gets near a mike and . . . well, Spud will change key a lot. Even with pitch compensation, the technology can't keep up with him."

"I should bring earplugs?"

"Nah, just brush up on those eighties power ballads and be there around nine." Hearing her hesitation and being an intuitive sort, he adds, "Oh and wear somethin schlumpy, don't want you upstaging Cornelia."

Which heads her straight for the closet and an understated yet tabloidworthy Dolce & Gabbana number she found at Filene's Basement for 70% off, being obliged in fact to separate it from the grasp of a Collegiate mother, East Side hairband and all, slumming her morning away after dropping the kids off, who was two sizes too big for it anyway, and which Maxine has since been waiting for an excuse to wear. Lincoln Center gala? Political fund-raiser? Forget it, a karaoke joint full of vulture capitalists, just the occasion.

Gathered that evening at the Lucky 18, in one of the larger rooms, Maxine finds Rocky's tone-deaf associate Spud Loiterman, Spud's girlfriend Letitia, assorted out-of-town clients in for the weekend, as well as a small party of actual Koreans wearing, possibly as ironic fashion statements, shiny yellowish outfits from the North made of Vinalon, a fiber derived, unless Maxine is hearing this wrong, from coal, who have wandered off a tour bus and are growing increasingly uneasy about finding their way back to it. And Cornelia, who shows up tonight comfortably bridge-attired and sporting pearls also. Taller than Rocky even without the heels she has on tonight, she radiates an unforced amiability you don't see in that many WASPs, though they claim they invented it.

Maxine and Cornelia are just getting into the social chitchat when Rocky, ethnic as always in a Rubinacci suit and Borsalino, muscles in, waving a cigar around. "Hey, Maxi, c'mere a minute, meet somebody." Cornelia silently flicks back a Do-you-mind-we're-busy-here glance with perhaps even less compassion than shuriken or throwing stars are launched with in martial-arts movies . . . and yet, and yet, what is the almost erotic edge with these two? "After the commercial, I hope," Cornelia with a shrug and the suggestion of a heavenward eyeroll, turning and sauntering elsewhere. Maxine has a glimpse of a Mikimoto clasp riding an attractive nape, yellow gold as usual, not everybody's choice with pearls, though try to tell the folks at Mikimouse-o, who think everybody in the U.S. is blond. Which Cornelia happens to be—the question then arising, does this blondness extend all the way through her head?

To be determined. Meantime, "Maxi, say hi to Lester, formerly of hwgaahwgh.com." Liquidation or whatever, seems like Rocky, being nothing if not a VC down to the bone, is apparently always in the market for bright ideas from any source.

Lester Traipse is square-rimmed and compact, uses some drugstore brand of hair gel, talks like Kermit the frog. The big surprise is his wingman tonight. Last seen stepping out of a Tim Horton's on René Lévesque into what Montreal calls "feeble snow" and the rest of the world a raging blizzard, Felix Boïngueaux tonight is sporting a strange do, which is either a triple-digit power haircut, carefully designed to lull observers into false complacency with their own appearance till it's too late, or else he cut it himself and fucked up.

Rocky and Lester have meantime silently moved on into the bar. "Nice seeing you again. Everything's working out? Listen," furtive glance after Rocky, "you won't mention, um . . ."

"The cash-register—"

"Sh-shhh!"

"Oh. Course not, why should I?"

"It's just that now we're trying to go legit."

"Like Michael Corleone, I understand, no problem."

"Seriously. We have this li'l start-up now. Me and Lester. Antizapper software, you install it on your point-of-sale system and it automatically disables all phantomware in a mile radius, anybody tries to use a zapper, it melts their disc. Well, no, maybe not that violent. But damn close? You're friends with Mr. Slagiatt? Hey, so put in a good word for us."

"Sure thing." Playing both ends against the middle, eh? Amoral youth, ain't it awful.

No sooner is the karaoke machine powered up than the Koreans have formed a queue at the sign-up book and conversation phatic or profitable must compete for a while with "More Than a Feeling," "Bohemian Rhapsody," and "Dancing Queen." On the screen, behind lyrics in Korean and English, appear enigmatic tape clips, masses of Asian people running around in faraway city streets and plazas, human kaleidoscopes filling the fields of gigantic sports arenas, low-res footage from Korean soap operas and nature documentaries and other strange peninsular visuals, often having little to do with the song on the machine or its lyrics, sometimes offering peculiar disconnects therebetween.

When it's Cornelia's turn she calls "Massapequa," the second-soprano showstopper from *Amy & Joey,* an Off-Broadway musical about

Amy Fisher that's been running since 1994 to packed houses. Giving it a sort of neo-country-music feel, Cornelia now, swaying, drenched in a salmon spot, in front of a screen showing koalas, wombats, and Tasmanian devils, proceeds to belt out—

Mass—a-pe-qua!
    in my
Dreams, I seek ya,
It's a long way back,
To that old Sunrise High-
Way—
  (Yeah,)
Thought . . . I'd leave you, but I
Still . . . receive you, like a
Station late at night,
From long ago . . .

Where's-a-pizza-when-you
need . . . one . . . ?
Where's-a-bar-a-girl-can . . . dance?
Where's 'ose kids we used to be?
Where's 'at extra second chance?
(Must've left em back in)
Mass—
sape-qua, never
Dreamed I'd keep ya,
Thought that growing up meant
Throwing you away . . .
But though I
Tried to toss ya, guess I
Never lost ya,
'Cause you're still right here, tucked

Safely, in my heart,
(Massapequa-ah!),
Still right here, tucked
Safely in my heart . . .

Well, the worst part about most "Massapequa" covers is when white voices attempt blues runs and end up sounding at best insincere. Cornelia has somehow avoided this difficulty. "Thank you," Maxine presently in the powder room or ladies' toilet finds herself kvelling, "I love it when that happens, soubrette material, leading-lady presence, like Gloria Grahame in *Oklahoma!*"

"That's kinder than you know," Cornelia demurely. "People usually say early Irene Dunne. Minus the vibrato of course. And Rocky speaks highly of you, which I always take as a good sign." Maxine raises an eyebrow. "Next to the ones he doesn't speak of at all, I mean." Activities at the matrimonial periphery not being Maxine's favorite topic, she smiles politely enough that Cornelia gets it. "Perhaps we could meet sometime, for lunch, do some shopping?"

"You're on. Gotta warn you, though, I'm not much into shopping for recreation."

Cornelia puzzled, "But you . . . you are Jewish?"

"Oh, sure."

"Practicing?"

"Nah, I know how to do it pretty good by now."

"I suppose I meant a certain . . . gift for finding . . . bargains?"

"Should be written into my DNA, I know. But somehow I still forget to fondle material or study the tags, and sometimes," lowering her voice and pretending to look around for disapproval, "I have even . . . paid retail?"

Cornelia pretending to gasp, faux paranoid, "Please don't tell anyone, but I have actually now and then . . . discussed the price of an item in a shop. Yes, sometimes—incredibly—they've even brought it down.

Ten percent. Nearly thirty once, but that was only the one time, at Bloomingdale's back in the eighties. Though the memory is still vivid."

"So . . . as long as we don't rat each other out to the ethnic police . . ."

They emerge from the ladies' to find the company grown noticeably rowdier, Soju Wallbangers in glasses and pitchers everywhere, Koreans horizontal on couches or, when vertical, singing with their ankles crossed, teenage obsessives with laptops playing Darkeden over in the corner, Cohiba smoke hanging in strata, waitresses laughing louder and cutting more slack for borderline lechery, Rocky at some point deeply invested in "Volare," having located the old kinescope of Domenico Modugno on *Ed Sullivan* back in '58, when the song was charting number one in the States week after week, and from this blurry video learning all Domenico's inflections and moves.

And who, really, is so fancy-schmancy they can't appreciate "Volare," arguably among the greatest pop tunes ever written? Young man dreams he's flying in the sky, above it all, defying gravity and time, like having midlife early, in the second verse he wakes up, back on earth, first thing he sees is the big blue eyes of the woman he loves. And that will turn out to be sky enough for him. All men should grow up so gracefully.

Sooner than expected, that phase of the evening arrives when Toto finds its way overwhelmingly onto the song queue.

"Spud, I don't think it's 'I left my brains down in Africa.'"

"Huh? But that's what it says on the screen." Where if you were expecting herds on the Serengeti, instead here's silent clips from the second season of the Korean TV hit *Gag Concert*. Mugging, studio-audience laughter. Enough smoke in the room now that images on the screen are pleasantly smeared.

Maxine has been in a lengthy though inconclusive discussion with one of the strayed Korean bus passengers about the number 18 in the name of this *noraebang*.

"Bad number," leers the Korean. "*Sip pal.* Means 'sell pussy.'"

"Yes, but if you're Jewish," Maxine unperturbed, "it's good luck.

Bar mitzvah money, for instance, you should always give it in multiples of 18."

"Sell pussy? for bar mitzvah?"

"No, no, in gematria, kind of . . . Jewish code? 18 computes to *chai* or life."

"Same thing with pussy!"

This intercultural dialogue is disrupted by commotion from the men's room. "Excuse me a moment." She has a look in and finds Lester Traipse in the thick of some Web-design discussion, or actually insane screaming match, with an oversize nerd impersonator who may actually, Maxine fears, be in some quite different line of work. Drowning out even the piped-in karaoke music, the row ostensibly has to do with tables versus CSS, a controversial issue of the time, which has always, given its level of passion, struck Maxine as somehow religious. She imagines it will be difficult, no matter which side prevails, to appreciate, ten years from now, the all-consuming nature of the dispute. But here, tonight, it isn't exactly what's going on. Content is not, in this toilet at the moment, king. The fake nerd, for one thing, shows too much criminal potential.

Naturally Maxine has brought only an evening purse tonight, with no room for a Beretta Tomcat, hoping for the soiree to pass pleasantly enough to keep everybody off of the front page of the *Daily News* with a headline such as NORAE-BANGBANG. Packing or not, her duty is clear. She goes wading into the tempest of testosterone and manages to drag Lester to safety by a peculiar necktie with multiple images of Scrooge McDuck color-separated into burnt orange and electric orchid.

"One of Gabriel Ice's badass entourage," Lester breathing heavily, "mutual history. Sorry. Felix is supposed to be keeping me out of trouble."

"Where'd he get to?"

"That's him singing 'September.'"

After politely allowing eight more bars of Earth, Wind, Fire and

Felix, whom you could call Fog, to occur, as if casually, "Known Felix long?"

"Not long. We kept showing up in the same outer offices to pitch the same VCs, found we had a common interest in phantomware, or more like I was at loose ends and got fascinated and Felix was looking for somebody with search-engine-promotion skills, so we figured we'd team up. Better than my old arrangement anyway."

"Sorry about hwgaahwgh.com."

"Me too, but the partners were all morphing into CSS nazis like that specimen in the toilet, and I'm just an old die-hard tables person, as you see—gray, left-justified, no apologies, there have to be dinosaurs or the little kids won't have nothing to look at in the museum, right?"

"So you're happy to be out of Web design for a while?"

"Why linger? On to whatever's next in the queue, just got to remember to keep clear of Gabriel Ice—unless of course he's a dear friend of yours, in which case oops."

"Never met him, but I hear very little good spoken. What'd he do, try to get cute with the term sheet?"

"No, strangely enough, that was all legit."

"The money was good?"

"Maybe too good." With some telltale fidgeting of the Florsheims indicating there's more, much more. "That was always a puzzler. We were way too narrowband, too slow, even you could say too Third World, for hashslingrz. CSS or whatever, bandwidth never came up as much of an issue with us. Whereas Ice, he's a bandwidth hog. Buying up all the budget-priced infrastructure he can find. Dotcoms that overbuilt their fiber networks, went broke doing it, their loss, Ice's gain."

Somebody who isn't Felix is now channeling Michael McDonald on "What a Fool Believes," and several people in the room are singing along. In this festive setting, the subtext of bitterness Maxine's hearing in Lester's story is so noticeable that her post-CFE/ESP alarm begins to beep. What can this mean?

"So your job for Ice . . ."

"Old-school HTML pages, in this case 'He's Taking More Lithium,' everything encrypted, nothin any of us knew how to read. Ice wanted robot meta tags on everything. NOINDEX, NOFOLLOW, no nothin. It's supposed to be for keeping pages away from Web crawlers, stashed deep enough down to be safe. But anybody could've done that in-house, there was more nerd delinquents hanging around that place than a Quake server."

"Yeah, I heard Ice was also running a sort of rehab clinic for ankle-biters. You've physically been to visit the hashslingrz HQ?"

"Shortly after he bought hwgaahwgh, Ice summoned me in for an audience. I thought at least I'd get lunch, which instead turns out to be instant coffee and health-food tortilla chips in a bowl. No salsa. No salt, even. All he does is sit there and eyeball me. We must have talked, but I can't remember about what. I still have nightmares. Not about Ice so much as his posse. Some of them ex-jailbirds. I'd bet on it."

"And I guess they made you sign some nondisclosure agreement."

"Not that anything was ever gonna be disclosed around there, no-body was exactly opening their kimono, even now, with hwgaahwgh .com liquidated, the NDA stays in force till the foreseeable end of the Universe or Daikatana finally comes out, whichever happens first. To-tally their call—having a bad day, little stomach episode, they can come take it out on me whenever they want."

"And so . . . that discussion in the gentlemen's lounge . . . may not have really been about Web design?"

He gives her one of those eyes-up glances that find enough light in the near distance to flash a specular warning. Like, I can't go there, and you better not either.

"Only," noodging, "that that guy in there doesn't fit the usual nerd profile."

"You'd think Ice would show more confidence, wouldn't you?" with a look both faraway and fearful, as if seeing something approach from a close-enough perimeter. "Him with his high-level connections. Instead here he is insecure, anxious, angry, like some loan shark or pimp who's just learned he can't depend for help on the cops he's paying off, or even on the higher levels he has to report to—no SEC to hear his sad complaint, no Fraud Unit, he's alone."

"So what you guys were really arguing about in there was somebody leaking information?"

"I should be so lucky. When information wants to be free, blabbing never counts as worse than a misdemeanor."

With something else then in the next sentence, just about to drop, which is when Felix shows up, just short of suspicious, as if he and Lester might have their own nondisclosure arrangements.

Lester has been trying to compose his face into an innocent blank, but some tell must've slipped through, because Felix now throws Maxine one of those "You better not be fucking anything up, here, eh?" sorts of look, grabs Lester, and hustles him off.

She is once again, as with the make-believe nerd in the men's toilet, visited by a strong hint of secret intention. As if customizing cash registers may all along have been a cover story for what Felix is really up to.

While for some the night is growing blurry, for Maxine it's turning staccato, breaking up into small microepisodes separated by pulses of forgetting. She remembers looking at the sign-up sheet and seeing she has apparently, not fully knowing why, called Steely Dan's up-tempo ballad of memory and regret, "Are You with Me Dr. Wu." Next thing she knows she's up at the mike, with Lester unexpectedly stepping in to sing harmony on the hook. During the saxophone break while Koreans holler "Pass the mike," they find themselves doing disco moves. "Paradise Garage," Maxine sez. "You?"

"Danceteria mostly." She risks a quick look at his face. He carries a furtive fantasizing gaze she's seen too many times before, an awareness of living not only on borrowed money but on borrowed time also.

Then she's out in the street and everybody is scattering, the Korean tour bus has shown up and the driver and hostesses are in a lively screamfest with their haewoned passengers, Rocky and Cornelia are waving and air-kissing their way into the back of a rented Town Car, Felix is talking earnestly into a mobile phone, and the disguised heavy from the men's toilet removes his thick plastic frames, puts on a ball cap, adjusts an invisible cloak, and vanishes halfway down the block.

Leaving behind them in the Lucky 18 an empty orchestra playing to an empty room.

15

Around 11:30 in the morning, Maxine spots a substantial black vehicle which reminds her of a vintage Packard only longer, parked near her office, disregarding the signs that say no parking for an hour and a half on that side to allow for street sweeping. Usual practice is for everybody to double-park on the other side and wait for the sweeper to come through, then move back in in its wake and park legally again. Maxine notices that nobody is waiting anywhere near the mystery limo and that, even more curiously, parking enforcement, usually found in this neighborhood like cheetahs at the fringes of antelope herds, is mysteriously absent. Here, in fact, even as she watches, comes the sweeper, wheezing noisily around the corner, then, catching sight of the limo, pausing as if to consider its options. Procedure would be for the sweeper to pull up behind the offending vehicle and wait for it to move. Instead, creeping nervously on up the block, it swerves apologetically around the lengthy ride and hastens to the corner.

Maxine notices a Cyrillic bumper sticker, which as she is shortly to learn reads MY OTHER LIMO IS A MAYBACH, for this vehicle here turns out, actually, to be a ZiL-41047, brought over piece by piece from Russia,

reassembled in Brooklyn, and belonging to Igor Dashkov. Maxine, peering through the tinted glass, is interested to find March Kelleher inside,
deep in confabulation with Igor. The window cranks down, and Igor
puts his head out, along with a Fairway bag which appears to be stuffed
with money.

"Maxi, *kagdila*. Madoff Securities advice was excellent! Just in time!
My associates are so happy! Over moon! They took steps, assets are safe,
and this is for you."

Maxine recoils, only partly out of the classic accountant's allergy to
real folding money. "You fuckin insane?"

"Amount you saved them was considerable."

"I can't accept this."

"Suppose we call it retainer."

"And who'd be hiring me exactly?"

Shrug, smile, nothing more specific.

"March, what's with this guy? And what are you doing in there?"

"Hop in." As she does so, Maxine notices that March is sitting there
counting a lapful of greenbacks of her own. "No and I'm not the GF
either."

"Let's see, that leaves what . . . dope dealer?"

"Shh-shh!" grabbing her arm. For as it turns out, March's ex-husband
Sid has in fact been running substances in and out of the little marina up
at Tubby Hook, at the river end of Dyckman Street, and Igor here it
seems is one of his clients. "I emphasize 'running,'" March explains. "Sid,
whatever the package might be, he's just the deliveryperson, never likes
to look inside."

"Because inside this package he doesn't look in . . . ?"

Well, for Igor it's methcathinone, also known as bathtub speed, "The
bathtub in this case being, my guess is it's over in Jersey."

"Sid always has good product," Igor nods, "not this cheap kitchen-
stove Latvian *shnyaga* which is pink from permanganate they don't get
rid of, before long you are deeply fucked up, like you don't walk right,

you shake? Latvian *dzhef,* do me a favor, Maxine! don't go near it, it ain't *dzhef!* it's *govno!*"

"I'll try and remember."

"You had breakfast? We got ice cream here, what kind you like?"

Maxine notices a sizable freezer under the bar. "Thanks, little early in the day."

"No, no, it's real ice cream," Igor explains. "Russian ice cream. Not this Euromarket food-police shit."

"High butterfat content," March translates. "Soviet-era nostalgia, basically."

"Fucking Nestlé," Igor rooting through the freezer. "Fucking unsaturated vegetable oils. Hippie shit. Corrupting entire generation. I have arrangements, fly this in once a month on refrigerator plane to Kennedy. OK, so we got Ice-Fili here, Ramzai, also Inmarko, from Novosibirsk, very awesome *morozhenoye,* Metelitsa, Talosto . . . today, for you, on special, hazelnut, chocolate chips, *vishnya,* which is sour cherry . . ."

"Can I maybe just take some for later?"

She ends up with a number of half-kilo Family Packs in an assortment of flavors.

"Thanks, Igor, this all seems to be here," March stashing the currency in her purse. She's planning to go uptown tonight to meet Sid and pick up his delivery for Igor. "You ought to come along, Maxi. Just a simple pickup, come on, it'll be fun."

"My grasp of the drug laws is a little shaky, March, but last time I checked, this is Criminal Sale of a Controlled Substance."

"Yes, but it's also Sid. A complex situation."

"A B felony. You and your ex—I gather you're still . . . close?"

"Don't leer, Maxi, it causes wrinkles," climbing out of the ZiL, waiting for Maxine. "Remember to count what's in your Fairway bag, there."

"Why, when I don't even know how much it's supposed to be to begin with, see what I'm saying."

There's a cart with coffee and bagels on the corner. It's warm today, they find a stoop to sit on and take a coffee break.

"Igor says you saved them a shitload of money."

"You think that 'them' includes Igor himself?"

"He'd be too embarrassed to tell anybody. What was going on?"

"Some kind of pyramid racket."

"Oh. Something a little different."

"You mean for Igor? like he has some history with—"

"No, I meant late capitalism is a pyramid racket on a global scale, the kind of pyramid you do human sacrifices up on top of, meantime getting the suckers to believe it's all gonna go on forever."

"Too heavy-duty for me, even the scale Igor's on makes me nervous. I'm more comfortable with people who hang around at ATMs, that level."

"So later for the gritty street drama, come on uptown for some high fantasy, these Dominican guys, you know?"

"Hmmm. I could manage some old-school merengue maybe."

MARCH IS MEETING SID at Chuy's Hideaway, a dance club near Vermilyea. The minute they step off the subway, which up here runs elevated high over the neighborhood, they can hear music. They go sashaying more than schlepping downstairs to the street, where salsa pulses deeply from the stereo systems of double-parked Caprices and Escalades, from bars, from shoulder-mounted boom boxes. Teenagers knock each other around good-naturedly. Sidewalks are busy, fruit stands open, arrays of mangoes and star fruit, ice-cream carts on the corners doing late business.

At Chuy's Hideaway behind a modest storefront, they find a deep lounge, bright, loud, violent, that seems to run all the way through to the next block. Girls in very high spike heels and shorts shorter than a doper's memory are gliding around with low-buttoned young men in gold chains and narrowbrim hats. Weedsmoke inflects the air. Folks are drinking rum and Cokes, Presidente beer, Brugal Papa Dobles. Deejay activities alternate with live local bachata groups, a bright, twangly mandolin/bottleneck sound, an impossible-not-to-want-to-dance-to beat.

March is in a loose red dress and eyelashes longer than Maxine re-calls, a sort of Irish Celia Cruz, with her hair all the way down. They know her at the door. Maxine inhales deeply, relaxes into sidekick mode.

The floor is crowded, and March without hesitating disappears onto it. Some possibly underaged cupcake who says his name is Pingo appears from nowhere, grabs Maxine in a courtly way, and dances off with her. At first she tries to fake it with what she can remember from the old Paradise Garage, but soon enough moves begin to drift back as she is taken into the beat . . .

Partners come and go in amiable rotation. Every now and then in the ladies' room, Maxine will find March regarding herself in the mirror with less than dismay. "Who sez Anglo chicks can't shake it?"

"Trick question, right?"

Sid shows up late, holding a Presidente longneck, avuncular, one of those bristling military haircuts, far from Maxine's admittedly warped image of a drug runner.

"Don't keep me waiting or anything," March beaming vexedly.

"Thought you'd need the extra time to score, angel."

"I don't notice Sequin anyplace. At the library or something, work-ing on a book report?"

The group on the stand is playing "Cuando Volverás." Sid pulls Max-ine to her feet and starts in with a bachata modified for reduced floor space, quietly singing the hook. "And when I lift your outside hand, it means we're gonna twirl, just remember go all the way around so you end up facing me."

"On this floor? twirls, you'll need a permit. Oh, Sid," she inquires politely a couple-three bars later, "are you by any chance hitting on me?"

"Who wouldn't?" Sid gallantly, "though you shouldn't rule out try-ing to piss off the ex."

Sid is a veteran of Studio 54, worked as a toilet attendant, got out on the floor during breaks, at shift's end gathered up $100 bills forgotten by patrons who'd been rolling them up all night to snort cocaine through, as many as he could get to before the rest of the staff, though he himself preferred to use the recessed filter on a Parliament cigarette as a sort of disposable spoon.

They don't quite close the joint up, but it's pretty late by the time they get out on Dyckman and down to the little Tubby Hook marina. Sid leads March and Maxine out to a low, 28-foot runabout with a triple cockpit, Art Deco sleek and all wood in different shades. "Maybe it's sexist," sez Maxine, "but I really have to wolf-whistle here."

Sid introduces them. "It's a 1937 Gar Wood, 200 horses, shakedown cruises on Lake George, honorable history of outrunning pursuit at every level . . ."

March hands over Igor's money, Sid produces an authentically distressed teenage backpack from the bilges.

"Can I drop you ladies anyplace?"

"Seventy-ninth Street marina," sez March, "and step on it."

They cast off silently. Thirty feet from shore, Sid angles an ear upriver. "Shit."

"Not again, Sid."

"Twin V-8s, Cats most likely. This time of night, it has to be the goldurn DEA. Jeez, what am I, Pappy Mason here?" He starts the engine, and off they go barrelassing into the night, roostertailing down the Hudson through a moderate chop, slapping against the water in a good solid rhythm. Maxine watches the 79th Street boat basin pass swiftly by on the port side. "Hey, that was my stop. Where we going now?"

"With this joker," March mutters, "it's probably out to sea."

The thought did enter Sid's mind, as he admits later, but that would have brought the Coast Guard into this too, so instead, gambling on DEA caution and hardware limitations, with the World Trade Center leaning, looming brilliantly curtained in light gigantically off their port quarter, and someplace farther out in the darkness a vast unforgiving ocean, Sid keeps hugging the right side of the channel, past Ellis Island and the Statue of Liberty, past the Bayonne Marine Terminal, till he sees the Robbins Reef Light ahead, makes like he's going to pass it too, then at the last minute hooks a steep right, nimbly and not always according to the rules of the road proceeding then to dodge anchored vessels towering in out of nowhere and oil tankers under way in the dark, sliding into Constable Hook Reach and on down the Kill Van Kull. Passing Port Richmond, "Hey, Denino's somewhere off the port beam here, anybody feel like grabbing a pizza?" Rhetorical, it seems.

Under the high-arching openwork of the Bayonne Bridge. Oil-storage tanks, tanker traffic forever unsleeping. Addiction to oil gradually converging with the other national bad habit, inability to deal with refuse. Maxine has been smelling garbage for a while, and now it intensifies as they approach a lofty mountain range of waste. Neglected little creeks, strangely luminous canyon walls of garbage, smells of methane, death and decay, chemicals unpronounceable as the names of God, the heaps of landfill bigger than Maxine imagines they'd be, reaching close to 200 feet overhead according to Sid, higher than a typical residential building on the Yupper West Side.

Sid kills the running lights and the motor, and they settle in behind Island of Meadows, at the intersection of Fresh and Arthur Kills, toxicity central, the dark focus of Big Apple waste disposal, everything the city has rejected so it can keep on pretending to be itself, and here unexpectedly at the heart of it is this 100 acres of untouched marshland, directly underneath the North Atlantic flyway, sequestered by law from development and dumping, marsh birds sleeping in safety. Which, given the real-estate imperatives running this town, is really, if you want to know, fucking depressing, because how long can it last? How long can any of these innocent critters depend on finding safety around here? It's exactly the sort of patch that makes a developer's heart sing—typically, "This Land Is My Land, This Land Also Is My Land."

Every Fairway bag full of potato peels, coffee grounds, uneaten Chinese food, used tissues and tampons and paper napkins and disposable diapers, fruit gone bad, yogurt past its sell-by date that Maxine has ever thrown away is up in there someplace, multiplied by everybody in the city she knows, multiplied by everybody she doesn't know, since 1948, before she was even born, and what she thought was lost and out of her life has only entered a collective history, which is like being Jewish and finding out that death is not the end of everything—suddenly denied the comfort of absolute zero.

This little island reminds her of something, and it takes her a minute to see what. As if you could reach into the looming and prophetic landfill, that perfect negative of the city in its seething foul incoherence, and find a set of invisible links to click on and be crossfaded at last to unexpected refuge, a piece of the ancient estuary exempt from what happened, what has gone on happening, to the rest of it. Like the Island of Meadows, DeepArcher also has developers after it. Whatever migratory visitors are still down there trusting in its inviolability will some morning all too soon be rudely surprised by the whispering descent of corporate Web crawlers itching to index and corrupt another patch of sanctuary for their own far-from-selfless ends.

A long, eerie wait to see if they've shaken the feds or whoever they are. Invisibly up yonder, moving around somewhere close, heavy machinery, much too deep into these early-morning hours. "I thought this wasn't an active dump anymore," Maxine sez.

"Officially the last barge came and went back around the end of the first quarter," Sid recalls. "But they're still busy. Grading it, capping it, sealing and covering it all up and turning it into a park, another family-friendly yup resource, Giuliani the tree hugger."

Presently March and Sid are into one of those low-volume elliptical discussions parents have about their children, in this case Tallis mostly. Who may, like her brothers, be a grown adult but somehow demands inflexible disbursements of time and worry, as if she were still a troubled teenager snorting Sharpie pen solvents back at the Convent of the Holy Ghost.

"Strange," Sid reflective, "to see the way Ice the kid morphed into what he is today. In college he was just this amiable geek. She brought him home, we figured, OK, horny kid, way too much screen time, socially ept as they ever get, but March thought she saw good-provider potential there."

"Sid having his little joke—hey, live forever, sexist pig. The idea was always for Tallis to know how to take care of herself."

"Pretty soon we were seeing them less and less, they had all this money, enough for a nice li'l crib down in SoHo."

"They were renting?"

"Bought it," March a little abrupt. "Paid cash."

"By then Ice had profiles in *Wired,* in *Red Herring,* then hashslingrz made the *Silicon Alley Reporter*'s '12 to Watch' list . . ."

"You were following his career."

"I know," Sid shaking his head, "it's pathetic ain't it, but what were we supposed to do? They cut us out. It was like they actively went seeking it, this life they have now, this faraway, virtual life, leaving the rest of us stuck back here in meatspace, blinking at images on a screen."

"Best-case scenario," March sez, "Ice was an innocent geek corrupted by the dotcom boom. Dream on. The kid was bent from the jump, under obligation to forces which do not advertise publicly. What did they see in him? Easy. Stupidity. A stupidity of great promise."

"And these forces—maybe alienating you guys was really part of their program, not Tallis's idea?"

Both of them shrug. March maybe a little more bitterly. "Nice thought, Maxi. But Tallis collaborated. Whatever it was, she bought in. She didn't have to."

The industrial racket from back in the marshland behind the giant cliffs of ruin has grown continuous. Now and then workers, in long-standing Sanitation Department tradition, have lengthy exhilarated screaming exchanges. "Strange shift to be working," it seems to Maxine.

"Yeah. Nice overtime for somebody. Almost like they're up to something they don't want anybody to know about."

"When did anybody ever want to know?" March lapsing for a

moment into the bag-lady character in her commencement speech at Kugelblitz, the one person dedicated to salvaging everything the city wants to deny. "Either they're playing catch-up or they're getting it ready to open for dump business again."

A presidential visit? Somebody's making a movie? Who knows.

Early seagulls show up from somewhere, begin inspecting the menu. The sky takes on a brushed-aluminum underglow. A night heron with breakfast in its beak ascends from its long watch at the edge of the Island of Meadows.

Sid starts up the motor finally, heads back up Arthur Kill and into Newark Bay, at Kearny Point bears right into the forsaken and abused Passaic River. "Let you two off when I can, then I'm gonna return to my secret undisclosed base."

Around Point No Point, under the black arching trusswork of the Pulaski Skyway. The light, inexorable as iron, growing in the sky . . . Tall brick stacks, railyards . . . Dawn over Nutley. Well, technically dawn over Secaucus. Sid pulls up to a boat dock belonging to the Nutley High rowing team, removes an imaginary yachting cap, and gestures his passengers ashore. "Welcome to Deep Jersey."

"Captain Stubing here," March yawns.

"Oh and you won't forget Igor's backpack, will you my Tomato Surprise."

Maxine's hair is a mess, she's been out all night for the first time since the 1980s, her ex and their children are somewhere out in the U.S. sure to be having a nice time without her, and for maybe a minute and a half she feels free—at least at the edge of possibilities, like whatever the Europeans who first sailed up the Passaic River must have felt, before the long parable of corporate sins and corruption that overtook it, before the dioxins and the highway debris and unmourned acts of waste.

From Nutley there's a New Jersey Transit bus to the Port of Authority by way of Newark. They grab a couple minutes of sleep. Maxine has one of those transit dreams. Women in shawls, a sinister light. Everybody speaking Spanish. A somehow desperate flight by antiquated bus through jungles to escape a threat, a volcano possibly. At the same time, this is also a tour bus full of Upper West Side Anglos, and the tour director is Windust, lecturing in that wise-ass radio voice, something about the nature of volcanoes. The volcano behind them, which hasn't gone away, grows more ominous. Maxine wakes up out of this someplace on the Lincoln Tunnel approach. In the terminal, March suggests, "Let's go out the other way, avoid Disney Hell and go find some breakfast."

They find a Latino breakfast joint on Ninth and dig in.

"Something on your mind, Maxine."

"Been meaning to ask you this for a while, what was going on in Guatemala back in 1982?"

"Same as Nicaragua, El Salvador, Ronald Reagan and his people, Schachtmanite goons like Elliott Abrams, turning Central America into a slaughterhouse all to play out their little anti-Communist fantasies. Guatemala by then had fallen under the control of a mass murderer and particular buddy of Reagan named Ríos Montt, who as usual wiped off his bloody hands on the baby Jesus like so many of these charmers do. Government death squads funded by the U.S., army sweeps through the western highlands, officially targeting the EGP or Guerrilla Army of the Poor but in practice exterminating any native populations they came across. There was at least one death camp, on the Pacific coast, where the emphasis may've been political, but up in the hills it was onsite genocide, not even mass burial, just bodies left for the jungle to take care of, which certainly must have saved the government a lot on cleanup costs."

Maxine is somehow not as hungry as she thought. "And any Americans who were there . . ."

"Either humanitarian kids, naïve and borderline idiotic, or 'advisers' sharing their extensive expertise at butchering nonwhites. Though by then, most of that was being outsourced to U.S. client states with the necessary technical chops. Why do you ask?"

"Just wondering."

"Yeah. When you're ready, tell me. I'm really Dr. Ruth Westheimer, nothing shocks me."

16

Waiting on her office doorstep is a case of wine, which when she sees its label causes her to observe, "Well, holy shit." An '85 Sassicaia? A case? Must be a mistake. There seems to be a note, however—"Turns out you saved us some money too," unsigned, yet who else can it be but Rocky, the ol' ethnoenologist? Good anyhow for enough guilt to get her back into the increasingly problematic hwgaahwgh/hashslingrz books.

Something today strikes her as odd. One of those nagging patterns that's not always welcome because it means uncompensated overtime, but what else is new. She puts on some coffee, has another look at the trail between hwgaahwgh and hashslingrz's account in the Emirates, and after a while sees what it is. A persistent shortfall, and of some size. As in somebody is tapping the pipeline. What's curious is the amount. It seems to match another sum, a puzzling persistent surplus related to the cash component of Ice's purchase of hwgaahwgh.com. The checks are being deposited into a business operating account at a bank on Long Island.

Since going rogue, Maxine has acquired a number of software kits, courtesy of certain less reputable clients, which have bestowed on her superpowers not exactly falling within Generally Accepted Accounting Practices, such as thou shalt not hack into anybody's bank account, thou shalt leave that sort of thing for the FBI. She roots around in a couple of desk drawers, finds an unlabeled disc in a sickly green metallic shade, and well before lunch is into Lester Traipse's private affairs. Sure enough, the mystery shortfall is exactly balanced by a sum being regularly transferred on into one of Lester's personal accounts.

Expressively exhaling, "Lester, Lester, Lester." Well. All that nondisclosure talk, just smoke to cover what he was really up to, something way more dangerous. Lester discovered the invisible underground river of cash flowing through his soon-to-be-defunct company and has been diverting a hefty chunk of Ice's ghost payments from their fate as riyals over into some secret account of his own. Figuring he's hit the big time.

So the other night at the karaoke joint, when he compared Gabriel Ice to a loan shark or a pimp, it was no idle figure of speech. Lester, endangered as a girl under a viaduct who's been holding out on the man running her, desperate for any kind of help, was sending Maxine a distress signal in a code that, shame on her, she didn't even bother to read . . .

And the hard part is that she knows better, knows that beneath the high-cap scumscapes created by the corporate order and celebrated in the media, there are depths where petty fraud becomes grave and often deadly sin. Certain types of personality get bent insanely out of shape, punishment is violent and—an anxious reflexive look at the clock on the wall—immediate. This guy might not know how much trouble he's in.

She's surprised when Lester picks up his mobile on the first ring. "You lucked out, this is the last call I was planning to take on this thing."

"Changing your carrier service?"

"Shitcanning the instrument. I think there's a tracking chip on it."

"Lester, I've come across something kind of serious, we should meet. Leave your cell phone at home." She can tell from his breathing that he knows what it is.

· · ·

ETERNAL SEPTEMBER, dating from the high nineties, is a disused techies' saloon tucked away between a barbershop and a necktie boutique half a block from a low-traffic station down one of the old IND lines.

"Some sentimental attachment," Maxine looking around trying not to make a face.

"No, I'm figuring anybody who actually comes in here in the middle of the day is so without clue that we can talk safely."

"You know you're in trouble, right, so I don't have to start in nagging about that."

"I wanted to tell you that night at the karaoke, but . . ."

"Felix kept putting in. Was he monitoring you? Protecting you?"

"He heard about my run-in in the bathroom and figured he should've had my back, that's all. I have to assume Felix is who he says he is."

A familiar ring to this. No point arguing. He trusts Felix, it's his lookout. "You have kids, Lester?"

"Three. One'll be starting high school in the fall. Keep thinking my math is wrong. How about you?"

"Two boys."

"You tell yourself you're doing it for them," Lester frowning. "As if it's not bad enough to use them for an excuse—"

Right, right. "Then again, you're not *not* doing it for them."

"Look, I'll pay it back. Sooner or later I would've. Is there some secure way for you to tell Ice that's what I really want to do?"

"Even if he believes you, which he may not, it's a lot of money . . . Lester. He'll want back more than just what you stole, he'll also want some vig, an aggravation fee, which could prove to be hefty."

"Cost of fucking up," quietly, no eye contact.

"I'll take that as an OK on the exorbitant-interest clause, shall I?"

"You think you can deal this?"

"He doesn't like me much. If it was high school I might get a little wistful, on the other hand Gabriel Ice, in high school . . ." shaking her head, why go there? "My brother-in-law works at hashslingrz, OK, I'll see if I can pass a message."

"Guess I'm the kind of greedy loser you're always in court testifying about."

"Not anymore, I'm decertified, Lester, out of forensics, the courts don't know me."

"And my fate is in your hands here? terrific."

"Chill, please, people are staring. There was never going to be recourse for you in the straight world. The only help you'll find now will be from some kind of outlaw, and I'm better than most."

"So now I owe you a fee."

"Do you see me waving invoices around here, forget it, maybe someday you'll be in a position."

"Don't like freebies," mutters Lester.

"Yeah, you'd rather steal it."

"Ice stole it. I diverted it."

"Exactly the kind of fine line that got me tossed out of the game and puts your own ass in danger now. You legal minds, I'm in awe."

"Please," this, to her surprise, not coming out really as glib as Maxine is used to, "make sure they know how sorry I am."

"As kindly as I can put it, Lester, they don't give a shit. 'Sorry' is for the local news channels. This is about crossing Gabriel Ice. He's got to be very unhappy with that."

She has said too much already and finds herself praying that Lester will not ask how much interest Ice is likely to charge. Because then, by her own code, post-CFE but just as unforgiving, she'll have to say, "I hope he only wants it in U.S. dollars." But Lester now, with enough else to worry about, only nods.

"You two do any business before he bought your company?"

"We only met the one time, but it was all over him then, like a smell. Contempt. 'I have a degree, a couple billion, you don't.' He understands right away I'm not even a self-educated geek, just a guy from the mail room got lucky. Once. How can he let somebody like that get away with even $1.98?"

No. No, Lester, that's not exactly it, is it. This is evasion she's hearing, and not the tax kind either, more in the area of life-and-death. "There's something you want to tell me," gently, "but it's worth your life if you do. Right?"

He looks like a little kid who's about to start crying. "What else would it be? The money isn't bad enough?"

"In your case I think not."

"I'm sorry. We can't go any further. It's nothing personal."

"I'll see what I can do about the money."

By which point they're breezing for the exit, Lester ahead of her like a feather in an air current, escaped from a pillow, as if in some domestic dream of safety.

YES, WELL, then there's still the videocassette Marvin brought. Sitting there on the kitchen table, as if plastic has suddenly figured out how to be reproachful. Maxine knows she's been putting off watching it, with the same superstitious aversion as her parents had to telegrams back in the day. There's a chance it could be business, and from bitter experience she can't rule out practical jokes either. Still, if it's too unpleasant to watch, maybe she can try to claim as business expenses the extra therapy sessions that might result.

Scream, Blacula, Scream, no, not exactly—a little more homemade. Opening with a jittery traveling shot out a car window. Late-afternoon winter light. The Long Island Expressway, eastbound. Maxine begins to grow apprehensive. Jumpcut to an exit sign—aahhh! Exit 70, this is going exactly where she was hoping it wouldn't, yes another jump now to Route 27, and we are heading, you could say condemned, to the Hamptons. Who would dislike her enough to send her something like this, unless Marvin got the address wrong, which never happens, of course.

She's relieved in a way to see it isn't going to be the Hamptons of legend, at least. She has spent more time there than it was worth. This is more like Fringehampton, where the working population are often angry to the point of homicide because their livelihoods depend on servicing the richer and more famous, up to whom they must never miss a chance to suck. Time-battered houses, scrub pine, roadside businesses. No lights or decorations up, so the winter here must be in the deep and dateless vacancy after the holiday season.

The shot enters a dirt road lined with shacks and trailers, and approaches what at first seems like a roadhouse because every window is pouring light, people are wandering around in and out of the place, sounds of jollification and a music track including Motor City psychobilly Elvis Hitler, at the moment singing the *Green Acres* theme to the tune of "Purple Haze" and providing Maxine an unmeasured moment of nostalgia so unlikely that she begins to feel targeted personally.

The camera moves up the front steps and into the house, shouldering aside partygoers, through a couple of rooms littered with beer and vodka bottles, glassine envelopes, unmatched shoes, pizza boxes and fried chicken containers, on through the kitchen to a door and down into the basement, to a particular concept of the suburban rec room . . .

Mattresses on the floor, a king-size fake angora bedspread in a shade of purple peculiar to VHS tape, mirrors everyplace, in a far corner a foul dribbling refrigerator that also buzzes loudly, in a stammering rhythm, as if providing a play-by-play on the hijinks in progress.

A young man, medium-long haircut, naked except for a dirt-glazed ball cap, an erection pointed at the camera. A woman's voice from outside camera range, "Tell them your name, baby."

"Bruno," almost defensive.

An ingenue in cowgirl boots and an evil grin, tattoo of a scorpion just above her ass, some time since her last shampoo, television screen-light reflecting off of a pale and zaftig body, introduces herself as Shae. "And this here is Westchester Willy, say hi to the VCR, Willy."

Nodding hello at the edge of the frame is a middle-aged, out-of-shape party who from mug shots faxed up to her from John Street Maxine recognizes as Vip Epperdew. Fast zoom in on Vip's face, with a look of undisguisable yearning, which he quickly tries to reset to standard party mode.

Gusts of laughter from topside. Bruno's hand comes into the shot with a butane lighter and a crack pipe, and the threesome now become affectionate.

Jules and Jim (1962) it isn't. Talk about double-entry bookkeeping! As erotic material, there are shortcomings, to be sure. Boy and girl quality could do with an upgrade, Shae is a jolly enough girl, maybe a little vacant around the eyes, Vip is years overdue for some gym time, and Bruno comes across as a horny little runt with a tendency to shriek and a dick, frankly, not big enough for the scenario, provoking expressions of annoyance from Shae and Vip whenever it approaches them for any purpose. Maxine is surprised to feel an unprofessional pulse of distaste for Vip, this needy, somehow groveling yup. If the other two are supposed to be worth the long schlep from Westchester, hours on the LIE, an addiction supposedly less negotiable than crack, not to their youth but to the single obvious thing their youth is good for, then why not kids who can pretend at least that they know what they're doing?

But wait. She realizes these are yenta reflexes, like, please Vip, you can do so much better, so forth. Doesn't even know him, already she's criticizing his sex-partner choices?

Her attention drifts back into a shot of them getting dressed again while chatting animatedly. What? Maxine's pretty sure she stayed awake, but it seems there was no money shot, instead, at some point, this has begun to diverge from canonical porn into, aaahh! improv! yes, they are now *giving themselves lines,* with deliveries of the sort that drive high-school drama teachers to drug abuse. Cut away to a close-up of Vip's credit cards, all laid out like a fortune-teller's tableau. Maxine pauses the tape, runs it back and forth, writing down what numbers she can, though the low resolution blurs some of them. The three get into a sub-vaudeville routine with Vip's plastic, handing the cards back and forth, passing witty remarks about each one, all except for a black card that Vip keeps flashing at Shae and Bruno, causing them to recoil in exaggerated horror like teen vampires from a bulb of garlic. Maxine recognizes the fabled AmEx "Centurion" card, which you have to charge at least $250K a year on or they take it away from you.

"You guys allergic to titanium?" Vip playfully, "c'mon, you afraid there's a chip in it, some lowlife detector gonna trigger a silent alarm on you guys?"

"Mall security don't scare me," Bruno all but whining, "been outrunning those 'suckers all my life."

"I just show em some skin," Shae adds, "they like that."

Shae and Bruno head out the door, and Vip collapses back on the phony angora. Whatever he's tired from, this ain't an afterglow.

"On to the Tanger Outlets, fuck yeah," cries Bruno.

"Anything we can get you, Vippy?" Shae over her shoulder with one of those Are-you-looking-at-my-ass-again? smiles.

"Off," Vip mutters, "would be nice sometime."

The camera stays on Vip till he turns to face it, resentful, reluctant. "Not too happy tonight, are we, Willy?" inquires a voice from behind it.

"You noticed."

"You have the look of a man things are closing in on."

Vip shifts his eyes away and nods, miserable. Maxine wonders why she ever quit smoking. The voice, something about the voice is familiar. Somehow she's heard it on television, or something close to it. Not a specific person, but a *type* of voice, maybe a regional accent . . .

Where could this tape have come from? Somebody who wants Maxine to know about Vip's household arrangements, some invisible Mrs. Grundy with a strong disapproval of threesomes? Or somebody closer, say more of a principal in the matter, maybe even a party to Vip's skimming activities. One of those Disgruntled Employees again? What would Professor Lavoof say beyond his trademark, "There has to be a world off the books"?

Same old sad template here—by now there's an unfriendly clock on

Vip's affairs, maybe he's already kiting checks, wife and kids as usual totally without clue. Does it ever end well? Ain't like it's jewel thieves or other charming scoundrels, there's nothing and nobody these fraud-feasors won't betray, the margin of safety goes on dwindling, one day they're overcome by remorse and either run away from their lives or commit terminal stupidity.

"Slow-Onset Post-CFE Syndrome, girl. Can't you allow for at least one or two honest people here and there?"

"Sure. Someplace. Not on my daily beat, however, thanks all the same."

"Pretty cynical."

"How about 'professional'? Go ahead, wallow in hippie thoughts if you want, meantime Vip is floating out to sea and nobody's told Search and Rescue about it."

Maxine rewinds, ejects, and, returning to realworld television programming, begins idly to channel-surf. A form of meditating. Presently she has thumbed her way into what seems to be a group-therapy session on one of the public-access channels.

"So—Typhphani, tell us your fantasy."

"My fantasy is, I meet this guy, and we walk on the beach, and then we fuck?"

After a while, "And . . ."

"Maybe I see him again?"

"That's it?"

"Yeah. That's my fantasy."

"Yes Djennyphrr, you had your hand up? What's *your* fantasy?"

"Being on top when we fuck? Like, usually he's on top? My fantasy is, is I'm on top for a change?"

One by one, the women in this group describe their "fantasies." Vibrators, massage oil, and PVC outfits are mentioned. It doesn't take long. Maxine's reaction is, is she's appalled. This is fantasy? Feeuhnt-uh-see? Her sisters in Romance Deficiency Disorder, this is the best they can come up with for what they think they need? Schlepping through her bedtime routine, she takes a good look in the bathroom mirror. "Aaaahh!"

It is not hair or skin condition tonight so much as the Knicks second-color road jersey she's wearing. With SPREWELL 8 on the back. Not even a gift from Horst or the boys, no, she actually went down to the Garden, stood in a line, and bought it for herself, paying retail, for a perfectly good reason, of course, having been in the habit of going to bed with nothing on, falling asleep reading *Vogue* or *Bazaar*, and waking up stuck to the magazine. There is also her mostly unavowed fascination with Latrelle Sprewell and his history of coach assault, on the principle that Homer strangling Bart we expect, but when Bart strangles Homer . . .

"Obviously," she remarks now to her reflection, "you are doing much, much better than those public-access losers. So . . . Makseenne! what's your fantasy?"

Um, bubble bath? Candles, champagne?

"Ah-ah? forgot that stroll by the river? all right if I just step over to the toilet here, do some vomiting?"

SHAWN NEXT MORNING is tons of help.

"There's this . . . client. Well, not really. Somebody I'm worried about. He's in twenty kinds of trouble, his situation is dangerous, and he won't let it go." She does a recap on Vip. "It's depressing the way I keep running into the same scenario time and again, every chance these clowns get to choose, they always bet on their body, never on their spirit."

"No mystery, quite common in fact . . ." He pauses, Maxine waits, but that seems to be it.

"Thanks, Shawn. I don't know what my obligations are here. It used to be I didn't care, whatever they got coming, they deserve. But lately . . ."

"Tell me."

"I don't like what's going to happen, but I'd feel bad ratting this guy out to the cops too. Which is what led me to wonder could I just pick your brain a little. Was all."

"I know what you do for a living, Maxine, I know it's all ethical trip-wires, and I don't like to put in. Do I. OK. Listen anyway." Shawn tells her the Buddhist Parable of the Burning Coal. "Dude is holding this burning-hot coal in his hand, obviously suffering a lot of pain. Somebody comes by—'Whoa, excuse me, isn't that a burning-hot coal in your hand, there?'

"'Ooh, ooh, ow, man, yes and like, like it really hurts, you know?'

"'I can see that. But if it's making you suffer, why do you keep hold-ing on to it?'

"'Well, duh-uhh? 'cause I need to, don't I—aahhrrgghh!'

"'You're . . . into pain? you're a nutcase? what is it? Why not just let it go?'

"'OK, check it out—can't you see how beautiful it is? lookit, the way it glows? like, the different colors? and aahhrrhh, shit . . .'

"'But carrying it around in your hand like this, it's giving you third-degree burns, man, couldn't you like set it down someplace and just look at it?'

"'Somebody might take it.'

"So forth."

"So," Maxine asks, "what happens? He lets go of it?"

Shawn gives her a nice long stare and with Buddhist precision, shrugs. "He lets go of it, and he doesn't let go of it."

"Uh, huh, I must've said something wrong."

"Hey. Maybe *I* said something wrong. Your assignment for next time is to find out which of us, and what."

Yet another one of these shadowy calls. She should get on to Axel and tell him Vip's a frequent visitor to the South Fork, then pass on the card-number fragments she was able to copy down off the videotape. But not so fast here, she cautions herself, let's just see . . .

She runs the tape again, especially the dialogue between Vip and whoever's behind the camera, whose voice is maddeningly just there at the edge of her memory . . .

Ha! It's a Canadian accent. Of course. On the Lifetime Movie Channel, you hear little but. In fact, it's Québéquois. Could that mean . . .

She gets on to Felix Boïngueaux's cellular. He's still in town chasing VC money. "Heard anything from Vip Epperdew?"

"Don't expect to."

"You have his phone number?"

"Got a few of them. Home, beeper, they all ring forever and never pick up."

"Mind sharing them?"

"Not at all. If you get lucky, ask him where our check is, eh?"

It's close. It's close enough. If it was Felix behind the camera, Felix who sent her the tape, then this is either what social workers like to call a cry for help from Vip or, more likely, seeing it's Felix, some elaborate setup. As to how this shuffles together with Felix being down here allegedly looking for investors—back burner, it'll keep, disingenuous li'l schmuck.

One of the phone prefixes is up in Westchester, no answer, not even a machine, but there's also a Long Island number, which she looks up in her crisscross at the office, already queasy with a suspicion, and sure enough, it's in the flip side of the Hamptons, all but certainly the amateur-porn set Shae and Bruno live in, where Vip has been making excuses to slide away to, to pay his dues to the other version of his life. The number brings an electronic squawk and a robot to tell Maxine sorry, this number is no longer in service. But there's something strange in its tone, as if incompletely robotized, that conveys inside knowledge, not to mention You Poor Idiot. A paranoid halo thickens around Maxine's head, if not a nimbus of certainty. Ordinarily there wouldn't be money enough in circulation to get her inside bomb-throwing distance of the east end of Long Island, but she finds herself now dropping the Tomcat in her bag, adding an extra clip, sliding into working jeans and a

beach-town-appropriate T-shirt, and next thing she's down on 77th renting a beige Camry. Gets on the Henry Hudson Parkway, hassles the
Cross Bronx over to the Throgs Neck Bridge, the line of city towers to
her right crystalline today, sentinel, onto the LIE. Cranks down the windows and tilts the seat back to cruising format and proceeds on eastward.

17

Since the mid-nineties when WYNY switched formats overnight from country to classic disco, decent driving music in these parts has been in short supply, but someplace a little past Dix Hills she picks up another country station, maybe from Connecticut, and presently on comes Slade May Goodnight with her early-career chartbuster, "Middletown New York."

I would send you, a sing-in cowgirl,
With her hat, and gui-tar band,
Just to let you know, I'm out here,
Anytime you need a hand—
                    But you'd start
Thinkin, about that ol' cowgirl,
And where she'll be after the show,
                    Same hopeless
story again,
same old sorrowful end, for-
-get-it, darlin, I already know—
                    And don't, tell, me,

How,
To eat, my heart out,
                            thanks, I, don't,
need no—knife, and fork,
                            list-nin to
trains . . . whistle through
The nights without you,
Down in Middletown, New York.
[After a pedal-steel break that has always reached in and found
Maxine's heart]
Sittin here, with a longneck bottle,
                            watchin car-
toons, in the after-school sun,
while the shadows stretch out like a story
about things that we never got done . . .
                            Never got a-
round, to groundin that Airstream,
                            and, so, we
kept, gettin shocks off the walls,
                            un-til we
neither could say, which particular day,
We weren't feelin nothin, at all.
                            So don't tell me
How, to eat, my heart out . . .

So forth. By which point Maxine is singing along in a pretty focused
way, with the wind blowing tears back into her ears, and she's getting
looks from drivers in adjoining lanes.

She hits Exit 70 about midday, and since Marvin's videotape wasn't
that attentive to what Jodi Della Femina might call shortcuts, Maxine has
to go intuitive with this, leaving Route 27 after a while and driving for
about as long as she recalls it taking on the tape, till she notices a tavern

called Junior's Ooh-La-Lounge with lunch-hour pickups and motorcycles out front.

She goes in, sits at the bar, gets a doubtful salad and a PBR longneck and a glass. The jukebox is playing music Maxine's unlikely ever to hear string arrangements of in any lunch venue in Manhattan. Presently the guy three stools down introduces himself as Randy and observes, "Well, the shoulder bag has a sway to it suggestive of small arms, but I don't smell cop somehow, and you're not a dealer, so what does that leave, I wonder." He could be described as roly-poly, though Maxine's antennas put him among that subset of the roly-poly who also carry weapons, maybe not on his person but certainly someplace handy. He has a neglected beard and wears a red ball cap with some Meat Loaf reference on it, out the back of which hangs a graying ponytail.

"Hey, maybe I *am* a cop. Working undercover."

"Nah, cops have 'at special somethin you get to recognize, least if you've been bounced around much."

"Guess I've only been dribbled up and down the back court a little. Am I supposed to apologize?"

"Only if you're here to get somebody in trouble. Who you lookin for?"

Okay. How about— "Shae and Bruno?"

"Oh, them, hey, you can get them in as much trouble's you want. Everybody around here's collected their share of karma, but those two . . . what in 'ee hell would you want with them?"

"It's this friend of theirs."

"Hope you don't mean Westchester Willy? Built kinda low to the ground, partial to that Belgian beer?"

"Maybe. Would you happen to know how to get to Shae and Bruno's place?"

"Oh, so . . . you're the insurance adjuster, right?"

"How's that?"

"The fire."

"I'm only a bookkeeper from this guy's office. He hasn't showed up for a while. What fire?"

"Place burned down a couple weeks ago. Big story on the news, emergency response from all over, flames lightin up the sky, you could see it from the LIE."

"How about—"

"Charred remains? No, nothin like that."

"Traces of accelerant?"

"Sure you're not one of these them crime-lab babes, like on TV."

"Now you're sweet-talking me."

"That was gonna be later. But if you—"

"Randy, if I wasn't so wired into office mode right now?"

A general pause. Colleagues in on breaks from work struggling not to laugh too loud. Everybody here knows Randy, pretty soon there is a schadenfreudefest in progress about who's having the worst time of it. Since last year when the tech boom collapsed, most homeowners out here who took hits in the market have been defaulting on contracts right and left. Only occasionally can you still find echoes of the nineties' golden age of home improvement and the name that keeps coming up, not to Maxine's surprise, is Gabriel Ice.

"His checks are still clearing," Maxine supposes. Randy laughs merrily, the way roly-poly folks do. "When he writes them." Renovating the bathrooms, Randy has found himself being stiffed invoice after invoice. "I owe all over the place now, four-figure showerheads as big as pizzas, marble for the bathtubs special-ordered from Carrara, Italy, custom glaziers for gold-streaked mirror glass." Everybody in the room chimes in with a story like this. As if at some point having had a fateful encounter with tabloid figure Donald Trump's cost accountants, Ice is now applying the guiding principle of the moneyed everywhere—pay the major contractors, blow off the small ones.

Ice has few fans in these parts—to be expected, Maxine supposes, but it's a shock to find opinion in the room unanimous that he also likely had a hand in torching Bruno and Shae's place.

"What's the connection?" Maxine squinting. "I always took him for more of a Hamptons person."

"Cheatin side of town, as the Eagles like to say, Hamptons ain't doin that for him, he needs to get away from the lights and the limos, out to some old fallindown house like Bruno and Shae's where a man can kick out the jambs."

"They think it's who they used to be," opines a young woman in painter's overalls, no bra, Chinese tats all up and down her bare arms, "nerds with fantasies. They want to go back to that, revisit."

"Oh, Bethesda, you're such a pussy, that's cuttin ol' Gabe way too much slack. Just like with everythin else, he's lookin to get laid on the cheap's all it is."

"But why," Maxine in her best insurance-adjuster voice, "burn the place down?"

"They had a reputation there for getting into odd behavior and whatever. Maybe Ice was bein blackmailed."

Maxine does a quick sweep of the faces in range but doesn't see anybody who thinks they know for sure.

"Real-estate karma," somebody suggests. "A crib as out of scale as Ice's would mean a lot of smaller houses somehow have to be destroyed, part of maintaining the overall balance."

"That's a lot of arson counts, Eddie," sez Randy.

"So . . . it's a sizable spread," Maxi pretends to ask, "the Ice home?"

"We call it Fuckingham Palace. Like to have a look at the place? I was headin out that way."

Trying to sound like a groupie, "Can't resist a stately home. But would they even let me in the gate?"

Randy produces a chain with an ID tag. "Gate's automatic, li'l transponder here, always carry an extra."

Bethesda clarifies. "Tradition around here, these big houses are great places to bring a date if your idea of romance is gettin rudely interrupted right in the middle."

"*Penthouse Forum* did that whole special issue," Randy footnotes.

"Here, let's just go detail you a little." They repair to the ladies' toilet, where Bethesda brings out a teasing brush and an eight-ounce can of Final Net and reaches for Maxine's hair. "Got to lose this scrunchy thing, right now you're lookin too much like these Bobby Van's people."

When Maxine emerges from the facility, "Mercy," Randy swoons, "thought it was Shania Twain." Hey, Maxine'll take that.

Minutes later Randy's wheeling out of the lot in an F-350 with a contractor's rack on it, Maxine close behind wondering how good of a plan this is and growing more doubtful as Junior's is replaced in the mirror by dismal residential streets gone tattered and chuckholed, full of small old rentals and dead-ending against chain-linked parking lots.

They make a brief stop to look at the site of Shae, Bruno, and Vip's old playhouse. It's a total loss. Green summer growth is vaporing back over the ashes. "Think it was an accident? Torched deliberately?"

"Can't speak for your pal Willy, but Shae and Bruno are not the most advanced of spirits, in fact pretty dumb fucks when you come to it, so maybe somebody did somethin stupid lightin up. Could've happened that way."

Maxine goes fishing in her bag for a digital camera to get a few shots of the scene. Randy peering in over her shoulder spots the Beretta. "Oh, my. That's a 3032? What kind of load?"

"Sixty-grain hollowpoint, how about yourself?"

"Partial to Hydroshocks. Bersa nine-millimeter?"

"Awesome."

"And . . . you're not really a bookkeeper in an office."

"Well, sort of. The cape is at the cleaner's today, and I forgot to bring along the spandex outfit, so you're missing the full effect. You can take your hand off my ass, however."

"My goodness, was I really—"

Which, compared to her usual social day, passes for a class act.

They continue out to the Montauk Point Lighthouse. Everybody is supposed to love Montauk for avoiding everything that's wrong with the Hamptons. Maxine came out here as a kid once or twice, climbed to the top of the lighthouse, stayed at Gurney's, ate a lot of seafood, fell asleep to the pulse of the ocean, what wasn't to like? But now as they decelerate down the last stretch of Route 27, she can only feel the narrowing of options—it's all converging here, all Long Island, the defense factories, the homicidal traffic, the history of Republican sin forever unremitted, the relentless suburbanizing, miles of mowed yards, contractor hardpan, beaverboard and asphalt shingling, treeless acres, all concentrating, all collapsing, into this terminal toehold before the long Atlantic wilderness.

They park in the visitors' lot at the lighthouse. Tourists and their kids all over the place, Maxine's innocent past. "Let's wait here for a minute, there's video surveillance. Leave your car in the lot, we'll pretend it's a romantic rendezvous, drive away together in my rig. Less suspicion from Ice's security that way."

Makes sense to Maxine, though this could still be some elaborate horse's-ass nooner he thinks he's pulling here. They drive out of the lot again, follow the loop around to Old Montauk Highway, presently hook a right inland on Coast Artillery Road.

Gabriel Ice's ill-gotten summer retreat proves to be a modest ten-bedroom what realtors like to call "postmodern" house with circle and pieces of circle in the windows and framing, open plan, filled with that strange lateral oceanic light that brought artists out here when the South Fork was still real. Obligatory Har-Tru tennis court, gunite pool which though technically "Olympic" size seems scaled more to rowing events than swimming, with a cabana that would qualify as a family residence in many up-Island towns Maxine can think of, Syosset, for example. Over the tops of the trees rises a giant old-time radar antenna from the days of anti-Soviet nuclear terror, soon to be a state-park tourist attraction.

Ice's place is swarming with contractors, everything smells like joint compound and sawdust. Randy picks up a paper container of coffee, a sack of grout, and a preoccupied expression, and pretends he's there about some bathroom question. Maxine pretends to tag along.

How could there be secrets here? Drive-through kitchen, state-of-the-art projection room, everything out in the open, no passages inside the walls, no hidden doors, all still too new. What could lie behind a front like this, when it's front all the way through?

That's till they get down to the wine cellar, which seems to've been Randy's destination all along.

"Randy. You're not going to—"

"I figure what I don't drink I can go on that eBay thing and turn for some bucks, start getting some of my money back here."

Randy picks up a bottle of white Bordeaux, shakes his head at the label, puts it back. "Dumb son of a bitch got stuck with a rackful of '91. A little justice, I guess, not even my wife would drink this shit. Wait, what's this? OK maybe I could cook with this." He moves on to reds, muttering and blowing dust off and stealing till his cargo pockets and Maxine's tote bag are full. "Gonna go stash these in the rig. Anything we missed?"

"I'll have another look around, meet you back outside in a minute."

"Just keep an eye out for rent-a-cops, they're not always in uniform."

It isn't vintage year or appellation that's caught her eye, but a shadowy, almost invisible door over in one corner, with a keypad next to it.

Soon as Randy's out the door, she pulls out her Filofax, which these days has evolved into an expensive folder full of loose pieces of paper, and in the dim light goes looking for a list of hashslingrz passwords Eric has found down in his Deep Web inquiries and Reg has passed along. She recalls some of them being flagged as key codes. Sure enough, only a couple-three fingerdances later, an electric motor whines and a bolt slams open.

Maxine doesn't think of herself as especially timid, she's walked into fund-raisers wearing the wrong accessories, driven overseas in rental cars with alien gearshifts, prevailed in beefs with bill collectors, arms dealers, and barking-mad Republicans without much hesitation bodily or spiritual. But now as she steps through the door, the interesting question arises, Maxine, are you out of your fucking mind? For centuries they've been trying to indoctrinate girls with stories about Bluebeard's Castle, and here she is once more, ignoring all that sound advice. Somewhere ahead lies a confidential space, unaccounted for, resisting analysis, a fatality for wandering into which is what got her kicked out of the profession to begin with and will maybe someday get her dead. Up in the world, it is the bright middle of a summer day with birds under the eaves and yellowjackets in the gardens and the smell of pine trees. Down here it's cold, an industrial cold she feels all the way to her toenails. Isn't only that Ice doesn't want her here. She knows, without knowing the reasons, that this is about the last door she should ever have stepped through.

She finds a long corridor, swept, austere, track lighting at wide intervals, shadows where they shouldn't be, leading—unless she's turned around somehow—toward the abandoned air base with the big radar antenna. Whatever's at the other end down here, across the fence, Gabriel Ice's access to it is important enough to be protected by a key code, making this likely more than some rich guy's innocent hobby.

She moves cautiously in, a trespasser's timer blinking silently in her head. Some of the doors along the corridor are shut and locked, some are open, the rooms behind them empty in a chill and unnaturally tended way, as if bad history could be stabilized somehow and preserved for decades. Unless of course this is simply protected office space in here, some physical version of the dark archive at hashslingrz that Eric has been looking into. It smells like bleach, as if recently disinfected. Concrete floors, channels leading to drains set at low points. Steel beams overhead, with fittings whose purpose she can't or doesn't want to figure out. No furniture except for gray Formica office tables and folding chairs. Some 220-volt wall outlets, but no sign of heavy appliances.

Has all the hair spray been somehow turning her head into an antenna? She's begun to hear whispering that soon resolves into radio traffic of some kind—looks around for speakers, can't locate any, yet the air is increasingly full of numerals and NATO phonetic letters including Whiskey, Tango, and Foxtrot, affectless voices distorted by radio interference, crosstalk, bursts of solar noise . . . occasionally a phrase in English she's never fast enough to catch.

She has come to a stairwell descending even deeper into the terminal moraine. Further than she can see. Her coordinates all at once shift ninety degrees, so that she can't tell now if she's staring vertically down uncountable levels or straight ahead down another long hallway. It lasts only a heartbeat, but how long dos it have to? She imagines somebody's idea of Cold War salvation down there, carefully situated at this American dead end, some faith in brute depth, some prayerful confidence that a blessed few would survive, beat the end of the world and the welcoming-in of the Void . . .

Oh shit, what's this— at the next landing down, something's poised, vibrating, looking up at her . . . in this light it isn't easy to say, she hopes she's only hallucinating, something alive yet too small to be a security person . . . not a guard animal . . . no . . . a child? Something in a child-size fatigue uniform, approaching her now with wary and lethal grace, rising as if on wings, its eyes too visible in the gloom, too pale, almost white . . .

The timer in her head goes off, jangling, urgent. Somehow, reaching for the Beretta right now will not be a wise idea. "All right Air Jordans— do your stuff!" She turns and sprints back up the corridor, back through the door she shouldn't have opened, back into the wine cellar to find Randy, who's been looking for her.

"You OK?"

Depending on how you define OK. "This Vosne-Romanée here, I was wondering . . ."

"Year don't matter much, grab it, let's go." For a wine thief, Randy is suddenly not acting too suave here. They scramble into the rig and head out the way they came. Randy is silent till they reach the lighthouse, as if he saw something back at Ice's too.

"Listen, do you ever get up to Yonkers at all? My wife's family's up there, and sometimes I'll do some shootin at this li'l ladies' target range called Sensibility—"

"'Men always welcome', sure, I know it, fact I'm a member."

"Well, maybe I'll catch you there sometime?"

"Lookin forward, Randy."

"Don't forget your burgundy there."

"Um . . . you were talking earlier about karma, maybe you should just go on ahead, take it."

SHE DOESN'T EXACTLY PEEL OUT, but neither does she dawdle, casting anxious glances in the mirror at least till about Stony Brook. Roll on, four-wheeler, roll on. Talk about fools' errands. Vip Epperdew's last known address a charcoal ruin, Gabriel Ice's compound ostentatious and unsurprising, except for a mystery corridor and something in it she doesn't want to know if she even saw. So . . . maybe she can deduct some of this, midsize daily rate, credit-card discount, one tank of gas, buck and a quarter a gallon, see if they'll go for $1.50. . . .

Just before the country station goes out of range, on comes the Droolin Floyd Womack classic,

Oh, my brain, it's
Lately started throbbin, and
Now and then, it's also
uh, squirmin too . . .
              and my
precious sleep at night, it's robbin,
'Cause it's throb-
bin, squirmin, just for you.
[female backup] Why, does, it
squirm? why does it
Throb, I wonder?
[Floyd] Uh, tell me please, it's driving
Me insane . . .

Can it be, some
evil spell I'm under? Oh be
Still, you squirmin,
Uh, throbbin brain . . .

That night she dreams the usual Manhattan-though-not-exactly she
has visited often in dreams, where, if you go far enough out any avenue,
the familiar grid begins to break down, get wobbly and interwoven with
suburban arterials, until she arrives at a theme shopping mall which she
understands has been deliberately designed to look like the aftermath of
a terrible Third World battle, charred and dilapidated, abandoned hovels
and burned-out concrete foundations set in a natural amphitheater so
that two or more levels of shops run up a fairly steep slope, everything
sorrowful rust and sepia, and yet here at these carefully distressed outdoor cafés sit yuppie shoppers out having a cheerful cup of tea, ordering
yuppie sandwiches stuffed full of arugula and goat cheese, behaving no
differently than if they were at Woodbury Common or Paramus. She is
supposed to be meeting Heidi here but abruptly finds herself at nightfall
on a path through some woods. Light flickers ahead. She smells smoke
with a strong toxic element, plastic, drug-lab fixins, who knows? comes
around a bend in the path and there is the house from the Vip Epperdew
videotape, on fire—black smoke in knots and whorls, battered among
acid-orange flames, pouring upward to merge with a starless overcast.
No neighbors have assembled to watch. No sirens growing louder in
the distance. Nobody coming to put the fire out or to rescue whoever
might still be inside, not Vip but, somehow, this time, Lester Traipse.
Maxine stands paralyzed in the jagged light, running through her options and responsibilities. The burning is violent, all-consuming, the heat
too fierce to approach. Even at this distance, she feels her oxygen supply
being taken. Why Lester? She wakes with this feeling of urgency, knowing she has to do something, but can't see what.

The day as usual comes sloshing in on her. Pretty soon she's up to
her ears in tax dodges, greedy little hotshots dreaming about some big

score, spreadsheets she can't make sense of. About lunchtime Heidi sticks her head in.

"Just the pop-culture brain I was looking to pick." They go grab a quick salad at a deli around the corner. "Heidi, tell me again about the Montauk Project."

"Been around since the eighties, part of the American vernacular by now. Next year they'll be opening the old air station to tourists. There's already companies running tour buses."

"What?"

"Another form of everything ends up as a Broadway musical."

"So nobody takes the Montauk Project seriously anymore, you're saying."

A dramatic sigh. "Maxi, earnest Maxi, forensic as always. These urban myths can be attractors, they pick up little fragments of strangeness from everywhere, after a while nobody can look at the whole thing and believe it all, it's too unstructured. But somehow we'll still cherrypick for the intriguing pieces, God forbid we should be taken in of course, we're too hip for that, and yet there's no final proof that some of it *isn't* true. Pros and cons, and it all degenerates into arguments on the Internet, flaming, trolling, threads that only lead deeper into the labyrinth."

Nor, it occurs to Maxine, does touristy mean detoxified, necessarily. She knows people who go to Poland in the summer on Nazi-death-camp tour packages. Complimentary Polish Mad Dogs on the bus. Out in Montauk there could be funseekers infesting every square inch of surface area, while underneath their idle feet, whatever it is, whatever Ice's tunnel connects with, goes on.

"If you're not eating that . . ."

"Fress, Heidi, fress, please. I wasn't as hungry as I thought."

18

ater in the afternoon, the sky begins to gather a lurid yellow tinge.
Something's on the way in from across the river. Maxine puts on Big
Apple news traffic and weather station WYUP, and after the usual
string of fast-mouth commercials, each more offensive than the last, on
comes the familiar teletype theme and a male voice, "You give us thirty-
two minutes—you don't get it back."

Seeming a bit too chirpy for the material, a newslady announces,
"A body found today in a deluxe Upper West Side apartment building has been identified as Lester Traipse, a well-known Silicon Alley
entrepreneur . . . an apparent suicide, though police say murder isn't
being ruled out."

"Meanwhile, week-old Baby Ashley, rescued yesterday from a dumpster in Queens, is doing well, according to—"

"No," the way someone much older and more demented might
shout back at the radio, "fuck no, you stupid bitch, not Lester." She just
talked to him. He's supposed to be alive.

She has seen the main sequence of embezzlers' remorse, tearful
press interviews, sidewise please-hit-me glances, sudden onsets of nerve
pain, but Lester is, was, one of those rare specimens, he was trying to

pay back what he took, to mensch up, seldom if ever do guys like this cancel their own series. . .

Leaving what? Maxine feels an unwelcome prickling along her jawline. None of the conclusions she's jumping to here look good. The Deseret? The Fucking Deseret? Something wrong with taking Lester over to Fresh Kills and leaving him on the landfill?

She finds herself gazing out the window. She squints past roofline contours, vents, skylights, water tanks and cornices under this pre-storm lighting, shining as if already wet against the darkening sky, down the street to where the cursed Deseret rears above Broadway, one or two storm-nervous lights already on, its stonework at this distance seeming too uncleansable, its shadows too many, ever to breach.

Insanely she begins to blame herself. Because she found Ice's tunnel. Ran away from whatever was approaching. It's Ice getting even, coming after her now.

IT DOESN'T HELP MUCH WHEN, later in the evening, she's out in the rain and sees Lester Traipse across the street, going down into the subway at Broadway and 79th, in the company of a blond bombshell of a certain age. Sure that this blonde is somehow Lester's handler, that they've been up on the surface for a while, taking care of business, and now she's bringing him back underneath, Maxine goes sprinting across the most dangerous intersection in the city, and by the time she gets through the moving obstacle course of murderous drivers sending up careless wings of filthy water and down to the subway platform, Lester and the blonde are nowhere to be seen in any direction. Of course, in NYC it is not uncommon to catch sight of a face that you know, beyond all argument, belongs to somebody no longer among the living, and sometimes when it catches you staring, this other face may begin to recognize yours as well, and 99% of the time you turn out to be strangers.

Next morning, after a shiftily insomniac night punctuated with dream clips, she shows up at her appointment with Shawn in something of a state. "I was like, 'Lester?' just about to yell across the street something stupid, you're supposed to be dead or something."

"First thing to suspect is," Shawn advises, "is that your memory's going?"

"No, uh-uh, this was Lester and nobody else."

"Well . . . I guess it happens sometimes. Ordinary unenlightened folks just like you, no special gifts or netheen, will see through all the illusion, just as well as a master with, like, years of training? And what they're able to see is, is the real person, the 'face before the face' we call it in Zen, and maybe then they attach some more familiar face to it?"

"Shawn, that's very helpful, thank you, but suppose it really *was* Lester?"

"Uh huh well was he walking in, like, third ballet position, by any chance?"

"Not cute, Shawn, the guy just—"

"What? Died? Didn't die? Made the news on WYUP? Got on the subway with some unidentified babe? Make up your mind."

In his ads, stuck to every newspaper machine in the city, Shawn promises, "Guaranteed No Use Of Kyosaku," these being the wooden "warning sticks" Soto Zen instructors use to focus your attention. So instead of hitting people, Shawn gets abusive with remarks. Maxine emerges from the session feeling like she's been one-on-one with Shaquille O'Neal.

In the outer office she finds another client waiting, light gray suit, pale raspberry shirt, tie and matching handkerchief in deep orchid. For a minute she thinks it's Alex Trebek. Shawn sticks his head out, gets all congenial. "Maxine, meet Conkling Speedwell, someday you'll think it was fate, but it's really just me being a busybody."

"Sorry if I cut in on your session," Maxine shaking hands, taking note of the guy's you could say agendaless grip, something rarely met with in this town.

"Buy me lunch sometime."

Enough with Lester for a while. He can wait. He has all the time in the world now. Pretending to consult her watch, "How's today looking?"

"Better than it was."

OK. "You know Daphne and Wilma's, down the street?"

"Sure, nice odor dynamic there. About one?"

Odor what? Turns out Conkling is a freelance professional Nose, having been born with a sense of smell far more calibrated than the rest of us normals enjoy. He's been known to follow an intriguing *sillage* for dozens of city blocks before finding the source is a dentist's wife from Valley Stream. He believes in a dedicated circle of hell for anybody who shows up at dinner or for that matter enters an elevator wearing an inappropriate scent. Dogs he hasn't met formally come up to him with inquiring looks. "A negotiable talent, sometimes a curse."

"So tell me, what am I wearing today?"

He's already smiling, shaking his head slightly, avoiding eye contact. Maxine understands that whatever this gift is, he doesn't go around showing it off.

"On second thought . . ."

"Too late." Some kind of jive nose manipulation, as if clearing his passages. "OK—first of all, it's from Florence . . ."

Uh-oh.

"The Officina in Santa Maria Novella, and you have on the original Medici formulation, Number 1611."

Aware that her mouth has dropped open a few millimeters further than she would like, "Don't tell me how you do it, don't, it's like card tricks, I don't want to know."

"I seldom run into that many Officina persons actually."

"More of them around than you'd think. You wander into this beautiful high old room full of these scents, people who've been to Florence a hundred times never heard of the place, you start to think maybe it's your own secret discovery—then suddenly, shopper's nightmare, it's all over town."

"People who wouldn't know a floral from a chypre," sympathetic. "Drives you nuts."

"And . . . being a Nose . . . it's nice work, the pay's good?"

"Well, most of it's with the larger corporations, we all keep revolving firm to firm, after a while you begin to notice the companies changing hands, getting restructured, just like the classic scents do, then you're out on the bricks again. For years it never occurred to me this might be what our mutual guru calls a message from beyond. 'Who is the person without rank, who goes in and out through the portals of the face?' is how he put it."

"He gave me that one too."

"'Portals' is supposed to mean eyes, but right away I figured nostrils, the koan turned out to be spot-on, gave me some room to think, and nowadays I'm freelance, my waiting list for new clients is about six months, which is longer than any of those company jobs ever lasted."

"And Shawn . . ."

"Steers an occasional client my way, takes a small fee. Enough to cover his Erolfa bill, which he tends to bathe in. Usual thing."

"In the Nose business. You have your own perfume line, or . . . ?"

He seems embarrassed. "More like an investigative agency."

Aahhh! "A private Nose."

"It gets worse. 90 percent of my business is matrimonial."

What else? "Goodness. How . . . would something like that work?"

"Oh, they show up, 'Smell my husband, my wife, tell me who they've been with, what'd they have for lunch, how many drinks, are they doing drugs, is there oral sex—' that seems to be the top FAQ—and so forth. Thing is, it's all in time sequence, each indication layered on top of the one before. You can put together a chronology."

"Strangely enough"—is this such a good idea?—"there's this situation I've had come up . . . Do you mind if I just pick your— let me put that another way, could one of you Nose people go in to a crime scene, like a police psychic, give it a snort, and reconstruct what went on?"

"Sure, Nasal Forensics. Moskowitz, De Anzoli, couple others, they specialize in that."

"How about you?"

Conkling angles his head, she'd have to say charmingly, and takes a minute. "Cops and me . . . You run a nasal scan, the boys get paranoid, they think maybe you're scanning them too, snorting into all those deep cop secrets. So we always end up at cross-purposes."

"This is never a problem for Moskowitz and them?"

"Moskowitz is a decorated bunco-squad veteran, De Anzoli has a D.Crim., and there's family members also on the job, it's a culture of trust. Me, I'm more comfortable as an independent."

"Oh, I can relate." She points her face across the room and then slides her eyeballs sideways to look at him. "Unless you already smelled that about me also?"

"Like is there some notorious pheromone, kicks in whenever—Wait, rewind, now you're gonna think—"

Maxine beams brightly and sips her Sudden Enlightenment Organic Bamboo tea. "Sure must make dating complicated, this snoot of yours."

"Is why I can generally keep quiet about it. Except when Shawn tries to fix me up."

They have a look at each other. Over the past year, Maxine has been out with hat fetishists, day traders, pool sharks, private-equity hotshots, and seldom has she been visited by anxieties about seeing any of them again. Now, a little bit late for it, she remembers to check out Conkling's left hand, which proves, like her own, to be innocent of a ring.

He catches her looking. "I forgot to check your finger too. Awful, ain't we." Conkling has a boy and a girl in middle school who show up on weekends, and today's Friday. "I mean, they have keys, but usually they find me there."

"Yeah I've got to go punch back in too. Here, this is my home, office, beeper."

"Here's mine, and if you're serious about a crime-scene job, I can either put you in touch with Moskowitz or . . ."

"Better if it was you." She allows for a heartbeat and a half. "I don't want to coordinate with the NYPD any more than I need to on this. Not that they ever take kindly to civilians poking their—sorry, I meant *inquiring into* police business."

SO WHAT THEY DO is meet for a noon swimming date at The Deseret pool, it having been proven scientifically, according to Conkling, that the human sense of smell tends to peak on average at 11:45 A.M. Maxine wears some midrange Trish McEvoy scent that's going to wash off anyway, so it shouldn't freak her out beyond some proper perimeter if Conkling guesses right again.

Conkling seems to be fit, in a frequent-swimmer way. Today he's wearing something from one of the WASP catalogs a couple sizes too big. Maxine resists any eyebrow commentary. She was expecting maybe a Speedo thong? She discreetly checks for dick size anyway, curious also about any reaction he might be having to how she looks in this number she has on today, a high-ticket reformatting of the LBD into a swimsuit, instead of the more or less disposable ones she gets through the mail in floral prints it is better not to think about . . . And whoop there it is. Isn't it?

"Something, uh . . ."

"Oh I was just looking for uh, my goggles."

"On your head?"

"Right."

From its looks, The Deseret pool could be the oldest one in the city. Overhead you can see soaring into the chlorine-scented mists a huge segmented dome of some translucent early plastic, each piece concave and teardrop-shaped, separated by bronze-colored cames—during the daytime, whatever the sun's angle, admitting the same verdigris light, its surface at nightfall growing ever more remote and less visible, vanishing before closing time into a wintry gray.

Joaquin the pool guy is on duty. Usually something of a motormouth, today he seems to Maxine a little, you'd say, unforthcoming.

"You heard anything more about the body they found?"

"Much as anybody, which is nothing. Not even the guys on the door, not even Fergus the nightman, who knows everything. Cops been and gone, now everybody's pretty creeped out, right?"

"It wasn't a tenant, I heard."

"I don't ask."

"Somebody must know something."

"Around here it's deaf and dumb. Policy of the building. Sorry, Maxine."

After a couple of token laps, Maxine and Conkling pretend to head for their respective locker rooms, but meet up again, sneak into a staff-only stairwell, presently they're underneath the pool, moving flip-flopped and semiclad through the shadows and mysteries of the unnumbered thirteenth floor, which belongs to a disaster always about to happen, a buffer space constantly under the threat of inundation from above if the pool—concrete, state of the art back then, grandfathered exempt from what today would be a number of code violations—should God forbid ever spring a leak. For now it's the outward and structural form of a secret history of payoffs to contractors and inspectors and signers of permits, dishonest stewards long gone who expected the deluge after them to take place well after any statute of limitations has run. Creaking underframe, early-20th-century trusswork and bracing. A range of animal life in which mice could be the least of one's worries. The only light comes shimmering from watertight observation windows in the pool, each enclosed in its private viewing booth, much like a peep show at an arcade, where according to an early real-estate brochure "admirers of the natatory arts may obtain, without themselves having to undergo immersion, educational views of the human form unrestricted by the demands of gravity." Light from above the pool comes down through the water and through the observation windows and out into this darkened level below, a strange rarefied greenish blue.

It was in one of these cubicles that the police found Lester's corpse propped up as if gazing into the pool, where earlier a swimmer had noticed him and after a couple more laps, getting the picture, freaked out. According to the papers, a knife-blade of some sort had been driven with great force into Lester's skull, apparently not by hand because part of the tang still protruded from Lester's forehead. The absence of a knife-handle suggested a spring-propelled ballistic blade, illegal in the U.S. since 1986, though said to be standard issue for Russian special forces. The *Post*, for whom the Cold War still emits a warm nostalgic glow, loves stories like this, so the screaming began, KGB assassination squads running loose through the city and so forth, and this sort of thing would go on for the better part of a week.

When she saw the headline, "GONE BALLISTIC!," Maxine rang up Rocky Slagiatt. "Your ol' Spetsnaz buddy Igor Dashkov. He would't happen to know anything about this."

"Already asked him. He says that knife is a urban myth. He was in the Spetsnaz for about a century and never saw one."

"Not quite my question, but—"

"Hey. Wouldn't rule out a Russian hit. On the other hand . . ."

Right. Wouldn't rule out somebody trying to set it up to *look* like a Russian hit, either.

The crime scene itself here, meanwhile, looks pretty picked over. There's yellow tape around, and chalk marks, along with discarded plastic evidence pouches and cigarette butts and fast-food packaging. Ignoring a background haze of cop aftershave, tobacco smoke, stomach effluxes from neighborhood saloons, crime-lab solvents, fingerprint powder, luminol—

"Wait, you can smell luminol? Isn't it supposed to be odorless?"

"Nah. Notes of pencil shavings, hibiscus, number-two diesel, mayonnaise—"

"Excuse me, that's wine-maven talk."

"Oops . . ."

Filtering, howsoever, these other odors out, Conkling enters orbit around the central fact of the stiff that was here, that in the one professional sense is still here, problematical now because of what forensic

Noses like to call the deathmask, the way the indoles of bodily decay assume precedence over all other notes that might be present. There are
differential techniques for getting around this, of course, one attends
oddly furtive all-weekend seminars in New Jersey to learn them, sometimes these have practical value, sometimes it's all just New Age gobbledygook from the eighties that the gurus presiding have found it difficult
to move comfortably on from, thus allowing the ever-hopeful attendee
to flush another $139.95 plus tax into the soil stack of his fiscal affairs.
Half of it IRS-allowable, but usually, vaguely, a disappointment.

"Just do a grab, here—" Conkling going in his duffel and pulling out
some heavy-duty plastic bags and a little pocket-size unit and a plastic
fitting.

"What's that?"

"Air-sampling pump—cute, huh? Runs off a rechargeable battery.
Just going to take a couple liters here."

Waiting till they step out of the guest or freight elevator onto
the street, the clamoring, soiled, innocent street, "So . . . what did you
smell up there?"

"Nothing too unusual, except . . . before NYPD got there, before the
gunsmoke, a scent, maybe a cologne, I can't ID right offhand, commercial, maybe from a few years back . . ."

"Somebody who was there."

Emerging from a moment of thought, "Actually I think it's time to
go check the library."

Meaning, it turns out, Conkling's own extensive collection of vintage perfumes, which Conkling keeps at his crib in Chelsea, where the
first thing Maxine notices is a glossy black instrument sitting in a battery
charger among a number of dramatically oversize ferns which may have
mutated because of the apparatus in their midst, humming in more than
one key, red and green LEDs glowing and blinking here and there, with
a Clint Eastwood–size pistol grip and a long discharge cone. A creature
hidden in jungle foliage, staring at her.

"This is the Naser," Conkling introduces them, "or olfactory laser."

Going on to explain that odors can be regarded as if they had periodic waveforms, like sound or light. The everyday human nose receives all smells in a jumble, like the eye receives the frequencies of incoherent light. "The Naser here can separate these into component 'notes,' isolate and put each in phase, causing it to 'cohere,' then amplify as needed."

Sounds a little West Coast, though the object looks intimidating enough. "This is a weapon? it . . . it's dangerous?"

"In the same way," Conkling supposes, "that sniffing pure rose attar will turn your brain into red Jell-O. Don't want to be messing with no Naser, necessarily."

"Can you, like, just set it on 'Stun'?"

"If I have to use it at all, it means I've made a mistake." He goes over to a glass-fronted cabinet full of flasks and atomizers, custom and commercial. "This scent—it's not one I could place immediately, not fresh soap so much as disinfectant. Not tobacco so much as stale cigarette butts. Some civet maybe, but Kouros it ain't. Nonhuman urine as well." Maxine recognizes this as magician's patter. Conkling opens one of the cabinet doors and reaches out a four-ounce spray bottle, holds it about a foot from his nose, and without hitting the plunger appears to inhale slightly. "Whooboy. Yep, this is it. Check it out."

"'9:30'," Maxine reads from the label, "'Men's Cologne.' Wait, is this the 9:30 Club down in D.C.?"

"The same, although it's no longer at the old F Street address, where it was located when this stuff was sold, back in the late eighties sometime."

"That's a while. This must be the last bottle in town."

"You never know. Even an example like this that comes and goes, there can still be thousands of gallons out there in the original packaging, just waiting to be found by scent collectors, nostalgists, in this case unreconstructed punk rockers, and don't rule out the insane. The original manufacturer got bought by somebody else, and 9:30 if I remember right was then relicensed. So we're pretty much left with the secondary market, discount houses, ads in the trades, eBay."

"How important is this?"

"It's the chronology that's bothering me here—too close to the gunsmoke not to be part of the event. If they've brought in Jabbering Jay Moskowitz on this, then he already knows of the connection, meaning so does everybody in the NYPD including meter readers. Jay is a top forensic Nose but isn't always clear on how professionally to share information."

"So . . . a guy wearing this . . ."

"Don't rule out a woman who might have been in close contact with a man wearing it. Someday there'll be search engines you can just input a little spritz of anything and voilà, nowhere to run to, nowhere to hide, the whole story will be there on the screen before you can scratch your head in amazement. Meantime there's the Nose community. Anecdotal material. I'll ask around."

There arrives the usual moment of awkward silence. Conkling still has an erection but, as if it's hardware he's lost the manual to, is hesitant about deploying it. Maxine herself is of two minds. Something seems to be going on that nobody's telling her. The moment, howsoever, passes, and before she knows it, she's back at the office. Ah well, as Scarlett O'Hara observes at the end of the movie . . .

SHE DREAMS SHE'S ALONE on the top floor of The Deseret, by the pool. Under the unnaturally smooth surface, visible through the optically perfect water, almost as an afterthought to the anxious vacancy of the space, a male Caucasian corpse in a suit and tie stretches face-up full length on the bottom as if taking a break from afterlife affairs, rolling, in some eerie semisleep, from one side to another. It is Lester Traipse, and it isn't. When she leans over the edge to get a closer look, his eyes open and he recognizes her. He doesn't have to rise up through the surface to speak, she can hear him from underwater. "Azrael," is what he's saying, and then again, with some urgency.

"Gargamel's cat?" Maxine inquires, "like on the Smurfs?"

No, and the disappointment in Lester/not-Lester's face tells her she should know better. In nonbiblical Jewish tradition, as she is perfectly aware, Azrael is the angel of death. In Islam also, for that matter . . . And briefly she is back in the corridor, Gabriel Ice's guarded mystery tunnel out in Montauk. Why? would be an interesting question to pursue, except that Giuliani, in his tireless quest for quality infrastructure, has caused not one but several jackhammers to start up well before working hours, figuring the taxpayers won't object to the extra overtime pay, and any message is corrupted, fragmented, lost.

19

Meantime Heidi, back from Comic-Con in San Diego, her head still teeming with superheroes, monsters, sorcerers, and zombies, has been visited by NYPD detectives looking into the address books of Heidi's old ex-fiancé Evan Strubel, who has recently been run in on charges of aggravated computer tampering, in connection with a federal insider-trading beef. Heidi's first thought is, He still has me in his Rolodex?

"You two were romantically involved?"

"Not romantically. Baroquely maybe. Years ago."

"Was that before or after he got married?"

"Thought you guys were from the precinct, not the Adultery Squad."

"Pretty touchy," it seems to the Bad Cop.

"Yep, and feely too," Heidi snaps back. "What's it to you, Your Eminence?"

"Just trying to get a chronology," soothes the Good Cop. "Whatever you're comfortable sharing, Heidi."

"'Sharing,' yo, Geraldo, I thought you got canceled."

And so forth, sort of like police handball.

As they are about to leave, Heidi finds the Bad Cop beaming strangely at her. "Oh, and Heidi . . ."

"Yes, Detective"— pretending to search her memory—"Nozzoli."

"These chick flicks from the fifties? Ever watch any of those?"

"On the movie channels now and then," Heidi somehow unable not to bat her eyelashes, "sure, I guess, who wants to know?"

"There's a Douglas Sirk festival next week down at the Angelika, and if you're interested, maybe we could go grab some coffee first, or—"

"Excuse me. Are you asking me—"

"Unless you're 'married,' of course."

"Oh, these days they allow married women to drink coffee, it even gets written into prenups."

"Heidi," Maxine, when she hears this, sighs as always, "desperate, unreflective Heidi, this Detective Nozzoli, he's, ah, he's married himself?"

"You are so the jaded cynic of the universe!" cries Heidi, "It could be George *Clooney* and you would find something wrong!"

"An innocent question, what."

"We went to see *Written on the Wind* (1956)" Heidi continues as if gone starry-eyed remembering, "and whenever Dorothy Malone came on the screen? Carmine got a hardon. A big one."

"Don't tell me—the old penis-in-the popcorn-box-routine. Just to keep in the fifties spirit."

"Maxi, hopelessly-West-Side-liberal Maxi, if you only knew what you were missing with these law-enforcement guys. Believe me, once you've tried cop, you never want to stop."

"Yes but tell me Heidi, what happened to your obsession with Arnold Vosloo from *The Mummy* and *The Mummy Returns,* and, and the interviews you keep trying to set up with his office—"

"Envy," supposes Heidi, "is so often all that stands between some of us and a sad, empty life."

Today Maxine is halfway through her file of take-out menus when Heidi sticks her head in with the latest episode of a continuing purse drama. Having survived an identity crisis brought on by her old Coach model, which has had observers attentive to bag signifiers mistaking her for various sorts of Asian, she is now deep in the basic princessly exercise of whether to go for a class image with Longchamps, for example, and live with never being able to find anything inside it, or schlep around a more comparmentalized model and accept a slight downgrade to her hipness rating.

"But that's history now, Carmine bless him has solved all that."

"Carmine is . . . he's some kind of . . . purse fetishist, Heidi?"

"No, but the man does pay attention. Look, check out what he bought me." It's an inexpensive tote in some autumnal print, with a gold-tone heart on it. "Fall and winter, right? Now watch." Heidi reaches inside and turns the whole thing inside out, presenting a totally different bag, light-colored and floral. "Spring and summer! it's convertible! you get a twofer, see?"

"How inventive. A bipolar bag."

"And well then of course it's a piece of living history also." Down in one corner Maxine reads MADE ESPECIALLY FOR YOU BY MONICA.

"New one on me, unless . . . oh. No, Heidi, wait. 'Monica'. He didn't get this at, at Bendel's?"

"Yep, right off the truck—it's the ol' Portly Pepperpot herself. Do you realize what this will fetch on eBay in a couple of years?"

"A Monica Lewinsky original. Tough call, but I'd err on the side of good taste is timeless."

"And who'd know better than you Maxi, all the seasons you've seen come and go."

"Oh but of course it's a hint isn't it, Carmine is suggesting a *particular act*, now let me think, what can that be, something you may not've been all that eager to perform . . ."

It's a fairly lightweight handbag, but Heidi does her best to assault Maxine with it in a meaningful way. They chase around the apartment screaming for a while before deciding to take a supper break and order in from Ning Xia Happy Life, whose take-out menus keep getting shoved under everybody's back door.

Heidi squints at the options. "There's a breakfast menu? Long March Szechuan Muesli? Magic Goji Longevity Shake? what, excuse me, the fuck?"

The delivery guy who shows up is not Chinese but Latino, which gets Heidi further confused. "*Seguro usted tiene el correcto apartmento? We were waiting for a Chinese delivery? Foodo Chineso?*"

Unpacking the bags, they can't remember ordering half of it. "Here, try this," passing Heidi a dubious egg roll.

"Strange . . . exotic burst of flavor . . . This is . . . meat? what kind, do you suppose?"

Pretending to look at the menu, "All it said was 'Benji Roll'? Sounded intriguing, so—"

"Dog!" Heidi jumping up and running over to the sink to spit out what she can. "Oh God! Those people eat dog over there! You ordered this, how could you? You never saw the movie? What kind of a child-hood did you— Aaaahhh!"

Maxine shrugs. "You want me to help induce vomiting, or can you remember how to do that OK?"

The Twelve Flavors Drunken Squid is a little overdone. They settle for dropping pieces from different heights onto their plates to see how high they'll bounce. The Green Jade Energetic Surprise comes in a plastic container molded to look like a jade box from the Qing dynasty. "The surprise," Heidi nervously, "is a shrunken head inside." It turns out to be mostly broccoli. The Gang of Four Vegetarian Combo, on the other hand, is exquisite, if mysterious. Anybody eating it at the physical Ning Xia restaurant impulsive enough to ask what's in it will only get a glare. The Chinese fortune-cookie fortunes are even more problematic.

"'He is not who he seems to be,'" Heidi reads.

"Carmine, obviously. Oh, Heidi."

"Please. It's a fortune cookie, Maxi."

Maxine cracks open her cookie. "'Even the ox may bear violence in his heart.' What?"

"Horst, obviously."

"Nah. Could be anybody."

"Horst never got . . . abusive with you, or anything . . . ?"

"Horst? a dove. Well, maybe except for that one time he started choking me . . ."

"He what?"

"Oh? He never told you about that."

"Horst actually—"

"Put it this way, Heidi—he had his hands around my neck, and he was squeezing? What would you call that?"

"What happened?"

"Oh, there was a game on, he got distracted, Brett Favre or somebody did something, I don't know, anyway he relaxed his grip, went off to the fridge, got a beer. Can of Bud Light, I believe. We kept arguing, of course."

"Wow, close call."

"Not really. I have always depended on the kindness of stranglers." A quick paradiddle with her chopsticks on Heidi's head.

DETECTIVE CARMINE NOZZOLI, with access to the federal crime database, turns out to be an unexpectedly obliging resource, allowing Maxine for example to run a quick make on Tallis's fiber-salesman BF. On first glance, Chazz Larday is an average lowlife from down in the U.S. someplace, come to NYC to make his fortune, having emerged out of a silent seething Gulf Coast petri dish of who knows how many local-level priors, a directoryful of petty malfeasance soon enough escalating into Title 18 beefs including telemarketing rackets via the fax machine, conspiracy to commit remanufactured toner cartridge misrepresentation, plus a history of bringing slot machines across state lines to where they are not necessarily legal, and cruising up and down the back roads of heartland suburbia peddling bootleg infrared strobes that will change red lights to green for rounders and assorted teenage offenders who don't like stopping for nothing, all at the behest allegedly of the Dixie Mafia, a loose confederacy of ex-cons and full-auto badasses very few of whom know or even like one another.

Carmine just shakes his head. "Mob arrangements I can understand, strong respect for family—but these good old boys, it's shocking."

"Has this Chazz guy done time?"

"Only for a couple of the little ones, county jail time, sheriff's wife bringin him casseroles and so forth, but all the big ones, he walked. Seems to have resources behind him. Then and now."

Mrs. Plibbler, high-school drama teacher from hell, once again must Maxine invoke thee here as guardian spirit of fraud police accredited and otherwise. "Oh hi, I'm calling from hashslingrz? Is this Mr. Larday?"

"You guys don't have this number."

"Uh huh, well this is Heather, from Legal? Trying to clear up one or two details about some arrangements you have with our company comptroller, Mrs. Ice?"

"Mizzis Ice." Pause. After some time in fraud work, you learn to read phone silences. They come in different lengths and depths, room ambiences and front-edge attacks. This one is telling Maxine that Chazz knows he shouldn't have blurted what he just did.

"I'm sorry, is that information not correct? Do you mean the arrangements are with *Mister* Ice?"

"Darlin, you are either so out of the loop or else you're one of these fuckin bloggers runnin a gossip page, either way be advised we have a trace on this instrument, we know who you are and where you are and our people will not hesitate to come after you. You have a good day now, you hear?" He hangs up and when she redials, there's no answer.

Good luck to him with the cop-show talk, but more important, what's up with Tallis, how innocent a party can she be in any of this? If she's in on something, how far in? And is that innocent pure or innocent stupid?

Given the likely level of corruption around here, Gabriel Ice may know all about that li'l lovebirds' *nidito* up in East Harlem, maybe even be springing for the rent. What else? Has he also been using Tallis as a mule to move money secretly to Darklinear Solutions? Why so secretly, for goodness' sakes? Too many questions, no theories. Maxine catches sight of herself in a mirror. Her mouth is not at the moment hanging open, but it might as well be. As Henny Youngman might diagnose it, ESP bypass.

VYRVA MEANWHILE IS BACK from Las Vegas and Defcon, not as poolside tan as expected, in fact striking Maxine as, what's the word, reserved? distraught? weird? As if something happened in Vegas that didn't all stay there, some ominous overflow, like alien DNA hitching a ride unnoticed back here to planet Earth, to perform its mischief in its own good time.

Fiona's still away at camp, working on a Quake-movie adaptation of *The Sound of Music* (1965). Fiona and her team are doing the Nazis.

"You must miss her."

"Of course I miss her," a little too quick.

Maxine puts her eyebrows into an I-said-something? asymmetry.

"Just as well she's not here, 'cause right now, it's starting to get crazy, everybody's after DeepArcher, the guys got seriously hit on in Vegas, one after another, the NSA, the Mossad, terrorist go-betweens, Microsoft, Apple, start-ups that'll be gone in a year, old money, new money, you name it."

Since it's been on her mind, Maxine names it. "Hashslingrz too, I suppose."

"Natch. There we are, Justin and me, an innocent tourist couple strolling through Caesars, suddenly here's Gabriel Ice lurking by a buffet table with an attaché case full of lobbying material."

"Ice was at Defcon?"

"At a Black Hat Briefing, some kind of security conference they hold every year the week before Defcon, a casino hotel full of guys who'd hack a lightbulb, corporate cops, crypto geniuses, sniffers and spoofers, designers, reverse engineers, TV network suits, everybody with something to sell."

They're down in Tribeca, a chance encounter at a street corner. "Come on, we'll grab an ice coffee."

Vyrva starts to look at her watch, suppresses the gesture. "For sure."

They find a place and duck into the blessed A/C. Something astrological going on, Jupiter, the money planet, in Pisces, the sign of all things fishy. "See—" Vyrva sighs. "There's a chance of some money."

Aww. "There wasn't before?"

"Honestly, should it matter who gets to own the damned old source code? Not as if it has a conscience, DeepArcher, it's just there, users can be anybody, no moral questionnaire 'r netheen? it's rilly only about the money. Who ends up with how much?"

"Except that in my business," Maxine gently, "what I see a lot of is innocent people making these deals with the satanic forces, for money way out of scale to anything they're used to, and there's a point where it all rolls in on them and they go under, and sometimes they don't come back up."

But Vyrva is far away now, the summer street outside, the cumulus piling up over Jersey, the rush hour bearing down, it's all country miles from wherever she is, rambling some DeepArcher of the unshared interior, her click history vanishing behind her like footprints in the air, like free advice unheard, so Maxine supposes it'll have to keep, whatever it is, whatever's finally on the term sheet.

20

With the gracious assistance as always of Detective Nozzoli, Maxine has obtained a license ID photo of Eric Jeffrey Outfield, and this, along with a brief list from Reg of places Eric is most likely to be found, sends her through a steamy August evening out to Queens to a strip club called Joie de Beavre. The place is located along a stretch of frontage road next to the LIE, its neon sign depicting a lewdly humanized beaver wearing a beret and winking its eyes alternately at a wiggling stripper.

"Hi, I was told to see Stu Gotz?"

"In back."

She was expecting a dressing room out of some movie musical? What she finds is a sort of casually upgraded ladies' toilet, stall partitions and so forth—some, to be sure, with glittery stars taped on the doors—a litter of pint liquor bottles, roaches both smokable and crawling, used Kleenex, not recognizably a Vincente Minnelli set.

Stu Gotz is sitting in his office, with a cigarette in one hand and a paper cup of something ambiguous in the other. Soon the cigarette will be in the cup. He runs a lengthy O-O. "You want to audition, MILF night is Tuesdays, come back then."

"Tuesday's my Tupperware party."

Drawing a thoughtful leer. "Then again, if you want to give it a shot right now . . ."

"This is more like an investigation I'm on? I need to locate one of your regular customers."

"Wait, you're a cop?"

"Not exactly, more like an accountant?"

"Well, don't let this family-type atmosphere fool you into thinking I know every one of them out there by name. Which I do, but it's like all the same name? Loser?"

"Wow. Some way to talk about your client base."

"Laid-off geeks who are more comfortable, hope I don't offend, jerking off in front of a screen than anything more real-life? Sorry if I don't get too sympathetic. Please, go on ahead, see for yourself, find a outfit, you're a what? a 2, maybe? Don' worry, some'n'll fit yiz."

Now, Maxine hasn't been a size 2 since back when a 2 was really a 2, instead of the current definition, which, for purposes of commerce, can run up to what used to be known as a 16. And beyond. To her credit, she does not blurt thanks for the pleasantry but shrugging begins to look through the contents of a beat-up armoire against the wall, full of somebody's notion of glamorous lingerie, outfits of subcultural interest— nun, schoolgirl, warrior princess—and spike heels, each pair more, you would have to say, alluring, than the last, not designer footwear exactly, maybe more in the Payless range, the sort of shoes that get podiatrists to daydreaming of Ferraris and personal golf lessons from Tiger Woods.

She settles on platform heels in neon aqua, plus matching sequined thong leotard and thigh-high stockings. Just the ticket, except . . . "Oh, Mr. Gotz?"

"Dry-cleaned and disinfected, my darling, my personal guarantee." Somehow not reassured, leaving her pantyhose on, she slides into the alluring getup, and after a few contemplative breaths, sashays out through a curtain of faux Swarovski crystals into the massively air-conditioned, high-decibel dimness of the Joie de Beavre. Two or three girls are spaced along the bar, massaging their pussies, staring semi-stoned into the distance. There appears to be a pole free, and Maxine heads for it, since oddly enough she does happen to know a couple of moves, thanks to a gym she works out at now and then, Body and Pole, far below 14th Street, down in cutting-edge country where pole dancing is already part of the exercise vernacular, though back on the Upper West Side it's still considered by many—well, by Heidi—to be fatally disreputable.

"Pitiful, thwarted Maxi, why not invest in a vibrator, I'm told there are several on the market that might do the trick even for you."

"Uptight, judgmental Heidi, why not come down some night yourself, give that pole a try, maybe rediscover your inner good-time girl."

Maxine's plan is to improvise a MILF-night routine while scanning faces and hoping for a match with Eric's license photo. According to Reg, owing to various Eric-conspiracy issues—some geek thing—the young computer whiz has shaved off the mustache in his official mug shot, but so far kept the same hair color.

She makes a point of taking from her purse a dispenser of Handi Wipes and with housewifely thoroughness disinfecting the pole, slowly fondling it up and down while casting demure glances along the bar. Their skins in the spill from this fluorescent indigo lighting register the same pallid hue, as if permanently stained from too much cathode radiation.

Considerately, Stu Gotz, or somebody, has put on a MILF-night mix, which includes a lot of disco, plus tracks from U2, Guns N' Roses, Journey. And pandering to this crowd, way too much Moby for Maxine's taste, except possibly "That's When I Reach for My Revolver."

Maxine's never had what you'd call Big Tits, although the connoisseurs here don't seem to mind as long as they're Bare Tits. The one body part they won't be staring at much is her eyes. This Male Gaze she's been hearing about since high school is not about to intersect its female counterpart anytime soon.

In the course of a dance routine somewhere between vanilla and cherry ripple, including leg hangs, helical descents, upside-down humping of the pole and so forth, Maxine notices this one party out on a remote curve of the bar, drinking you'd say relentlessly what will prove to be Jägermeister and 151, through a Day-Glo straw out of a twenty-ounce convenience-store cup he has brought in with him, and showing no signs of alcohol poisoning, which could mean either unnatural immunity or unreachable despair. She undulates over for a closer look, and sure enough it's him, Eric Jeffrey Outfield, übergeek, looking, except for the bare upper lip and a newly acquired soul patch, just like his ID photo. He is wearing cargo pants in a camo print whose color scheme is intended for some combat zone very remote, if not off-planet, and a T-shirt announcing, in Helvetica, <P> REAL GEEKS USE COMMAND PROMPTS </P>, accessorized with a Batbelt clanking like a charm bracelet with remotes for TV, stereo, and air conditioner, plus laser pointer, pager, bottle opener, wire stripper, voltmeter, magnifier, all so tiny that one legitimately wonders how functional they can be.

About then on comes Jamiroquai's "Canned Heat," whose bass line Maxine has never found a way to resist, and seized in some post-disco swoon she forgets temporarily what she's come here for, ignores the pole, and succumbs to just dancing, and by the time the music has segued into "Cosmic Girl," she's squatting on the bar in front of Eric, who seems more fascinated by her glittery aqua shoes than anything, staying there till the tape ends and everybody takes a break, then slithering over the bar and down onto a barstool next to him.

"I'm out of singles," he begins.

"Honey, it's them NASDAQ blues, we all took a bath, it sucks, but maybe you can do me a favor, I'm new in here and you look at least like a semiregular, maybe you can tell me where the Champagne Lounge is in this joint?"

"I'm out of twenties too."

"No obligation."

"Next you're gonna say, 'But wait!'" He looks quizzically into his lethal drink for a while, as if for the answer to some personal problem to come floating into view printed on one face of a dodecahedron, then in a slow lurch gets carefully to his feet. "I'm headed for the toilet, c'mon, it's on the way."

He leads her toward the back and down a flight of stairs. The lighting drifts more and more into the red end of the spectrum. From below ooze romantic string arrangements Maxine thought had been retired in the seventies, no more inviting tonight than they were then.

"I'll be in here, in case you want to talk. No fees. Promise."

The Champagne Lounge is cozy in scale, more like a Mad Dog Utility Room. Video screens, some showing only noise, others flickering porno tapes of a low-res Kodachrome vintage, are mounted here and there on wall brackets. Girls sit alone at tables taking smoke breaks. Others straddle clients in the stained velour shadows of "privacy booths" in back. There's a miniature bar with a couple shelves of bottles whose labels are not immediately familiar to Maxine. "You're new," observes the fashion-doll-faced bartender, in a perky voice at some odds with the sullen set of enhanced lips it emerges from. "Welcome to geek heaven. You get one mojito on the house, then you're on your own."

"Full disclosure," sez Maxine, "I'm a civilian, thought tonight was MILF night, guess I got it wrong."

"You bring a customer?"

"Just my neighbor's nephew, she asked me to keep an eye on him. Sweet kid, basically, too much time on the Internet maybe."

At which point Eric puts his head through the bead curtains.

"*Oh* no not this guy, uh-uh, he's been 86'd, hey creepazoid, you want me to call Porfirio down here again, show you where the sidewalk is?"

"It's cool," Maxine smiling, shrugging, sliding out the doorway. "All good."

"Assholes," Eric mutters, "can I help it if I like feet?"

"Where do you live? I'll take you back."

"Manhattan, downtown."

"Come on, I'll spring for a cab. Just let me run in and change."

"I'll wait outside."

"What's with Footboy," Stu Gotz wants to know when she's street legal again. "Nice company you keep."

"Oh, it's business."

"Which reminds me—at this time we are delighted to offer you a one-month contract, provided only that you attend our Introductory Profiling Seminar, which will acquaint you with the many varieties of technoscum and psychosocial misfit all too sadly apt to be overrepresented among our clientele."

She takes his card, which may come in handy someday though in ways neither can see right at the moment.

ERIC LIVES IN A FIFTH-FLOOR walk-up studio in Loisaida, a doorless bathroom wedged in one corner and in another a microwave, coffeemaker, and miniature sink. Liquor-store cartons full of personal effects are stacked around haphazardly, and most of the limited floor space is littered with unwashed laundry, Chinese take-out containers and pizza boxes, empty Smirnoff Ice bottles, old copies of *Heavy Metal, Maxim,* and *Anal Teen Nymphos Quarterly,* women's shoe catalogs, SDK discs, game controllers and cartridges for Wolfenstein, DOOM, and others. Paint peels from selected ceiling areas, and window treatments are basically street grime. Eric finds a cigarette butt a little longer than the others in a running shoe he's been using for an ashtray and lights up, lurches over to the electric coffee mess, pours out some cold day-old sludge into a mug with a rectangular outline on it and the words CSS IS AWESOME running outside the frame. "Oh. Want some?"

They light up a joint, Eric comfortable on the floor. "Now," in a voice she hopes is firm enough, "about this foot situation."

"Here, let's just get your shoes off, don't worry. You don't have to deal with the floor, you can rest them on me."

"My thought also."

It has been a while, like forever, since her feet have received attention like this. She has a moment of panic, wondering, am I weird, allowing this? Eric, with an extrasensory grin, looks up and nods. "Yeah, you are."

Her feet seem to have been resting in his lap for a while, and she can't help noticing he has this, well, hardon. Out of his trousers and between her feet, actually, and sort of moving back and forth . . . Not that this happens to her a lot, which may account for why she begins tentatively now to explore, whatever the foot equivalent of handle is, maybe "footle" the aroused organ, her toes always having been prehensile enough to pick up socks, keys, and loose change, her soles, could it be the cannabis? unaccountably sensitized, particularly the insides of her heels, which reflexologists have told her connect directly with the uterus . . . she slides the polished toes of one foot under his balls and with the pads of the others begins caressing his penis, after a while switching feet, just to see what will happen, all out of experimental curiosity of course . . .

"Eric, what's this, did you just . . . come, on my feet?"

"Um, yeah? well not 'on' exactly, coz I'm wearing a condom?"

"You're worried about what, funguses?"

"No offense, I just like condoms, sometimes I'll wear one just to have it on, you know?"

"OK . . ." Maxine glances quickly at his dick, and her contacts flip inside out and go sailing across the room. "Eric, excuse me, is that some loathsome skin disease?"

"This? oh it's a designer condom, from the Trojan Abstract Expressionist Collection I believe, here—" He takes it off and waves it at her.

"No need, no need."

"Was that OK for you?"

Why, the sweetheart. Well? Was it? She angles her head and smiles, she hopes not too sitcomically.

"You don't do this a lot."

"Not that often, as Daddy Warbucks always sez . . ." Now he has that attentive kid-on-a-date look. So Maxine don't be a schmuck all your life, "Listen. Eric. Total honesty here, all right?" She tells him about her arrangements with Reg.

"What? You came out to that strip joint deliberately, to look for me? Hey Reg, thanks buddy. What's he doing, he's checking up on me?"

"Rest easy, just think of me as the straightworld version of you, see what I'm saying. You're the one gets to be the outlaw, adventures down in the Deep Web, which of us do you think's having more fun?"

"Sure." He flicks a quick look at her—she's been watching him, otherwise she wouldn't have seen it. "You think it's fun, maybe sometime I should bring you down there. Show you around."

"OK. It's a date."

"Really?"

"It could be romantic."

"Most of the time it ain't, just pretty straightforward, directories you have to access and search by yourself, because no crawler knows how to, no links into it exist. Now and then it can get weird, stuff somebody like hashslingrz wants to keep hidden. Or sites lost to linkrot, to bankruptcy, to who-gives-a-shit-anymore . . ."

The Deep Web is supposed to be mostly obsolete sites and broken links, an endless junkyard. Like in *The Mummy* (1999), adventurers will come here someday to dig up relics of remote and exotic dynasties. "But it only looks that way," according to Eric—"behind it is a whole invisible maze of constraints, engineered in, lets you go some places, keeps you out of others. This hidden code of behavior you have to learn and obey. A dump, with structure."

"Eric . . . say there was something down there I might want to hack into . . ."

"Ehhh. Here I thought you loved me for my psychosexual profile. Should've known. Story of my life."

"Sh-sh, no, nothing like that—the site I'm thinking about, it may not even be there, one of those old Cold War sites, maybe some fringe fantasy, time travel, UFOs, mind control—"

"Sounds awesome so far."

"It could be heavily encrypted. If I did want to get in, I'd need some alphageek crypto whiz."

"Sure, that'd be me, but . . ."

"Hey, I'll hire you, I'm legit, Reg will vouch."

"Sure he will, he's the one who fixed us up. He should be charging me a finder's fee." Holding one of her shoes now in you could say a hopeful way.

"You weren't planning to . . ."

"I was, but if you have to get back, I understand, here, let me just slide these back on for you . . ."

"I mean, these are a little too casual anyway, don't you think? You seem like more of a Manolo Blahnik person."

"Actually, there's this guy Christian Louboutin? Does these five-inch stilettos? Awesome."

"Think I've seen knockoffs around."

"Hey, knockoffs, no problem."

"Next time, maybe . . ."

"Promise?"

"No?"

When she gets home, the phone is ringing. Off the hook. A number of previous messages on the machine, all from Heidi.

Who basically wants to know where Maxine's been.

"Networking. Something important, Heidi?"

"Oh. Just wondering . . . who's the new fella?"

"The . . ."

"You were seen over at the Chinese-Dominican joint the other day. Quite intense, it is reported, eyes only for each other."

"Like," she probably shouldn't be blurting, "he's FBI or something, Heidi, it was work . . . I put it on Travel & Entertainment."

"You put everything on T&E, Maxine, breath mints, newsstand um-

brellas, the thing neither Carmine nor I can understand is why you keep
asking us for so much help getting into the NCIC database, especially if
you're seeing Eliot Ness and whatever."

"Which reminds me actually . . ."

"What, again? Carmine, not that he begrudges, far from it, is wondering if possibly you might like to return some of these favors he's
doing you."

"By . . . ?"

"Well, for instance in connection with The Deseret corpse and this
mafioso you're apparently also dating concurrently?"

"Who—Rocky Slagiatt? he's some kind of a suspect now? What do
you mean, dating?"

"Well of course we assumed you and Mr. Slagiatt are . . ." Heidi by
now with that trademark smirk all over her voice.

Maxine drops for a minute into one of Shawn's visualizing exercises
in which her Beretta, within easy reach, has been transformed to a color-
ful California butterfly dedicated, like Mothra, to purposes of peace.
"Mr. Slagiatt has been helping me with an embezzlement beef, mutual
trust here being of the essence, which I doubt would include ratting him
out to the authorities, do you think, Heidi."

"Carmine only wants to know," Heidi implacable, "is, has Mr.
Slagiatt ever mentioned his former client the late Lester Traipse."

"VC talk? We don't do much of that, sorry."

"Wrecks the afterglow, I quite understand, though where you find
the time for some D.C. bureaucrat on the side—"

"Maybe he's more interesting than that—"

"'Interesting.' Ah." The annoying staccato Heidi *ah*. "And Hitler was
a good dancer, a wonderful sense of humor, I can't fuckin believe this,
we watch the same movies on the Lifetime channel, these are always the
ones who turn out to be the sociopathic rat, shtupping the receptionist,
embezzling the children's lunch money, slowly poisoning the innocent
bride with the bug spray in the breakfast food."

"That's like . . ." innocently, "a cereal killer?"

"Just 'cause I once pitched you a commercial about cops? You believed that?"

"He's not a cop. We're not newlyweds. Remember? Heidi, chill, for goodness sakes."

21

After a day of wandering around in the vast shopping basin of the SoHo-Chinatown-Tribeca interface, Maxine and Heidi find themselves one evening in the East Village looking for a bar where Driscoll is supposed to be singing with a nerdcore band called Pringle Chip Equation, when sudden gusts of smell, not yet at this distance intense but strangely contoured in their purity, begin as they walk through the humid twilight to accost them. Presently from down the block, screaming in panic, dramatically clutching their noses and occasionally heads, civilians come running. "I think I saw the movie," Heidi sez. "What's that smell?"

Turns out to be Conkling Speedwell, packing his Naser tonight, which looks in fact to've been recently deployed, its LED-studded delivery cone blinking truculently. He is accompanied by a small detachment of corporate security in designer fatigues each with a shoulder patch shaped like a flask of Chanel No. 5, with FRAGRANCE FORCE written across the stopper part and on the label the mirrored-C logo flanked by a couple of Glocks.

"Sting operation," Conkling explains. "Truckful of Latvian counterfeit product, we were supposed to make a buy, but it all went stinko." He nods at a forlorn trio of Pardaugava mini-mobsters semiconsciously collapsed in a doorway. "They'll be OK, just aldehyde shock, caught 'em with the main lobe, maximized the prewar nitro musk and jasmine absolute, right?"

"Anybody would've done the same." And on the topic of chemistry, what, excuse me, is suddenly up with Heidi and Conkling here?

"Say . . . is that Poison you're wearing?" Conkling's nose, in the dim light, having acquired a slowly pulsing glow.

"How could you tell?" with the eyelashes and so forth. Annoying enough, more so given the Poison issue, which has long simmered between Heidi and Maxine, especially Heidi's practice of wearing it into elevators. All over the city, sometimes even years later, elevators have still not gotten over Heidi occupancies however brief, some even being obliged to attend special Elevator Recovery Clinics to be detoxified. "You have to stop blaming yourself for this, you were the victim . . ."

"I should've just closed the doors on her and defaulted to the roof . . ."

Meantime here comes the precinct, plus the bomb squad, a couple ambulances, and a SWAT team.

"Why, sure and if it isn't the kid."

"Moskowitz, what brings you out?"

"Schmoozin with some o' the b'ys down to the Krispy Kreme, happened to pick this up on the scanner— Why, and is it itself theer with the blinkin lights, that infamous Neaaaser, now?"

"Oh . . . what, this? Nah, nah, just a toy for the kids, listen," pressing a decoy button to activate a sound chip, which begins to play "Baby Beluga."

"Lovely, and what sort of eedjit would you be takin me for, young Conkling?"

"The savant kind, I guess, but meanwhile look, Jay, there's a whole van full of Chanel No. 5 over there that might get lost on the way to the property room unless somebody keeps an eye on it."

"Why, it's me dear wife's own favorite scent, it is."

"Well, in that case."

"Conkling," Maxine'd love to stay and chat, but, "you happen to know a bar in the neighborhood called Vodkascript, we're looking for it."

"Passed it, just a couple blocks that way."

"You're welcome to join us," Heidi struggling with the overeagerness.

"Don't know how long we'll be here . . ."

"Ah, c'mon." Sez Heidi. She is wearing jeans tonight and a twinset in some ill-advised tangerine shade, despite, or because of, which, Conkling is enchanted.

"Guys, we'll finish up the paperwork back at 57th, OK?" Sez Conkling.

That was quick. Thinks Maxine.

At Vodkascript they find a roomful of trustafarians, cybergoths, out-of-work codefolk, uptowners ever in search of a life less vapid, all jammed into a tiny ex–neighborhood bar with no A/C and too many amplifiers, listening to Pringle Chip Equation. The band are all wearing nerd eyeglass frames and, like everybody else in the room, sweating. The lead guitarist plays an Epiphone Les Paul Custom and the keyboardist a Korg DW-8000, and there is also a reedperson with assorted horns and a percussionist with a wide range of tropical instruments. In a special guest appearance tonight, Driscoll Padgett is heard on an occasional vocal. Maxine never imagined that Driscoll's universe of three-letter acronyms might include "LBD," but now look at this latest edition. Hair pinned up, revealing to Maxine's surprise one of those sweetly hexagonal junior-model faces, eyes and lips underdone, the chin resolute as if she were getting serious about her life. A face, Maxine can't help thinking, come into its own . . .

Remember the Alley,
    each day was a party, and
    we were the new kids in town . . .

geeks on a joyride,
all rowdy and red-eyed,
and too high, to ever come down . . .

South of the DoubleClick
welcome sign, hard to find
much status quo in the house,
techies just chillin there
morphing to millionaires
all at the wave of a mouse . . .

Was it real?
            was it
anything more than a
dream through a lunch break, a
prayer on the fly,
Could we feel . . .
off the edge of the screen, somethin
meatspace and mean, that was passing us by . . .

When all of those high times
and lowlifes and good news
And bad moves have drifted away,
these streets are still thronging
With hustling and longing
just like they were
back in the day . . .
I'm in a new place now,
the rent's high, the dates lie,
The town's not as cozy as then,
Call me, keep try'n me,
Maybe you'll find me . . .

Maybe you'll find me,
Again . . .

After the set, Driscoll waves and comes over.

"Driscoll, Heidi, and this is Conkling."

"Oh, sure, the guy with the Hitler," quick look at Maxine, "uh, thing. How'd that work out?"

"Hitler," Heidi violently with the eyelashes, scattering pieces of mascara, as if it's a pop star she and Conkling might have in common.

Fuck here we go, Maxine half-subvocalizes, having only herself recently learned of Conkling's longtime obsession with, not so much Hitler in general as the even more focused question of, what did Hitler smell like? Exactly? "I mean obviously like a vegetarian, like a nonsmoker, but . . . what was Hitler's cologne, for example?"

"I always figured it was 4711," Heidi taking her beat a little faster than a normal person might.

Conkling is instantly mesmerized. The sort of thing you see in older Disney cartoons. "Me too! Where did you—"

"Only a wild guess, JFK used it, right? and both men, mutatis mutandis, had the same kind of, you know, charisma?"

"Exactly, and if young Jack borrowed his father's cologne—in the literature we often find a father-to-son transmission model—we know the elder Kennedy admired Hitler, even plausibly enough to want to smell like him, add to that that every U-boat in Admiral Dönitz's fleet got spritzed continuously with 4711, barrels full of it every voyage, and furthermore Dönitz was *personally* named by Hitler as his *successor*—"

"Conkling," Maxine gently and not for the first time, "that doesn't make Hitler a big U-boat lover, by that point there was nobody else he trusted, and somehow, the logic here?"

At first, assuming Conkling was only developing a thesis out loud, Maxine was willing to cut him some slack. But soon she began to grow vaguely alarmed, recognizing, behind a pose of wholesome curiosity, the narrow stare of the zealot. At some point he showed Maxine a "period press photo" in which Dönitz is presenting Hitler with a gigantic bottle of 4711, its label clearly visible. "Wow," careful not to agitate Conkling, "talk about product placement, huh? Mind if I pull a Xerox of this?" Just a hunch, but she wanted to show it to Driscoll.

It drew an instant eyeroll. "Photoshopped. Look." Driscoll opened her computer, clicked around some Web sites, typed in a couple of search terms, finally pulled up a photo from July 1942 of Dönitz and Hitler, identical to Conkling's, except that the two men are only shaking hands. "Angle Dönitz's arm down a couple of degrees, find an image of the bottle, scale it any size you want, put it in his hand, leave Hitler's where it is, looks like he's reaching for the bottle, see?"

"Think there's any point in telling Conkling any of this?"

"Depends where he got the picture from and how much he spent."

When Maxine, not shy, asked, Conkling looked embarrassed. "Swap meets . . . New Jersey . . . you know how there's always Nazi memorabilia . . . Look, there could be an explanation—it could still be a genuine *Nazi propaganda photo*, right? which they altered themselves, for a poster or . . ."

"You'd still need to get it expertized— Oh, Conkling, there's somebody on the other line here, I have to take this."

Maxine has tried since to keep their conversations professional. Conkling does ease up some with the Hitler references, but it only makes Maxine nervous. Wild talents like überschnozz here, she learned long ago at the New York campus of Fraud University, can often be nutcases also.

Heidi of course thinks it's cute. When Conkling slides off to the toilet, she leans till their heads are touching and murmurs, "So Maxine, is there an issue here?"

"You mean," switching to loyal sidekick, "as in 'Bird Dog' by the Everly Brothers, well, far as I know, Conkling is nobody's quail at the moment, and besides you only poach husbands, isn't that right, Heidi."

"Aahhh! You will never—"

"And what about Carmine, passionate, Italian, goes without saying jealous, a recipe for Naser versus Glock at high noon, no?"

"Carmine and I are deliriously happy, no I'm only thinking of you, Maxine, my best friend, don't want to get in your way . . ."

At which point Conkling comes back and the saccharimeter readings drop to a less alarming level.

"Fascinating toilet. Not quite the complexity of a Welcome to the Johnsons, say, but plenty of stories old and new."

CALL FROM AXEL DOWN at the tax office, latest on Vip Epperdew, seems he's jumped bail and fled the jurisdiction. "His young friends have also disappeared. Maybe in another direction, maybe they're still all together."

"You want me to fix you up with a good skiptracer?"

"What's to go after? Not our problem anymore. Muffins and Unicorns is in receivership, Vip's accounts are all frozen, the tax liability's being negotiated, the wife is filing for divorce and about to get her real-estate license, happy endings all around. Excuse me while I go find a tissue."

Maxine, for whom the Uncle Dizzy ticket is a kind of tutorial in annoyance control, spends an hour or two with Xeroxes of Diz's receipts and journals, takes a break, finds Conkling browsing through back issues of *Fraud* magazine. "Why didn't you say something?"

"You looked pretty busy. Didn't want to interrupt. Just an update on that 9:30 product—I consulted one of my associates, we go back to the old days at IF&F. She's proösmic—she can foresmell things that're going to happen. Sometimes a scent can act as a trigger. In this case more like a detonator—she took one pass at the air sample I showed her and went nitrous." For weeks already she'd been going around in a state of panic, short of breath, waking up for no reason, probed gently but insistently by a reverse *sillage*, a wake from the future. "She says no one alive has smelled it before, this toxic accord she's been picking up, bitter, indolic, caustic, 'like breathing in needles,' is how she puts it. Proprietary molecules, synthetics, alloys, all subjected to catastrophic oxidization."

"Which means what, like a fire?"

"Could be. She has a pretty good record with fires, including some big ones."

"And?"

"She's getting out of town. Telling everybody she knows to do the same. Because 9:30 cologne's connected with D.C., she's not going near D.C. either."

"How about you, you staying in town?"

Misunderstanding, "This weekend? I wasn't going to, but then I met somebody and changed my mind."

"'Somebody.'"

"Your friend the other night, wearing the Poison."

Bashful the Dwarf here. "Heidi. Well, I do congratulate you on your taste in women."

"I hope this won't come between you."

A double take she has trained over the years down to a less noticeable take and a half, "What. You think we might get into some Alexis-and-Krystle-by-the-poolside, over who gets to date you, Conkling? Tell you what, I'll do the noble thing, go back to my husband if he'll have me."

"You seem . . . annoyed somehow, I'm sorry."

"With Horst due back any day, some impatience maybe, but not with you."

"Your husband was always in the picture, I knew that right away—well, actually, I smelled it, so I made the effort from then on to keep things strictly business with us, case you didn't catch that."

"Aw, Conkling. I hope it hasn't been too inconvenient for you."

"It has. But what I really came over to ask, is have you seen her today?"

"Heidi? Heidi is . . ." But there she has to put it on pause. Doesn't

she. The ethical thing about now might be to, well, not warn, maybe just *happen to mention* one or two of Heidi's minor character zits. But Conkling, poor zhlub, is so desperate here to talk about her, oh and what's her sign and who's her favorite band, and, and . . .

Please. "You want what, my blessing? Thinks I'm the Rabbi here. How about I write you an audit opinion, I could manage that."

Wistfully though rehearsed, "I think you and I took it about as far as it was going."

"Yes we could've been an item," Maxine pretends to reflect.

"With Heidi you don't think—it's just the Naser, do you?"

"You want to be appreciated for yourself."

"Bring out the Naser once, people jump to conclusions. Some women can't resist a military connection, however remote. I was never a field type, in my heart I'm always behind some desk. Not like—"

"What?"

"Never mind."

It is insanely unlikely he was about to mention Windust. Insane, right? But who else, then?

22

A t three in the morning, the phone rings, in the dream it seems to be the siren of some cops who are chasing her. "You don't have all the evidence," she mumbles. Gropes for the instrument and picks up.

Sound effects on the other end suggesting an unfamiliarity with telephones, "Wow, these things are weird. Hey, now what's it doing—is it gonna time out on me, jeez . . ." It seems to be Eric, who's been up since the previous 3:00 A.M. and is about to grind and snort another fistful of Adderall.

"Maxine! You talked to Reg lately?"

"Hmm, what?"

"His e-mail, his phone, his doorbell, it's all dangling links anymore. Can't find him at work or on his mobile. Like everyplace I look, suddenly no Reg."

"When were you in touch with him last?"

"Last week. Should I be starting to worry?"

"He could've just split for Seattle."

Eric hums a few bars of the Darth Vader theme. "You don't think it's anything else."

"Hashslingrz? They fired him, you knew that."

"Yeah, meaning I got fired too, Reg being a class act sent me a nice severance check, but you know what, with core privileges now that let me go anywhere inside hashslingrz, lately the more of my business it ain't, the more I can't stay away from it. Fact, I was just about to go down there again but thought I'd better call you . . ."

"While I was asleep, thanks."

"Oh shit, right, you guys sleep, hey, I'm—"

"It's OK." She gets out of bed and shuffles over to the computer. "You mind some company? Show me around the Deep Web, maybe? We did have a date."

"Sure, you can come on my network, I'll give you the passwords, walk you through it . . ."

"Just putting coffee on here . . ."

Presently they're linked and slowly descending from wee-hours Manhattan into teeming darkness, leaving the surface-Net crawlers busy overhead slithering link to link, leaving behind the banners and pop-ups and user groups and self-replicating chat rooms . . . down to where they can begin cruising among co-opted blocks of address space with cyber-thugs guarding the perimeters, spammer operation centers, video games one way or another deemed too violent or offensive or intensely beauti-ful for the market as currently defined . . .

"Some nice foot-lover sites too," Eric comments casually. Not to mention more forbidden expressions of desire, beginning with kiddie porn and growing even more toxic from there.

It surprises Maxine how populated it is down here in sub-spider country. Adventurers, pilgrims, remittance folks, lovers on the run, claim jumpers, skips, fugue cases, and a high number of inquisitive entrepre-nerds, among them Promoman, whom Eric introduces her to. His avatar is an amiable geek in square-rim glasses wearing a pair of old-school sandwich boards that carry his name, as do those of his curvaceous co-adjutor Sandwichgrrl, her hair literally flaming, a polygon-busy GIF of a bonfire on top of a manga-style subteen face.

"Deep Web advertising, wave of the future," Promoman greets Maxine. "Thing is to get position now, be in place, already up and running when the crawlers show up here, which'll be any minute."

"Wait—you're actually seeing revenue from ads on sites down here?"

"Right now it's weapons, drugs, sex, Knicks tickets . . ."

"All that real recherché shit," puts in Sandwichgrrl.

"It's still unmessed-with country. You like to think it goes on forever, but the colonizers are coming. The suits and tenderfeet. You can hear the blue-eyed-soul music over the ridgeline. There's already a half dozen well-funded projects for designing software to crawl the Deep Web—"

"Is that," Maxine wonders, "like, 'Ride the Wild Surf'?"

"Except summer will end all too soon, once they get down here, everything'll be suburbanized faster than you can say 'late capitalism.' Then it'll be just like up there in the shallows. Link by link, they'll bring it all under control, safe and respectable. Churches on every corner. Licenses in all the saloons. Anybody still wants his freedom'll have to saddle up and head somewhere else."

"If you're looking for bargains," advises Sandwichgrrl, "there are some nice ones around the Cold War sites, but prices may not stay reasonable for long."

"I'll bring this up at our next board meeting. Meantime maybe I will just go have a look."

It isn't a promising neighborhood. If there was a Robert Moses of the Deep Net, he'd be screaming, "Condemn it already!" Broken remnants of old military installations, commands long deactivated, as if transmission towers for ghost traffic are still poised out on promontories far away in the secular dark, corroded, untended trusswork threaded in and out with vines and leaves of faded poison green, using abandoned tactical frequencies for operations long defunded into silence . . . Missiles meant for shooting down Russian prop-driven bombers, never deployed, lying around in pieces, as if picked over by some desperately poor population that comes out only in the deepest watches of the night. Gigantic vacuum-tube computers with half-acre footprints, gutted, all empty sockets and strewn wiring. Littered situation rooms, high-sixties plastic detailing gone brittle and yellow, radar consoles with hooded circular screens, desks still occupied by avatars of senior officers in front of flickering sector maps, upright and weaving like hypnotized snakes, images corrupted, paralyzed, passing to dust.

Maxine notices that one of these maps is centered on eastern Long Island. The room has a familiar look, austere and unmerciful. She is visited by one of those rogue hunches. "Eric, how do we get into this one?"

A brief tapdance over the keyboard and they're in. If it isn't one of the underground rooms she saw out at Montauk, it'll do. The ghosts here are more visible. Strata of tobacco smoke hang unstirred in the windowless space. Scope wizards attend radar displays. Virtual underlings pass in and out with clipboards and coffee. The officer on duty, a bird colonel, regards them as if about to ask for a password. A message box appears. "Access is limited to properly cleared individuals attached to ADC from AFOSI Region 7."

Eric's avatar shrugs and smiles. The soul patch pulses incandescent green. "Crypto's all pretty old-school, give me a minute here."

The colonel's face fills the screen, broken up sporadically, smeared, pixelated, blown through by winds of noise and forgetfulness, failing links, lost servers. Its voice was synthesized several generations back and never updated, lip movements don't match the words, if they ever did. What it has to say is this.

"There is a terrible prison, most informants believe it's located here in the U.S., though we also have Russian input comparing it unfavorably to the worst parts of the gulag. With classic Russian reluctance they will not name it. Wherever it is, brutal is too kind a description. They kill you but keep you alive. Mercy is unknown.

"It's supposed to be a kind of boot camp for military time travelers. Time travel, as it turns out, is not for civilian tourists, you don't just climb into a machine, you have to do it from inside out, with your mind and body, and navigating Time is an unforgiving discipline. It requires years of pain, hard labor, and loss, and there is no redemption—of, or from, anything.

"Given the lengthy schooling, the program prefers to recruit children by kidnapping them. Boys, typically. They are taken without consent and systematically rewired. Assigned to secret cadres to be sent on government missions back and forth in Time, under orders to create alternative histories which will benefit the higher levels of command who have sent them out.

"They need to be prepared for the extreme rigors of the job. They are starved, beaten, sodomized, operated on without anesthetic. They will never see their families or friends again. If by accident this should ever happen, during an assignment or simply as a contingency of the day, their standing orders are immediately to kill anyone who recognizes them.

"Standard strategies for deflecting public attention are considered to be in effect. Rapture by UFOs, disappearance into the correctional system, MKUltra-type programs have all proven useful as diversionary narratives."

Supposing . . . OK, say a preadolescent boy was abducted circa 1960. Forty-some years ago. He'd be fifty by now, give or take. Walking among us though liable to disappear without notice, sent again and again into the cruel wilderness of Time, to overwrite destiny, to rewrite what others believe is written. Probably these wouldn't have been local eastern–Suffolk County kids, better to snatch them from further away, thousands of miles from home, they'd be disoriented, easier to break.

Now and who, among the previously unsuspected hundreds in Maxine's Rolodex, would fit a description like that? Long after she's surfaced again, left Eric to get on with his early morning, back among the unpoetic demands of the day, she finds herself imagining a backstory for Windust, an innocent kid, abducted by earth-born aliens, by the time he's old enough to understand what's being done to him, it's too late, his soul is theirs.

Maxine, please. Where has she picked up the cockamamie idea that nobody is beyond redemption, not even a murderous stooge for the IMF? Even allowing for Internet unreliability, Windust can be ticketed with a harvest of innocent souls that puts him easily into the company of more renowned Guinness Book murderers, except it's all happened slowly, amortized one murder at a time, in faraway jurisdictions where neither the law nor the media will discommode him. Then you finally get to see him in person, the scholarly demeanor, the not exactly endearing fatality for wrong fashion choices, and you can't get the two stories to connect. Against her better judgment, possibly because there's nobody else to take it to, Maxine knows this has to be brought to Shawn's attention.

Shawn's out seeing his own therapist, so Maxine sits in the outer office looking through surfing magazines. He comes breezing in ten minutes late poised on some wave of blessedness.

"One with the universe, thanks," he greets her, "and yourself?"

"You don't have to get pissy, Shawn."

From what Maxine can gather, Shawn's therapist, Leopoldo, is a Lacanian shrink who was forced to give up a decent practice in Buenos Aires a few years ago, due in no small part to neoliberal meddling in the economy of his country. The hyperinflation under Alfonsín, the massive layoffs of the Menem-Cavallo era, plus the regimes' obedient arrangements with the IMF, must have seemed like the Law of the Father run amok, and after enough of it Leopoldo came to see too little future in the haunted city he loved, so he gave up his practice, his luxury suite in the shrinks' quarter known as Villa Freud, and split for the States.

One day Shawn was in a phone booth here in town, out on the street, one of those calls he really needed to make, everything possible was going wrong, he kept shoveling quarters, no dial tone, robots giving him shit, finally working himself up into the usual NYC rage, slamming the receiver against the unit while screaming *fucking Giuliani,* when he heard this voice, human, real, calm. "Having a little trouble, there?" Later on of course Leopoldo copped to drumming up business this way, hanging around places where mental-health crises are likely to occur, like NYC phone booths, after first removing any out-of-order signs. "Maybe a little ethical shortcutting," Shawn figures, "but it's fewer sessions per week, and they don't always last the full fifty minutes. And after a while I began to see how much Lacanian is like Zen."

"Huh?"

"Total bogosity of the ego, basically. Who you think you are isn't who you are at all. Which is much less, and at the same time—"

"Much more, yes, thanks for clearing that up, Shawn."

Considering Leopoldo's history this does seem like a good moment to bring up the topic of Windust. "Does your shrink ever talk about the economy down there?"

"Not much, it's a painful subject. Worst insult he can think of is to call somebody's mother a neoliberal. Those policies destroyed the Argentine middle class, fucked with more lives than anybody's counted so far. Maybe not as bad as getting disappeared, but totally sucks *loquesea*. Why do you ask?"

"Somebody I know who was in on all that, back in the early nineties, nowadays working out of D.C., still up to the same nasty kinds of business and I'm worried about him, I'm like the guy with the red-hot coal. I can't let it go. It's hazardous to my health, there isn't even anything beautiful about it, but I still need to hold on to it."

"You've developed a thing for, like, Republican war criminals now? Using condoms, I hope?"

"Cute, Shawn."

"Come on, you're not really offended."

"'Not really'? Wait a minute. This is a cast-iron Buddha here, right? watch this." Reaching for the Buddha's head, which of course, as soon as she touches it, will turn out to fit her grasp perfectly, as if designed expressly as a weapon handle. In the instant all unfriendly impulses are calmed.

"I've seen his rap sheet," trying not to edge into Daffy Duck mode here, "he tortures people with electric cattle prods, he pumps aquifers dry and forces farmers off their land, he destroys entire governments in the name of a fucked-up economic theory he may not even believe in, I have no illusions about what he is—"

"Which is what, some misunderstood teenager, only needs to hook up with the right girl, who turns out to know even less than he does? This is high-school again? competing for boys who're going to be doctors or end up on Wall Street, but all the time secretly yearning to run with the dopers, the car thieves, the convenience-store badasses . . ."

"Yes Shawn and don't forget surfers. What, excuse me, gives you authority here? What happens in your practice, when you want to save somebody but lose them instead?"

"All I do is try for what Lacan calls 'benevolent depersonalization.' If I got hung up trying to 'save' clients, how much good do you think I'd do?"

"A lot?"

"Guess again."

"Um . . . not so much?"

"Maxine, I think you're afraid of this guy. He's the Reaper, he's on your case, and you're trying to charm your way out of it."

Oof. Isn't this the moment to go stomping out the door with a dignified yet unequivocal over-the-shoulder fuck-you? "Well. Let me think about that."

23

rooke and Avi finally show up back in the States looking like they've spent the year at some strange anti-kibbutz dedicated to screen-staring, keeping out of the sun, and not missing too many meals, Elaine taking one look at Brooke promptly conveys her over to Megareps, a neighborhood health club, and negotiates a trial membership while Brooke loiters at the snack bar on the ground floor, contemplating muffins, bagels, and smoothies in a less than objective way.

Maxine isn't that eager to see her sister but figures she has to do at least a drop-by. Turns out at the moment Elaine and Brooke are down at the World Trade Center eyeballing the unexplored shopping potential of Century 21. Ernie is supposed to be at Lincoln Center watching some well-received Kyrgyz movie but has actually snuck over to *The Fast and the Furious* at the Sony multiplex, so Maxine finds herself for an enchanted hour and a half in the company of her brother-in-law, Avram Deschler, who is minding a Tongue Polonaise of Elaine's, which has been slowly cooking all day in the kitchen, filling the place with a smell initially intriguing, soon compelling. The matter of the federal visits can't help but come up.

"I think it's only about my clearance."

"Your . . . ?"

"You heard of a computer-security firm called hashslingrz?"

A pointed look at the bottom of her shoe. "Dimly."

"They get a lot of federal work, NSA and so forth, and they've offered me a job, and in fact I'm starting week after next." Waiting for at least dazzled admiration.

That's all the federal house calls were about? Sorry, somehow Maxine doubts it. Security clearances are routine low-level chores, and there is some deeper horseshit in progress here.

"So . . . you met the big guy, Gabriel Ice."

"He actually showed up in person, in Haifa, to recruit me. We did breakfast at a falafel joint in Wadi Nisnas. He seemed to know the owner. I told him what I wanted for salary, benefits, and he said OK. No hondeling. Tahini all over his shirt."

"Just a regular guy."

"Exactly."

As if only ditzing from topic to topic, "Avi, you know anything about a piece of software called Promis?"

A pause maybe a week or two further along than blue lines on a stick. "Kind of an old story in the business. The scheming and counter-scheming at Inslaw, the court cases, the FBI stealing it away, and so forth. A cash cow for Mossad, however. From what people tell me."

"And the rumor about a backdoor . . ."

"There wasn't one originally, but certain customers insisted, so the program got modified. More than once. In fact, it's an ongoing evolution. Today's version, you wouldn't recognize it. Or so I'm told."

"Long as I'm picking your brain here, somebody also told me about a computer chip, some Israeli vendor, maybe you've run across it, sits quietly in a customer's machine absorbing data, from time to time transmitting what it's gathered out to interested parties?"

Not that he jumped or anything, but his eyes have begun to roam the room. "Elbit makes one that I know of."

"Ever run across one, like, physically?"

He finally meets her gaze and then sits staring at her, as if she's some kind of a screen, and she figures the point of diminishing returns has arrived.

Soon Brooke and Elaine come back from downtown with a number of Century 21 bags plus a strange vegan p'tcha into whose crystalline depths one can gaze with growing albeit perplexed fascination. "Lovely," according to Elaine, "like a three-dimensional Kandinsky. Perfect with the tongue."

Tongue Polonaise is a childhood favorite around here. Maxine used to think it meant some classical-piano novelty act. All day, a pickled beef tongue has been out in the kitchen simmering in an elaborate tsimmis of chopped apricots, mango puree, pineapple chunks, cherries with the pits out, grapefruit marmalade, two or three different varieties of raisin, orange juice, sugar and vinegar, mustard and lemon juice, and of the essence, for reasons lost in some snoozy nimbus of tradition, gingersnaps—Nabisco by default, since Keebler dropped the old Sunshine variety a couple of years back.

"She forgets the gingersnaps again," Ernie likes to pretend to growl, "you're gonna read about it in the *Daily News.*"

The sisters warily exchange a hug. The conversation avoids all contact with the controversial until onto the living-room tube comes a Channel 13 yakker hosted by Beltway intellectual Richard Uckelmann called *Thinking with Dick,* whose guests today include an Israeli cabinet official Brooke and Avi used to run into at parties. Under discussion is the always-lively topic of West Bank settlements. After a minute and a half, though it seems longer, of government propaganda, Maxine blurts, "This guy didn't try to sell you any real estate, I hope."

Just what Brooke has been waiting for. "Miss Smartmouth," a little screechy, "always with a remark. Try going out on night patrol sometime, arabushim throwing bombs at you, see how far that mouth gets you."

"Girls, girls," murmurs Ernie.

"You mean 'girl, girl,' I think," Maxine sez, "I'm the one suddenly being trashed here."

"Brooke only means she's been to a kibbutz and you haven't," Elaine soothingly.

"Right, all day long at the Grand Canyon Mall in Haifa, spending her husband's money, some kibbutz."

"You, you don't even have a husband."

"Oh, look, a screamfest. Just what I came over here for." She blows a kiss at the p'tcha, which seems to wobble in reply, and looks around for her purse. Brooke stomps off to the kitchen. Ernie goes after her, Elaine gazes sorrowfully at Maxine, Avi pretends to be absorbed in the television.

"All right, all right, Ma, I'll behave, just . . . I was gonna say do something about Brooke, but I think that moment passed thirty years ago." Presently, Ernie comes out of the kitchen eating a gingersnap, and Maxine goes in to find her sister shredding potatoes for latkes. Maxine finds a knife and starts chopping onions and for a while they prep in silence, neither willing to be the first to talk, God forbid it should be anything like "I'm sorry."

"Hey, Brooke?" Maxine eventually. "Pick your brain a minute?"

A shrug, like, I've got a choice?

"I was out on a date with a guy who says he's ex-Mossad. I couldn't tell if he was bullshitting me or what."

"Did he take off his right shoe and sock and—"

"Hey, how'd you know?"

"Any given night in any singles bar in Haifa, you can always find some loser who's taken a Sharpie and put three dots on the bottom of his heel. Some old folklore about a secret tattoo, total bullshit."

"And there are still girls who fall for it?"

"Didn't you ever?"

"Come on, Jews and tattoos? I'm desperate, but not unobservant."

Everybody makes nice for the rest of the evening. The Tongue Polonaise comes in on a Wedgwood platter Maxine only remembers seeing at seder. Ernie dramatically sharpens a knife and begins carving the tongue as ceremoniously as if it's a Thanksgiving turkey.

"So?" inquires Elaine, after Ernie takes a bite.

"A time machine of the mouth, my darling, Proust Schmoust, this takes a man straight back to his bar mitzvah." Singing a couple bars of "Tzena, Tzena, Tzena" just to prove it.

"It's his mother's recipe," clarifies Elaine, "well, except for the mangoes, they hadn't been invented yet."

EDITH FROM YENTA EXPRESSO is out in the hallway, lounging in front of her door as if soliciting customers. "Maxine, some guy was here the other day looking for you? Daytona was out also, he asked me to tell you he'd be back."

"Uh-oh," having one of those intuitive flashes. "Nice shoes?"

"High three figures, Edward Greens, snakeskin, appropriately enough. You might want to be careful though, he's problematic."

"Client?"

"Known to the community. Don't get me wrong, lonely is OK, it's my bread and butter, I'm down with lonely, I'm down with desperate. But this guy . . ."

"Not that look, Edith please. This isn't romantic."

"I'm in the business thirty years, trust me, how romantic is it? As romantic as it gets."

"Creeping me out here. You're saying I should expect him back?"

"Don't worry, I already gave them a heads-up at the *Times,* they'll spell your name right."

SO, SURE ENOUGH, as if Edith's wearing a wire, a phone call from Nicholas Windust. He wants to do brunch at some faux-Parisian brasserie over on the East Side. "Long as you're springing," Maxine shrugs, thinking of it as a modest federal tax rebate.

Windust seems to think it's a date. He is done up, otherwise inexplicably, in somebody's idea of hipster gear—jeans, vintage sharkskin sport

coat, Purple Drank T-shirt, enough dress-code violations to get him
thrown off the L train. Maxine peers at this for as long as she has to,
shrugs, "It's a look."

He wants to sit inside, Maxine feels safer close to the street and it's
nice out today, so, cozy schmozy, outside it shall be. Windust orders a
soft-boiled egg and a Bloody Mary, Maxine wants half a grapefruit and
coffee in a bowl. "Amazed you could find the time, Mr. Windust," with a
smile of shameless bogosity, "So! my brother-in-law's back in the USA
now, I can't imagine what else this could be about."

"We were intrigued to learn he's hired on at hashslingrz.com. Like
your turnout by the way, Armani, isn't it?"

"Just some schmatte from H&M, but how nice of you to notice."
And what is with the getting cute here, stop, stop, Maxine when will
you . . . ?

"Suggesting an interesting hookup of interests, if Avram Deschler is,
as we suspect, a Mossad sleeper."

Maxine makes with a Blank Stare she has learned from Shawn and
often found useful. "Too academic for me."

"Play dumb if you like, but I ran a search on you, you're the little
lady who sent Jeremy Fink up the river. Busted the Manalapan Ponzoids
gang over in Jersey. Went down to Grand Cayman disguised as a reggae
backup singer, firebombed ten and a half billion in physical Swiss francs,
and exfiltrated in the perps' own Gulfstream jet."

"That was Mitzi Turner, actually. They're always getting us confused. Mitzi's the asskicker, I'm just a working mom."

"Regardless, given the number of U.S. government contracts
hashslingrz is involved with—"

"Look, either Avi's some fantasy of yours, darkside hacker-saboteur,
Mossad assassin, or he's just another standard-issue geek trying to get
through like the rest of us here outside the Beltway—whatever, I still
don't see how I come into it."

Windust opens and reaches into an aluminum attaché case which he
seems to be living out of, judging from the shaving kit and changes of

underwear inside, and finds a folder. "Before his next tête-à-tête with Gabriel Ice, here's something you might want to look over."

Without being able to see his eyes, she watches his mouth for, what, some footnote? but no, he's only smiling at her not even in a sociable way, more like he's holding some winning hand, or a weapon aimed at her heart.

Though unenthusiastic about touching anything that's been in contact with Windust's intimate apparel, she's also a fraud investigator whose prime directive is You Never Know, so she takes the folder gingerly and stashes it in her Kate Spade satchel.

"On the clear understanding," Maxine quickly adding, "as Deborah Kerr, or Marni Nixon, might say, or actually sing—that this is none of my—"

"Am I making you nervous?"

She risks a fast sideways peek and is astonished to catch on his face now a look that would not be out of place in a pickup joint south of 14th Street, some late Saturday night when the hotter inventory has been squired away out the door and the pickings have grown unhelpfully slimmer. What's up with this? She is not about to react to such a face. A silence arises, and lengthens, and not only a silence, as her glance, inadvertently wandering to that other indicator of the inward, confirms. It's in fact a hardon of some size, and worse, he's caught her looking.

"That's it, back to work," is what, in heedless idiocy, she finds herself unable to much more than croak. But doesn't move, doesn't even reach for her bag.

"Here, maybe this'll be easier," writing something on a napkin. In a more wholesome, or maybe only earlier, era it might have been the name of a good restaurant, or an idea for a start-up. Today the best you can call this is an invitation to step into airheadedness and error. An address inconvenient to the subway, she notices. "Say about rush hour, better chances for invisibility, that work for you?"

Among many things she hasn't picked up before is this note in his voice, demanding, not what you'd call especially seductive. And yet still not a deal killer. And what would that have to be, she wonders. He gets up, nods, and splits leaving her with the check. After saying he'd pay for it. What is she thinking, again?

AS IF HE'S A KINDLY angel bringing a last chance to act responsibly, Conkling materializes in the waiting room unannounced, the way he usually does. "Whoo," Daytona with a dramatic flinch, "scared the shit out of me, what you be lettin all these ghetto-ass g's walk in here all the time?" Conkling meantime has gone all weird, for his own reasons.

"What. You smell something."

"That masculine again–9:30 Cologne for Men. Something here is giving off indicia." Like a hound dog in a jailbreak movie, Conkling follows the *sillage* into Maxine's office, zeroing in on her purse. "Pretty slow drydown on this stuff, so it's from sometime in the last couple hours."

Oh, what else. Windust. She digs in her bag, brings out the folder he gave her. Conkling riffles the pages. "This is it."

"Guy I, hmm, just had brunch with, he's in from D.C."

"You're sure there's no connection here with Lester Traipse?"

"Just somebody I went to college with," Oh? what's this, a sudden reluctance to share information with Conkling about Windust? For some reason? That she doesn't want to get into right now? "Works in middle management now at the EPA, maybe the stuff is on some list of toxic pollutants?"

Her thoughts go wandering off, and nobody tries to summon them back. Did Windust, once in a more sympathetic-juvenile day, actually hang out at the old 9:30 Club the way Maxine did at the Paradise Garage? Maybe on Stateside breaks from doing evil all around the world, maybe he caught Tiny Desk Unit and Bad Brains in their local-band period, maybe the smell of 9:30 Cologne is his last, his only link with the under-corrupted youth he was? Maybe Conkling is coming down with a seasonal allergy and his nose is a little off today? Maybe Maxine is sliding deeper into a sentimental idiocy attack? Maybe's ass, OK? Circumstantial schmircumstantial, Windust was there when Lester was taken out, and maybe he even did it.

Damn.

What happened to the chances for a giddy romantic episode today? Suddenly it looks a lot more like field research.

Meantime Conkling wants to talk about, who else, Princess Heidrophobia. By the time Maxine is able to get his unwholesomely obsessed ass back out the door, she's left with a scant half hour to get put together for her, what would you call it, working rendezvous with Windust. Somehow she finds herself home, and immobile in front of the bedroom closet, and wondering why her mind has gone this blank. Polyvinyl chloride, something in bright red perhaps, though not inappropriate, is somehow absent from the inventory. Jeans are out of the question also. At length, deep in, at the event horizon of closet oblivion, she notices a chic cocktail-hour suit in a subdued aubergine shade, discovered long ago at the Galeries Lafayette going-out-of-business sale and kept for reasons that probably don't include nostalgia. She tries to think of ways in which Windust might read it. If he reads it, if he doesn't just grab and start ripping . . . Repeated messages from her Vertex, or does she mean Vortex, of Femininity are piling up unanswered.

24

The address is in a far-west-side piece of lower Hell's Kitchen among trainyard and tunnel approaches plowed indifferently through a neighborhood whose disconnected fragments have been left to survive as they might, lofts, recording studios, pool-table showrooms, movie-equipment rental places, chop shops . . . Wised-up real-estate mavens of Maxine's acquaintance assure her that this is the next hot neighborhood. Redevelopment is in the air. Someday the Number 7 subway will be extended over here and the Javits Center will have its own stop. Someday there will be parks and soaring condos and luxury tourist hotels. Right now it is still a windswept hard-to-get-to region that visitors from other planets, arriving in centuries to come after New York has been long forgotten, will assume was ceremonial, even religious, used for public spectacles, mass sacrifices, lunch breaks.

Today there is a huge gathering of police up and down 11th Avenue and seething all among the blocks over to Tenth. Maxine is just as happy not to be on foot at the moment. The cabdriver, whose problem this has become, thinks it might be a police exercise, based on a scenario where terrorists take over Javits Center.

"Why," Maxine wonders, "would anybody want to?"

"Well, spoze it happened during the Auto Show. Then they'd have all those cars and trucks. They could sell off some of that for money to buy bombs and AKs and shit," the driver clearly with a scenario of his own here, "keep the cool units like the Ferraris and Panozes, use the trucks for military vehicles, oh, and they'd also need to hijack a fleet of car carriers, Peterbilt 378s, somethin like that. And . . . and the really good vintage stuff, Hispano-Suizas, Aston Martins, they could hold them for ransom."

"'Give us ten million or we'll trash this car'?"

"Bend the aerial at least, nothin that would seriously fuck with the resale value, understand." All around them the Finest flock, swarm, stand guard, run in formation up and down the street. Above in the bright pre-autumnal sky, UFOs carry out their patient cloaked reconnaissance. Now and then a cop with a bullhorn will approach, glaring, and yell at the cab to move on.

Finally they pull up in front of the address, which seems to be a six-story rental building, unfashionable, forsaken, due someday for demolition and replacement by some high-rise condo scheme. At night maybe one lighted window per floor. It reminds her of her own part of town back in the eighties, when the neighborhood was being co-opped. Tenants who can't or won't move out. Developers who're itching to tear the place down acting very unpleasant.

When she hits the buzzer, it seems like ten minutes of being stared and smirked at by a sudden gathering of half the neighborhood, before a shrill noise that could be anything comes out of the undersize speaker.

"It's me—Maxine."

"Nnggahh?"

She shouts her name again and peers through the unwashed glass. The door remains unbuzzed. Finally, just as she's turning away, here comes Windust to open it.

"Buzzer doesn't work, never has."

"Thanks for sharing that."

"Wanted to see how long you'd wait."

Desolate corridors, unswept and underlit, that stretch on for longer than the building's outside dimensions would suggest. Walls glisten un-healthily in creepy yellows and grime-inflected greens, colors of medical waste . . . Open to all sorts of penetration besides the squatters who now and then step out into a sight line and immediately back, like targets in a first-person shooter. Carpeting has been removed from the hallways. Leaks are not being fixed. Paint hangs. Fluorescent bulbs on borrowed time buzz purplishly overhead.

According to Windust, wild dogs live in the basement and begin to come out at sundown, to roam the halls all night. Brought in originally to intimidate the last tenants into moving out, left on site to fend for themselves as soon as the Alpo bill outgrew the relocation budget.

Inside the apartment, Windust doesn't waste time. "Get down on the floor." Seems to be in a sort of erotic snit. She gives him a look.

"Now."

Shouldn't she be saying, "You know what, fuck yourself, you'll have more fun," and walking out? No, instead, instant docility—she slides to her knees. Quickly, without further discussion, not that some bed would have been a better choice, she has joined months of unvacuumed debris on the rug, face on the floor, ass in the air, skirt pushed up, Windust's not-exactly-manicured nails ripping methodically at sheer taupe panty-hose it took her easily twenty minutes in Saks not so long ago to decide on, and his cock is inside her with so little inconvenience that she must have been wet without knowing it. His hands, murderer's hands, are gripping her forcefully by the hips, exactly where it matters, exactly where some demonic set of nerve receptors she has been till now only semi-aware of have waited to be found and used like buttons on a game controller . . . impossible for her to know if it's him moving or if she's doing it herself . . . not a distinction to be lingered on till much later, of course, if at all, though in some circles it is held to be something of a big deal . . .

Down on the floor, nose level with an electrical outlet, she imagines for a second she can see some great brightness of power just behind the parallel slits. Something scurries at the edge of her vision, the size of a mouse, and it is Lester Traipse, the shy, wronged soul of Lester, in need of sanctuary, abandoned, not least by Maxine. He stands in front of the outlet, reaches in, parts the sides of one slit like a doorway, glances back apologetically, slides into the annihilating brightness. Gone.

She cries out, though not for Lester exactly.

IN THE MELANCHOLY LIGHT, Maxine scans Windust's face for evidence of emotion. For a quickie, it was OK even if God forbid there should be anything like eye contact around here. On the other hand, at least he used a condom—wait, wait, junior-prom reflexes aren't bad enough, she's doing credits and debits on this now also?

Out the window, instead of a sweeping panorama of lights, each illuminating a different Big Apple drama, there's a modest low-rise view, water tanks poised like antique skyrockets on rooftops whose last water-proofing got mopped on by immigrant hands generations dead, light from other windows mediated by nailed-up bedcovers, bookshelves full of wrecked paperbacks, the backsides of TV sets, shades pulled all the way down tenancies ago and never raised.

There is a kitchen of sorts in here, whose cupboards, in the tradition of accommodation addresses, are full of items some invisible long train of nameless reps and troubleshooters and traveling folk must have thought they needed to get through their stays, the nights they didn't have the will or the permission to venture out in the streets . . . strange forms of pasta, cans with pictures in unfamiliar color processes of hard-to-identify foodstuffs, soups with unpronounceable names, snack products with official-looking waivers where the nutritional information is usually found. In the fridge all she sees is a single beet, sitting, one would have to say insolently, on a plate. There are suggestions of blue-green mold, interesting visually, but . . .

"Time for coffee?"

"It's all right, I have to get back."

"School night, of course. I should give Dotty a call myself."

"Dotty, who would be . . ."

"My wife."

Ha. With an internal double take at herself along the lines of, so what? And this makes how many wives now, two? and what's it to you, Maxine? Finally, the underlying question, He's deliberately waited till right now to mention a wife?

Windust has found a box covered in Japanese writing of what appear to be seaweed snacks, into which he now dives, with every appearance of an appetite. Maxine watches, not nauseous exactly, or not yet.

"Care for one of these, they're . . . special. . . . And, Maxine . . . I'm not upset."

Talk about romantic outbursts. Not upset, imagine. On the other hand, what about "set up"? Some uncharted gust of interior wind brings her the scent of 9:30, reminding her of The Deseret roof, and Lester Traipse again.

"I may be a little distracted today," she sees no harm in mentioning, "there's a case, technically not my area, but it's been on my mind. Maybe you caught it on the news. A murder, Lester Traipse?"

Cold, cold customer. "Who?"

"It happened just down the street from me, at The Deseret. You've never been there, by any chance? I mean considering your deep interest in Gabriel Ice, who happens to own a piece of the building."

"Really."

She was expecting a courtroom-drama confession? He knows I know, she figures, so enough work for one day.

Once inside a cab he has not come downstairs to see her off in, headed uptown, What, she is just able to mentally inquire of herself, was I, the fuck, thinking? And the worst, or does she mean the best, part of it is that even right now it will take very little, yes, all pivoting here on

FDR's silvery small cheekbone in fact, to lean forward, interrupt the call-in hatefest on the cabbie's radio, and in a voice sure to be trembling ask to be brought back to the homicidal bagman in his dark savage squat, for more of the same.

SHE DOESN'T GET AROUND to reading the folder Windust brought till later that evening. There are all these suddenly fascinating fringe chores to be done, sorting the sponges under the sink by size and color, running a head-cleaner tape through the VCR, going through the take-out menus for excess duplication. Finally she picks the thing up, with its faded punk-rock aura. The cover is innocent of title, author, logo, any ID at all. Inside she finds a sort of mini-dossier in which we learn right away, and seemingly a big deal to whoever compiled this, that Gabriel Ice is Jewish, while also continuing to be instrumental in the illegal transfer of millions of $US to an account in Dubai controlled by the Wahhabi Transreligious Friendship (WTF) Fund, which, according to this anyway, is a known terrorist paymaster.

"Why," the account wonders plaintively, "being Jewish, would Ice provide aid and comfort on this lavish scale to the enemies of Israel?" Possible theories include Simple Greed, Double Agency, and Self-Hating Jew.

There are a dozen pages on attempts to follow the money through the *hawala* setup Eric discovered, beginning with Bilhana Wa-ashifa Import-Export in Bay Ridge, thence via the re-invoicing of shipments into the U.S. of halvah, pistachios, geranium essence, chickpeas, several kinds of ras el hanout, and shipments outbound of mobile telephones, MP3 players, and other light electronics, DVDs, old *Baywatch* episodes in particular—these data, assembled by some committee of the clue-challenged, alarmingly unacquainted even with GAAP, all thrown together so haphazardly that after half an hour Maxine's eyeballs are rotating in opposite directions and she has no idea if the document is meant as self-congratulation or some thickly disguised confession of failure. Bottom line, they seem to know about the *hawala*—hey, awesome. What else? The last page is headed "Recommendations for Action" and runs down the usual list of sanctions against hashslingrz, withdrawal of security clearance, prosecution, cancellation of outstanding contracts, and a disturbing footnote, "Option X—Consult Manual." Manual not, of course, included.

Why would Windust want to show her this? The probability of a setup continues to increase. Close to dawn, she finds herself in a dream rerun of *Now, Voyager* (1942) in which versions of Paul Henreid, as "Jerry," and Bette Davis, as "Charlotte," are about to take another smoke break. As always, "Jerry" suavely puts two cigarettes in his mouth and lights them both, but this time as "Charlotte" expectantly reaches for hers, "Jerry" keeps them both in his mouth, continuing to puff away, beaming pleasantly, sending up huge clouds of smoke, till there's only a couple of soggy cigarette butts hanging off of his lower lip. In her reverse shots, "Charlotte" is seen to grow more and more anxious. "Oh . . . oh well . . . of course if you . . ." Maxine comes awake screaming, under the impression there is something in bed with her.

HAVING LATELY DISCOVERED in the yuppie collectors' market a credulity that may be limitless, a gang of cigar forgers have been working out of a smoke shop on West 30th, offering "smuggled" Cuban cigars for $20 a pop, an attractive price for the time, along with a line of "rare antique" cigars, including alleged selections from J. P. Morgan's private stock, original chewed-on props from Groucho Marx movies, and cigar incunabula such as Christopher Columbus's first Cuban, mentioned by de las Casas in *Historia de las Indias*. Incredibly, these fakes are all fetching their asking prices, and a boutique hedge fund in town has been paying these knock-off artists huge sums, writing it off to travel and entertainment, then taking what when the media get hold of it will be called Lavish Kickbacks. One morning a couple days later, Maxine is just getting comfortable with this perennially active ticket when Daytona comes in shaking her head back and forth, with her eyes angled downward and to the right. Recalling a neurolinguistic workshop she once attended in Atlantic City, Maxine observes, "You're talking to yourself again."

"Don't be playin that woowoo shit on me, call's on line one. See if you can talk his ass down."

Connected to the phone these days, thanks to her brother-in-law, Avi, Maxine now has a miraculous Israeli voice analyzer, whose algorithm is supposed to be able to tell the difference between "offensive" and "defensive" lying, plus Only Kidding Around. No telling what kind of routine Windust has been up to with Daytona, but whatever is bothering him today, it does not fall into the category of playful.

"You've read the material I left you?"

How about I had such a nice time the other day, haven't been able to get you out of my mind, so forth? Terminate this fucking conversation forthwith, why don't you. Instead, Miss Congeniality, "I knew most of it already, but thanks."

"You knew about Ice being Jewish."

"Yes and Superman too, so what, excuse me, it's 1943 again? what's the obsession with you people?"

"He did hire your brother-in-law."

"So? You're saying these Jews, they really stick together? That's it?"

"The thing about Mossad—they're America's allies, but only up to a point. They cooperate, and they don't cooperate."

"Yes Jewish Zen, quite common, Al Jolson in blackface one minute, singing in temple the next, remember that one? Let me invite your attention to Gershom Scholem, *Major Trends in Jewish Mysticism,* which should clear up any lingering questions you might have, plus allow me to get back to a demanding workday which does not grow any less so with phone calls like this one. Unless you would like to just what we call spit it out?"

"We know how much money Ice has been diverting, where it's going, we're almost sure of who it's going to. But so far we still only have the separate threads. You've read those pages, you see how scattered it all is. We need somebody with fraud-investigating skills to weave it together into some shape we can take upstairs."

"Please, I'm struggling here, that is so fucking lame. Are you saying that nowhere in your own vast database can you find contact information for even one professional liar? It's what you people do, it's your hometown industry." Try to remember also, Maxine noodged herself, romantic history aside, this is the party who was there when Lester Traipse got dumped underneath the pool at The Deseret.

"Oh and by the way." Casual as a sanitation truck. "You've heard of the Civil Hackers' School in Moscow?"

"No, uh-uh."

"According to some of my colleagues, it was created by the KGB, it's still an arm of Russian espionage, its mission statement includes destroying America through cyberwarfare. Your new best friends Misha and Grisha are recent graduates, it seems."

Surveillance, OK, russophobic reflexes to be expected, and yet what goes on here, the chutzpah. "You don't like me socializing with Russkies. Excuse me, I thought all that Cold War drama was over. Is it mob allegations, what?"

"These days the Russian mob and the government share many interests. I'm only advising you to be more reflective about the company you keep."

"Worse than high school, I swear, one date they think they own you."

An exasperated click and the line goes dead.

25

Waiting for her at home in the mailbox is a small square jiffy bag with a postmark from somewhere out in the deep interior of the U.S. Some state beginning with an M maybe. At first she thinks it's from the kids or Horst, but there's no note, just a DVD in a plastic sleeve.

She pops the disc into the DVD player, and abruptly onto the screen comes a Dutch-angled view of a rooftop, somewhere on the far West Side, and the river and Jersey beyond. Early-morning light. A burned-in time stamp reads 7:02:00 A.M., a week or so back, staying frozen for a moment before it begins to increment. On comes a track full of broken sound, distant ambulance sirens, garbage collection down in the street, a helicopter passing or maybe hovering. The shot is from either behind or inside some piece of structure that houses the building's water tank. Out on the roof are two men with a shoulder-mounted missile, maybe a Stinger, and a third who is spending most of his time hollering into a cellular phone with a long whip antenna.

There are time gaps when nothing much is happening. The dialogue isn't too clear, but it's in English, the accents not especially local, from someplace out between the coasts. Reg (it has to be Reg) is back to his old zoom-happy ways, taking note of every passenger jet that shows up in the sky before returning to the standby routine on the roof.

At around 8:30, noticing movement on the roof of another building close by, the camera pans over toward it and zooms in on a figure with an AR15 assault rifle, who now attaches a bipod, gets down in prone firing position, gets up, removes the bipod, goes over to the roof parapet and uses that for support instead, moving around this way to different positions till he finds one he likes. His only targets appear to be the Stinger guys. Even more interesting, he is making no efforts at concealment, as if the Stinger guys know he's there, all right, and aren't doing anything about it.

A short while later, the guy with the mobile points into the sky and everything tightens into action, the crew aiming at and acquiring their target, which looks like a Boeing 767, heading south. They track the plane and go through motions like they're preparing to fire, but they don't fire. The plane continues, presently vanishing behind some buildings. The guy on the phone yells "OK, let's wrap it," and the crew pack up everything and they all vacate the roof. The shooter on the other roof has likewise vanished. There's wind noise and a brief spell of silence from below.

Maxine gets on the phone to March Kelleher. "March, do you know how to post video material on your Weblog?"

"Sure, bandwidth allowing. You sound strange, got something interesting?"

"Something you ought to see."

"Come on over."

March lives between Columbus and Amsterdam a few blocks away, on a cross street that Maxine can't remember the last time she's been on. If ever. A cleaner's, an Indian place she never noticed. This old *boricua* neighborhood survives, scraped and soiled, driven indoors, done with, its original texts being relentlessly overwritten—the gangs of the fifties, the drug dealing twenty years ago, all publicly fading into yup indifference, as high-rise construction, free of all self-doubt, continues its march northward. Someday very soon this will all be midtown, as one by one the sorrowful dark brickwork, the Section 8 housing, the old miniature apartment buildings with fancy Anglo names and classical columns flanking their narrow stoops, and arch-shaped window openings and elaborate wrought-iron fire escapes rapidly going to rust, are demolished and bulldozed into the landfill of failing memory.

March's building, known as The St. Arnold, is a medium-size prewar intrusion on a block of brownstones, with a consciously seedy look Maxine has learned to associate with frequent changes of ownership. Today there's an off-brand moving van outside, painters and plasterers at work in the lobby, Out of Order sign on one of the elevators. Maxine gets more than the usual number of suspicious O-Os, before being allowed to go in the elevator that's working. Security this tight of course could also result if enough tenants here were into shady activities and paying off the staff.

March is wearing novelty slippers each shaped like a shark, with sound chips in the heels so when she walks around, they play the opening of the *Jaws* (1975) theme. "Where can I find these, price is no object, I can write it off."

"I'll ask my grandson, he bought them with his allowance—Ice's money, but I figure if it went through the kid, then maybe it's laundered enough."

They go into the kitchen, old Provençal tiles on the floor and an unpainted pine table that the two of them can sit at and still leave room for March's computer and a pile of books and a coffeemaker. "My office here. Whatcha got?"

"Not sure. If it's what it looks like, it should carry a radiation warning."

They start up the disc, and March, getting the situation from frame one, mutters holy shit, sits fidgeting and frowning till the guy with the rifle shows up, then leans forward intently, slopping a little coffee onto that morning's overpriced copy of the *Guardian*. "I don't fucking believe it." When the scene is done, "Well." She pours coffee. "Who shot this?"

"Reg Despard, documentary guy I know who was doing a project on hashslingrz—"

"Oh, I remember Reg, we met during the blizzard of '96, down at the World Trade Center, there was a janitors' strike, all kinds of weird shit going on, secrets, payoffs. By the end of it, we felt like old veterans. We had a standing deal, anything interesting, I'd get to post it first on my Weblog. Bandwidth allowing. We lost touch, but what goes around comes around. Does this look to you what it looks like to me?"

"Somebody nearly shoots down an airplane, changes their mind at the last minute."

"Or maybe it's a dry run. Somebody *planning* to shoot down an airplane. Say, somebody in the private sector, working for the current U.S. regime."

"Why would they—"

Irish people are not known for silently davening, but March sits for a short while appearing to. "OK, first of all maybe this is a fake, or a setup. Pretend I'm the *Washington Post*, OK?"

"Sure." Maxine reaches toward March's face and begins to make page-turning motions.

"No. No, I meant like in that Watergate movie? Responsible journalism and so forth. First of all, this disc is a copy, right? So Reg's original could've been messed with in any number of ways. That date-and-time stamp in the corner could be fake."

"Who would fake this, do you think?"

March shrugs. "Somebody who wants to nail Bush's ass, assuming 'Bush' and 'ass' is a distinction you make? Or maybe it's one of Bush's people playing the victim card, trying to nail somebody who wants to nail Bush—"

"OK but suppose it is some kind of a dress rehearsal. Who's the sharpshooter over on the other roof?"

"Insurance to see that they go through with it?"

"And on the other end of the phone that guy's yelling into?"

"Excuse me, you already know what I think. Those Stinger guys were talking English, my guess is civilian contractors, because that's GOP ideology, whenever possible privatize—and when the spook sound labs have the dialogue all cleaned up and transcribed, those mercs are gonna be in some deep shit for not doing enough of a sweep of the roof. How did Reg get this to you, if I may ask?"

"Over the transom."

"How do you know Reg sent it? Maybe it's CIA."

"OK March it's all a fake, I just came over here to waste your time. What do you advise, do nothing?"

"No, we find out where this roof is, for starters." They scan through the footage again. "OK, so that's the river . . . that's Jersey."

"Not Hoboken. No bridge, so it's south of Fort Lee—"

"Wait, freeze it. That's the Port Imperial Marina. Sid goes in and out of there sometimes."

"March, I hate to even mention this, I've never been up there, but I have a creepy feeling about this roof, that . . ."

"Don't say it."

". . . it's the fuckin . . ."

"Maxi?"

"Deseret."

March squints at the screen. "Hard to tell, none of these angles are that clear. Could be any of a dozen buildings in that stretch of Broadway."

"Reg was stalking the place. Trust me, that's where this was shot. Just something I know."

Carefully, as to a nutcase, "Maybe you only want it to be The Deseret?"

"Because . . . ?"

"It's where they found Lester Traipse. Maybe you want to believe there's a connection."

"Maybe there is, March, all my life the place has given me bad dreams, and them I've learned to trust."

"Shouldn't be too hard to check out if it's the same rooftop."

"I'm a regular on the freight elevator there, I'll get you a guest pass for the pool, then we can figure a way on up to the roof."

AFTER THREADING A MAZE of unfrequented hallways and fire stairs, they emerge into the open, high up near a catwalk between two sections of the building, suitable for teen adventurers, clandestine lovers, well-heeled wrongdoers on the run, and take this vertiginous crossover to a set of iron steps that bring them finally around up onto the roof, into the wind above the city.

"Look sharp," March ducking behind a vent. "Some gents with metal accessories."

Maxine crouches down next to her. "Yeah I've got their album, I think."

"Is it that missile crew again? What's all that that they're carrying?"

"Doesn't look like Stingers. Wouldn't it be easier to just go over and ask them?"

"Am I your husband, is this a gas station? Go on ahead, it makes you happy."

They have no sooner got to their feet when here comes yet another group stepping off the elevator.

"Wait," March angling her shades, "I know her, that's Beverly, from the Tenants' Association."

"March!" A wave too vigorous not to be prescription-drug-assisted. "Glad you're here."

"Bev, what's up?"

"Scumbag co-op board again. Went behind everybody's back, leased some space up here to a cellular-phone outfit. These guys," indicating the work crew, "are trying to put in microwave antennas to irradiate the neighborhood. Somebody doesn't stop em we're all gonna end up with glow-in-the-dark brains."

"Count me in, Bev."

"March, um . . ."

"Come on, Maxi, in or out, it's your neighborhood too."

"OK, for a while, but that's another guilt trip you owe me."

"For a while" of course turns out to be the rest of the day Maxine's stuck on the roof. Every time she starts to leave, there's a new mini-crisis, installers, supervisors, building management to argue with, then Eyewitness News shows up, shoots some footage, then more lawyers, late-rising picketers, flaneurs and sensation seekers drifting in and out of the picture, everybody with an opinion.

In that slack corner of the afternoon when it's too discouraging even to look at a clock, March, as if remembering she came up here to check for clues, stoops and picks up a screw cap of some kind, weathered gray, two-, two-and-a-half-inch diameter, dings here and there, some faded writing in marker pen. Maxine squints at it. "What's this, Arabic?"

"Has a sort of military look, doesn't it?"

"You think . . ."

"Listen . . . do you mind if we show this to Igor? Just a hunch."

"Igor could be some kind of criminal mastermind, you're OK with that?"

"Remember Kriechman, the slumlord?"

"Sure. First time we met, you were picketing him."

"At some point a couple years later, business motives no doubt, Igor took a dislike, went up to Pound Ridge, introduced piranhas into the Doctor's swimming pool."

"And they all became best friends forever?"

"The message was conveyed, the Doctor ceased and desisted whatever it was and has been very well-mannered since then. So I've come to think of Igor as a benevolent mobster for whom real estate is only a sideline."

. . .

THEY TAKE A MEETING in the ZiL, on its way through Manhattan from one piece of monkey business to another.

"Sure, blast from past, part from Stinger missile launcher. Battery-coolant receptacle cap."

"You used to get shot at with Stingers," March is thoughtful enough to point out.

"Me, my friends, nothing personal. After Afghanistan, Stingers stayed there with mujahedeen, went on black market, many got bought back by CIA. I arranged a few deals, CIA didn't care how much they spent, you could get up to $150,000 a pop."

"That was a long time ago," Maxine sez. "Are there any of them still around?"

"Plenty. Worldwide, maybe 60, 70,000 units plus Chinese knockoffs . . . Not so much in U.S., which makes this one interesting. Mind my asking—where'd you find it?"

March and Maxine exchange a look. "What could hurt?" Maxine supposes.

"Actually the last time somebody said that . . ."

"You know you want to tell me," Igor beams.

They tell him, including a quick synopsis of the DVD. "And who videos this?"

Turns out Reg and Igor have also done some business. They met in Moscow around the peak of the Russian-baby-adoption craze in the U.S., when Reg was taping eligible babies to help pediatricians stateside to advise prospective parents. Because of the potential for fraud here, the idea was not to have these babies just sit there and pose for close-ups but actually do things like reach for objects, roll or crawl around, which meant some direction or at least wrangling from Reg. "Very sympathetic young man. Great appreciation for Russian cinema. Always at Gor-bushka Market buying up kilos of DVDs, *piratstvo*, of course, but no Hollywood movies, only Russian—Tarkovsky, Dziga Vertov, *Lady with*

Little Dog, not to mention greatest animated film ever made, *Yozhik v Tumane* (1975)."

Maxine hears spasmodic sniffling and looks in the front seat to find Misha and Grisha both with tears in their eyes and quivering lower lips. "They, ah, like that one too?"

Igor shakes his head impatiently. "Hedgehogs, Russian thing, don't ask."

"This writing on the battery cap, what's it say, can you read it?"

"Pashto, 'God is great,' maybe legit, maybe CIA forgery to look like mujahedeen, covering up some caper of their own."

"Well now that you've brought it up, there's another . . ."

"Let me read your mind. Spetsnaz knife, right?"

"With the flying blade, that allegedly did in Lester Traipse—"

"Poor Lester." A strange mixture of compassion and warning in his face.

"Uh-oh." Yet another relationship here, it figures. "The knife story is a frame-up, I gather."

"Spetsnaz don't shoot knives through air at people, Spetsnaz *throw* knives. Ballistic knife is weapon for *chainik*, with no throwing skills, afraid to get close up, wants to avoid gunshot noise. And—" pretending to hesitate "—blade they took out of Lester, OK, my distant cousin works downtown at Police Plaza, he saw it in property room, guess what. Fucking podyobka, totally, ain't even Ostmark blade, maybe Chinese, maybe cheaper. Let's hope someday I tell you more, but it still ain't what Flintstones call page right out of history. Too much payback to deal with right now."

"Whatever you feel comfortable sharing, of course, Igor. Meantime, what are we supposed to be doing about the other weapon? The hi-tech one on the roof? Suppose there's a clock on this?"

"Mind letting me watch DVD? Simple nostalgia, you understand."

26

Cornelia rings up and as previously threatened wants to go shopping. Maxine is expecting Bergdorf's or Saks, but instead Cornelia hustles her into a cab and next thing she knows they're headed for the Bronx. "I've always wanted to shop at Loehmann's," Cornelia explains.

"But they never let you in because you . . . have to be accompanied by somebody Jewish?"

"I'm offending you."

"Nothing personal. Little history, is all. You realize, I hope, that this is not the Loehmann's of legend. That one moved, back in, I don't know, late 80's?"

When Maxine and Heidi were girls, the store was still on Fordham Road, and every month or so their mothers would take them up there to learn how to shop. Loehmann's in those days had a no-returns policy, so you had to get it right the first time. It was boot camp. Gave you discipline and reflexes. Heidi took to it as if in a previous life she had been a rag-trade superstar. "I feel like I'm weirdly home, that this is who I really am, I can't explain it."

"I can," Maxine said, "you're a compulsive shopper."

For Maxine it was less cosmic. The changing room was short on privacy, what people liked to call "communal," crowded with women in different stages of undress and attitude trying on clothes half of which didn't fit but nevertheless offering free fashion advice to whoever looked like they needed it, meaning everybody. Like the locker room back at Julia Richman without the envy and paranoia. Now here's this pearl-wearing WASP wants to drag her back into it all again.

The new Loehmann's has been moved northward, into a former skating rink, it seems, almost to Riverdale, right up against the relentless roar of the Deegan, and Maxine has to struggle not to let out a scream of recognition—same endless aisles of heaped and picked-over garments, same old notorious Back Room as well, stuffed, she bets, with the same buyers' mistakes and horror-story prom gowns with sequins shedding everywhere. Cornelia, on the other hand, the minute she steps in the store, is under its spell. "Oh, Maxi! I love it!"

"Yes, well . . ."

"Meet you by the registers, say around one, we'll go have lunch, OK?" Cornelia disappearing into a miasma of whatever formaldehyde product retailers put on garments to make them smell this way, and Maxine, feeling not exactly claustrophobic, more like flashback-intolerant, wanders outside again, into the streets, at least to see what's what, and then remembers that only a little way up the Deegan, just over the Yonkers line, is Sensibility, the ladies' shooting range she's just mailed in another year's membership dues to, and that for this excursion to Loehmann's she has somehow remembered to bring along the Beretta.

Hey. Cornelia will be hours. Maxine finds a cab letting off a fare, and twenty minutes later she's all signed in at Sensibility, on the firing line in goggles, earplugs, and head muffs, with a convenience-store cup full of loose rounds, blasting away. Let the gamer have his zombies, Han Solo his TIE fighters, Elmer Fudd his elusive rabbit, for Maxine it has always been the iconic paper target figure known to cops as The Thug, here rendered in fuchsia and optical green. He has the look of an aging juvenile delinquent, with one of those shiny high-fifties haircuts, a scowl, and a possibly nearsighted squint. Today, even with his image cranked all the way back to the berm, she manages to place some nice groups in his head, chest, and, actually, dick area—which long ago may have been an issue, though after a while it seemed to Maxine the number of trouser wrinkles the artist shows radiating from the target's crotch could be read as an invitation to shoot there as well. She takes some time practicing double taps. Pretends briefly—only a bit of fun, you know—that it's Windust she's shooting at.

In the lobby on the way out, she's at the pay phone calling a cab when who does she run into but her old partner in wine theft, Randy, last seen driving away from the parking lot at the Montauk lighthouse. He seems a little preoccupied today. They withdraw to a settee beneath a mural-size screen grab from the opening of *The Letter* (1940) in which Bette Davis is pretending to pump six rounds into an uncredited though perhaps not altogether unthanked "David Newell."

"Guess what, that son of a bitch Ice? Pulled my access to his house. Somebody must've took a wine inventory. Got my license plates off the closed-circuit video."

"Bummer. No legal follow-ups, I hope."

"Not so far. Tell the truth, I'm just as happy to be clear of the place. Been hearing about some weird shit lately." Strange lights at dark hours, visitors with funny-looking eyes, checks that bounce and come back with unreadable writing all over them. "Film crews showing up around Montauk suddenly from the paranormal channels. Cops pullin all kinds of overtime, working mysterious incidents includin that fire at Bruno and Shae's place. I guess you heard about ol' Westchester Willy by now?"

"On the run's the last I heard."

"He's out in Utah."

"What?"

"The three of em, I got some snail mail yesterday, they're getting married. To each other."

"They didn't just skip, they eloped?"

"Here, check this out." An engraved card featuring flowers, wedding bells, cupids, some kind of not-all-that-easy-to-make-out hippie typeface.

Maxine, beginning to feel nauseous, reads as far as she has to. "This is an invitation to their *shower,* Randy? It's what, legal in Utah for three people to get married?"

"Probably not, but you know how it is, run into somebody in a bar, bullshit level starts to rise, pretty soon, crazy impulsive kids, they're hoppin in the rig and headin out yonder."

"You're, ah, planning to attend this get-together?"

"It's tough enough figuring out what to give them. A His, His, and Hers bath ensemble? A triple-sink vanity?"

"Thirty-piece set of cookware."

"There you go. Must be a federal fugitive warrant out on em, you could pick up some quick change, fly out there, maybe I could come along for muscle."

"I'm not a bounty hunter, Randy. Just a bookkeeper who's a little surprised the relationship lasted more than ten minutes after the money got frozen. In fact, I think it's kinda cute. I must be turning into my mother."

"Yeah, somethin how Shae and Bruno stepped up for ol' Willy that way. You start feelin a little bitter about human nature, then people fool you."

"Or in my business," Maxine reminds herself more than Randy, "people fool you and then after a while you start to get bitter."

She arrives back at Loehmann's just about the time Cornelia resurfaces from the crowds of women in the Back Room who've been molesting racks of discounted clothing, squinting doubtfully at designer labels, seeking advice by way of cellular phone from their size-zero teenage daughters. Maxine recognizes in Cornelia signs of advanced DITS, or Discount Inventory Tag Stupor.

"You're starved, let's find something before you pass out," and off they go looking for lunch. Back in the old Fordham Road era, as she recalls, you could at least find a decent knish in the neighborhood, a classic egg cream. Around here there's a Domino's Pizza and a McDonald's, and a possibly make-believe Jewish delicatessen, Bagels 'n' Blintzes, which is of course where Cornelia simply must do lunch, having heard of it no doubt from some Junior League newsletter, and where they are presently in a booth, surrounded by a dumpsterload of Cornelia's purchases, which "impulsive" is maybe too kind a word for.

At least this isn't some midtown ladies' tearoom. The waitress, Lynda, is a classic deli veteran, who only needs to hear two seconds' worth from Cornelia to start muttering, "Thinks I'm the downstairs maid," Cornelia meantime making a point of asking for "Jewish" rye bread for her turkey-pastrami and roast-beef combo. Sandwich arrives, "And you're quite sure this is *Jewish* rye bread."

"I'll ask it. Hello!" Holding the sandwich up to her face, "You're Jewish? The customer wants to know before she eats you. What? No, she's goyishe, but they don't have kosher so maybe this pick-pick-pick is what they do instead," so forth.

Maxine introduces Cornelia to Dr. Brown's Cel-Ray, pours it in a glass for her. "Here, Jewish champagne."

"Interesting, a bit on the demi-sec side—excuse me, oh Lynda? would you happen to have this drier, brut perhaps . . . ?"

"Sh-shh," goes Maxine, though Lynda, recognizing WASP jocularity here, ignores.

In the course of lunchtime yakking, Maxine gets an earful of Slagiatt marriage history. Though the attraction was perverse and immediate, Cornelia and Rocky, it seems, did not so much fall in love as stumble into a classic NYC folie à deux—she, charmed at the notion of marrying into an Immigrant Family, expecting Mediterranean Soul, matchless cooking, an uninhibited embrace of life including not-quite-imaginable Italian sex activities, he meanwhile looking forward to initiation into the Mysteries of Class, secrets of elegant dress and grooming and high-society repartee, plus a limitless supply of old money to borrow against without having to worry too much about debt collection, or not the kind he was used to anyway.

Imagine their mutual dismay on learning the real situation. Far from the Channel 13 upper-class dynasty he expected, Rocky discovered in the Thrubwells a tribe of nosepicking vulgarians with the fashion sense and conversational skills of children raised by wolves, and with a collective net worth Dun & Bradstreet barely acknowledged. Cornelia was equally stunned to find that the Slagiattis, most of whom were distributed along a suburban archipelago well east of the Nassau line, and for whom the closest thing to an Italian feast was to order in from Pizza Hut, did not "do warmth," even among themselves, regulating the children, for example, not with the genial screaming or smacking around one might have expected from an adolescence spent at the Thalia watching neorealist films but with cold, silent, indeed one must say pathological glaring.

As early as their honeymoon in Hawaii, Rocky and Cornelia were exchanging What-have-we-done gazes. But it was heaven there, with ukuleles for harps, and sometimes heaven has its way. One evening, as they watched a postcoital sunset, "WASP chicks," declared Rocky, an adoring note already throbbing in his voice. "Well."

"We are dangerous women. We have our own crime syndicate, you know."

"Huh?"

"The Muffya."

A sort of compassionate clarity dawned, and grew. Cornelia went on insisting dramatically that for Thrubwells most of the Social Register was rather too impossibly ethnic and arriviste, and Rocky went on singing "Donna non vidi mai" while ogling her in the shower, often eating a Sicilian slice as he sang. But in growing closer they also came to know who it was they thought they were kidding.

"Your husband tends to run to extra dimensions," Maxine supposes.

"Down in K-Town they call him '4-D.' He's also psychic, by the way. He thinks you're having some trouble at the moment, but he's reluctant to what he calls 'put in.'" Cornelia with one of those WASP eyebrow routines, possibly genetic, sympathy with a subtext of please, not another loser to deal with . . .

Still, however unintended, a potential mitzvah should be looked into. "Without getting too cute, it's some video I've come across. I wouldn't even be wondering how worried I should get, except it's political in the worst way, maybe international, and I guess I'm to the point where I really could use some advice."

With no hesitation Maxine can see, "In that case you must get in touch with Chandler Platt, he has a genius for facilitating outcomes, and he's really very sweet."

Which sets off a game-show buzzer, actually, for if Maxine's not mistaken, she's already run into this Platt customer, a financial-community big shot and fixer of some repute with upper-echelon access and what strikes her as a sense, finely calibrated as an artillery map, of where his best interests lie. Over the years they've met at various functions at the junction between East Side largesse and West Side guilt, and as it's coming back to her now, Chandler may even once have grabbed her tit briefly, more of a reflex than anything, some cloakroom situation, no harm no foul. She doubts he even remembers.

And, well, there are fixers and fixers. "This genius of his—it extends to knowing how to dummy up?"

"Ah. One cannoli hope, as the Godfather always sez."

CHANDLER PLATT HAS a roomy corner office midtown, at the high-muzzle-velocity law firm of Hanover, Fisk, up in one of the glass boxes along the Sixth Avenue corridor, with a view conducive to delusions of grandeur. Dedicated elevator, a traffic-flow design that makes it impossible to tell how much, forget what kind of, business is afoot. There seems to be a lot of deep amber and Czarist red in the picture. An Asian child intern shows Maxine into the presence of Chandler Platt, who is installed behind a desk made of 40,000-year-old New Zealand kauri,

more like a piece of real estate than a piece of furniture, leading the casual observer, even one with a vanilla view of these matters, to wonder how many secretaries might fit comfortably beneath it and what
amenities the space would be furnished with—restroom conveniences,
Internet access, futons to allow the li'l cuties to work in shifts? Such un-
wholesome fantasies are only encouraged by the smile on Platt's face,
uneasily located between lewd and benevolent.

"A pleasure, Ms. Loeffler, after how long's it been?"

"Oh . . . last century sometime?"

"Wasn't it that clambake at the San Remo for Eliot Spitzer?"

"Might be. Never could figure you at a Democratic fund-raiser."

"Oh, Eliot and I go back. Ever since Skadden, Arps, maybe longer."

"And now he's Attorney General and he's going after you guys as
much he ever went after the mob." If there's a difference, she almost
adds. "Ironic, huh?"

"Costs and benefits. On balance he's been good for us, put away
some elements that would have eventually turned and bit us."

"Cornelia did imply that you have friends all over the spectrum."

"In the long run, it's less to do with labels than with everyone coming
out happy. Some of these folks really have become my friends, in the pre-
Internet sense of the term. Cornelia, certainly. Long ago I briefly courted
her mother, who had the good judgment to show me the door."

Maxine has brought Reg's DVD and a tiny Panasonic player, which
Platt, not sure of where the wall outlets are exactly, allows her to plug in.
He beams at the little screen in a way that makes her feel like a grand-
child showing him a music video. But about the time the Stinger crew
get set up,

"Oh. Oh, wait just a minute, is this the pause button here, would
you mind—"

She pauses it. "Problem?"

"These weapons, they're . . . Stinger missiles or something. A bit out
of my ground, I hope you appreciate."

And if she wanted a runaround, she'd be over in Central Park.

"Right, I keep forgetting, you people tend to be Mannlicher-Carcano types."

"Jackie and I were dear friends," he replies coolly, "and I'm not sure I oughtn't to resent that."

"Resent, resent, please, I knew this was a mistake." She's on her feet, picking up her Kate Spade bag, noticing an unaccustomed lightness. Naturally, the one fucking day she probably should have brought the Beretta. Reaches to eject the DVD. By now Platt's diplomatic reflexes have taken over, or maybe WASP control freakery. Murmuring something like "There, there," he hits a hidden call button, which rapidly brings in the intern with a pot of coffee and an assortment of cookies. Maxine wonders if Girl Scouts were inappropriately involved in this. Platt watches the rest of the rooftop footage in silence.

"Well. Provocative. Perhaps if you could spare me a couple of minutes?" Withdrawing to an inner office and leaving Maxine with the intern, who is leaning in the doorway now gazing at her, she wants to say inscrutably, but that would be racist. Absent a full ingredient list, she is of course not about to start scarfing cookies.

"So . . . how's the job? your first step in a legal career here?"

"I hope not. What I really am is a rap artist."

"Like uh, who, Jay-Z?"

"Well, actually I'm more of a Nas person. As you may know they're in this feud at the moment, that old Queens-versus-Brooklyn thing again, hate to take sides, but—"The World Is Yours," how can anything even compare?"

"You perform in public, like clubs?"

"Yeah. Got a club date coming up soon, in fact, here, check this out." From somewhere he has produced a TB-303 clone with built-in speakers, which he now plugs in and powers up, and starts fingering a major pentatonic bass line. "Dig it,"

Tryin to do Tupac and Biggie thangs
With red velvet Chairman Mao piggy banks,

like Screamin Jay in Hong Kong
jumpin to wrong conclusions
old-movie confusions, yo who be dat
Scandinavian brand of Azian
ya dig wid some Sigrid be
the daughter of Kublai Khan,
Warner Oland, Charlie Chan, General Yan
bitter tea, for her stupidity pullin rank
Bette Davis shanked by Gale Sondegaard
like they was on the yard
or down in some forgotten cell
far, far from the corner of
Mott and Pell—

"Yes oh and Darren," Chandler Platt reentering a little brusquely, "when you have a chance, could you please bring me those copies of the Braun, Fleckwith side letter? And get Hugh Goldman for me over there?"

"Mad cool, yo," unplugging his digital bass and heading for the door.

"Thanks, Darren," Maxine smiles, "nice song—from what little Mr. Platt has allowed me to hear."

"Actually, he's unusually tolerant. Not everyone in his demographic goes for what we like to think of as Gongsta Rap."

"Y— I thought I might have caught one or two, I'm not sure, racial overtones . . ."

"Preemptive. They gonna be give me all rice-nigga remarks and shit, this way I beat 'em to it." He hands her a disc in a jewel case. "My mix tape, enjoy."

"He gives them away," Chandler Platt blinking his eyes at regular intervals and without motive, like faces in low-budget cartoons. "I made the mistake of asking him once how he expects to make money. He said that wasn't the point, but has never explained what is. To me, I'm appalled, it strikes at the heart of Exchange itself." He reaches for and sits contemplating a chocolate-chip cookie. "Back when I was getting into the business, all 'being Republican' meant really was a sort of principled greed. You arranged things so that you and your friends would come out nicely, you behaved professionally, above all you put in the work and took the money only after you'd earned it. Well, the party, I fear, has fallen on evil days. This generation—it's almost a religious thing now. The millennium, the end days, no need to be responsible anymore to the future. A burden has been lifted from them. The Baby Jesus is managing the portfolio of earthly affairs, and nobody begrudges Him the carried interest . . ." Suddenly, and from the cookie's point of view, rudely, chomping into it and scattering crumbs. "Sure you won't have one, they're quite . . . No? All right, thanks, don't mind if I . . ." Grabbing another, two or three actually, "I just spoke with some people. A most puzzling conversation, I have to say. At least they picked up."

"Not the standard corporate chitchat, then."

"No, something else, something . . . peculiar. Not out loud, or in so many words, but as if . . ."

"Wait. If you don't want to tell me—"

". . . as if they know already what's going to happen. This . . . event. They know, and they're not going to do anything about it."

Is this all yet another exercise in freaking out the common folk so we'll keep bleating and begging for protection? How scared is Maxine supposed to feel? "I didn't get you in any trouble, I hope."

"'Trouble.'" She thinks she's seen most of the looks of despair available to men of this pay grade, but what now briefly appears on his face you'd have to open a new file for. "In trouble with that bunch? Never that easy to tell, really. Even if there were to be unpleasantness, I could rely without hesitation upon young Darren, who's board-certified in everything from nunchaku up through . . . well, Stinger missiles, I'm sure, and beyond. Rest easy as to my safety, young lady, and look instead to your own. Try to avoid terrorist-related activities. Oh, and would you mind going out the back way? You weren't here, you see."

The back exit happens to be near Darren's cubicle. Maxine glances in and finds him standing by a window, turned away in quarter profile, looking, *sighting*, down fifty stories into New York, down into that specific abyss, with an intensity she recognizes from the DeepArcher splash screen. Should she run in, break his concentration with questions like, Do you know Cassidy, did you pose for the Archer, provoking him into who knows what don't-be-in-my-face-bitch gongsta displeasure . . . Is she that desperate for a literal link between this kid and some screen image? when she knows all the time there is none, that the figure was there, has always been there, that's all, that Cassidy thanks to some intervention nobody knows how to name found her way to the silent, stretched presence at the edge of the world and copied what she remembered and immediately forgot the way back there . . . .

Jangling with unquiet thoughts, Maxine emerges onto the street and notices it's only a short walk to Saks. Maybe a half hour of fashion-related fugue, don't call it shopping, will soft-sell her back down. She cuts across to Fifth Avenue by way of Forty-Seventh Street. It being the Diamond District, who wouldn't? Not only on the chance however remote of glimpsing from afar exactly the stones, the setting she's been looking for all her life, but also for the general air of intrigue, the feeling that nothing, nobody on this block is positioned where they are by accident, that saturating the space, invisible as the wavelengths that carry soap operas into the home, dramas of faceted intricacy are teeming all around.

"Maxine Tarnow? Isn't it?" Seems to be Emma Levin, Ziggy's krav maga teacher. "Just down here to meet my boyfriend for lunch."

"So you two are what—shopping for diamonds? maybe . . . *the* diamond? Oh! What's that . . . dingdong sound I hear? Could it be . . ." No. She didn't actually say this out loud. Did she? is she really turning into Elaine, nonconsensually as Larry Talbot into the Wolf Man, for example?

Naftali, the ex-Mossad boyfriend, works security for a diamond merchant here on the street. "You'd think we'd've met years ago on the job, field guy in on a visit to the office, kaplotz! Magic! but no, it was a fixer-upper. Same lightning bolt, however . . ."

"Ziggy's been bringing home Naftali stories since he started krav maga. Big impression, which on Ziggy it's hard to make."

"There he is. My dreamboat." Naftali is pretending to lounge against a storefront, a flaneur who can be triggered silently, instantly into the wrath of God. According to Ziggy, the first time Naftali visited the studio, Nigel immediately asked him how many people he'd killed, and he shrugged, "I lost count," and when Emma glared, added, "I mean . . . I can't remember?" Maybe a case of kidding a kidder, but Maxine wouldn't want to have to find out. Flabless and close-cropped, a black suit, a face amiable from half a block away reacquiring as it comes into focus its history of laceration and breakage and feelings kept at a professional distance. Though for Emma Levin he makes exceptions. They smile, they embrace, and for a second they're the two brightest sparklers on the block.

"Ah, you're Ziggy's mom. The tough guy. How's his summer going?"

Tough? her little Ziggurat? "He's somewhere off in Iowa, Illinois, one of them. Practicing his moves every day, I'm sure."

"Good place to be," Naftali speeding his beat a little, and Emma flashing him the look.

As an ex-blurter, Maxine can relate, but still, wondering what he's almost saying, she tries, "Wish I could figure a way to get out of town for a while."

He's watching her intently, not exactly smiling but pleased, like somebody who's been in on enough interrogations to appreciate the etiquette. "Out here in the open, you know, you get all these stories. The problem is, most of it's garbage."

"Which doesn't help that much, if you're a worrier."

"You're a worrier? I wouldn't have thought."

"Naftali Perlman," Emma growls, "now you stop hustling her, she's married."

"Separated," Maxine batting her eyelashes.

"See, how possessive," Naftali beaming. "We're going to lunch, you want to join us?"

"I'm due back at work, but thanks."

"Your work . . . you're . . . a model?"

In a very precise way, Emma Levin draws one foot to the side, cocks an elbow, puts on her kung fu–movie face.

"My kinda woman!" An explicit squeeze which Emma cannot be said to avoid.

"Behave, guys. Shalom."

27

The boys call in one night from Prairie du Chien or Fond du Lac or someplace to tell her they'll be home in two days.

All, as Ace Ventura sez, and even sings, righty then. Maxine wanders uneasily around the place, convinced she has left evidence of misbehavior out in glaringly plain sight that will, not exactly get her in trouble with Horst, but oblige her to be heedful of his feelings, which despite appearances, he may actually have. She runs through the company she's kept—aside from Windust—since Horst left town. Conkling, Rocky, Eric, Reg. In every case she can claim legitimate work reasons, which would be fine if Horst was the IRS.

Though Heidi is likely to be less than helpful, "Maybe you and Carmine could drop by, say, accidentally?" Maxine wonders.

"You're expecting trouble?"

"Emotions, maybe."

"Mm-hmm? . . . so what you're really saying is you want Horst to see me in a relationship with another person, because you're paranoid Horst and I may still be an item? Maxi, insecure Maxi, when will you be able to just let it go?"

Heidi seems on edge these days, even for Heidi, so Maxine isn't too surprised when her girlhood chum makes a point of not showing up, with Carmine or without, when the Loeffler menfolk at last come rough-housing home again, loud and sugar-high, down the hall and through the door.

"Hey Mom. Missed you."

"Oh, guys." She kneels on the floor and holds the boys till everybody gets too embarrassed.

They're all wearing red Kum & Go ball caps and have brought Maxine one too, which she puts on. They've been everywhere. Floyd's Knobs, Indiana. Duck Creek Plaza in Bettendorf. Chuck E. Cheese and Loco Joe's. They sing her the Hy-Vee commercial. More than once.

Arriving in Chicago, they promptly got a tour down memory lane, which for Horst was the LaSalle Street canyon, his first and oldest home turf, where he'd been one of those handjiving adventurers who dared the pit every trading day. Started at the Merc trading three-month Eurodollar futures, both for clients and for himself, wearing a custom trader's jacket with tastefully muted green and magenta stripes and a three-letter name tag pinned to it. After the pits closed around three in the afternoon, he shifted to civvies and walked over to the Chicago Board of Trade and checked in at the Ceres Cafe. When the CME decided to ban double trading, Horst joined a good-size migration over to the CBOT, where no such qualms existed, though Eurodollar activity was noticeably less intense. For a while he shifted to Treasuries, but soon, as if answering some call from deep in the tidy iterations of Midwest DNA, he had found his way into the agricultural pits, and next thing he knew, he was out in deep American countryside, inhaling the aroma from handfuls of wheat, scrutinizing soybeans for purple seed stain, walking through fields of spring barley squeezing kernels and inspecting glumes and peduncles, talking to farmers and weather oracles and insurance adjusters—or, as he put it to himself, rediscovering his roots.

Still, farm fields Kum & farm fields Go, but it's Chicago that really pulls you back. Horst took his sons to the traders' cafeteria at the CBOT, and to the Brokers Inn, where they ate the legendary giant fish sandwich, and to old-school steak houses in the Loop where the beef is hung aging in the front window and the staff address the boys as "Gentlemen." Where the steak knife next to your plate is not some flimsy little serrated blade with a plastic handle but whetstoned steel riveted into custom-hewn oak. Solid.

The Loeffler grandfolks, all through their visit, were over the moon, the specifically Iowa moon, which from the front porch was bigger than any moon the boys had ever seen, rising over little trees whose silhouettes were shaped like lollipops, making everybody forget about what they might've been missing on the tube, which was on inside but more as an accent light than anything.

They ate at malls all across Iowa, at Villa Pizza and Bishop's Buffet, and Horst introduced them to Maid-Rites as well as to local variations on the Louisville Hot Brown. Further into the summer and days to the west, they watched the wind in different wheat fields and waited through the countywide silences when it grows dark in the middle of the afternoon and lightning appears at the horizon. They went looking for arcade games, in derelict shopping plazas, in riverside pool halls, in college-town hangouts, in ice-cream parlors tucked into midblock micromalls. Horst couldn't help noticing how the places had, most of them, grown more ragged since his time, floors less swept, air-conditioning not as intense, smoke thicker than in the midwestern summers of long ago. They played ancient machines from faraway California said to be custom-programmed by Nolan Bushnell himself. They played Arkanoid in Ames and Zaxxon in Sioux City. They played Road Blasters and Galaga and Galaga 88, Tempest and Rampage and Robotron 2084, which Horst believes to be the greatest arcade game of all time. Mostly, wherever they could find it, they seemed to be playing Time Crisis 2.

Or Ziggy and Otis were. The big selling point of the game was that both boys could play at the same machine and keep an eye on each other, while Horst went off on various commodities-related chores.

"I'm just gonna zip in this bar here for a minute, guys. Some business."

Ziggy and Otis continuing to blast away, Ziggy usually with the blue handgun and Otis the red one, jumping on and off the foot pedals depending on whether they need to seek cover or come out shooting. At some point, going after more tokens, they notice a couple of local kids who've been lounging nearby watching them play, but strangely, for these arcades, reluctant to kibitz. While not actually drooling or packing any real-life weapons that Ziggy or Otis can see, they still radiate this aura of blank menace with which the Midwest so often fails to endear itself. "Something?" inquires Ziggy as neutrally as possible.

"You fellas 'nerds'?"

"Nerds, how's that?" sez Otis, who is wearing a midnight blue porkpie hat and Scooby-Doo shades with green lenses. "This is the package, live wid it."

"We're nerds," the shorter of the two announces.

Ziggy and Otis look carefully and see a pair of suburban normals. "If you guys are nerds," Ziggy cautiously, "what do the non-nerds around here look like?"

"Not sure," sez the bigger one, Gridley. "They're kind of hard to see most of the time, even in the daylight."

"Especially in the daylight," adds Curtis, the other one.

"Nobody scores this high on Time Crisis. Usually."

"Ever, Gridley. Except that kid from Ottumwa."

"Sure, but he's a space alien. One of those distant galaxies. You guys space aliens?"

"It's mostly just piling up bonus points." Ziggy demonstrates. "These guys in the orange suits? New on the job, worst shots in the game, worth 5000 a pop, but 5000 here," Pow! "5000 there," Pow! "pretty soon it begins to add up."

"We never find that many."

"Oh," Ziggy suavely as if everybody knew, "next time you see the Boss heading away from you—"

"There!" Otis points.

"Right, well, you shoot his hat off—see? real quick, four times, lead him and aim a little above his head—so now you don't have to go straight for that tank there, first you can go in this alleyway full of all these lame bonus guys. Get em in the head, you pick up extra points."

"You guys from New York?"

"You noticed," sez Ziggy. "It's why we're into shooters."

"How about powerboats?"

"Sounds kind of wholesome, somehow."

"You ever try Hydro Thunder?"

"Seen it," Otis admits.

"Come on," Gridley sez. "We can show you how to get into the bonus boats right away. There's a police boat with a cannon on it, Armed Response, that ought to be your kind of thing."

"And you get to sit on a subwoofer."

"My brother's a little strange."

"Hey, forget you, Gridley."

"You guys are brothers? Us too."

So Horst, returning from the bar after covering a margin call, arranging a July-November soybean spread, social-engineering an update on Kansas City hard red winter wheat, and putting away an indeterminate number of Berghoff longnecks, finds his sons screaming with, you would have to say, unaccustomed abandon, blasting souped-up powerboats through a postapocalyptic New York half underwater here, suffocating in mist, underlit, familiar landmarks picturesquely distressed. The Statue of Liberty wearing a crown of seaweed. The World Trade Center leaning at a dangerous angle. The lights of Times Square gone dark in great irregular patches, perhaps from recent urban warfare in the neighborhood. Intact buildings are draped in black scaffold netting all the way to the waterline. Ziggy is in the Armed Response, and Otis has the helm of the *Tinytanic*, a miniature version of the famous doomed ocean liner. Gridley and Curtis have vanished, as if they were shills not quite of this earth, whose function in the realworld was to steer Ziggy and Otis into the ruinous waterscapes of what might lie in wait for their home city, as if powerboat skills will be necessary for Big Apple disasters to come, including but not limited to global warming.

"So Mom, we were thinking, maybe we could move to someplace less at risk? Murray Hill? Riverdale?"

"Well . . . we're up six floors . . ."

"So at least a lifeboat, keep it near the window?"

"With what floor space, give us a break you goofballs will *you.*"

After the boys are in bed, Maxine trying to settle in in front of another homicidal-baby-sitter TV movie, Horst approaches diffidently. "Would it be OK if I stuck around for a while?"

Resisting anything like a double take, "You mean tonight."

"Maybe a little longer?"

What's this? "Long as you like, Horst, we're still splitting the maintenance here." Gracious as it is possible at the moment to be, when she'd rather be watching a former sitcom actress pretending to be a youngish Mom in Peril.

"If it's problematic, I can stay someplace else."

"The boys will be thrilled, I think."

She watches his mouth begin to open and then close again. He nods and withdraws to the kitchen, from which soon can be heard sounds of refrigerator entry and plundering.

The drama on the tube is approaching a crisis, the babysitter's evil scheme has begun to fall apart, she has just grabbed the Baby and is trying to make a run for it, in inappropriate heels, into some kind of alligator-intensive terrain, a squad of police who look like catalog models with no firm idea of which end of the gun do you point at the suspect are speeding to the rescue—all night shots, natch—when Horst emerges from the kitchen with a chocolate mustache, holding an ice-cream package.

"There's Russian writing all over it. This Igor guy, correct?"

"Yeah, he gets it shipped in, always more than he can use, I get to help with some of the overrun."

"And in exchange for his generosity—"

"Horst, it's business, he's," smoothly, "eighty years old and looks like Brezhnev, you already ate half a kilo, you want me to call this in, find a stomach pump for you?"

Horst semimiraculously getting a grip, "Not at all, fact, this stuff is terrific. Next time you talk to that ol' Igor, can you find out if they have chocolate macadamia over there? passion fruit swirl maybe?"

MAXINE SPENDS NEXT MORNING at Morris Brothers looking at back-to-school gear for the boys, popping into the apartment around lunch-time. She's just about to open a half-pint of yogurt when Rigoberto buzzes up on the intercom. Even over the low-fidelity speaker, you can hear some swooning in his voice. "Mrs. Loeffler? You have a visitor?" A pause as if working on how to say it. "I'm, like pretty sure it's Jennifer Aniston, is down here to see you?"

"Rigoberto, please, you're a sophisticated New Yorker." She goes to the peephole and sure enough presently out the elevator and down the hall comes this wide-angle version of Rachel "I Love Ross, I Love Ross Not" Green herself. Maxine opens the door before negative thoughts like *psychopath in latex celebrity mask* can arise.

"Ms. Aniston, first of all let me just say, I am such a huge fan of the show—"

Driscoll shakes her hair. "You think?"

"You look just like her. Don't tell me Murray and Morris actually—"

"Yep, and thanks totally for that tip, it's changed my life. The guys said to tell you they miss you and they hope you're not still upset about that li'l dryer malfunction?"

"Nah, federal emergency, half of Con Ed out in the street with jack-hammers, what's to be upset? Come on in the kitchen, I just ran out of Zima, but there's beer. Maybe."

Rolling Rock, two bottles Horst has somehow overlooked, way in the back of the fridge. They go in and sit at the dining-room table.

"Here," Driscoll sliding over a gray-and-burgundy envelope about the size and shape of an old floppy disc, "this is for you."

Inside is a card on expensive stock with calligraphic hand-lettering.

Ms. Maxine Tarnow-Loeffler

The pleasure of your company is requested at

The First Annual

Grande Rentrée Ball, or

Geeks' Cotillion

Saturday night, the eighth of September, 2001

Tworkeffx.com

Open Bar

Clothes Optional

"What's this?"

"Oh I'm on some committee."

"Looks like a big deal, who can afford a party on this scale anymore?"

Well, seems Gabriel Ice, who else, having as it turns out recently acquired Tworkeffx, which builds and maintains virtual private networks, has discovered among the company assets a special Party Fund which has been sitting for years in escrow waiting for something like this particular End of the World As We Know It.

Maxine's annoyed. "All that time and nobody thought to raid the account? How idealistic is that? The crooks I deal with every day, not one—lame, idiotic, whatever—would have passed this up. Until fucking Ice, of course. So now he's the genial host and not spending a nickel out of his own pocket."

"Still, we could all use a wingding about now, even if it's only the Alley's biggest pink-slip party. It'll be about the open bar if nothing else."

· · ·

AS LABOR DAY APPROACHES, everybody in the world begins calling in, people Maxine hasn't heard from for years, a classmate from Hunter who reminds her at length how at just the right moment in an evening of irresponsible stupor she saved this person's life by hailing a taxi, folks from out of town making their annual autumn pilgrimages into NYC, eager as any city-dwelling leafers headed the other way to gaze at spectacles of decadence, sophisticated travelers who have been away all summer at fabulous tourist destinations, back now to bore everybody they can round up with camcorder tapes and tales of fantastic bargains, travel upgrades, living with the natives, Antarctic safaris, Indonesian gamelan festivals, luxury tours of the bowling alleys of Liechtenstein.

Horst, though not exactly hanging around the house all day, is finding time for the boys, more time, it seems from Maxine's increasingly out-of-focus memories of the Horst Years, than he has ever spent before, taking them up to see a Yankee game, discovering the last skee-ball parlor in Manhattan, even volunteering to bring them around the corner for a seasonal drill he has always avoided, back-to-school haircuts.

The barbershop, El Atildado, is below street level. There's a noisy subarctic air conditioner, back copies of *OYE* and *Novedades,* and 90 percent of the conversation, like the commentary to the Mets game on the TV, in Caribbean Spanish. Horst has just gotten absorbed in the game, which is with the Phillies, when in off the street, down the steps, and through the door comes a party in a Johnny Pacheco T-shirt, schlepping a full-size outdoor barbecue complete with propane tank, which he is looking to sell at an attractive price. This happens a lot at El Atildado. Miguel, the owner, always sympathetic, patiently tries to explain why nobody in here is likely to be too interested, pointing out the logistics of walking home with it on the street, not to mention the police, who have El Atildado on their list and keep sending the same beefy Anglos in plainclothes getups that wouldn't fool your baby sister screeching up to the curb to jump out and into action. Indeed, according now to a doorman from down the street on a break, who sticks his head in with the latest cop-watch update, this very scenario is nearly upon them. There is some tense low-volume conversation. Laboriously the barbecue guy maneuvers his sale item back out the door and up the steps, and no more than a minute later here comes the Twentieth Precinct in the form of a cop in a Hawaiian shirt which does not not entirely cover his Glock, hollering, "Ahright, where is he, we just saw him on Columbus, I find out he was in here I'm gonna have your ass, you understand me what I'm sayin here, all you motherfuckers, gonna be in some deep shit, *mierda honda, tu me comprendes,*" and so forth.

"Hey, look," sez Otis, as his brother makes dummy-up signals, "it's Carmine—hey! hey, Carmine!"

"Yo, guys," Detective Nozzoli's eyes flicking to the TV screen. "How they doin?"

"Five–nothin," Ziggy sez. "Payton just homered."

"Wish I could watch. Gotta go chase a perp instead. Say hi to your mom."

"'Say hi to your mom'?" Horst inquires after the inning has ended and commercials come on.

"Him and Heidi are dating," Ziggy calmingly. "She used to bring him around sometimes."

"And your mom . . ."

So it comes out also that Maxine has been coordinating with the cops, some kind of cops, the boys aren't sure which. "She's into criminal cases now?"

"Think it's about a client."

Horst's screenward gaze grows melancholy. "Nice clients . . ."

Later Maxine finds Horst in the dining room trying to assemble a particleboard computer desk for Ziggy, blood already streaming from several fingers, reading glasses about to slide off the sweat on his nose, mysterious metal and plastic fasteners littering the floor, instruction sheets torn and flapping everywhere. Screaming. The default phrase being "Fucking IKEA."

Like millions of other men around the world, Horst hates the Swedish DIY giant. He and Maxine once blew a weekend looking for the branch in Elizabeth, New Jersey, located next to the airport so the world's fourth-richest billionaire can save on lading costs while the rest of us spend the day getting lost on the New Jersey Turnpike. Also off it. At last they arrived at a county-size parking lot, and shimmering in the distance a temple to, or museum of, a theory of domesticity too alien for Horst fully to be engaged by. Cargo planes kept landing gently nearby. An entire section of the store was dedicated to replacing wrong or missing parts and fasteners, since with IKEA this is not so exotic an issue. Inside the store proper, you walk forever from one bourgeois context, or "room of the house," to another, along a fractal path that does its best to fill up the floor space available. Exits are clearly marked but impossible to get to. Horst is bewildered, in a potentially violent sort of way. "Look at this. A barstool, named Sven? Some old Swedish custom, the winter kicks in, weather gets harsh, after a while you find yourself relating to the furniture in ways you didn't expect?"

It was years into the marriage before Horst admitted to not being a domestic person—by then, to nobody's big surprise. "My ideal living space is a not too ratty motel room in the deep Midwest, somewhere up in the badlands, about the time of the first snows." Horst's head in fact is a single nationwide snowdrift of motel rooms in far windswept spaces that Maxine will never know how to find her way to, let alone inhabit. Each crystalline episode fallen into his night, once, unrepeatable. The aggregate a wintry blankness she can't read.

"Come on. Take a break." She puts the tube on, and they sit and watch the Weather Channel for a while, with the sound off. One anchor meteorologist says something and the other looks over and reacts and then looks back into the camera and nods. Then they switch, and the other talks, and the first one nods.

Maybe the formal amiability is catching. Maxine finds herself talking about work, and Horst, improbably, listening. Not that it's any of his business, of course, but then again, a recap, what could hurt? "This documentary guy Reg Despard—his twice-as-paranoid IT genius, Eric—they spot something cute in the bookkeeping at hashslingrz.com, OK, Reg comes to me with it, thinks it's sinister, global in scope, maybe to do with the Mideast, but it could be too much *X-Files* or whatever." Pause, skillfully disguised as taking a breath. Waiting for Horst to get all pissy. But he's only blinking, slowly yet, which may signal some interest. "Now, it seems Reg has disappeared, mysteriously, though maybe only out to Seattle."

"What do you think's going on?"

"Oh. Think? I have time to think? The feds are now on *my* case also, supposedly because of Brooke and her husband and some alleged Mossad connection, which may be total, how do they say out where you come from, horseshit."

Horst by now is holding his head in both hands, as if about to attempt a foul shot with it. "Jemima, Keziah, and Kerenhappuch! What can I do to help?"

"Actually, you know what?" Where is this coming from, and how serious is she really, "Saturday night there's this big nerd clambake downtown? and, and I could use an escort, how about that. Huh?"

He kind of squints. "Sure thing." Half a question. "Wait . . . will I have to dance?"

"Who can say, Horst, sometimes when the music is right? you know, a person just has to?"

"Um, no I meant . . ." Horst is almost cute when he fidgets. "You never forgave me for not learning how to dance, right?"

"Horst, I am supposed to be what, here, tiptoeing around your regrets? If you like, I can teach you a couple of real simple steps right now, would that help?"

"Long as I don't have to swing my hips, a man's got to draw the line someplace."

She roots through the CD collection, pops on a disc. "OK. This is merengue, real simple, all you have to do is stand there like a silo, if you feel like moving a foot now and then, why so much the better."

The kids look in after a while and find them in a formal clinch, slow-dancing to every other beat of "Copacabana."

"Vice-principal's office, you two."

"Yeah, on the double."

28

I t's a warm evening. Just around the time sunset colors are developing over Jersey and food-delivery bike traffic in the neighborhood approaches its peak and city trees are filled with bird dialogue that reaches a crescendo as the streetlights come on, contrails of evening departures hanging brightly in the sky, Horst and Maxine, having dropped the kids at Ernie and Elaine's, are on the subway headed down to SoHo.

The recently acquired Tworkeffx, paying top-of-the-market rent, has occupied for a handful of glittering years a species of Italian palazzo, its cast-iron façade faking the look of limestone, ghostly tonight in the streetlight. What must be everybody from down in the Alley, past and present, is converging on it. You can hear the festivities for blocks before you get there. A crowd track of party-prepped voices with soprano highlights, bass lines from the music inside, punctuated by crackling and high-volume distortion from security-cop walkie-talkies.

One cannot help noticing a certain emphasis tonight on instant nostalgia. Nineties irony, a little past its sell-by date, is in full bloom again down here. Maxine and Horst are swept past the bouncers at the door in a vortex of fauxhawks and fades and emo hair, mops and crops and Japanese princess cuts, Von Dutch trucker-cap knockoffs, temporary tattoos, spliffs hanging off lips, *Matrix*-era Ray-Bans, Hawaiian shirts, the only shirts in sight with collars, except for Horst's. "Good grief," he exclaims, "it looks like Keokuk around here." Those in earshot are too hip to tell him that's the point.

Even though the dotcom bubble, once an eye-catching ellipsoid, now droops in vivid pink collapse over the trembling chin of the era, perhaps no more than a vestige of shallow breath left inside it, no expense tonight has been spared. The theme of the gathering, officially "1999," has a darker subtext of Denial. It soon becomes clear that everybody's pretending for tonight that they're still in the pre-crash fantasy years, dancing in the shadow of last year's dreaded Y2K, now safely history, but according to this consensual delusion not quite upon them yet, with all here remaining freeze-framed back at the Cinderella moment of midnight of the millennium when in the next nanosecond the world's computers will fail to increment the year correctly and bring down the Apocalypse. What passes for nostalgia in a time of widespread Attention Deficit Disorder. People have pulled their pre-millennial T-shirts back out of the archival plastic they've been idling in—Y2K IS NEAR, ARMAGED- DON EVE, Y2K COMPLIANT LOVE MACHINE, I SURVIVED . . . Determined, as Prince can be heard repeatedly urging, to party like it's 1999.

The Soviet-era sound system, looted from a failed arena somewhere in Eastern Europe, is also blasting Blink-182, Echo and the Bunnymen, Barenaked Ladies, Bone Thugs-n-Harmony, and other sentimental oldies while vintage stock quotations from the boom-years NASDAQ crawl along a ticker display on a frieze running the full perimeter of the ballroom, beneath giant four-by-six-meter LED screens onto which bloom and fade loops of historical highlights like Bill Clinton's grand-jury testimony, "It depends upon what the meaning of the word 'is' is," the other Bill, Gates, getting a pie in the face in Belgium, the announcement trailer for Halo, clips from the *Dilbert* animated TV series and the first season of SpongeBob, Roman Coppola's Boo.com commercials, Monica Lewinsky hosting *SNL*, Susan Lucci finally winning a Daytime Emmy for Erica

Kane, with Urge Overkill's song of the same name deejayed in as accompaniment.

The antique bar, elaborately carved in a number of neo-Egyptian motifs, was salvaged by Tworkeffx from the headquarters lodge of a semimystical outfit uptown being converted, like every structure of its scale in NYC, to residential use. If occult mojo still permeates the ancient Caucasian walnut, it is waiting its moment to manifest. What remains tonight is an appeal to fond memories of all the open bars of the nineties, where everybody here can remember drinking for free, night after night, simply by claiming affiliation with the start-up of the moment. The bartenders behind it tonight are mostly out-of-work hackers or street-level drug dealers whose business dried up after April 2000. Those who can't help making with the free booze advice, for example, turn out to be Razorfish alumni, still the smartest people in the room. There is no bottom-shelf product here, it's all Tanqueray No. Ten, Patrón Gran Platinum, The Macallan, Elit. Along with PBRs, of course, in a washtub full of crushed ice, for those who cannot easily deal with the prospect of an irony-free evening.

If there's business being talked tonight, it's someplace else in town, where time is too valuable to waste on partying. Third-quarter earnings are in the toilet, deal flow is down to a slow drip, corporate IT budgets are as frozen as machine margaritas in a Palo Alto bar, Microsoft XP has just emerged from beta, but already there is nerdal muttering and geekish discontent over security and backward-compatibility issues. Recruiters are out discreetly prowling the crowd, but with none of the usual color-coded bracelets visible tonight, hackers looking to work for short money have to default to intuition about who's hiring.

Later those who were here will remember mostly how vertical it all was. The stairwells, the elevators, the atria, the shadows that seem to plunge from overhead in repeated assaults on the gatherings and ungatherings beneath . . . the dancers semi-stunned, out under the strobing, not dancing exactly, more like standing in one place and moving up and down in time to the music.

"Doesn't look that complicated," Horst observes, sort of to himself, wandering away into the bright commotion of temporal aliasing.

"Maxi, hi?" It's Vyrva, with her hair up, eyes dramatized, wearing basic black and spike heels. Justin puts his head around from somewhere behind her and with a stoner's smile wiggles his eyebrows. Even in this pullulating decadence, he's still his reliable West Coast sweetheart self, wearing a T-shirt that reads JUSTIN \ NOTHER PERL HACKER. Lucas is along, wearing roomy homeboy jeans and an I-spotted-the-fed Defcon shirt.

"Wow, back off Kim Basinger. Making me feel even frumpier than usual here, Vyrva."

"What, this old schmatte, the dog likes to sleep on it, she let me borrow it for the evening." No direct eye contact, decidedly off-profile for Vyrva, her gaze wandering instead to the giant screens overhead as if waiting for something there, some possibly fateful film clip. Maxine doesn't perform brain scans but does have a longtime acquaintance with jumpy.

"Quite a ballroom ain't it. Bar mitzvah theme ideas everywhere you turn. The Ice individual has spared no expense, he must be lurking around someplace."

"Don't know, haven't been looking."

"Myself," sez Lucas, "I think he's in some creepy retro-pissing contest with Josh Harris. Remember that millennium-eve party at pseudo? Went on for months?"

"You mean," sez Justin, "like, people in clear plastic rooms fucking in public view, where? Where?"

"Yo, Maxi." Eric, hair dyed a sort of pale electric green, a flirtatious eye, a grin that on analysis might test over in the shit-eating part of the scale. Maxine senses Horst, invisibly nearby, gazing at them, about to lapse into sad-sack mode. Oy vey "Did you see *my husband* around here anyplace?" Loud enough for Horst if he's there to hear.

"Your what?"

"Oh," normal tone, "sort of quasi ex-husband, did I not ever mention that?"

"Big surprise," mumbling cheerfully, "and whoa, what's this we've got here tonight, Giuseppe Zanotti, right?"

"Stuart Weitzman, smartass, but wait, somebody you should meet here, partial to Jimmy Choo if I'm not mistaken." It's Driscoll, the all-out Anistonian version, causing a screen to begin blinking on Maxine's Lobodex of Love, or in-brain matchmaking app. "Unless you guys know each other already . . ."

At it again, Maxine, why can't she resist these ancient yenta forces that seek to control her? enough, please, with the meddling, parties take care of yenta business better than yentas do, economies of scale or something, no doubt. Eric squints in a charming way. "Didn't we . . . one of those Cybersuds affairs, you tried to throw me in the river or something? No, wait, she was shorter."

"Maybe a nonbeer event?" crypto-Rachel-to-Ross-wise, "some Linux installfest?" Phone numbers in marker pen on palms or some such ritual, and Driscoll is off again.

"Listen, Maxi," Eric turning serious, "there's somebody we need to find. Lester Traipse's partner, the Canadian guy."

"Felix? He's still in town?" Somehow, not such good news. "What's his problem?"

"He needs to see you, something about Lester Traipse, but he's also acting paranoid, keeping on the move, partying heavily."

"Security through immaturity." Lester, what about Lester?

Not a word from Felix since that night at the karaoke and suddenly now he wants to talk. Where was he when his trusting business partner got murdered? Conveniently back in Montreal? How about out in Montauk with Gabriel Ice, scheming how to set Lester up? What's so urgent tonight that Felix needs to tell Maxine, she wonders.

"Come on, we'll do a pseudo-random sweep of the toilets."

She follows him into the strummed and seething maw of this work space now fallen into event space, scanning the crowd, getting a quick glimpse of Horst out on the floor doing the same Z-axis Bounce as everybody else, and at least not *not* enjoying himself.

Eric motions her through a door and down a corridor to a toilet that proves to be unisex and privacy-free. Instead of rows of urinals, there are continuous sheets of water descending stainless-steel walls, against which gentlemen, and ladies so inclined, are invited to piss, while for the less adventurous there are stalls of see-through acrylic which in more prosperous days at Tworkeffx also allowed slacker patrols to glance in and see who's avoiding work, custom-decorated inside by high-ticket downtown graffiti artists, with dicks going into mouths a popular motif, as well as sentiments like DIE MICROSOFT WEENIES and LARA CROFT HAS POLYGON ISSUES.

No Felix here. They hit the stairs and proceed upward floor by floor, ascending into these bright halls of delusion, prowling offices and cubicles whose furnishings have been picked up from failed dotcoms at bargain prices, too soon in their turn destined for looting by the likes of Gabriel Ice.

Partying everywhere. Sweeping into it, swept . . . Faces in motion. The employees' lap pool with champagne empties bobbing in it. Yuppies who appear only recently to have learned how to smoke screaming at each other. "Had a brilliant Arturo Fuente the other day!" "Awesome!" A parade of restless noses snorting lines off of circular Art Deco mirrors from long-demolished luxury hotels dating back to the last time New York saw a market frenzy as intense as the one just ended.

In and out of a number of theme restrooms, gigantic all but wraparound Irish-bar urinals, vintage embossed toilets from a hundred years ago, wall-mounted tanks and pull chains, other spaces, dimmer and less elegant, seeking to evoke classic downtown club toilets, without a spritz of Lysol since the mid-nineties and only one toilet bowl, distressed and toxic, which people have to queue up for.

Felix meanwhile is in none of these. Reaching the top floor at last, Eric and Maxine enter the godfather of postmodern toilets, a piazza-size expanse of Belgian encaustic tiling in ocher, pale blue and faded burgundy, recycled from a mansion on lower Broadway, with three dozen stalls, its own bar, television lounge, sound system, and deejay, who at

the moment, while a six-by-six matrix of dancers perform the Electric Slide across the antique tiling, is playing Nazi Vegetable's once-
chartbusting disco anthem

In the Toilet [Hustle tempo]

Such a weird 'n' wack-y feeling, wit' your
Brains up on th' ceiling, in the
Toi-let!
[Girl backup]—In the toi-let!
Coke and Ecstasy and weed,
Never know when you might need
Them in the toi-let
(All in-that, toi-let!)
Just come in to take a peek, end up
Stayin' for a week, down in the
Toi-let! . . .
(Toilet! Toilet!)
All those mirrors, lotsa chrome, stuff you'd
Never try at home, here in thuhuh
Toi-let—
Whoa, oh, girl a-nd
[Release]
Boy, let
The night have its way,
Wave bye-bye to the day,
Don't use nothin too much,
Have a look but don't touch, or you'll
Spoil it,
Just be cool, it's the toi-hoi-let—
That expectant, disinfectant-heavy
Rest-room rendez-vooo . . .
Urinal smoothies, just like in the movies,

'll charm ya right outta your, pants—come
To the
Toilet! flush all those
Troubles and dance!

Not everybody benefits from a misspent youth. Teen contemporaries of Maxine's got lost in the club toilets of the eighties, went in, never came out, some with luck grew too hip or not hip enough to appreciate the scene at all, others, like Maxine, went on only to flash back to it now and then, epileptigogic lighting, Quaaludes for sale on the floor, outerborough hair statements . . . the Aqua Net fogs! The girl-hours lost sitting in front of mirrors! The strange disconnects between dance music and lyrics, "Copacabana," "What a Fool Believes," heartbreaking stories, even tragic, set to these strangely bouncy tunes . . .

The Electric Slide is a four-wall line dance that Maxine recognizes from the many bar mitzvahs gone blurring by since the old Paradise Garage of her teen years and the only fraction of the week really that mattered, Saturday nights when she would sneak out of the house at one or one-thirty, take the subway down to Houston and the endless, endless block to King, teleport in past the bouncers to rejoin for a while the other core Garageheads, and dance all night in the conjured world, and wait till breakfast at some diner to try to figure out what kind of a story to tell her parents this time . . . and next thing you're in your purse looking for tissues because it's all gone, of course, another of those expulsions on out into a colder season, where not everybody made it through, there was AIDS and crack and let's not forget late fuckin capitalism, so only a few really found refuge of any kind . . .

"Um, Maxine, are you . . . ?"

"Yes. No. I'm good . . . what?"

Eric gestures with his head, and there among the Art Nouveau intricacies of the floor, in the middle of the formation, Maxine spots the elusive potential homicide accomplice Felix Boïngueaux, wearing a

double-knit disco-era suit in some screamingly saturated coral, almost
certainly picked up on sale, a store buyer's impulse soon regretted, over
a T-shirt with a Canadian maple-leaf logo and THE EH? TEAM on it. The
dance formation reformats into couples, and Felix comes over, sweating
and jittery.

"Yo, Felix, *ça va?*"

"Bummer about Lester, eh?" Unblinking chutzpah-heavy eye
contact.

"This is what you wanted to see me about, Felix?"

"I was out of town when it happened."

"Did I say anything? Even if Lester did seem, well, under the impression you had his back."

Chances of rattling this customer are about as fat as Ally McBeal.
"You're still following the case, then."

"We're keeping a file open on it." The investigatorial "we." Let
him think there's a third party who's hired her. "Anything you can help
us with?"

"Maybe. Maybe you'd just go runnin to tell the cops or something."

"I'm not a cop lover, Felix, that's Nancy Drew, actually not too flat-
tering a comparison, you need to work on that."

"Hey, you're the one who tried to get the ol' Vipster popped," Felix
meantime having begun to squint suspiciously at Eric, who withdraws amiably enough into the ebb and flow of dancers, drinkers, and
dopers.

She pretends to sigh. "It's about the poutine isn't it, you'll never
forgive me, once again, Felix, I'm sorry I said that—dumb remark, cheap
shot."

Going along with it, "In Montreal it's a diagnostic for moral
character—if somebody resists poutine, they resist life."

"Can I think about," having a look around at the partying, "that
later? Monday? I promise."

"Look, look, it's Gabriel Ice." Nodding in the direction of the bar, where sure enough their gracious host stands, expressing himself to a small knot of admirers.

"Ever meet him?"

She understands that this may've been the whole point. "We've talked on the phone. I got a sense that his time is precious to him."

"Come on, I'll introduce you, we've been doing a little business together."

Of course you have, bitch. They sidle across the teeming square footage till they're in earshot of the trim tycoon, who is not so much chatting as delivering some kind of sales pitch.

His eyes, framed by Oliver Peoples horn-rims, are less expressive than many Maxine has noted at the fish market, though sometimes a party who may appear immune to desire is in fact oversusceptible, dangerously so, no least idea of how to deal with it once it jumps the fence, as it must, and heads for the ridgeline. Thin and careful lips. In the business you run into far too many of these faces, don't know what they want, or how much of it, or what to do with it once they have it.

"More and more servers together in the same place putting out levels of heat that quickly become problematic unless you spend the budget on A/C. Thing to do," Ice proclaims, "is to go north, set up server farms where heat dissipation won't be so much of a problem, take your power from renewables like hydro or sunlight, use surplus heat to help sustain whatever communities grow up around the data centers. Domed communities across the Arctic tundra.

"My geek brothers! the tropics may be OK for cheap labor and sex tours, but the future is out there on the permafrost, a new geopolitical imperative—gain control of the supply of cold as a natural resource of incomputable worth, with global warming, even more crucial—"

There is something creepily familiar about this go-north argument. By a corollary of Godwin's law valid only on the Upper West Side, Stalin's name, like Hitler's, is 100% certain to enter a discussion of any length, and Maxine now recalls Ernie telling her about the genocidal

Georgian and his plans back in the 1930s for colonizing the Arctic with domed cities and armies of young technicians, otherwise known, Ernie was always careful to point out, as forced labor, bringing out for multimedia emphasis his 78rpm album of *The Attractive Schoolgirl of Zazhopinsk,* an obscure opera from the purge era, strangled Russian bass-tenor duets invoking steppes of ice, thermodynamic night. And now here's Gabriel Ice, in a capitalist party mask, with a neo-Stalinist rerun.

Aah, God help us, how sleazy is it, and how has it come to this? a rented palace, a denial of the passage of time, a mogul on the black-diamond slopes of the IT sector thinks he's a rock star. It isn't so much that Maxine can't be fooled, it's more that she hates to be, and when she finds anybody trying too hard to fool her, she reaches for her revolver. Or in this case, turns and heads for the stairs, leaving Felix and Gabriel Ice to shmooze as they will, rogue to rogue.

Does Nora Charles ever have to put up with this sort of thing? Even Nancy Drew? The parties they go to, it's all catered hors d'oeuvres and beautiful strangers. But let Maxine try to step out and enjoy herself a little, forget it, it always ends up like this. Weekday-type obligations, guilt, ghosts.

For some reason, however, she manages to stay all night and close the joint down. Horst, perhaps from secondhand smoke, regressing to his old party-animal ways, is affably all over the place. Maxine finds herself tangled in and presently refereeing nerd disputes she can't understand a word of. She nods out in the toilet once or twice, and if she dreams at all, it's hard to separate from the great invisible wheeling around her, decelerating, board-fading to all-but-silent black and white, till it's time at last to CD tilde home. For recessional music there's "Closing Time" by Semisonic, a four-chord farewell to the old century. Former and future nerdistocracy slowly, and to look at them you'd think reluctantly, filtering back out into the street, into the long September which has been with them in a virtual way since spring before last, continuing only to deepen. Putting their street faces back on for it. Faces already under silent assault, as if by something ahead, some Y2K of the work-week that no one is quite imagining, the crowds drifting slowly out into the little legendary streets, the highs beginning to dissipate, out into the casting-off of veils before the luminosities of dawn, a sea of T-shirts nobody's reading, a clamor of messages nobody's getting, as if it's the true text history of nights in the Alley, outcries to be attended to and not be lost, the 3:00 AM kozmo deliveries to code sessions and all-night shredding parties, the bedfellows who came and went, the bands in the clubs, the songs whose hooks still wait to ambush an idle hour, the day jobs with meetings about meetings and bosses without clue, the unreal strings of zeros, the business models changing one minute to the next, the start-up parties every night of the week and more on Thursdays than you could keep track of, which of these faces so claimed by the time, the epoch whose end they've been celebrating all night—which of them can see ahead, among the microclimates of binary, tracking earthwide everywhere through dark fiber and twisted pairs and nowadays wire-lessly through spaces private and public, anywhere among cybersweat-shop needles flashing and never still, in that unquiet vastly stitched and unstitched tapestry they have all at some time sat growing crippled in the service of—to the shape of the day imminent, a procedure waiting exe-cution, about to be revealed, a search result with no instructions on how to look for it?

In the taxi on the way home, there's loud traffic in Arabic on the radio, which Maxine figures at first for a call-in show till the cabbie picks up a handset and joins in. She glances at the ID up on the Plexiglas. The face in the photo is too indistinct to make out, but the name is Islamic, Mohammed somebody.

It's like hearing a party from another room, though Maxine notices there's no music, no laughing. High emotion all right, but closer to tears or anger. Men talking over each other, shouting, interrupting. A couple of the voices might be women's, though later it will seem they could have belonged to high-pitched men. The only word Maxine recognizes, and she hears it more than once, is *Inshallah*. "Arabic for 'whatever,'" Horst nods.

They're waiting at a light. "If it is God's will," the driver corrects him, half turning in his seat so that Maxine happens to be looking him in the face. What she sees there will keep her from getting to sleep right away. Or that's how she'll remember it.

29

The spread on the Jets-Indianapolis game Sunday is 2 points. Horst, regionally loyal as always, bets Ziggy and Otis a pizza that the Colts will win, which in fact they do in a 21-point walkover. Peyton Manning can do no wrong, Vinny Testaverde is a little less consistent, managing in the last five minutes for example to fumble on the Colts' 2-yard line to a defensive end who then proceeds to run the ball 98 yards to a touchdown, as Testaverde alone chases him up the field while the rest of the Jets look on, and Ziggy and Otis lapse into intemperate language their father doesn't see how he can call them out for.

It's a warm evening, and they all decide instead of ordering the pizza in to walk over to Columbus, to Tom's Pizza, a local soon to fade into Upper West Side folk memory. First time in years, it occurs to Maxine later, that they've done anything all together as a family. They sit at a table outside. Nostalgia lurks, ready to ooze from ambush. Maxine thinks back to when the boys were little, the local practice in neighborhood pizza parlors then being to cut slices into small bite-size squares as an accommodation for little kids. When the kid can handle a whole slice, it's a kind of coming-of-age. Later on, with braces, there's a return to smaller squares. Maxine glances over at Horst for any outward signs of an active memory, but no dice, old Stolid Geometry is occupied with stuffing pizza into his face at a steady rhythm and trying to make the boys lose count of how many slices they've had. Which itself, Maxine supposes, you could call family tradition, not specially admirable, but hell, she'll take it.

Later, back home, Horst settled in in front of his computer screen, "Guys, come here, look at this. Darnedest thing."

The screen is full of numbers. "This is the Chicago Exchange, toward the end of last week, see? there was a sudden abnormal surge of put options on United Airlines. Thousands of puts, not a heck of a lot of calls. Now, today, the same thing happens for American Airlines."

"A put," Ziggy sez, "that's like selling short?"

"Yeah, when you're expecting the stock price to go down. And trading volume meanwhile is way, way up—six times normal."

"Just those two airlines?"

"Yep. Weird, huh?"

"Insider trading," it seems to Ziggy.

MONDAY NIGHT VYRVA CALLS MAXINE with panic in her voice. "The guys are freaking out. Something about this random-number source they've been hacking into suddenly going nonrandom."

"And you're telling me this because . . ."

"OK if Fiona and I come over there for a little?"

"Sure." Horst is out at a sports bar someplace way downtown watching *Monday Night Football*. Giants and Broncos, at Denver. Planning to sleep over at the apartment of his colleague in arrested adolescence Jake Pimento, who lives in Battery Park City, and then go in to work at the Trade Center from there.

Vyrva shows up all loose ends. "They're screaming at each other. Never a good sign."

"How was camp, Fiona?"

"Awesome."

"Didn't suck."

"Exactly."

Otis, Ziggy, and Fiona settle in in front of Homer Simpson, playing an accountant of all things, in a film noir, or possibly jaune, called "*D.O.H.*"

Vyrva showing signs of early parent bewilderment. "She's suddenly doing Quake movies. Some of them are online, she has a following already. We've been cosigning distribution deals. More clauses than a North Pole family reunion. No idea what we're agreeing to, of course."

Maxine makes popcorn. "Stay over, why don't you. Horst won't be back tonight, plenty of room."

Just one more of these into-the-night schmoozathons, nothing special, kids off to bed without too much drama, television programming that's better with the sound off, no deep confessions, business chatter. Vyrva checks in with Justin around midnight. "They're bonding again, now. Worse than the other. I think I will stay over."

TUESDAY MORNING THEY ALL CONVOY over to Kugelblitz together, hang around the stoop till the bell rings, Vyrva peels away to grab a bus across town, Maxine heads for work, puts her head in a local smoke shop to grab a newspaper, and finds everybody freaking out and depressed at the same time. Something bad is going on downtown. "A plane just crashed into the World Trade Center," according to the Indian guy behind the counter.

"What, like a private plane?"

"A commercial jet."

Uh-oh. Maxine goes home and pops on CNN. And there it all is. Bad turns to worse. All day long. At around noon the school calls and says they're shutting down for the day, could she please come and collect her kids.

Everybody's on edge. Nods, headshakes, not a lot of social conversation.

"Mom, was Dad down there at his office today?"

"He was staying over at Jake's last night, but I think he's mostly been working from his computer. So chances are he didn't even go in."

"But you haven't heard from him?"

"Everybody's been trying to get through to everybody, lines are swamped, he'll call, I'm not worrying, don't you guys, OK?"

They're not buying it. Of course they're not. But they both nod anyway and just get on with it. A class act, these two. She holds their hands, one on either side, all the way home, and though this sort of thing belongs to their childhood and generally annoys them, today they let her.

The phone starts ringing after a while. Each time Maxine jumps to pick it up, hoping it's Horst, it turns out instead to be Heidi, or Ernie and Elaine, or Horst's parents calling from Iowa where everything is an hour closer to the innocence of sleep. But from the slab of beef who still, she hopes, shares her life, no word. The boys stay in their room watching the single constant telephoto shot of the smoking towers, already too distant. She keeps sticking her head in. Bringing snack food, mom-approved and otherwise, that they don't touch.

"Are we at war, Mom?"

"No. Who says we are?"

"This Wolf Blitzer guy?"

"Usually countries go to war with countries. I don't think whoever did this, that they're a country."

"It said on the news they're Saudi Arabians," Otis tells her. "Maybe we're at war with Saudi Arabia."

"Can't be," Ziggy points out, "we need all that oil."

As if by ESP, the phone rings, and it's March Kelleher.

"It's the Reichstag fire," she greets Maxine.

"The what?"

"Those fucking Nazis in Washington needed a pretext for a coup, now they've got it. This country is headed up shit's creek, and it isn't rugriders we should worry about, it's Bush and the gang."

Maxine isn't so sure. "It seems like none of them know what they're doing right now, just caught by surprise, more like Pearl Harbor."

"That's what they want you to believe. And who says Pearl Harbor wasn't a setup?"

They're actually discussing this? "Forget doing it to your own people, why would anybody do this to their own economy?"

"You never heard of 'You've got to spend money to make money'? Tithing back to the dark gods of capitalism."

Then something occurs to Maxine. "March, that DVD of Reg's, the Stinger missile . . ."

"I know. We got snookered."

THE PHONE RINGS. "Are you all right?"

Asshole. What the fuck does he care? Not a voice she's been that anxious to hear from. In the background a bureaucratic pandemonium, ringing phones, lower pay grades being verbally abused, shredders working full-time.

"Who's this again?"

"You want to talk, you've got my number." Windust hangs up. "Talk," does that mean "fuck"? Wouldn't surprise her, that level of desperation, of course, there have to exist losers who would actually use the tragedy unfolding downtown to get laid on the cheap, and no reason Windust as she's come to know him couldn't be one.

Still no word from Horst. She tries not to worry, to believe her own pitch to the boys, but she's worried. Late that night, after they're in bed, she sits awake in front of the tube, nodding off, being wakened by microdreams of somebody coming in the door, nodding off again.

Sometime during the night, Maxine dreams she's a mouse who's been running at large inside the walls of a vast apartment building she understands is the U.S., venturing out into kitchens and pantries to scavenge for food, scuffling but free, and in these small hours she has been attracted by what she recognizes as a sort of humane mousetrap yet cannot resist the bait, not traditional peanut butter or cheese but something more from the gourmet section, pâté or truffles maybe, and the moment she steps into the enticing little structure, her simple body weight is enough to unlatch a spring-loaded door that closes, not that loudly, behind her, and is impossible to open again. She finds herself inside a multilevel event space of some kind, at a gathering, maybe a party, full of unfamiliar faces, fellow mice, but no longer exactly, or only, mice. She understands that this place is a holding pen between freedom in the wild and some other unimagined environment into which, one by one, each of them will be released, and that this can only be analogous to death and afterdeath.

And wants desperately to wake up. And once she's awake to be someplace else, even a meretricious geeks' paradise like DeepArcher.

She gets out of bed, sweating, looks in to find the boys snoring away, drifts into the kitchen, stands staring at the fridge like it's a television set that will tell her something she needs to know. She hears sound from the spare room. Trying not to hope, not to hyperventilate, she tiptoes in and there yes it's Horst, snoring in front of his BioPiX channel, alone of all channels tonight not providing twenty-four hour coverage of the disaster, as if it's the most natural thing in the world to be alive, and home.

"DENVER WON IT 31–20. I fell asleep on Jake's couch. Sometime in the night, I woke up, couldn't get back to sleep right away." So strange down there, Battery Park at night. Made Horst think of the night before Christmas when he was a kid. Santa Claus up there invisible, on route, someplace up in that sky. So quiet. Except for Jake snoring in the bedroom. And that neighborhood, even when you can't see the Trade Center towers, you feel them, felt them, like somebody in an elevator shouldering up against you. And out in the sunlight the soaring hazy aluminum presence . . .

Next morning all hell's broken loose outside, by the time Jake remembers where the coffee is and Horst puts the news on the tube, there's sirens, helicopters, all through the neighborhood, pretty soon they notice people out the window, heading for the water, figure it might be a good idea to join them. Tugboats, ferries, private boats, pulling in, taking people out from the yacht basin, all on their own, amazing coordination of effort, "I don't think anybody was in charge, they just came in and did it. I ended up over in Jersey. Some motel."

"Your kind of place."

"The television didn't work too good. Nothing on but news updates."

"So if you guys hadn't decided to sleep in . . ."

"Back in the pits, I used to know this Christer coffee trader who told me it was like grace, something you don't ask for. Just comes. Of course it can also be withdrawn at any time. Like when I always knew which way to bet on Eurodollars. The times we shorted Amazon, got out of Lucent when it went to $70 a share, remember? It wasn't me that ever 'knew' anything. But something did. Sudden couple extra lines of brain code, who knows. I just followed along."

"But then . . . if it was that same weird talent that kept you safe . . ."

"How could it be? How could predicting market behavior be the same as predicting a terrible disaster?"

"If the two were different forms of the same thing."

"Way too anticapitalist for me, babe."

Later he reflects, "You always had me figured for some kind of idiot savant, you were the one with the street smarts, the wised-up practical one, and I was just some stiff with a gift, who didn't deserve to be so lucky." First time he's said this to her in person, though it's a pitch he's made more than once to an imaginary ex-wife, alone at night in hotel rooms in the U.S. and abroad, where sometimes the television speaks in languages he doesn't know any more of than he needs to get around, the room service always brings him somebody else's food, which he has learned to go along with in a spirit of adventurous curiosity, reminding himself that he would otherwise never have experienced, say, blackened alligator casserole with fried pickles or sheep's-eyeball pizza. Daytime business for him is duck soup (which they also brought him once, for breakfast, in Ürümqi) with no connection he can clearly see to the other, the backstreets of the day, the 3:00 AM retranslations appropriate to fear of unwelcome dreams, the unreadable vistas of city shadow out the windows. Poisonous blue masses he doesn't want to see but keeps drawing back the drapes a little to blink through at for as long as he has to. As if something is happening out there he mustn't miss.

NEXT DAY AS MAXINE and the boys are heading out to Kugelblitz, "Mind if I come along?" sez Horst.

Sure. Maxine notices other sets of parents, some who haven't spoken for years, showing up together to escort their children, regardless of age or latchkey status, safely to and from. Headmaster Winterslow is there on the stoop, greeting everybody one by one. Grave and courtly and for once refraining from educated speech. He is touching people, squeezing shoulders, hugging, holding hands. In the lobby is a table with sign-up sheets for volunteer work down at the site of the atrocity. Everybody is still walking around stunned, having spent the previous day sitting or standing in front of television screens, at home, in bars, at work, staring like zombies, unable in any case to process what they were seeing. A viewing population brought back to its default state, dumbstruck, undefended, scared shitless.

ON HER WEBLOG, March Kelleher has wasted no time shifting into what she calls her old-lefty tirade mode. "Just to say evil Islamics did it, that's so lame, and we know it. We see those official close-ups on the screen. The shifty liar's look, the twelve-stepper's gleam in the eye. One look at these faces and we know they're guilty of the worst crimes we can imagine. But who's in any hurry to imagine? To make the awful connection? Any more than Germans were back in 1933, when Nazis torched the Reichstag within a month of Hitler becoming chancellor. Which of course is not at all to suggest that Bush and his people have actually gone out and staged the events of 11 September. It would take a mind hope-

lessly diseased with paranoia, indeed a screamingly anti-American nutcase, even to allow to cross her mind the possibility that that terrible day
could have deliberately been engineered as a pretext to impose some
endless Orwellian 'war' and the emergency decrees we will soon be
living under. Nah, nah, perish that thought.

"But there's still always the other thing. Our yearning. Our deep
need for it to be true. Somewhere, down at some shameful dark recess
of the national soul, we need to feel betrayed, even guilty. As if it was us
who created Bush and his gang, Cheney and Rove and Rumsfeld and
Feith and the rest of them—we who called down the sacred lightning of
'democracy,' and then the fascist majority on the Supreme Court threw
the switches, and Bush rose from the slab and began his rampage. And
whatever happened then is on our ticket."

A week or so later, Maxine and March do breakfast at the Piraeus
Diner. There is now a huge American flag in the window and a UNITED
WE STAND poster. Mike is being extra solicitous to the cops who come in
looking for free meals.

"Check this out." March hands over a dollar bill, around the margins
of whose obverse somebody has written in ballpoint, "World Trade Center was destroyed by CIA—Bush Senior's CIA is making Bush Jr. Prez for
life & a hero." "I got this in change at the corner grocery this morning.
That's well within a week of the attack. Call it what you like, but a historical document whatever." Maxine recalls that Heidi has a collection of
decorated dollar bills, which she regards as the public toilet wall of the
U.S. monetary system, carrying jokes, insults, slogans, phone numbers,
George Washington in blackface, strange hats, Afros and dreadlocks and
Marge Simpson hair, lit joints in his mouth, and speech-balloon remarks
ranging from witty to stupid.

"No matter how the official narrative of this turns out," it seemed
to Heidi, "these are the places we should be looking, not in newspapers
or television but at the margins, graffiti, uncontrolled utterances, bad
dreamers who sleep in public and scream in their sleep."

"This message on this bill doesn't surprise me so much as how promptly it showed up," March sez now. "How fast the analysis has been."

Like it or not, Maxine has become March's official doubter, and happy to help, usually, though these days like everybody else she's feeling discombobulated. "March, since it happened, I don't know what to believe."

But March, relentlessly on the case, brings up Reg's DVD. "Suppose there was a Stinger crew deployed and waiting for orders to shoot down the first 767, the one that went on to hit the North Tower. Maybe there was another team stationed over in Jersey to pick up the second one, which would've been circling around and coming up from the southwest."

"Why?"

"Anti-compassion insurance. Somebody doesn't trust the hijackers to go through with it. These are Western minds, uncomfortable with any idea of suicide in the service of a faith. So they threaten to shoot the hijackers down in case they chicken out at the last minute."

"And if the hijackers do change their minds, what if the Stinger team do the same and *don't* shoot the plane down?"

"Then that would explain the backup sniper on the other roof, who the Stinger people know is there, keeping them in his sights till their part of the mission is over. Which is as soon as the guy with the phone gets word the plane's committed—then everybody cleans up and clears out. It's full daylight by then, but not that much risk of being seen 'cause all the attention is focused downtown."

"Help, too byzantine, make it stop!"

"Trying, but is Bush answering my calls?"

HORST MEANTIME IS PUZZLED ABOUT something else. "Remember the week before this happened, all those put options on United and American Airlines? Which turned out to be exactly the two airlines that got hijacked? Well, it seems on that Thursday and Friday there were also lopsided put-to-call ratios for Morgan Stanley, Merrill Lynch, couple others like them, all tenants of the Trade Center. As a fraud investigator, what does that suggest to you?"

"Foreknowledge of a decline in their stock prices. Who was doing all this trading?"

"Nobody so far has stepped forward."

"Mystery players who knew it was going to happen. Overseas maybe? Like the Emirates?"

"I try to keep hold of my common sense, but . . ."

Maxine goes over to her parents' for lunch, and Avi and Brooke are there as expected. The sisters embrace, though you could not say warmly. There's no way not to talk about the Trade Center.

"Nobody that morning had anything to say," Maxine, noticing at some point that there's a NY Jets logo on Avi's yarmulke, 'Ain't it awful' is about as profound as it got. Just the one camera angle, the static telephoto shot of those towers smoldering, the same news that's no news, the same morning-show airhead idiocy—"

"They were in shock," Brooke mutters, "like everybody that day, what, you weren't?"

"But why keep showing us that one thing, what were we supposed to be waiting for, what was going to happen? Too high up to run hoses, OK, so the fire will either burn itself out or spread to other floors or—or what else? What were we being set up for, if not what happened? One comes down, then the other, and who was surprised? Wasn't it inevitable by then?"

"You think the networks knew ahead of time?" Brooke, offended, glowering. "Whose side are you on, are you an American or what are you?" Brooke now in full indignation, "this horrible, horrible tragedy, a whole generation traumatized, war with the Arab world any minute, and even this isn't safe from your stupid little hipster irony? What's next, Auschwitz jokes?"

"Same thing happened when JFK was shot," Ernie belatedly trying to defuse things with geezer nostalgia. "Nobody wanted to believe that official story either. So suddenly here were all these strange coincidences."

"You think it was an inside job, Pa?"

"The chief argument against conspiracy theories is always that it would take too many people in on it, and somebody's sure to squeal. But look at the U.S. security apparatus, these guys are WASPs, Mormons, Skull and Bones, secretive by nature. Trained, sometimes since birth, never to run off at the mouth. If discipline exists anywhere, it's among them. So of course it's possible."

"How about you, Avi?" Maxine turning to her brother-in-law. "What's the latest on 4360.0 kilohertz?" Nice as pie. But he gives a violent jump. "Oops, or do I mean megahertz?"

"What The Fuck?"

"Language," Elaine automatically before realizing it's Brooke, who seems to be looking around for a weapon.

"Arab propaganda!" Avi cries. "Anti-Semitic filth. Who told you about this frequency?"

"Saw it on the Internet," Maxine shrugs, "ham operators have known about it forever, they're called E10 stations, operated by Mossad out of Israel, Greece, South America, the voices are women who figure in the erotic daydreams of radio hobbyists everywhere, reciting alphanumerics, encrypted, of course. Widely believed to be messages to agents, salaried and otherwise, out in the Diaspora. Word is that in the run-up to the atrocity, traffic was pretty heavy."

"Every Jew hater in this town," Avi making with the aggrieved tone, "is blaming 9/11 on Mossad. Even a story going around about Jews who worked down at the Trade Center all calling in sick that day, warned away by Mossad through their"—air quotes—secret network.'"

"The Jews dancing on the roof of that van over in Jersey," Brooke fuming, "watching it all collapse, don't forget that one."

Later as Maxine prepares to leave, Ernie catches up with her in the foyer. "Ever call that FBI guy?"

"I did, and you know what? He thinks Avram really is Mossad, all right? On station, tapping his foot to a klezmer beat only he can hear, waiting to be activated."

"Evil Jewish conspiracy."

"Except you'll notice Avi never talks about what he was doing over in Israel, neither of them do, any more than what he's doing here now for hashslingrz. The one thing I can guarantee you is, is it'll be well compensated, wait and see, he'll give you guys a Mercedes for your anniversary."

"A Nazi car? Good, so I'll sell it . . ."

30

f you read nothing but the Newspaper of Record, you might believe that New York City, like the nation, united in sorrow and shock, has risen to the challenge of global jihadism, joining a righteous crusade Bush's people are now calling the War on Terror. If you go to other sources—the Internet, for example—you might get a different picture. Out in the vast undefined anarchism of cyberspace, among the billions of self-resonant fantasies, dark possibilities are beginning to emerge.

The plume of smoke and finely divided structural and human debris has been blowing southwest, toward Bayonne and Staten Island, but you can smell it all the way uptown. A bitter chemical smell of death and burning that no one in memory has ever in this city smelled before and which lingers for weeks. Though everybody south of 14th Street has been directly touched one way or another, for much of the city the experience has come to them mediated, mostly by television—the farther uptown, the more secondhand the moment, stories from family members commuting to work, friends, friends of friends, phone conversations, hearsay, folklore, as forces in whose interests it compellingly lies to seize control of the narrative as quickly as possible come into play and dependable history shrinks to a dismal perimeter centered on

"Ground Zero," a Cold War term taken from the scenarios of nuclear war so popular in the early sixties. This was nowhere near a Soviet nuclear strike on downtown Manhattan, yet those who repeat "Ground Zero" over and over do so without shame or concern for etymology. The purpose is to get people cranked up in a certain way. Cranked up, scared, and helpless.

For a couple of days, the West Side Highway falls silent. People between Riverside and West End miss the ambient racket and don't get to sleep so easily. On Broadway meanwhile it's different. Flatbeds carrying hydraulic cranes and track loaders and other heavy equipment go thundering downtown in convoys day and night. Fighter planes roar overhead, helicopters hang battering the air for hours close above the rooftops, sirens are constant 24/7. Every firehouse in the city lost somebody on 11 September, and every day people in the neighborhoods leave flowers and home-cooked meals out in front of each one. Corporate ex-tenants of the Trade Center hold elaborate memorial services for those who didn't make it out in time, featuring bagpipers and Marine honor guards. Child choirs from churches and schools around town are booked weeks in advance for solemn performances at "Ground Zero," with "America the Beautiful" and "Amazing Grace" being musical boilerplate at these events. The atrocity site, which one would have expected to become sacred or at least inspire a little respect, swiftly becomes occasion instead for open-ended sagas of wheeling and dealing, bickering and badmouthing over its future as real estate, all dutifully celebrated as "news" in the Newspaper of Record. Some notice a strange underground rumbling from the direction of Woodlawn Cemetery in the Bronx, which is eventually identified as Robert Moses spinning in his grave.

After maybe a day and a half of stunned suspension, the usual ethnic toxicities, fierce as ever, have resumed. Hey, it's New York. American flags appear everywhere. In apartment-building lobbies and up in apartment windows, on rooftops, in storefronts and corner groceries, in eateries, on delivery trucks and hot-dog stands, on motorcycles and bikes, on cabs driven by members of the Muslim faith, who between shifts are taking courses in Spanish as a Second Language with a view to posing as a slightly less disrespected minority, though whenever Latino people try putting out some variation like the Puerto Rican flag, they are reflexively cursed and denounced as enemies of America.

That terrible morning, so it was later alleged, for a radius of many blocks surrounding the towers, every pushcart disappeared, as if the population of pushcart owners, at that time believed to be most of them Muslim, had been warned to keep away. Through some network. Some evil secret rugrider network possibly in place for years. The pushcarts stayed away, and so the morning began that much less comfortably, obliging folks to go in to work without their customary coffees, danishes, donuts, bottles of water, so many bleak appoggiaturas for what was about to happen.

Beliefs like this take hold of the civic imagination. Corner newsagents are raided and Islamic-looking suspects hauled away by the busload. Sizable Mobile Police Command Centers appear at various flashpoints, especially over on the East Side, wherever, for example, a high-income synagogue and some Arab embassy happen to occupy the same block, and eventually these installations grow not so mobile, becoming with time a permanent part of the cityscape, all but welded to the pavement. Likewise, ships with no visible flags, pretending to be cargo vessels, though with more antennas on them than booms, appear out in the Hudson, drop the hook, and become, effectively, private islands belonging to unnamed security agencies and surrounded by stay-away zones. Roadblocks keep appearing and disappearing along the avenues leading to and away from the major bridges and tunnels. Young Guardsfolk in clean new camo fatigues and carrying weapons and ammunition clips are patrolling Penn Station and Grand Central and the Port of Authority. Public holidays and anniversaries become occasions for anxiety.

Igor on the answering machine at home. Maxine picks up. "Maxi! Reg's DVD—you got copy there?"

"Someplace." She puts him on speaker, finds the disc, pops it into the machine.

She hears a bottle clink against a glass. Kind of early in the day. *"Za shastye."* Followed by a rhythmic wood thumping, as of a head against a table. *"Pizdets*! New Jersey vodka, 160 proof, keep away from open flame!"

"Um, Igor, you wanted to—"

"Oh. Real cute Stinger footage, thank you, takes me back. You know there was more."

"Besides the scene on the roof?"

"Hidden track."

No, she didn't know that. March didn't either.

It's raw footage from Reg's Unnamed Hashslingrz Project, nerds staring at screens, as expected, plus an officescape of cubicles, lab and recreational spaces, including a full-size indoor half court inside whose chain-link fencing white and Asian yups, all flagrant elbows and missed jump shots, run around authentically distressed city asphalt screaming inner-city insults.

What she's still been only half expecting is the shot where Reg walks in the wrong door and we see young men of Arab background, intensely breadboarding together something electronic.

"You know what that is, Igor?"

"Vircator," he informs her. "Virtual-cathode oscillator."

"What's it for? It's a weapon? It makes an explosion?"

"Electromagnetic, invisible. Gives you big pulse of energy when you want to disable other guy's electronics. Fries computers, fries radio links, fries television, anything in range."

"Broiled is healthier. Listen," she takes a chance, "you ever used one of these, Igor? In the field?"

"After my time. Bought a few since, maybe. Sold a few."

"There's a market?"

"Very hot area of military procurement right now. Many forces worldwide are deploying short-range vircators already, research is funded big time."

"These guys in the picture here—Reg said he thought they were Arab."

"No surprise, most of tech articles on pulse weapons are in Arabic. For really dangerous field-testing, of course, you must look at Russia."

"Russian vircators, they're what, highly thought of?"

"Why? You want one? Talk to padonki, they work on commission, I take a percent of that."

"Only wondering why, if these guys are as well funded as Arabs are thought to be, they have to build their own."

"I looked at it frame by frame, and they aren't building unit from scratch, they are modifying existing hardware, possibly Estonian knock-off they bought someplace?"

So maybe only busywork without an end product here, nerds in a room, but suppose it's one more thing to worry about, now. Would somebody really try to set off a citywide electromagnetic pulse in the middle of New York, or D.C., or is this device on the screen meant for transshipment somewhere else in the world? And what kind of a piece of the deal could Ice be duked in for?

There's nothing else on the disc. Leaving everybody up against an even larger question about to lift its trunk and start in with the bellowing. "OK. Igor. Tell me. You think there might be some connection with . . . ?"

"Ah, God, Maxi, I hope not." Self-administering another shot of Jersey vodka.

"What, then?"

"I'll think about it. You think about it. Maybe we won't like what we come up with."

ONE NIGHT, without any buzz on the intercom, there's a tentative knock at the door. Through the wide-angle peephole, Maxine observes a trembling young person with a fragile head sporting a buzz cut.

"Hi, Maxi."

"Driscoll. Your hair. What happened to Jennifer Aniston?" Expecting yet another 11 September story about frivolities of youth, newfound seriousness. Instead, "The maintenance was more than I could afford. I figure a Rachel wig's only $29.95, and you can't tell it from the real thing. Here, I'll show you." She shrugs out of her backpack, which Maxine notices now does seem to run to Himalayan-expedition scale, roots through it, finds the wig, puts it on, takes it off. A couple of times.

"Let me guess why you're here." It's been happening all over the neighborhood. Refugees, prevented from entering their apartments in Lower Manhattan, whether fancy-schmancy or modest, have been showing up at the doors of friends farther uptown, accompanied by wives, kids, sometimes nannies, drivers, and cooks also, having after exhaustive research and cost-benefit analysis concluded that this is the best refuge currently available to them and their entourage. "Next week who knows, right? We'll take it one week at a time." "Day at a time'd be better." Yupper West Side folks in their greatness of heart have been taking these real-estate casualties in, what choice do they have, and sometimes fast friendships grow even deeper and sometimes are destroyed forever . . .

"No problem," is what Maxine tells Driscoll now, "you can have the spare room," which happens to be available, Horst shortly after 11 September having shifted his sleeping arrangements into Maxine's room, to the inconvenience of neither and to what, if in fact she ever went into it with anybody, would be the surprise of very few. On the other hand, whose business is it? It's still too much for her to get her own head around, how much she's missed him. How about what they call "marital relations," is there any fucking going on? You bet, and what's it to you? Music track? Frank Sinatra, if you really need to know. The most poignant B-flat in all lounge music occurs in Cahn & Styne's song "Time After Time," beginning the phrase "in the evening when the day is through," and never more effectively than when Sinatra reaches after it on vinyl that happens to be in the household record library. At moments like this, Horst is helpless, and Maxine long ago has learned to seize the moment. Allowing Horst to think it's his idea, of course.

Driscoll is followed within two hours by Eric, staggering underneath an even more sizable backpack, evicted without notice by a landlord for whom the civic tragedy has come as a convenient excuse to get Eric and the other tenants out so he can convert to co-ops and pocket some public money also.

"Um, yeah, there's room if you don't mind sharing. Driscoll, Eric, you met at that party, down at Tworkeffx, remember, work it out, don't fight . . ." She goes off muttering to herself.

"Hi." Driscoll thinks about tossing her hair, thinks twice.

"Hi." They soon discover a number of interests in common, including the music of Sarcófago, all of whose CDs are present among Eric's effects, as well as Norwegian Black Metal artists such as Burzum and Mayhem, soon established as sound-track accompaniment of choice for spare-room activities which begin that evening within about ten minutes of Eric observing Driscoll in a T-shirt with the Ambien logo on it. "Ambien, awesome! You got any?" Does she. Seems they share a partiality to this recreational sleeping pill, which if you can force yourself to stay awake will produce acidlike hallucinations, not to mention a dramatic increase in libido, so that soon they are fucking like the teenagers they technically were only a short time back, while yet another side effect is memory loss, so that neither remembers what went on exactly till the next time it happens, whereupon it is like first love all over again.

On meeting Ziggy and Otis, the frolicking twosome exclaim, more or less in unison, "You guys are real?"—among widely reported Ambien hallucinations being numbers of small people busy running around doing a variety of household tasks. The boys, though fascinated, as city kids know how to maintain a perimeter. As for Horst, if he even remembers Eric from the Geeks' Cotillion, it's been swept downstream by recent events, and in any case the Eric-Driscoll hookup helps with any standard Horstian reactions of insane jealousy. His reasonably serene domestic setup being invaded by forces loyal to drugs, sex, rock-and-roll doesn't seem to register as any threat. So, figures Maxine, we'll all be on top of each other for a while, other people have it worse.

Love, while in bloom for some, fades for others. Heidi shows up one day beneath deep clouds of an all-too-familiar disgruntlement.

"Oh no," cries Maxine.

Heidi shakes her head, then nods. "Dating cops is like so over. Every chick in this town regardless of IQ is suddenly a helpless little airhead who wants to be taken care of by some big stwong first wesponder. Trendy? Twendy? Meh. Totally without clue's more like it."

Ignoring the urge to inquire if Carmine, unable to resist the attention, has perhaps also been running around, "What happened exactly? Or no, not exactly."

"Carmine's been reading the papers, he's bought into the whole story. Thinks he's a hero now."

"He's not a hero?"

"He's a precinct detective. A second or third responder. In the office most of the time. Same job he was always on, same petty thieves, drug dealers, domestic abusers. But now Carmine thinks he's out on the front line of the War Against Terror and I'm not being respectful enough."

"When were you ever? He didn't know that?"

"He appreciated attitude in a woman. He said. I thought. But since the attack . . ."

"Yeah, you can't help noticing some attitude escalation." New York cops have always been arrogant, but lately they've been parking routinely on the sidewalk, yelling at civilians for no reason, every time a kid tries to jump a turnstile, subway service gets suspended and police vehicles of every description, surface and airborne, converge and linger. Fairway has started selling coffee blends named after different police precincts. Bakeries who supply coffee shops have invented a giant "Hero" jelly donut in the shape of the well-known sandwich of the same name, for when patrol cars show up.

Heidi has been working on an article for the *Journal of Memespace*

Cartography she's calling "Heteronormative Rising Star, Homophobic Dark Companion," which argues that irony, assumed to be a key element of urban gay humor and popular through the nineties, has now become another collateral casualty of 11 September because somehow it did not keep the tragedy from happening. "As if somehow irony," she recaps for Maxine, "as practiced by a giggling mincing fifth column, actually brought on the events of 11 September, by keeping the country insufficiently serious—weakening its grip on 'reality.' So all kinds of make-believe—forget the delusional state the country's in already—must suffer as well. Everything has to be literal now."

"Yeah, the kids are even getting it at school." Ms. Cheung, an English teacher who if Kugelblitz were a town would be the neighborhood scold, has announced that there shall be no more fictional reading assignments. Otis is terrified, Ziggy less so. Maxine will walk in on them watching *Rugrats* or reruns of *Rocko's Modern Life,* and they holler by reflex, "Don't tell Ms. Cheung!"

"You notice," Heidi continues, "how 'reality' programming is suddenly all over the cable, like dog shit? Of course, it's so producers shouldn't have to pay real actors scale. But wait! There's more! Somebody needs this nation of starers believing they're all wised up at last, hardened and hip to the human condition, freed from the fictions that led them so astray, as if paying attention to made-up lives was some form of *evil drug abuse* that the collapse of the towers cured by scaring everybody straight again. What's that going on in the other room, by the way?"

"Couple kids I do some business with off and on. Used to live downtown. Another of these relo stories."

"Thought it might be Horst watching porn on the Internet."

Once Maxine would have zinged back, "He was only driven to do that while he was seeing you," but feels reluctant these days to include Horst in the back-and-forth she and Heidi like to get into, because of . . . what, it can't be some kind of loyalty to Horst, can it? "He's over in Queens today, that's where they evacuated the commodity exchange to."

"Thought he'd be long gone by now. Back out there someplace," waving vaguely trans-Hudson. "Everything all right otherwise?"

"What?"

"You know, in terms of, oh, Rocky Slagiatt?"

"Copacetic, far 's I know, why?"

"I guess ol' Rocky's a lot chirpier these days, huh?"

"How would I know?"

"With the FBI shifting agents off of Mafia duty and over to antiterrorism, I mean."

"So 11 September turns out to be a mitzvah for the mob, Heidi."

"I didn't mean that. The day was a terrible tragedy. But it isn't the whole story. Can't you feel it, how everybody's regressing? 11 September infantilized this country. It had a chance to grow up, instead it chose to default back to childhood. I'm in the street yesterday, behind me are a couple of high-school girls having one of these teenage conversations, 'So I was like, "Oh, my God?" and he's like, "I didn't say I wasn't see-een her?"' and when I finally turn to look at them, here are these two women my own age. Older! *your* age, who should know better, really. Like trapped in a fuckin time warp or something."

Oddly enough, Maxine's just had something like it happen around the corner on Amsterdam. Every schoolday morning on the way to Kugelblitz, she's been noticing the same three kids waiting on the corner for a school bus, Horace Mann or one of them, and maybe the other morning there was some fog, maybe the fog was inside her, some incompletely dissipated dream, but what she saw this time, standing in exactly the same spot, was three middle-aged men, gray-haired, less youthfully turned out, and yet she knew, shivering a little, that these were the *same kids*, the same faces, only forty, fifty years older. Worse, they were looking at her with a queer knowledgeable intensity, focusing personally on her, sinister in the dimmed morning air. She checked the street. Cars were no more advanced in design, nothing beyond the usual police and military traffic was passing or hovering overhead, the low-rise holdouts hadn't been replaced with anything taller, so it still had to be "the present," didn't it? Something, then, must've happened to these kids. But next morning all was back to "normal." The kids as usual paying no attention to her.

What, then, the fuck, is going on?

31

When she goes to Shawn with this, she finds her guru, in his own way, freaking out also. "You remember those twin statues of the Buddha that I told you about? Carved out of a mountain in Afghanistan, that got dynamited by the Taliban back in the spring? Notice anything familiar?"

"Twin Buddhas, twin towers, interesting coincidence, so what."

"The Trade Center towers were religious too. They stood for what this country worships above everything else, the market, always the holy fuckin market."

"A religious beef, you're saying?"

"It's not a religion? These are people who believe the Invisible Hand of the Market runs everything. They fight holy wars against competing religions like Marxism. Against all evidence that the world is finite, this blind faith that resources will never run out, profits will go on increasing forever, just like the world's population—more cheap labor, more addicted consumers."

"You sound like March Kelleher."

"Yeah, or," that trademark sub-smirk, "maybe she sounds like me."

"Uh-huh, listen, Shawn . . ." Maxine tells him about the kids on the corner and her time-warp theory.

"Is that like the zombies you said you were seeing?"

"One person, Shawn, somebody I know, maybe dead maybe not, enough with the zombies already."

Hmm yes, but now another, you'd have to say insane, suspicion has begun to bloom in all the California sunshine around here, which is, suppose these "kids" are really operatives, time troopers from the Montauk Project, abducted long ago into an unthinkable servitude, grown solemn and gray through years of soldiering, currently assigned to Maxine expressly, for reasons never to be made clear to her. Possibly in strange cahoots also, and why not, with Gabriel Ice's own private gang of co-opted script kiddies . . . aahhh! Talk about paranoid jitters!

"OK", soothingly, "like, total disclosure? It's been happenin to me too? I'm seeing people in the street who are supposed to be dead, even sometimes people I know were in the towers when they went down, who can't be here but they're here."

They gaze at each other for a while, down here on the barroom floor of history, feeling sucker-punched, no clear way to get up and on with a day which is suddenly full of holes—family, friends, friends of friends, phone numbers on the Rolodex, just not there anymore . . . the bleak feeling, some mornings, that the country itself may not be there anymore, but being silently replaced screen by screen with something else, some surprise package, by those who've kept their wits about them and their clicking thumbs ready.

"I'm sorry, Shawn. What do you think it could be?"

"Besides how much I miss them, beats me. Is it just this miserable fucking city, too many faces, making us crazy? Are we seeing some wholesale return of the dead?"

"You'd prefer retail?"

"Do you remember that piece of footage on the local news, just as the first tower comes down, woman runs in off the street into a store, just gets the door closed behind her, and here comes this terrible black billowing, ash, debris, sweeping through the streets, gale force past the window . . . that was the moment, Maxi. Not when 'everything changed.' When everything was revealed. No grand Zen illumination, but a rush of blackness and death. Showing us exactly what we've become, what we've been all the time."

"And what we've always been is . . . ?"

"Is living on borrowed time. Getting away cheap. Never caring about who's paying for it, who's starving somewhere else all jammed together so we can have cheap food, a house, a yard in the burbs . . . planetwide, more every day, the payback keeps gathering. And meantime the only help we get from the media is boo hoo the innocent dead. Boo fuckin hoo. You know what? All the dead are innocent. There's no uninnocent dead."

After a while, "You're not going to explain that, or . . ."

"Course not, it's a koan."

THAT EVENING UNACCUSTOMED LAUGHTER from the bedroom. Horst is horizontal front of the tube, helplessly, for Horst, amused. For some reason he's watching NBC instead of the BioPiX channel. A diffident long-haired person in amber sunglasses is doing stand-up on some late-night show.

A month after the worst tragedy in everybody's lifetime and Horst is laughing his ass off. "What is it Horst, delayed reaction you're alive?"

"I'm happy to be alive, but this Mitch Hedberg guy is funny, too."

Not a hell of a lot of occasions she's seen Horst really laugh. Last time must've been Keenan and Kel's "I dropped the screw in the tuna" episode four or five years ago. Sometimes he'll chuckle at something, but rarely. Whenever somebody asks how come everybody's laughing at something and he isn't, Horst explains his belief that laughter is sacred, a momentary noodge from some power out in the universe, only cheapened and trivialized by laugh tracks. He has a low tolerance for unmotivated and mirthless laughter in general. "For many people, especially in New York, laughing is a way of being loud without having to say anything." So what's he still doing in town, by the way?

GOING IN TO WORK one morning, she runs into Justin. It seems accidental, but there may be no accidents anymore, the Patriot Act may have outlawed them along with everything else. "Mind if we talk?"

"Come on up."

Justin slouches into a chair in Maxine's office. "It's about DeepArcher? Remember back just before the attack on the Trade Center, Vyrva must've told you, everything got a little weird with the random numbers we were using?"

"Dimly, dimly. Did that ever get back to normal?"

"Did anything?"

"Horst says the stock market went crazy too. Just before."

"You heard of the Global Consciousness Project?"

"Some . . . California thing."

"Princeton, as a matter of fact. These folks maintain a network of thirty to forty random-event generators all around the world, whose outputs all flow into the Princeton site 24/7 and get mixed together to produce this random-number string. First-rate source, exceptional purity. On the theory that if our minds really are all linked together somehow, any major global event, disaster, whatever, will show up in the numbers."

"You mean, somehow, make them less random."

"Right. Meantime, for DeepArcher to be untraceable, we happen to need a high-quality supply of random numbers. What we've done is create globally a set of virtual nodes on volunteer computers. Each node only exists long enough to receive and resend, and then it's gone—we use the random numbers to set up a switching pattern among the nodes. Soon as we found out about this Princeton source, Lucas and I were into the site, bootlegging the product. All goes well till the night of September 10th, when suddenly these numbers coming out of Princeton began

to depart from randomness, I mean really abruptly, drastically, no explanation. You can look it up, the graphs are posted on their Web site for
anybody to see, it's . . . I'd say scary if I knew what any of it meant. It
kept on that way through the 11th and a few days after. Then just as mysteriously everything went back to near-perfect random again."

"So . . ." and like why is he telling her this exactly, "whatever it was,
it's gone away?"

"Except that for those couple of days, DeepArcher was vulnerable.
We did our best with serial numbers off dollar bills, which do pretty
good as seeds for a low-tech pseudorandom-number generator, but still,
DeepArcher's defenses began to disintegrate, everything was more visible, easier to access. It's possible some people may have found their way
in then who shouldn't have. Soon as the GCP numbers got random
again, the way back out would've become invisible to any intruders.
They'd be caught inside the program. They could still be there."

"They can't just click on 'Quit'?"

"Not if they're busy trying to reverse-engineer their way to our
source code. Which is impossible, but still they can compromise a lot of
what's in there."

"Sounds like another reason to go open source."

"Lucas says the same thing. I wish I could just . . ." He looks so perplexed that Maxine against her better judgment sez, "Stop me if you've
heard this one. Guy's walking around holding a blazing-hot coal . . ."

THAT EVENING, first thing in the door, she notices something sure smells
good. Horst is cooking supper. Seems to be coquilles Saint-Jacques
and daube de boeuf provençal. Again. Of course, the Guilt Special. By a
strange invariance in the parameters of wedlock, Horst lately has been
turning, all but insufferably, into a homebody. The other night she came
in late, all the lights were off, wham, she's suddenly assaulted at ankle
level by a mechanical device, which turns out to be a robot vacuum
cleaner. "Trying to kill me here!"

"Thought you'd be pleased," sez Horst, "it's the Roomba Pro Elite, brand-new from the factory."

"With the spousal-attack feature."

"Actually, it won't be released till fall, got this one at an early-adopters preview sale. Wave of the future, honeybunch."

Irony-free. Unthinkable a year or two ago. Meantime it's Maxine's turn now to have these, hmm, undomestic urges. Which, for those to whom balanced books appeal, seems fair. Guilt? What's that?

Eric and Driscoll are in and out of the house together and separately and unpredictably, though they do respect school nights and an informal curfew of 11:00 P.M. Out any later than that and they make other sleeping arrangements, which everybody is cool with, besides relieving Maxine of some worry. The boys, in any case, like their father, continue to sleep so unperturbed that next to them the average sawmill inventory is insomniac.

One day Maxine finds Eric in the spare room with a 27-ounce spray bottle of Febreze, spritzing his dirty laundry, item by item. "There's a laundry room in the basement, Eric. We can lend you detergent."

He drops the T-shirt he's holding on to a pile of already-Febrezed laundry and remains pointing the bottle at his ear, as if about to shoot himself with it. "Does it come with Downy April Fresh Scent?" Diminishing returns. But he also has a worried look.

Angling an antenna, "Something else, Eric?"

"I was up all night with this again. Fuckin hashslingrz. Can't let it go."

"You want some coffee? I'm going to make some coffee."

Following her into the kitchen, "That hashslingerz money pipeline to the Emirates, remember? banks in Dubai and shit, I couldn't stop going back, over and over it, what if that was helping finance the attack on the Trade Center? then Ice isn't only just another dotcom douchebag, he's a traitor to his country."

"Somebody in Washington agrees with you." She gives Eric a quick recap of the dossier that Windust handed her, with his punk-rock cologne all over it.

"Yeah, how about this 'Wahhabi Transreligious Friendship,' they happen to mention them?"

"They think it's some kind of front for moving money into jihadist operating accounts."

"Even cuter than that. It's a front, all right, but it's really the CIA, pretending to be jihadist."

"Get outta here."

"Maybe it was the Ambien, maybe it was always there right in front of me and I just didn't see it, but somehow this time all the veils go droppin one by one, and there's Mata Hari herself. It's all been a way to get funds out to different anti-Islamic undergrounds in the region. In return Ice gets to keep a commission on everything moving through, plus some heavy-ass consultancy fees."

"Why, the man's a patriot."

"He's a greedy little shit," Eric's head now in a halo of Daffy Duck froth droplets, "eternity in a motel lounge in Houston Texas with a Andrew Lloyd Webber mix repeating forever on the stereo is too good for his sorry ass. Just totally trust me on one thing, Maxine. I'm gonna fuck him up."

"Sounds like an exploit in the wind."

"Maybe."

"One brush with Rikers isn't enough already, now you're planning denial-of-service attacks?"

"Way too good for Ice. If every company with an asshole in charge deserved a DOS hit? be nothing left of the tech sector. But here, let me share with you my latest invention, this is like a hors d'oeuvre."

He shows her on his laptop. Seems he has recently launched the Vomit Kurser, named in homage to the ill-regarded Comet Cursor of the nineties and developed in partnership with a *bruja* from one of his old neighborhoods. Via eye-catching but fake pop-up ads promising health, wealth, happiness &c, the Kurser will surreptitiously lay old-school curses on selected targets—click in once, your ass is grass. Somehow, as the Latina sorceress has explained to Eric, the Internet as it turns out exhibits a strange affinity for the dynamics of curses, especially when written in the more ancient languages predating HTML. Through the uncountable cross-motives of the cyberworld, the fates of unreflective click-happy users are altered for the worse—systems crash, data are lost, bank accounts are looted, all of which being computer-related you might expect, but then there are also the realworld inconveniences, such as zits, unfaithful spouses, intractable cases of Running Toilet, providing the more metaphysically inclined further evidence that the Internet is only a small part of a much vaster integrated continuum.

"This will bring down Ice's system? He's Jewish, he doesn't know from Santería, this sounds over toward the woowoo end of the spectrum even for you, Eric."

"You may chill, it's not the main event, only a trailer, meantime not only have I been corrupting his malloc(3), I've turned it out trickin in the street, years of therapy before it's straight again."

"Please just watch your ass, I think I saw the movie, it ends on a sort of vindictive note. Something in the tail credits about 'is currently serving a life sentence in the federal pen'?"

She hasn't seen this look on his face before. Scared but resolute also. "There's no Escape key here. No way back to Game Shark hex cheats and them high-spirited li'l overflow stunts, no more happy times, now the only way left for me to go is deeper."

Unhappy kid. She wants to touch him but is unsure of where. "Sounds like that could be tricky."

"All good. Do you have any idea how many large-cap bad guys there are on Ice's client list? I can at least show other hackers and crackers how to get into some useful places. Be a outlaw guru."

"And if some of those colleagues turn out to be already bent? and shop you to the feds?"

He shrugs. "So I'll have to be a little more careful than I was back in my script-kiddie days."

"Someday, Eric, they're going to have the time machine, we'll be able to book tickets online, we'll all get to go back, maybe more than once, and rewrite it all the way it should have gone, not hurt the ones we hurt, not make the choices we made. Forgive the loan, keep the lunch date. Of course, at first tickets'll be an arm and a leg, till the product-development costs get amortized . . ."

"Maybe there'll be a frequent-time-traveler program, where you get bonus *years*? I could pile up a lot of those."

"Please. You're too young to have that many regrets."

"Hey, I'm even feeling bad about us."

"Us, what."

"That night after we got back from Joie de Beavre."

"A warm memory, Eric. I don't think it's in the criminal code yet, foot-related infidelity? Nah."

"Did you ever tell Horst?"

"Somehow the moment has never been right. Or to put it another way, why? Have you mentioned it to Driscoll?"

"Nah, pretty sure I didn't . . ."

"'Pretty sure' you . . ." Realizing she's slipped her shoes off and has been rubbing her feet together. At least, you'd say, wistfully.

"Can I ask you something else?"

"Maybe . . ."

"You know, there really are these little tiny people who come out from under the radiator with . . . with little brooms, and dustpans, and—"

"Eric, no. I don't want to hear about it."

32

Next morning Reg Despard calls from over the western horizon. "Watching the Space Needle as we speak."

"What's it doing?"

"The Macarena. Are you OK? I would've called sooner, right after the towers, but I was on the road, and then when I got finally out here, I was house hunting and—"

"Just as well you got away in time."

"Came on the car radio, I thought about hooking a U-turn and heading back. Didn't, just kept going. Survivor's guilt here."

"Interstate hypnosis. Don't overthink it, Reg. You're out there now in Riot Grrrl country with the wholesome evergreen trees and charcoal briquettes pretending to be coffee and whatever, right? please. Release yourself."

"All I see is what's on the news, but it looks grim back there."

"Lot of grieving, everybody's still nervous, cops stopping anybody they want to, looking through backpacks—about what you'd expect. But in terms of attitude, life goes on, in the street nothing's too different. Did you find work yet?"

Hesitation. "I'm temping at Microsoft."

"Oof."

"Yeah, the dress code takes some getting used to, all the breathing apparatus and stormtrooper gear . . ."

"Seen your kids yet?"

"Trying not to push anything, but . . ."

"You're from New York, they're expecting pushy."

"Got invited over to dinner last night. Hubby did the cooking. Bouillabaisse, local ingredients. Some kind of Yakima Valley chenin blanc. Gracie still has that awesome-new-man-in-her-life glow, like I need to see that. But the girls . . . I can't tell you . . . They're quieter than I remember. Not sullen quiet, no scowls, no lower lips, once or twice they even smiled. Maybe even at me, couldn't be sure."

"Reg, I hope this works out."

"Listen. Maxine." Uh-oh. "This phone line we're on, is it—"

"If it ain't, we're all doomed. What."

"That DVD."

"Interesting footage. One or two shots you maybe could've used a spirit level . . ."

"I keep waking up at three A.M."

"It could've been anything, Reg."

"Those guys on the roof, those A-rabs in that closed room at hashslingrz. Training sessions. Had to be."

"If Gabriel Ice is playing a part in some large-scale secret operation, then . . . you're suggesting . . ."

"Even though the Stinger crew look like private-sector mercs, it would still have to be with encouragement from higher levels of U.S. government."

"Eric thinks so too. And March Kelleher, well, goes without saying. You're OK with her posting the video?"

"That was always the idea, I tried to spread around ten, twenty DVDs hopin somebody with the bandwidth would post one at least. Someday there'll be a Napster for videos, it'll be routine to post anything and share it with anybody."

"How could anybody make money doing that?" Maxine can't quite figure.

"There's always a way to monetize anything. Not my department. I'm happy enough with the exposure."

"Build up your traffic, hope that network effects kick in, yes, sounds like an all-too-familiar sad but true business plan."

"As long as the material gets out there. Long as somebody puts in some HTML that'll make it easy to repost."

"You really think Bush's people are behind this."

"You don't?"

"I'm just a fraud examiner. Bush, don't get me started. The Arab angle, I have these Jewish reflexes, so I have to work to avoid paranoia on that subject also."

"Hear ya. It's all good in the brotherhood, don't intend no disrespect to nobody, too busy workin on my new packaging, Reg 2.0, nonviolent, West Coast and stress free."

"Just step careful. Send me some footage sometime. Oh, and Reg?"

"Anything, my sister."

"Think I ought to short Microsoft?"

NEXT TIME MAXINE AND CORNELIA do lunch, they agree to meet down at Streetlight People. Maxine brings Rocky a Xerox of the hashslingrz file Windust gave her.

"Here, the latest on how hashslingrz is spending your money."

Rocky scans a page or two with a quizzical face. "Who generated this thing?"

"No-name agency down in D.C., obviously with some ax to grind, but I can't figure out what it is. Hiding behind some jive-ass think tank."

"Comes at a good time anyway, we've been looking at our exit options from hashslingrz, it's OK I show this to Spud and the board?"

"If they can follow it, sure, what are you guys thinking these days, recapitalize?"

"Probably, there's no IPO in the works, no M&A, they got plenty of government work, frankly it's just time to get out. The cash, naturally, but there's something else about them over there, like . . . can I say evil?"

"This is what, Mister Rogers's neighborhood? I assume you mean IBM- or Microsoft-type evil."

"You ever had eye contact with this guy? It's like he knows you know how bad it could be and he don' give a shit?"

"Thought it was only me."

"None of us know how complicated this is gonna get, who they're really workin for, but if even people in D.C. are gettin worried now," tapping the dossier, "it's cash-for-equity time."

"So I take it I'm off the case."

"But on my Rolodex forever."

"Spare her," Cornelia breezing in. "He's always telling me the same thing, don't listen."

"Git outta here, ya ditzy broads, I got woik ta do."

Owing to Cornelia's impression that Maxine somehow observes kosher eating guidelines, they end up at another "Jewish" deli, Mrs. Pincus's Chicken Soup Emporium. A chain, yet. Everybody seems to be from out of town. Fortunately, the appetites Maxine and Cornelia have brought with them are more for schmoozing than for authenticity-challenged gefilte fish.

Presently Cornelia, with the skill of an accomplished close-up card artist, has out of what seems a randomly shuffled deck of lunch conversation lightly brought them to the topic of families and the eccentrics to be found lurking therein.

"My policy," Maxine sez, "is don't get me started, all too soon we're back in the shtetl with some dark magic in progress."

"Oh, tell me. My family, well . . . 'Talk about dysfunctional!' pretty much sums it up. We've even got one in the CIA."

"One? I thought all you people worked for the CIA."

"Only Cousin Lloyd. Well, that I know of."

"He's allowed to talk about what he does?"

"Perhaps not. We're never sure. It's . . . it's Lloyd, you see."

"Y— Well, not exactly."

"You must understand these are Long Island Thrubwells, not at all to be confused with the Manhattan branch of the family, and though we have never embraced eugenics or anything of that sort, it is often difficult not to entertain some DNA-based explanation for what, after all, does present rather a pattern."

"High percentage of . . ."

"Idiots, basically, mm-hmm . . . Don't mistake my meaning, Cousin Lloyd was always an agreeable child, he and I got along well, at family gatherings none of the food he threw would actually ever strike me personally . . . But beyond mealtime assault, his true gift, one might say compulsion, was for tattling. He was always creeping about, observing the less supervised activities of his peers, taking detailed notes, and when these weren't convincing enough, I'm embarrassed to say, making things up."

"So, perfect CIA material."

"Ever so long on their wait list, till last year a position in the Inspector General's office fell vacant."

"And this is like Internal Affairs, he actually snitches on the CIA? that's not dangerous for him?"

"It's mostly inventory theft, they're forever stealing bullets to use in their own private weapons? that seems to be one of Cousin Lloyd's pet peeves."

"So he's working in 'D.C. now,' as Martha and the Vandellas might say. Does he ever do any moonlighting? Like, consultation?"

"I shouldn't wonder. Idiots have expenses, after all, the medications, the frequent blackmail payments and police bribes, the pointed hats, which of course have to be custom-fitted . . . but I do hope, Maxi, that you aren't in any sort of difficulty with the Agency?"

Why are disingenuousness alarms suddenly going off here? "Some agency, maybe not that one, but coming from down in that direction at least, yes indeed, and you know, come to think of it, suppose there was something I might like to talk over with your cousin . . ."

"Shall I ask him to get in touch?"

"Thanks, Cornelia, I owe you one . . . or, without having met Lloyd yet, say at least half of one."

"No, thank *you*, Maxi, this has all been so wonderful. So . . ." gesturing around Mrs. Pincus's as if at a loss for words.

Maxine, lips closed and eyes narrowed, one more than the other, smiles. "Ethnic."

COUSIN LLOYD, luckily not into the NYC dating scene, where haste like this would earn him instant rejection, calls Maxine early the next day. He sounds so nervous that Maxine decides to lull him with generic accounting-fraud talk. "Right now it's all converging on a think tank down there called TANGO? You've heard of them?"

"Oh. Very much the hot property in town right now. Quite popular with Double-U and his crowd."

"One of their people, an operative named Windust, is proving a little problematic, I can't seem to find anything about him, not even an official bio, he's password-protected to the max, firewalls behind firewalls, I don't have the resources to get past any of that." Little me. "And if it turns out he was involved in, oh, let's say . . . embezzling . . ."

"And, not wishing to presume . . . you two are . . . chums?" managing to surround the word with guttural slime.

"Hmm. Once again, whoever's listening, I am not numbered among Mr. Windust's fan base and know next to nothing about him, except he's some kind of Friedmanite hit man, working 24/7 to keep the world convenient for people perhaps much like yourself, Mr. Thrubwell."

"*Oh,* dear, no offense I hope . . . I will try to see what I can do from this end. Our databases—they're world-famous, you know. I'm cleared pretty much all the way to Eyes Only, it shouldn't be a bother."

"I so look forward."

Thanks to the thumb drive Marvin delivered, of course, Maxine has most of Windust's résumé already, so putting Lloyd on his case is not for informational purposes, especially . . . In fact, Maxine, why *are* you harassing the man? Some honorable obsession about nailing the likely murderer of Lester Traipse, or just feeling neglected, missing the old pantyhose ripper's curious notions about foreplay? Talk about ambivalent!

At least, if Lloyd is half the idiot his cousin Cornelia thinks he is, Windust should become aware of CIA interest in a fairly short time. No reason he shouldn't start watching his back like everybody else. Right now petty molestation is about all that's available to Maxine, down here in the small time, without anything you could call a moral sight line, no way to know how to compete at that elite level, that planetary pyramid scheme Windust's employers have always bet everything on, with its smoothly delivered myths of the limitless. No idea of how to step outside her own history of safe choices and dowse her way across the desert of this precarious hour, hoping to find what? some refuge, some American DeepArcher . . .

33

Maxine has a purseful of time-sensitive passwords from Vyrva, changed every fifteen minutes on average, for getting into Deep-Archer. She can't help noticing this time how different the place is. What was once a train depot is now a Jetsons-era spaceport with all wacky angles, jagged towers in the distance, lenticular enclosures up on stilts, saucer traffic coming and going up in the neon sky. Yuppified duty-free shops, some for offshore brands she doesn't recognize even the font they're written in. Advertising everywhere. On walls, on the clothing and skins of crowd extras, as pop-ups out of the Invisible and into your face. She wonders if— Sure enough, here they are, lurking around the entrance to a Starbucks, a pair of cyberflaneurs who turn out to be Eric's ad-business acquaintances Promoman and Sandwichgrrl.

"Nice place to hang out," sez Sandwichgrrl.

"Not to mention do business," adds Promoman. "Joint's jumpin. A lot of these folks who look like only virtual background? they are real users."

"Really. There's supposed to be all kinds of deep encryption."

"There's also the backdoor, you didn't know about that?"

"Since when?"

"Weeks . . . months?"

So that 11 September window of vulnerability Lucas and Justin were so worried about, for good reason apparently, has allowed not only unwelcome guests to sneak in but somebody—Gabriel Ice, the feds, fed sympathizers, other forces unknown who've had their eye on the site—to install a backdoor also. And easy as that, there goes the neighborhood. She clicks away, reaching at length a strange creepy nimbus like a follow spot in a club where you know you'll get sick before the evening ends, has a moment of doubt, ignores it, clicks on into the heart of the nauseous blear of light, and then everything for a while goes black, blacker than anything she's seen on a screen before.

When the picture returns, she seems to be traveling in a deepspace vehicle . . . there's a menu for choosing among views, and, switching briefly to an exterior shot, she discovers it's not a single vehicle but more like a convoy, not quite simply-connected, spaceships of different ages and sizes moving along through an extended forever . . . Heidi, if asked, would say she detected some *Battlestar Galactica* influence.

Inside Maxine finds corridors of glimmering space-age composite, long as boulevards, soaring interior distances, sculptured shadows, traffic through upwardly thickening twilight, pedestrians crossing bridges, airborne vehicles for passengers and for cargo busily glittering . . . Only code, she reminds herself. But who of all these faceless and uncredited could have written it and why?

Popping up in midair, a paging window appears, requesting her presence on the bridge, with a set of directions. Somebody must have seen her log in.

On the bridge she finds empty liquor bottles and used syringes. The captain's chair is a La-Z-Boy recliner of distant vintage, hideous beige and covered with cigarette burns. There are inexpensive posters of Denise Richards and Tia Carrere Scotch-taped to the bulkheads. Some sort of hip-hop mix is coming from hidden speakers, at the moment Nate Dogg and Warren G, doing the huge mid-nineties West Coast hit

"Regulate." Personnel come and go on various errands, but the pace is not what you'd call brisk.

"Welcome to the bridge, Ms. Loeffler." A loutish youth, unshaven, in cargo shorts and a stained *More Cowbell* T-shirt. There is a shift in the ambience. The music segues to the theme from Deus Ex, the lights dim, the space is tidied by invisible cyberelves.

"So where's everybody? the captain? the exec? The science officer?"

Raising one eyebrow and fingering the tops of his ears as if testing for pointiness, "Sorry, prime directive, No Fuckin Officers." Gesturing her over to the forward observation windows. "The grandeur of space, dig it. Zillions of stars, each one gets its own pixel."

"Awesome."

"Maybe, but it's code's all it is."

An antenna swivels. "Lucas, is that you?"

"Bus-tiiid!" The screen filling for a moment with psychedelic iTunes Visualizer patterns.

"So you're in here dealing with what, backdoor issues, I hear?"

"Um, not exactly."

"They tell me it's wide open these days."

"Downside of being proprietary, always guarantees a backdoor sooner or later,"

"And you're all right with this? How about Justin?"

"We're good, fact we were never comfortable with that old model anyway."

Old model. Which must mean . . . "Some big news, let me guess."

"Yep. We finally decided to go open source. Just sent the tarball out."

"Meaning . . . anybody . . . ?"

"Anybody with the patience to get through it, they want it, they got it. There's already a Linux translation on the way, which should bring the amateurs in in droves."

"So the big bucks . . ."

"No longer an option. Maybe never was. Justin and me'll have to keep on being working stiffs for a while."

She watches the unfolding flow of starscape, Kabbalistic vessels smashed at the Creation into all these bright drops of light, rushing out from the singular point that gave them birth, known elsewhere as the expanding universe . . . "What would happen if I started to click on some of these pixels here?"

"You could get lucky. It's nothin *we* wrote. There could be links to somewhere else. You could also spend your life dowsing the Void and never getting much of anywhere."

"And this ship—it isn't on the way to DeepArcher, is it?"

"More like out on an expedition. Exploring. When the earliest Vikings started moving into the northern oceans, there's one story about finding this huge fuckin opening at the top of the world, this deep whirlpool that'd take you down and in, like a black hole, no way to escape. These days you look at the surface Web, all that yakking, all the goods for sale, the spammers and spielers and idle fingers, all in the same desperate scramble they like to call an economy. Meantime, down here, sooner or later someplace deep, there has to be a horizon between coded and codeless. An abyss."

"That's what you're looking for?"

"Some of us are." Avatars do not do wistful, but Maxine catches something. "Others are trying to avoid it. Depends what you're into."

MAXINE CONTINUES TO WANDER corridors for a while, striking up conversations at random, whatever "random" means in here. She begins to pick up a chill sense that some of the newer passengers could be refugees from the event at the Trade Center. No direct evidence, maybe only because she has 11 September on her mind, but everywhere now she looks, she thinks she sees bereaved survivors, perps foreign and domestic, bagmen, middlemen, paramilitary, who may have participated in the day or are only claiming to've done so as part of some con game.

For those who may be genuine casualties, likenesses have been brought here by loved ones so they'll have an afterlife, their faces scanned in from family photos, . . . some no more expressive than emoticons, others exhibiting an inventory of feeling ranging from party-euphoric through camera-shy to abjectly gloomy, some static, some animated in GIF loops, cyclical as karma, pirouetting, waving, eating or drinking whatever it was they were holding at the wedding or bar mitzvah or night out when the shutter blinked.

Yet it's as if they want to engage—they get eye contact, smile, angle their heads inquisitively. "Yes, what was it?" or "Problem?" or "Not right now, OK?" If these are not the actual voices of the dead, if, as some believe, the dead can't speak, then the words are being put there for them by whoever posted their avatars, and what they appear to say is what the living want them to say. Some have started Weblogs. Others are busy writing code and adding it to the program files.

She stops at a corner café and has soon fallen into conversation with a woman—maybe a woman—on a mission to the edge of the known universe. "All these know-nothings coming in, putting in, it's as bad as the surface Web. They drive you deeper, into the deep unlighted. Beyond anyplace *they'd* be comfortable. And that's where the origin is. The way a powerful telescope will bring you further out in physical space, closer to the moment of the big bang, so here, going deeper, you approach the border country, the edge of the unnavigable, the region of no information."

"You're part of this project?"

"Only here to have a look. Find out how long I can stay just at the edge of the beginning before the Word, see how long I can gaze in till I get vertigo—lovesick, nauseous, whatever—and fall in."

"You have an e-mail address?" Maxine wants to know.

"Kind of you, but maybe I won't come back. Maybe one day you'd look in your in-box and I won't be there. Come on. Walk with me."

They reach a sort of observation platform, dangerously cantilevered out from the ship into high hard radiation, vacuum, lifelessness. "Look."

Whoever she is, she's not carrying a bow and arrows, her hair isn't long enough, but Maxine can see she's gazing downward at the same steep angle, the same space-rapt focus at infinity, as the figure on the DeepArcher splash page, gazing into a void incalculably fertile with invisible links. "There's a faint glow, after a while you notice it—some say it's the trace, like radiation from the big bang, of the memory, in nothingness, of having once been something . . ."

"You're—"

"The Archer? No. That one is silent."

BACK IN MEATSPACE, needing somehow to talk to somebody about the new, and soon she guesses unrecognizable, DeepArcher, Maxine calls Vyrva's mobile number. "I'm just headed down into the subway, I'll get back to you when I have reception again." Maxine is not an old hand at cell-phone shenanigans but knows nervous when she hears it. A half hour later Vyrva, allegedly just back from the East Side, shows up at the office in person dragging a heavy-gauge trash bag stuffed full of Beanie Babies. "Seasonal!" she cries, pulling out one by one little Hallowe'en bats, grinning jack-o'-lanterns in witch hats, ghost bears, bears in capes done up as Dracula, "Ghoulianne the Girl Ghost, see, with the little pumpkin, isn't she cute!"

Hmmm yes something slightly manic about Vyrva this morning, the East Side to be sure can have this Munchkinetic effect on people, but—retro-CFE circuits now fully kicked in—it occurs to Maxine that the Beanie Babies could have been a cover all the time, couldn't they, for activities less in the public interest . . .

Phatic how's Justin, how's Fiona, all fine thanks—a shifty flicker of the eyeballs here?— "The guys . . . I mean, we're all stressed lately, but . . ." Vyrva putting on a pair of lavender-lens wire-rims, five dollars on the street, any number of reasons why right now, "We came to New York, we all did, so innocent . . . Back in California it was fun, just write the code, go for the cool solution, the elegance, party when you can, but here, more and more it's like—"

"Growing up?" maybe a little too reflexive.

"OK, men are children, we all know that, but this is like watching them give in to some secret vice they don't know how to stop. They want to hang on to those old innocent kids, you can see it, it's this terrible disconnect, the childlike hope and the depravity of New York meatspace, it's becoming unbearable."

Dear Abby, I have this friend with a big problem . . .

"You mean, unbearable for you . . . somehow . . . emotionally."

"No," Vyrva with a rapid flash of eye contact, "for everybody, as in a-little-goes-a-long-way, pain-in-the-ass unbearable." Chirpy yet snarling delivery, all too familiar in Maxine's line of work. Maybe also an appeal for understanding, hopefully on the cheap. This is how they get when the audit hooks start pulling up evidence they thought they'd deep-sixed forever, when the tax man sits there across the desk with his office thermostats cranked all the way up, stone-faced, puffing on an IRS-issue stogie, waiting.

Careful to keep it subtext-free for the moment, "Maybe it's business that's getting to them?"

"No. Can't be pressure about the source code, not anymore, they're out from under all that now. You can't tell anybody, but they're going open source."

Pretending not to have heard the news already, "Giving it away? Have they looked at the tax situation?"

According to Vyrva, Justin and Lucas were out one evening at the brightly lit bar of some tourist motel way over in the West Fifties. Huge-screen TVs tuned to sports channels, fake trees, some of them twenty feet tall, long-haired blond waitresses, an old-school mahogany bar. A lot of convention traffic. The partners are drinking King Kongs, which are Crown Royal plus banana liqueur, and reviewing the room for familiar faces when they hear a voice to which time has been at best disrespectful going, "A Fernet-Branca, please, better make that a double, with a ginger-ale chaser?" and Lucas does a spit take with his drink. "It's him! That crazy motherfucker from Voorhees, Krueger! He's after us, he wants his money back!"

"You're being paranoid?" Justin hopes. They hide behind a plastic bromeliad and observe squintingly. The packaging is a little different these days, but it seems to be Ian Longspoon all right, last seen years ago just having spun out in the Sand Hill soapbox derby. Being approached now by a compact individual in Oakley M Frames and a neon avocado lounge suit. Justin and Lucas instantly recognize Gabriel Ice in some notion of deep disguise.

"What would Ice be meeting our old VC, on the sly, to talk about?" Lucas wonders.

"What would they have in common?"

"Us!" Both at once.

"We need to look at those cocktail napkins, and quick!" They happen to know the motel security guy here and are presently back in his office scrutinizing a bank of CCTV displays. Zooming down on the Ice / Longspoon table, they can make out strange soggy diagrams full of arrows, boxes, exclamation points plus what sort of look like giant letter J's, not to mention L's . . .

"You think?"

"It could stand for anything, couldn't it?"

"Wait, I'm trying to think . . ." Each picking it up in turn, tossing it back and forth to be reamplified, till before long it's totally paranoid panic and their security friend, grown grumpy, is showing them the back way out.

"What the boys concluded," Vyrva summarizes, "is that Ice was trying to get Voorhees, Krueger to invoke protective covenants, take the business away, and then sell off the assets—the DeepArcher source code, basically—to Ice."

"Fuck it," Justin later in the night, with unexpected bitterness, "he wants it, let him have it."

"Ain't like you, bro, what'll happen next time we need to get lost?"

"I won't." Justin sounding a little melancholy about it.

"Maybe I will," Lucas declares.

"We can invent someplace else."

"Justin, what is this town doing to our heads, man, we never used to be like this."

"I don't think it's any better back in California anymore. Just as corrupt, we've been up and down the same streets together, you know where it all leads to, there or here."

Vyrva, though technically a shiksa, let them go on, drifting in and out in a motherly way, offering snacks and keeping her annoyance to herself. Now, to Maxine, "Talk about lost. Sometimes . . ."

Here it comes, the fraudster's lament. Maxine could run workshops in Conquering Eyeroll. "And . . ."

"And if they're lost, then I think," barely audible, "it could be my fault."

In comes Daytona with a sack full of Danishes and a plastic coffee carafe. "Yo Vyrva, surf's up, baby!"

Vyrva is enough of a sport to stand and bump butts with Daytona and contribute eight bars of backup on the seldom-heard oldie "Soul Gidget" before Daytona, giving her a look, remarks, "Should be singin 'A Whiter Shade of Pale,' you lookin a little anorexic, girl, need some them *po'k chops*! Collard greens!"

"Fried peach pies," Vyrva wan but game.

"What I'm talk'n about," waving herself back out the door. *"Hold that mayo!"*

"Vyrva—"

"No. It's OK. I mean it's not OK, oh, Maxi . . . I've been going through such guilt?"

"If you're not Jewish, you have to have a license, cause we hold the patent, see."

Shaking her head, "What should I do, I'm like so scared now, I'm in so deep?"

"How about Lucas, how deep is he?"

"Lucas? No? Not Lucas?" Pissed off that Maxine isn't getting it.

"Uh-oh. We're talking about somebody else? Who?"

"Please . . . I really thought I could help. It was supposed to be for Fiona, for Justin, for all of us. He said the guys could write their own ticket."

"Somebody," as dinosaur-size scales at long last fall clattering from Maxine's eyes, "somebody who wanted to acquire the DeepArcher source code, assumed that dating the wife of one of the partners would give him a foot in the door, am I following this so far?"

"Maxi, you've got to believe—"

"No, that was the '69 Mets, it'll be on your Big Apple citizenship exam, and meantime who now, I wonder, who of all the dozens of suits and suitors, would be enough of a total shit to try something like that, wait, wait, it's right here at the edge of my brain . . ."

"I might have told you, but you hate him so much . . ."

"Everybody hates Gabriel Ice, so I guess that means you haven't told anybody."

"And he's such a vengeful little prick, if I tried to call things off, he'd tell Justin all about it, destroy my marriage, my family . . . I'd lose Fiona, everything—"

"There, there, don't dwell, that's worst-case. Could play out any number of ways. How long's it been going on for?"

"Since Las Vegas last summer. We even got in a quickie on September 11th, which makes it that much worse . . ."

Maxine unable not to squint a little, "I hope you're not saying you caused that somehow? That would be really crazy, Vyrva."

"Same kind of carelessness. Isn't it?"

"Same as what? Is this the listen-up-all-you-slackers speech? American neglect of family values brings al-Qaeda in on the airplanes and takes the Trade Center down?"

"They saw how we are, what we've become. How soft, how neglectful. Self-indulgent. They figured us for an easy target, and they were right."

"Somehow I don't see the cause and effect, but maybe it's just me."

"I'm an adulteress!" Vyrva wails quietly.

"Ah, come on. Adolescentress, maybe."

Yet who can help, in these situations, wanting to hear a detail or two? Ice's cozy bachelor pad down in Tribeca, for example, a bathroom running to about the square footage of a pro basketball court, featuring a wide collection of tampons of every make, size, and absorbency, bottles of shampoo and conditioner whose labels you can't read a word of because they're imported from so far away, hair equipment from bobby pins to an enormous retro salon dryer you not only sit under but apparently actually have to climb inside, plus a condom selection that makes the checkout at Duane Reade look like a machine in a gas-station men's room.

"Thing is," after some nose blowing, "the sex is always so great."

"A sensitive, considerate lover."

"Fuck no, he's a son of a bitch. Did you ever try anal?"

Does Maxine really want to hear about this?

Does Delman's sell shoes?

"It figures," encouragingly. "His specialty, I bet?"

34

Hallowe'en arrives. Below 14th Street this has become over the years a major city festival, with a parade whose TV coverage rivals that of Macy's on Thanksgiving. Up on the Yupper West Side activities tend more toward the scale of a block party, 69th cordoned off, areaways converted into haunted houses, street entertainment and food pitches, bigger crowds every year, which is usually where Maxine takes the boys trick-or-treating, finishing up along 79th and sometimes 86th, working the lobbies of the different apartment buildings. But this year, it is rumored, post-9/11 jitters may have curtailed or even canceled some of these street activities, despite the mayor's face all over the local channels, looking strangely like the rubber mask of it currently appearing in seasonal pop-up stores, talking tough as ever, recommending that New Yorkers stand up to terror by celebrating Hallowe'en as usual.

"Jagdeep's folks are having this Hallowe'en party," it occurs to Ziggy, what you'd call disingenuously.

This is the kid in Ziggy's class who was writing code when he was four, Maxine recalls, and also happens to live in The Deseret. "How appropriate. The whole place is a haunted house."

"Something wrong with The Deseret, Mom?" Otis wide-eyed and so in cahoots.

"Everything," Maxine replies.

"Aside from that, though," Zig serenely.

"You guys'd be trick-or-treating strictly inside the building?"

"No need to go anyplace else, Hallowe'en there is legendary. Every apartment gets done up in a different horror theme."

"And . . . this is nothing to do with Jagdeep's sister. With the several years' premature, uh . . ."

"Rack," Otis suggests, being then obliged to dodge a brotherly krav maga sucker punch. "You won't see her anyway, Zig, she'll be party-ing," running off, Ziggy in pursuit, "down in the Village, she only dates NYU guys—"

Horst with a straight face not unmodulated by a shit-eating grin, "Series'll be on tonight, El Duque's starting, maybe against Curt Schil-ling, we could stay in and watch the game . . ."

"Buy me some peanuts and Cracker Jack?"

Otis has decided he'll go as Vegeta, his hair radically gelled up tonight into spikes, his silver-and-blue outfit obtained from some strange Asian site, fulfilled and delivered almost before he clicked "Add to Cart." Ziggy's going as the Empire State Building, with a stuffed toy ape at-tached about neck-high. Vyrva and Justin agree to be chaperones and will meet them at The Deseret.

Eric and Driscoll are headed down to the Village parade, got up re-spectively as a NAND gate ("I say yes to everything") and Aki Ross, from the *Final Fantasy* movie, "The haircut of everybody's dreams, sixty thou-sand strands, each one animated separately, serious bandwidth, though this wig here," Driscoll headshaking a short demo, "has to go under the heading of Desperate Tie-ins."

"No more Rachel, huh?"

"Moving on."

Heidi does a fast drop-by, done up in a tropical-weight beige dress, short tousled darkish wig, glasses with oversize wire rims, and a strange plastic perhaps glow-in-the-dark lei hanging around her neck. "You look dimly familiar," Maxine greets her, "you would be . . . ?"

"Margaret Mead," Heidi replies. "Taking my anthro plunge into the urban primitive tonight, babe, it's all out there and I'm totally immersing in it. Dig what I found down on Canal Street."

"Open up your hand, I can't see it, what is it?"

"Digital camcorder, usually you can only find these in Japan. Hours of battery time, and I'm bringing spares, so I can record all night."

"Yet you seem anxious."

"Who wouldn't be, it's every pop impulse in history, concentrated into one night a year, what if I don't know which way to point the lens, what if I miss something really crucial?"

"Listen to my voice," something they used to get into as girls, "you are not becoming hysterical, chill, there's a good princess."

"Oh, Lady Maxipad, thanks ever so much, you're so practical . . ."

"Yes and I just went to the cash machine, so I'm also good for bail money, if that should come up."

As evening falls, Maxine and Horst take the biggest wastebasket in the house and fill it with fun-size candies of different brands, including Swedish Fish, PayDays, and Goldenberg's Peanut Chews, set it outside in the hall, hang a Do Not Disturb sign on the doorknob, and retire to the bedroom, allowing Hallowe'en to develop as it will, which out in the streets of the Upper West Side means into a pseudopod of exotic Greenwich Village, after having had to settle the rest of the year for being a vague sort of uptown Dubuque.

Indoors, the evening gets you'd say festive, with Maxine riding Horst for the better part of an hour, not that it's anybody's business of course, and coming a number of times, at last fiercely in sync with Horst, not long after which, owing to some extrasensory cue from the television, whose mute feature has been engaged, they surface from their post-orgy daze in time to witness Derek Jeter's clutch tenth-inning homer and another trademark Yankee win. "Yes!" Horst beginning to scream in delighted disbelief. "And it better be Keanu Reeves in the biopic!"

"Uh, huh. You hate everything about New York," Maxine reminds him.

"Oh. Well I've driven through Arizona, nothin against Arizona, but I did have a little money on the Yanks, judgment call, really . . ." About to drift off into directionless cozy talk here . . .

"Really"? Maybe not, Horst. "Listen, being it's a school night? I think I'm gonna just zip down the street and see how everybody's doing."

"Well my darlin, can't say it wasn't a blast, shoat but sweet as they say around the pigpen, maybe I'll just catch some highlights, then."

From Horst, she is aware, this amounts to a declaration of love. But something is now focusing her out of the house, on to The Deseret, and what's likely to be a peculiar vertical creepfest over there.

A full moon still a little lopsided and not yet at its zenith, and her girlhood nemesis, doorman Patrick McTiernan, on duty at the gate, wearing a dark blue uniform with The Deseret name in gold, along with gold chevrons hash-marking each sleeve, gold braid epaulets, a gold fourragère drooping over his right shoulder. His own name above the left-hand breast pocket. In gold. Maybe this is a Hallowe'en getup. Or else years have passed, enough of them for Patrick to pick up the extra hash marks, plus the suave chops of a Distinguished Older Gentleman. He does not, of course, recognize Maxine, either from back in the day or as a faceless pool guest, and observing that she is not a group of drunken teenagers, waves her on in.

The Singhs are up on the tenth floor, the elevators are all either busy or broken down from overloading, and Maxine, having heard fitness-benefit rumors, is OK with taking the stairs. The somber old landmark is certainly jumping tonight. Stairwells and corridors are thronged with all manner of pint-size Statues of Liberty, Uncle Sams, firefolks, cops and GIs in fatigues, not to mention Shreks, Bob the Builders, SpongeBobs and Patricks and Sandy the Squirrels, Queen Amidalas, Harry Potter characters in Quidditch goggles, Gryffindor robes, and witch hats. Apartment doors are all wide open, and inside you can hear a range of sound tracks, including Steely Dan's "Ain't Never Gonna Do It Without the Fez On." The tenantry have as usual gone all out, spending thousands on haunted-house effects, black light and fog generators, arena sound, animatronic zombies as well as live actors working for insultingly less than scale, treat assortments from Dean & DeLuca and Zabar's, and gift bags stuffed with high-end digital tchotchkes, Hermès scarves, and free airplane tickets to places like Tahiti and Gstaad.

Up at the Singh residence, Prabhnoor and Amrita are dressed as Bill Clinton and Monica Lewinsky. Rubber masks and everything. Prabhnoor is handing out cigars. Amrita, in a blue dress of course, is holding a dead karaoke mike and sweetly singing "I Did It My Way." They seem like perfectly pleasant people. Everybody is drunk, mostly on vodka, judging from the empties piled up around and behind the bar, though catering staff dressed as Battle Droids are also going around with trays of champagne, plus filet mignon canapés and lobster sandwiches. Vyrva, done up as a Pikachu Beanie Baby, it figures, approaches Maxine gushing, "What a wonderful costume! You look just like a big, grown-up lady!"

"How're the kids making out so far?"

"Pretty good, we may have to rent a U-Haul. Justin's going around with them, working door-to-door. Some Hallowe'en, huh?"

"Yeah. Can't understand why I'm feeling all this class hostility."

"This? next to the Alley a couple years ago? the average start-up party? this is a footnote, my dear. Commentary."

"You've been in New York too long, Vyrva, you're starting to talk like my father."

"Justin's got his mobile, you want me to call and—"

"It's The Deseret, off-planet, likely to be roaming charges here nobody can afford, I'll just cruise around, thanks."

Out into this overdue-for-exorcism building she has never found even marginally likable. Lining the streetlike corridors, where a hundred years ago pony-drawn delivery wagons, cranked up here on massive hydraulic lifts, brought directly to the doorsills of tenants cans of milk, bushels of flowers, cases of champagne, tonight Maxine finds elaborate mock-ups of Camp Crystal Lake, mummies' tombs, Frankenstein's Art Deco lab all in black and white. Tenant hospitality is you'd have to say proactive. Before long, without so much as raising an eyebrow, she finds herself schlepping sacks full of Hallowe'en plunder too heavy for a child even to lift.

As the evening advances, so does the median age of the crowd of walk-ins, with much more emphasis on eye makeup, glitter, fishnet hose, axes in skulls, fake blood. It is inevitable that somebody should be masquerading as Osama bin Laden, and here in fact are two of them, whom Maxine recognizes sooner than she wants to as Misha and Grisha.

"We were going to go as World Trade Center," Misha explains, "but decided OBL would be even more offensive."

"So how come you're not down in the Village someplace, where the TV coverage is?"

They exchange a Can-we-trust-her look.

"It's for a reason," she guesses, "private not public."

"It's fuckin Hallowe'en, right?" sez Grisha.

"Paying respects," explains Misha.

To whom? Here at The Deseret, of course, to whom else but Lester Traipse, the real Hallowe'en ghost tonight, Lester the jive-ass ballistic blade victim with the unfinished business, doomed to wander those century-old corridors until accounts are balanced, or for eternity, whichever comes first. Lester was a creature of Silicon Alley, Alley to the core, and down the Alley the stories are never that short let alone sweet, down there it's not only a mediagenic neighborhood of dreams recently faded but also the latest in a tradition of New York Alleys It Is In Fact Best To Avoid, shadows full of mentally unstable voices, echoes off the masonry, cries of city desolation, metallic noises less innocent than ancient trash cans in the wind.

"You guys were friends with Lester? Did business?" Or to put it another way, what earthly connection . . . unless that's the point, and the connection is anything but earthly. It's fuckin Hallowe'en.

"Lester was fellow *podonok,*" Misha blushing a little, as if embarrassed at how lame this sounds, "friend of scumbag hackers everywhere."

"Including," a thought occurring to her, "the former Soviet Union. Maybe this was even some secret-police business?"

Misha and Grisha begin to giggle, watching each other's face to see, as it turns out, who is going to slap whom first back into sobriety and respect for the departed. A prison thing.

"You two," noodging cautiously, "really did attend that Civil Hackers' School in Moscow, didn't you?"

"Umnik Academy!" cries Misha, "those guys, no, uh-uh!"

"Not us! We're only *chainiki!*"

"From Bobryusk!" Misha nodding vigorously.

"Don't even know how to sit facing keyboard!"

"Not that I mean to pry, it's only that Lester may have fallen afoul of Gabriel Ice, who as you must know is practically synonymous with U.S. security arrangements. So Russian intelligence would naturally have an interest in his activities."

"He owns this building," Grisha sort of blurts, getting a look from his coadjutor. "If he's here tonight, maybe we'll run into him. Him or one of his people. Maybe they won't like seeing Osama twins. Who knows? Little Mortal Kombat maybe."

Note to self. Noodge Igor, who must know what the fuck this is all about. Scribbled illegibly on a virtual Post-it, stuck on a little-frequented brain lobe it presently falls off of, but there for marginal nagging value at least.

A flamboyance of French maids, street hookers, and baby dominatrices, none of then in junior high yet, comes jittering up the stairs. "Look! What'd I tell you?"

"OhmyGod?"

"Eeew, creepy?"

Misha and Grisha beam, puts their hands on their hearts, and bow slightly. *"Tha tso kalan yee?"*

"Tha jumat ta zey?"

Sending the young ladies into rewind, all in a frenzy, back down the stairs, Misha and Grisha calling genially after them, *"Wa alaikum u ssalam!"*

"That's Hebrew?" sez Maxine.

"Pashto. Wishing them peace, also how old are you, do you go to mosque regularly."

"Here come my kids."

Ziggy's Empire State Building outfit has acquired spray-painted graffiti, and somebody has slipped a miniature souvenir Red Sox cap onto King Kong's head. Otis's hair is still defiantly vertical, and like the gent he is, he's schlepping Fiona's bag along with his own.

"Fiona, nice getup, help me out, you're supposed to be—"

"Misty?"

"The girl in Pokémon. And this is—"

Fiona's friend Imba, who's got up as Misty's chronically bummed-out companion Psyduck.

"We flipped for it," Fiona sez.

"Misty's a gym leader," Imba explains, "but she has impatience issues. Psyduck has powers, but such unhappiness." Synchronized, she and Fiona grab the sides of their heads like S. Z. Sakall and utter the characteristic "Psy, psy, psy." It occurs to Maxine that Psyduck, though Japanese, could be Jewish.

"Good evening, Tech Support, how may I abuse you?" Justin has come tonight as Dilbert's power-freak dog, Dogbert, wearing indigo shades instead of clear lenses. Maxine introduces everybody.

"You are *the* Justin McElmo?" First time Maxine has heard either of these goons say "the."

"Don't know, there's probably more of em out there."

"Of DeepArcher," Grisha amplifies.

"Just a couple of Game Boy fans," Maxine mutters.

"You guys have been down there? Since how long?" Justin not alarmed so much as curious.

"Since 11 September maybe? Before then, was much harder to hack in. Then suddenly, day of attack, gets easier. Later, gets impossible again."

"But you're still getting in."

"Can't stay away!"

"*Pizdatchye,*" kvells Grisha, "always some new story, new graphics, different each time."

"Everything evolving," Misha sez. "Tell us, Justin. Did you design it that way?"

"To evolve?" Justin looking surprised. "No, it was only supposed to be the one thing, like, timeless? A refuge. History-free is what Lucas and I were hoping for. Now you guys are seeing, what?"

"Usual *govno,*" sez Grisha. "Politics, markets, expeditions, asskicking."

"Not gamer scenarios, you understand. Down there we cannot be gamers, we must be travelers."

A good enough basis to exchange business cards.

Just before moving on to further shenanigans, the torpedoes draw Maxine aside. "DeepArcher—you know it too. You've been there."

"Um," nothing to lose, "see, it's only, like, code?"

"No! Maxine, no!" with what could be either naïve faith or raving insanity, "it's real place!"

"It is asylum, no matter, you can be poorest, no home, lowest of jailbirds, *obizhenka,* condemned to die—"

"Dead—"

"DeepArcher will always take you in, keep you safe."

"Lester," Grisha whispers, eyes angling upstairs toward the pool, "Lester's soul. You understand? Stingers on roof. That." A head gesture out into the All Saints night, toward far downtown where the Trade Center used to stand, past the invisible swarming hundreds of thousands of masked celebrants in streets lighted and semi-lit, out to the reeking hole with the Cold War name at the lower edge of the island.

Maxine nods, pretending to see what she can't see. "Thank you. Go easy, guys." She collects Ziggy and Otis, who are already scarfing down

Teuscher truffles like they're Hershey Kisses, and they make their way out the forbidding portals of The Deseret and homeward.

"Top of the evening to yese," calls Patrick McTiernan.

Yeah and where was all that leprechaun jive when she could've used it.

Horst is still awake, now watching Anthony Hopkins in *The Mikhail Baryshnikov Story*, intensely absorbed, a spoonful of Urban Jumble ice cream poised a foot away from his mouth and dribbling onto his shoe.

"Dad, Dad! Snap out of it!"

"Will you look at this," blinks Horst. "Ol' Hannibal dancin up a storm here."

AFTER HER HALLOWE'EN ANTHRO EXPEDITION, Heidi has come back a changed person. "Children of all ages enacting the comprehensive pop-cultural moment. Everything collapsed into the single present tense, all in parallel. Mimesis and enactment." She may've been having a little incoherence after a while. Nowhere did she see a perfect copy of anything. Not even people who said, "Oh, I'm just going as myself" were authentic replicas of themselves.

"It's depressing. I thought Comic-Con was peculiar, but this was Truth. Everything out there just a mouseclick away. Imitation is no longer possible. Hallowe'en is over. I never thought people could get too wised up. What'll happen to us all?"

"And because you tend to be a blamer . . ."

"Oh I blame the fuckin Internet. No question."

THE PHONE CALL TO IGOR isn't one she's looking forward to. Whatever the karmic balance is outstanding between him and Gabriel Ice, she was deliberately avoiding it till Misha and Grisha, noodges from beyond the daytime envelope she would much rather keep inside, made this impossible anymore. Plus which, the happy torpedoes have now it seems been stalking hashslingrz for hidden reasons, and it probably behooves her to find out what, though she isn't expecting much in the way of details.

Igor is chirpy. Too chirpy. Acting like he's been waiting for this call forever.

"Look, Igor, it's not as if anybody is paying me to find out who did Lester—"

"You know who did it. So do I. Cops will not act. It becomes matter of . . ." Is he trying to get her to say it?

"Justice."

"Restoration."

"He's dead. What's to restore?"

"You'd be surprised."

"I would indeed. Especially if it's KGB business and you and your posse are embedded assets."

A silence she has to categorize as amused. "They don't say KGB anymore, they say FSB, they say SVU. Since Putin, KGB means old guys in government."

"Whatever. Ice was deep into funding anti-jihadists. Russia has its own Islamic issues. Is it so crazy to imagine the two countries cooperating? Getting upset when Lester started collecting unauthorized bonuses?"

"Maxine. No. It wasn't only because of money."

"Excuse me? What then?"

He waits a fraction of a beat too long. "Lester saw too much."

She tries to remember that last time she and Lester talked, in Eternal September. There must have been a tell she missed, a lapse, something. "If he understood what he was seeing, wouldn't he have told somebody?"

"He tried to. He called me on my mobile. Night before they got him. I couldn't pick up. Left long message on voice mail."

"He had your mobile number."

"Everybody does. Cost of doing business."

"What was the message?"

"Pretty crazy shit. Black Escalades trying to run him off LIE. Phone calls to wife, threats to kids. Me, my people, he thought we might have connections. Help broker some understanding."

"As in . . . ?"

"He forgets about what he saw, they don't kill him. Good luck."

"And what he saw . . . ?"

"He was crazy by then. They already had his sanity. They didn't have to kill him. One more thing which must be restored. You want secular cause and effect, but here, I'm sorry, is where it all goes off books. Lester said, 'Only choice I have left is DeepArcher.' I heard about DeepArcher site from *padonki,* so I have rough idea what it means, but not what he's talking about."

Sanctuary. While she was being dogfucked by one of his murderers.

THE DAY OF THE NYC MARATHON, seven weeks into post-atrocity, the fearful day still reverberating, what you could call a patriotic atmosphere, thousands of runners come out in memory of 11 September and its victims in defiance of any chance it'll happen again, security super tight, Verrazano Bridge deeply guarded, all harbor traffic suspended, nothing visible in the skies overhead but helicopters keeping industrious watch . . .

Around midday, headed for the weekly flea market at a nearby middle school, Maxine begins to notice, first one by one, then in a stream, yuppies in Mylar capes—the superhero business suddenly gone low-rent here—beginning to filter over from the park. By the corner of 77th and Columbus, it's grown into a mob scene. Whooping and hollering and hugging and flags waving everyplace.

Sitting exhausted on the sidewalk against a wall with a row of other runners recovering from the event their shiny official wraps announce they have just run, here seems to be Windust.

First time face-to-face since that romantic evening down on the far West Side. "Don't tell anybody you saw me," still a little short of breath, "it's a vice, especially this soon after eleven September, too much mortality around already, why go out of the way to embrace even more? And yet," waving around wearily, "here we all are." Unless he bought his souvenir cape from somebody down the street and Maxine's in for another setup here.

"Too deep for me."

A flirtatious smirk. "Yes, I remember."

"Then again, sometimes a centimeter is way too much. It's all right, you're having some chemicals from the running. Can you get up yet? I'll buy you a cup of coffee." Of course, Maxine, why not, maybe a cheese danish also? Is she crazy, this is the last thing she should be doing. But the Jewish Mother, sitting silent in the dark, has suddenly chosen this moment to jump up, switch on the tasteful lamp from Scully & Scully, and blindside Maxine into yet another shameful display of *eppes-essen* solicitude. For a second she hopes Windust is too exhausted. But fitness prevails, and he's on his feet, and before she can think up an excuse they are sitting in a retro lunchwagon on Columbus, dating from the eighties when the neighborhood was hot, now more of interest to tourists who are into subcultural history. The place today is jittering with recaffeinating marathoners. Nobody is talking too loud, however, so the chances for conversation are at least fifty-fifty, for a change.

What kind of ex, she wonders, would Windust ever have qualified as? ex-heavy date, ex-mistake, ex-quickie, maybe just x for unknown? By now she ought to be well into pretending none of it ever happened, instead here's this lurid Day-Glo folder icon blinking at her, Unbalanced Accounts.

Crowds outside push past the window screaming congratulations, laughing too loud, stuffing their faces, flourishing their capes. On triumph's home screen, Windust is a solitary pixel of discontent. "Guess they showed those rugriders, huh. Look at them. An army of the clueless, who think they own 11 September."

"Hey, why shouldn't they, they bought it from you, we all did, you took our own precious sorrow, processed it, sold it back to us like any other product. Ask you something? When it happened? The Day Every-thing Changed, where were you?"

"In my little cubicle. Reading Tacitus." The warrior-scholar routine. "Who makes a case that Nero didn't set fire to Rome so he could blame it on the Christians."

"Sounds familiar, somehow."

"You people want to believe this was all a false-flag caper, some invis-ible superteam, forging the intel, faking the Arabic chatter, controlling air traffic, military communications, civilian news media—everything coordinating without a hitch or a malfunction, the whole tragedy set up to look like a terror attack. Please. My wised-up civilian heartbreaker. Guess what. Nobody in the business is that good."

"You're saying I don't need to get too excited about this anymore? Well. Ain't that a relief. Meantime you people have what you want, your War on Terror, war without end, and job security up the ol' wazoo."

"For somebody maybe. Not me."

"Goonsquad skills no longer in demand? Aw."

He looks downward, at his abs, his dick, his shoes, some vintage Mizuno Waves in an eye-assaulting color scheme the years have not been kind to. "Retirement looming, basically."

"There's exit options for *you* guys? Quit kidding."

"Well . . . considering what the exits are, we do try to make private arrangements instead."

"Saving up your spare change, Florida Keys, little skiff with an ice chest full of Dos Equis sort of thing . . ."

"Wish I could be more specific."

According to the flash-drive dossier Marvin brought around last summer, Windust's portfolio is stuffed with privatized state assets all across the Third World. She imagines a few blessed hectares down in the trackless retrocolonial, someplace "safe," whatever that means, off the surveillance matrix, spared somehow from U.S.-engineered regime changes, children with AKs, deforestation, storms, famines, and other late-capitalist planetary insults . . . with somebody he can trust, some ultimate Tonto, keeping an eye on its perimeters for him as the years unroll . . . In the lives variously reported of Windust, are loyalties like that possible?

She should have tumbled before this to the peculiar lightlessness in his eyes today, a deficit beyond secular fatigue. "Retirement" is a euphemism, and somehow she doubts he's up here on any midlife cardiofitness program. This is coming more and more to feel like a checklist of winding-up chores he's running through before moving on.

In which case, Maxine, enough with the date-night ditzing around, she can feel a cold draft through some failing seam in the fabric of the day, and there is no payoff here worth any further investment beyond, "Let's see, you had how many, three? Gigaccinos, and then the bagels . . ."

"Three bagels, plus the Denver omelet deluxe, you had the plain toasted . . ."

Out on the sidewalk, neither can find a formula that will let them separate with any grace. After another half minute of silence, they end up nodding and turning in different directions.

On the way home she passes the neighborhood firehouse. They're in working on one of the trucks. Maxine recognizes a guy she sees all the time in the Fairway buying huge amounts of food. They smile and wave. Cute kid. Under different circumstances . . .

Of which as usual there are not enough. She threads among the daily bunches of flowers on the sidewalk, which will be cleared in a while. The list of firefighters here who were lost on 11 September is kept back someplace more intimate, out of the public face, anybody wants to see it they can ask, but sometimes it shows more respect not to put such things out on a billboard.

If it isn't the pay, isn't the glory, and sometimes you don't come back, then what is it? What makes these guys choose to go in, work twenty-four hour shifts and then keep working, keep throwing themselves into those shaky ruins, torching through steel, bringing people to safety, recovering parts of others, ending up sick, beat up by nightmares, disrespected, dead?

Whatever it is, would Windust even recognize it? How far has he journeyed from working realities? What sanctuary has he sought, and what, if any, given?

AS THANKSGIVING APPROACHES, the neighborhood, terrorist atrocities or whatever, reverts to its usual insufferable self, reaching a peak the night before Thanksgiving, when the streets and sidewalks are jammed solid with people who have come in to town to view The Blowing Up Of The Balloons for the Macy's parade. Cops are everywhere, security is heavy. In front of every eatery, there are lines out the door. Places you can usually step inside, order a pizza to go, and wait no more than the time it takes to bake it are running at least an hour behind. Everybody out on the sidewalk is a pedestrian Mercedes, wallowing in entitlement—colliding, snarling, shoving ahead without even the hollow-to-begin-with local euphemism "Excuse me."

This evening Maxine finds herself abroad in this pageant of classic NYC behavior, having made the mistake of offering to spring for a turkey if Elaine will cook it, and compounded it by putting in an advance order at Crumirazzi, a gourmet shop down toward 72nd. She gets there after supper to find the place jammed tighter than a peak-period subway with anxious citizens gathering supplies for their Thanksgiving feasts, and the turkey line folded on itself eight or ten times and moving very, very slowly. People are already screaming at each other, and civility, like everything on the shelves, is in short supply.

A serial line jumper has been making his way forward along the turkey line, a large white alpha male whose social skills, if any, are still in beta, intimidating people one by one out of his way.

"Excuse me?" Shoving ahead of an elderly lady waiting in line just behind Maxine.

"Line jumper here," the lady yells, unslinging her shoulder bag and preparing to deploy it.

"You must be from out of town," Maxine addressing the offender, "here in New York, see, the way you're acting? It's considered a felony."

"I'm in a hurry, bitch, so back off, unless you want to settle this outside?"

"Aw. After all your hard work getting this far? Tell you what, you go out and wait for me, OK? I won't be too long, promise."

Shifting to indignation, "I have a houseful of children to feed—" but he's interrupted by a voice someplace over by the loading dock hollering, "Hey asshole!" and here cannonballing over the heads of the crowd comes a frozen turkey, hits the bothersome yup square in the head, knocking him flat and bouncing off his head into the hands of Maxine, who stands blinking at it like Bette Davis at some baby with whom she must unexpectedly share the frame. She hands the object to the lady behind her. "This is yours, I guess."

"What, after it touched him? thanks anyway."

"I'll take it," sez the guy behind her.

As the line creeps forward, everybody makes sure to step on, not over, the fallen line jumper.

"Nice to see the ol' town gettin back to normal, ain't it." A familiar voice.

"Rocky, what are you doing over in this neck of the woods?"

"It's Cornelia, she can't get through Thanksgiving without this one brand of stuffing mix she grew up with, Dean & DeLuca ran out of it and Crumirazzi's is the only other place in NYC."

Maxine squints at the giant plastic sack he's carrying. "'Squanto's Choice, Authentic Old-Tyme WASP Recipe.'"

"Uses antique white bread."

"'Antique' . . ."

"Wonder Bread from back before they started sellin it sliced?"

"That's seventy years, Rocky, it doesn't get moldy?"

"It gets hard as cement. They have to take jackhammers and break it up. Gives it that extra something. Why are you waiting in this line, I took you for more of a Swift Butterball person."

"Thought I'd try and help my mom out. Wrong as usual. Look at this fuckin zoo. Karmic crime scene. You think it won't find its way into the food?"

"Family all gettin together this year, huh?"

"You'll be seeing it in the *Post*. 'Among those being held for observation . . .'"

"Hey, your friend from Montreal? That Felix guy with the antizapper? We're givin him some bridge money, Spud Loiterman has a sixth sense, he says go."

"So you want to hire me now, or wait till Felix is what Bobby Darin calls 'beyond the sea'?"

"Yeah, OK, he's working a hustle, so what, I was like that once, I can relate, and anyway who am I to second-guess the Dean Martin of Dissonance?"

35

As things turn out, Thanksgiving is not so horrible after all. Probably 11 September has something to do with it. There is an empty space set seder fashion at the table, not for the prophet Elijah but for one or any of the unknown souls whom prophecy failed that day. The sound ambience is subdued, edgeless. Ernie and the boys settle in in front of the annual *Star Wars* marathon, Horst and Avi talk sports, smells of cooking fill the rooms, Elaine glides in and out of dining room, pantry, and kitchen, a one-woman army of woodwork-dwelling elves, Maxine and Brooke by the end of the afternoon have reached zinger parity with no lethal weapons appearing, the food is, as so often with Elaine, a form of time travel, the turkey mercifully unjinxed despite its Crumirazzi origins, the pastries somehow escaping Brooke's fatality for the overelaborate and even including what Otis in a rave review calls a normal pumpkin pie. Ernie spares everybody a speech and only gestures at the empty chair with a glass of apple cider. "Everybody who should've been celebrating today but isn't."

As they're leaving, Avi draws Maxine aside. "Your office—is there some kind of a back entrance?"

"You want to drop by without anybody seeing you. Maybe . . . should we do breakfast someplace?"

"Um . . ."

"Too public, OK, here's what you do, go around the corner, there's a delivery gate that's usually open, go in the courtyard, bear to the right, you'll see a door painted with red lead, the service elevator's right inside, I'm on three. Call first."

AVI COMES CREEPING up to the office in disguise, jeans way too skinny for him, T-shirt reading ALL YOUR BASE ARE BELONG TO US, a fuzzy white Kangol 504 at which Daytona does a triple take, pretending to adjust her glasses. "Thought it was Sam the King of Cool in here, walkin amongst us. Clients is gettin way too hip for *my* ass, Miz Maxine!"

"You never met my brother-in-law?" Avi takes off his hat, and there's his yarmulke. The two shake hands warily.

"I'll just whup up a mess of coffee, then, shall I."

"Good timing, Avi, the danish guy was just here a minute ago."

"Been meaning to ask, where in this neighborhood anymore? We come back to the city, now the Royale on 72nd is gone."

"Tell me. We have to get these schlepped up from 23rd Street. Sit, please, here, coffee, thanks, Daytona."

"Only got a minute, have to go punch in. I'm supposed to pass on a message to you."

"From the Ice Man himself, I bet. Neither of you could just phone?"

"Well, it's not only that. Something weird I need to ask you about, also."

"If your boss's message is stop looking into the audit trails at hashslingrz, consider it done, that ticket's been dormant really since September 11th."

"I think he has a job for you."

"Respectfully decline."

"Just like that?"

"Everybody's different, Avi, maybe I've worked for a lowlife or two over the years, but this Ice specimen, I hope you guys haven't become dear friends, he's how shall I put it—"

"He speaks highly of you also."

"So what kind of a gig could he be offering me—get run over by a truck?"

"He thinks he's being ripped off by persons unknown, inside the company."

"Oh, please. And needs an ex-CFE to make that story look legit? Let you in on a big secret, Avi, these persons unknown happen to be Ice himself, along with the missus possibly duked in, being you'll recall company comptroller? Sorry to be the bearer, but Ice for months, maybe years, has been robbing his own shop blind."

"Gabriel Ice is . . . embezzling?"

"Yes contemptible enough, but now he's whining about Dishonest Employees? oldest con in the book, he wants to pin it on some poor zhlub who can't afford a good enough lawyer. My diagnosis? Classic fraud, your employer is a fraudster. That's ten billable seconds, I'll send an invoice."

"He's under investigation? He'll be charged?" So plaintive that Maxine finally reaches over and pats her brother-in-law on the shoulder.

"Nobody's about to go forensic with it, maybe some curiosity at federal level, but Ice has his own friends down there, likely at some point they'll all be dealing in secret and nothing'll ever get as far as the courts or outside the Beltway. You and me, the taxpayer, will of course end up a tiny percent more impoverished, but who gives a shit about us. Your job is safe, don't worry."

"My job. Well, that's the other thing."

"Ooh, somebody's not happy?" in a voice she likes to use in the street with screaming toddlers she hasn't necessarily been introduced to.

"No, and I'm not Dopey or Doc either. If this city was a nuthouse, hashslingrz would be the paranoid ward—help, help, the enemy, look, they're out there, they're all around us! Like being back in Israel on a bad day."

"And as seen from inside your workplace, this business-world analogy to being surrounded on all sides by criminally insane Arabs would be . . ."

An uncoordinated, slightly desperate shrug. "Whoever it is, it's no delusion, somebody's actively engaged, mystery stalkers, hacking into our networks, social-engineering us at bars."

"OK, setting aside what could be a, forgive me, deliberate company policy of keeping all the employees paranoid . . . How about Brooke, any reports there of stalking, molestation, lapses of taste above and beyond the usual in this town?"

"There's these two guys."

"Uh-oh." Hoping this time her intuition circuit board really is on the fritz, "A sort of Russian hip-hop act?"

"Funny you should mention."

Pizdets. "Listen, if it's who I think, they're probably not into inflicting harm."

" 'Probably.' "

"Can't give you a figure, but I can make a phone call. Let me see what's going on, meantime tell Brooke not to worry."

"Actually, I haven't been sharing any of this with her."

"Such a mensch, Avi, always thinking of her stress level, lucky her."

"Well, not exactly . . . the nondisclosure agreement says no wives?"

As he's going out, Daytona flashes her nails. "Loved you in *Pulp Fiction*, baby. That Bible quote? Mm-hmmm!"

ABOUT 5:00 A.M. MAXINE WAKES from one of those annoying recursive subnightmares, this time something about Igor and an oversize bottle of vodka, named after a Lithuanian basketball player, which he keeps trying to introduce her to as if it's a person. She slips out of bed and goes into the kitchen, where she finds Driscoll and Eric sharing their usual breakfast, a bottle of Mountain Dew with two straws in it. "Been meaning to mention this," Driscoll begins, and gazing at each other like two country singers at a benefit, she and Eric start to sing the old *Jeffersons* sitcom theme, "Movin on out."

"Wait. Not 'to the East Side.'"

"Williamsburg," Eric sez, "actually."

"It's all goin over to Brooklyn. Feels like we're the last of the old-time Alley folks."

"Hope it's nothing we've done."

"Isn't you guys, it's Manhattan in general," Driscoll explains. "Not like it used to be, maybe you've noticed."

"Greed situation," Eric amplifies. "You'd think when the towers came down it would've been a reset button for the city, the real-estate business, Wall Street, a chance for it all to start over clean. Instead lookit them, worse than before."

Around them, the City That Doesn't Sleep is beginning to not sleep even more. Lights come on in windows across the street. Drunks out too long after closing time scream in discontent. Down the block a car alarm starts in with a medley of attention signals. Over in the flanking avenues, heavy machinery roars into standby mode, preparing to move into position beneath the windows of citizens incautious enough to still be in bed. Birds too clueless or stubborn to get out of town before the winter now creeping upon the city begin discussing why they're not in avian therapy yet.

Maxine, busy with the coffee routine, observes her own migratory birds with regret. "So in Brooklyn will you guys be living together or separately?"

"True," reply Eric and Driscoll in unison.

Maxine regards the ceiling briefly.

"Sorry. Nonexclusive 'or.'"

"Geek thing," Driscoll explains.

. . .

THERE HAVE ALREADY BEEN a number of panicked, not to mention abusive, calls from Windust by the time Maxine shows up at work. Daytona is strangely amused.

"Sorry you had to deal with that . . . he didn't get racial, I hope."

"Maybe not him, but . . ."

"Oh, Daytona." Maxine takes the next one. Windust certainly seems perturbed. "Calm down, you're blowing out my speakerphone here."

"That fucking destructive irresponsibile bitch, what does she think she's doing? Does she know how many people she's just put at risk?"

"'She' being . . ."

"You know what I'm talking about, goddamn it, Maxine, did you have anything to do with this?"

"With . . ." She can't help it, it does her spirit good to see him this way. Eventually she gets him to splutter it out. Seems March Kelleher has finally gotten around to posting Reg's footage from The Deseret roof on the Internet. Well, thanks for the heads-up, March, though it is about time.

"Let me just look, here."

March—Maxine can imagine with what kind of a mischievous glint—trying to maintain a class-act approach, "Many of us need the comfort of a simple story line with Islamic villains, and co-enablers like the Newspaper of Record are delighted to help. Poor, poor America, why do these evil foreigners hate us, must be all this freedom of ours, and how twisted is that, to hate freedom? Really thinking about all those buildable lots where the demolition's already been done. If you're interested in counternarratives, however, click on this link to the video of a Stinger crew on a Manhattan rooftop. Check out theories and countertheories. Contribute your own."

No invitation needed, really. The Internet has erupted into a Mardi Gras for paranoids and trolls, a pandemonium of commentary there may not be time in the projected age of the universe to read all the way through, even with deletions for violating protocol, plus home videos and audio tracks including a lilting sound bite from Deseret spokesman Seamus O'Vowtey, "Our buildin security's the best in the city. This has to be an inside job, likely somethin to do with certain o' these tenants."

"Wow, bummer," Maxine somewhat insincerely.

"That doesn't begin to—"

"No I mean The Deseret, it took me years to get in their front gate, and here's a whole missile crew just moseys on in and up to the roof."

"No use telling her to take the video down, I imagine?"

"There's already a million copies out there."

"Shit's hit the fan down here. I've come in for an episode of inconvenience myself, effectively I'm a fugitive now, need to sneak in and out of my own house, last I heard from Dotty was back in the middle of the night, reporting unmarked vans out in front, now she's gone totally offline and who knows when I'll see her—"

"Where are you calling from, I keep hearing Chinese in the background?"

"Chinatown."

"Ah."

"I don't suppose you could meet me down here."

"No?" Whatdafuck. "I mean, what for?"

"None of my ATM cards seem to be working anymore."

"And, excuse me, you want to borrow money? From me?"

"I wouldn't say borrow, because that assumes a future in which I might pay it back."

"You're beginning to scare me a little."

"Good. Can you bring enough just to get me down to D.C. again?"

"Yeah I saw that movie, I think Elizabeth Taylor was playing you?"

"I knew this would come up."

Today, she reminds herself heading downtown, all the fortune cookies are screaming, "Err on the side of no schmucks!" This man deserves no mercy, Maxine, your best course here is to just let him go fuck himself. He's short of cash, boo hoo, given his skill sets, knocking over a convenience store shouldn't be such a stretch for him, preferably one in New Jersey, he'd already be halfway to D.C. So of course here she is, hurrying to him with a valise full of greenbacks. The apparent cause and effect in this may be worth a look, however. March posts the footage, Windust is forced into flight and his money supply frozen. The links between are hard to resist—Windust, if not ramrodding the whole Deseret roof operation, must've been at least in charge of security, and he fucked up. Anybody plugged into the Internet, any bleating sheep of a civilian, can now see what it was Windust's job to keep hidden. So, big surprise any sanctions should turn out to be serious, maybe extreme?

She sits watching on the backseat video display their snail's progress through the streets of Manhattan, as tracked by GPS, drifting into unprofitable thoughts. Is it that American Indian curse about, if you save somebody's life you're responsible for what happens to them from then on? Setting aside fringe theories about Indians being lost tribes of Israel and so forth, did she save Windust's life once long ago without knowing it and now invisible karmic bureaucracy is passing her these messages—he wants you, so go!

She finds Windust under an awning with a number of Chinese people, waiting for the bus, the Manhattan Bridge looming nearby. After watching from across the street for a minute, Maxine realizes that the people on either side of Windust aren't talking to each other directly, but through him. Smart-assed as ever, he seems to be translating back and forth from one kind of Chinese to another. He spots her looking at him, nods, gestures, Stay where you are, threads his way across to her. Not looking that great. In fact, a man on the edge.

"Good timing. Just spent my last U.S. dollars on the bus to D.C."

"There's a bus terminal around here?"

"Street pickup, savings passed on to the customer, bargain of the century, you're Jewish, I'm amazed you haven't heard of this."

"Your envelope."

Instead of counting the bills like a normal person, Windust with a small practiced hand move hefts the envelope, the sort of thing that over time, for a career bagman, gets to be automatic.

"Thanks, angel. Don't know when—"

"Reimburse when you can, something I don't have to declare as income. Maybe from the street floor at Tiffany's— no, wait, what's her name, Dotty? Nah, you wouldn't want her finding out."

He's examining her face. "Earrings. Simple diamond studs. With your hair up . . . ."

"Actually, I'm a Eurowire type gal." She has barely time to think about adding, "How squalid is this?" when the round comes in, invisible, silent till it hits a piece of wall, whereupon it finds its voice and ricochets droning brightly off into Chinatown, by which time Windust has grabbed Maxine and pulled her down behind a skip full of construction debris.

"Holy shit. Are you—"

"Wait," he advises, "just give it a minute, I'm not sure about the angle, it could've come from anyplace. Up in any of those," gesturing with his head at the upper stories surrounding them. They watch the pavement fragment further into what will later be taken for only a few more city potholes. The people across the street don't seem to notice. On the incoming breeze, a distant slow stammering. "Somehow I've been expecting three-round bursts. This sounds more like an AK. Hold steady."

"I knew I should've worn the Kevlar outfit today."

"Among your friends in the Russian mob, distance equals respect, so we should consider assassination by AK-47 an honor."

"Gee, you must be some hot shit."

"In fifteen seconds," glancing at his watch, "I plan to disappear and get on with my day. You might want to wait here for a bit before resuming your own."

"Class act, I figured you'd grab my arm and we'd run someplace, like in movies? Chinese people jumping out of the way? Or was I supposed to be blond?" Scanning upper windows meantime, reaching into her purse, bringing out the Beretta, thumbing off the safety.

"Good," Windust nodding like it's about time. "You can cover me."

"That one there, the one that's open, that look good to you?" No reply. Already, as the Eagles say, gone. She crab-steps out from behind the skip anyway and lets go a couple of double taps at the window, screaming, "Motherfuckers!"

Goodness, Maxine, where'd that come from? Nobody's returning fire. The people waiting for the bus begin to point and pass remarks. Keeping an eye on the street traffic, she waits for a vehicle tall enough to take cover behind, which turns out to be a moving van with MITZVAH MOVERS in mock-Hebrew lettering and a cartoon of what appears to be an insane rabbi with a piano on his back, and vacates the area.

Well, as Winston Churchill always sez, there is nothing more exhilarating than getting shot at without result, though for Maxine there is also a flip side or payback, which arrives a few hours later, on the afterschool stoop at Kugelblitz, in front of an assortment of Upper West Side moms whose life skills include an eye for the slightest uptick in the distress of others, not that Maxine quite collapses in tears, though her knees feel unreliable and she may be experiencing a certain lightness of head . . .

"Everything all right, Maxine? you look so . . . inexplicable."

"One of those having-it-all moments, Robyn, and yourself?"

"Going crazy with Scott's bar mitzvah, you have no idea, the work, caterers, deejay, invitations. And Scott, his aliyah, he's still struggling to memorize it, with the Hebrew running the other way we're worried now it's making him dyslexic?"

"Well," in the most rational voice available to her at the moment, "why not go off-Torah and choose a passage from, I don't know, Tom Clancy? not really that traditional, true, not even I guess Jewish, but something with, you know, maybe Ding Chavez in it?" noticing after a short time lag that Robyn is looking at her funny and people are beginning to edge away. Providentially at this point, the kids all come charging out of the lobby and onto the stoop, and parental subroutines kick in, carrying her and Ziggy and Otis down the steps and into the street, where she notices Nigel Shapiro busy poking with a little stylus at the tiny keyboard of a wavy-shaped pocket-size green-and-purple unit. Doesn't look like a Game Boy. "Nigel, what is that?"

Looking up after a while, "This? it's a Cybiko, my sister gave itta me, everybody at La Guardia has em, the big selling point is the silence. It's wireless, see, you can send text messages back and forth in class and nobody hears you."

"So if Ziggy and I each had one, we could message back and forth?"

"If you're in range, which is only like a block and a half. But trust me, Mizzus Loeffler, it's da wave o' da fyootch."

"You'll be wanting one, I imagine, Ziggy."

"Already got one, Mom." And who knows who else. Maxine has a moment of eyebrow oscillation. Talk about private networks.

THE OFFICE PHONE LETS LOOSE with some robotic theme, and Maxine picks up. It's Lloyd Thrubwell, in some agitation. "The subject you inquired after? I'm so sorry. There's not much further I can take this."

Yeah let me look in my Beltway-to-English phrasebook here . . . "You're being ordered to back off of it, right?"

"This person has been the topic of an internal memo, several actually. I can't say any more than that."

"You probably heard already, but Windust and I got shot at yesterday."

"His wife," only having a spot of fun, "or your husband?"

"I'll take that as WASP for 'Thank God you're both all right.'"

Muffled mouthpiece passage. "Wait, I'm sorry, it's a serious event, of course. We're already looking into it." A beat of silence, which on Avi's stress analyzer is clearly registering far over in the Lying Through Ass range. "Do either of you have any theories as to the shooter's identity?"

"Out of all the enemies Windust has made during a long career doing his country's shitwork, jeepers Lloyd, personally, any thoughts on that would so be a chore."

More muffled yakking. "No problem. If you have any contact with the subject, however indirect, we would strongly advise against continuing it." The display on Avi's gizmo has now turned a vivid cadmium red and begun to blink.

"Because they don't want me meddling in Agency business, or something else?"

"Something else," Lloyd whispers.

The sound background changes as an extension is picked up, and another voice, one she has never heard, at least not in the waking world, advises, "He means your personal safety, Ms. Loeffler. The assessment here on Brother Windust is that he's a highly educated asset, but doesn't know everything. Lloyd, that's all, you can get off the line now." The connection goes dead.

36

Some holiday season someday, Maxine would like to find featured on the tube a revisionist *Christmas Carol*, where Scrooge is the good guy for a change. Victorian capitalism has hustled him over the years for his soul, turning him from an innocent entry-level kid into a mean old man who treats everybody like shit, none worse than his apparently honest bookkeeper Bob Cratchit, who in reality has been systematically skimming off of poor haunted and vulnerable Scrooge, cooking the books, and running off periodically to Paris to squander what he's stolen on champagne, gambling, and cancan girls, leaving Tiny Tim and the family in London to starve. At the end, instead of Bob being the instrument of Scrooge's redemption, it turns out to be by way of Scrooge that Bob is ransomed back to the side of humanity again.

Every year when Christmas and Hanukkah roll around, this story begins to slop over into work. Maxine finds herself reversing polarities, overlooking obvious Scrooges and zooming in on secretly sinful Cratchits. The innocent are guilty, the guilty are beyond hope, everything's on its head, it's a Twelfth Night of late-capitalist contradiction, and not especially relaxing.

Having listened through the window to the same heartfelt street-trumpet rendition of "Rudolph the Red-Nosed Reindeer" a thousand times, each identical, note-for-note, finding this at last, what's the phrase—fucking tiresome, Maxine, Horst, and the boys decide to take a break together and roll a couple of frames down at the Port Authority bus terminal, which houses the last unyuppified bowling alley in the city.

At the terminal, on the way upstairs, amid the swarm of travelers, hustlers, shoulder surfers, and undercover cops, Maxine notices a sprightly figure beneath a gigantic backpack, possibly bound for some-place he thinks has no extradition treaty with the U.S. "Be right with you guys." She makes her way through the traffic and brings out the socia-ble smile. "Why, Felix Boïngueaux, *ça va*, heading back up to Montreal, are we?"

"This time of year, are you crazy? Heading for sunshine, tropical breezes, babes in bikinis."

"Some friendly Caribbean jurisdiction, no doubt."

"Only going as far as Florida, thanks, and I know what you're thinking, but that's all in the past, eh? I'm a respectable businessman now, paying for employee health insurance and everything."

"Heard about your bridge round from Rocky, congratulations. Haven't seen you since the Geeks' Cotillion, recall you being into some deep discussion then with Gabriel Ice. Were you able to drum up any business?"

"Maybe a little consulting work." No shame. Felix is now an account payable of the guy who may have whacked his former partner. Maybe has been all along.

"Tell you what, get a Ouija board and ask Lester Traipse what he thinks about that. You told me once, you strongly implied, you knew who did Lester —"

"No names," looking nervous. "You want it to be uncomplicated, but it's not."

"Just one thing—total honesty, OK?" Looking for furtive eyeballs with this one? forget it. "After Lester was hit—did you ever have any rea-son to think there was somebody after you too?"

Trick question. Saying no, Felix admits he's being protected, which makes the next question "Who by?" Saying yes leaves open the possibility he'll produce documentation, however embarrassing, if the price is right. He stands there processing this, stolid as a take-out container of poutine, amid the swarm of holiday travelers, fake Santas, children on leashes, drink-sodden victims of lunchtime office partying, commuters hours late and days early, "Someday we'll be friends," Felix shifting his backpack, "I promise."

"I so look forward. Bon voyage. Have a frozen mai tai in memory of Lester."

"Who was that, Mom?"

"Him? Uh, one of Santa's elves, down here on a business trip from Montreal, which is like a regional hub for North Pole activities, same weather conditions and so on?"

"Santa's elves don't exist," proclaims Ziggy, "In fact—"

"Dummy up, kid," mutters Maxine, about the same time Horst advises, "That's enough."

Seems various NYC junior know-it-alls of Otis and Ziggy's acquaintance have been putting around the story there's no Santa.

"They don't know what they're talking about," sez Horst.

The boys squint at their father. "You're what, forty, fifty years old, and you believe in Santa Claus?"

"I do indeed, and if this miserable city is too wised up to deal with it, then they can shove it up their own," looking around dramatically, "butthole, which last time I checked was someplace over on the Upper East Side."

While they check in at Leisure Time Lanes, get bowling shoes, examine the fried-food inventory and so forth, Horst goes on to explain that just like the Santa clones out on the street corners, parents are also Santa's agents, acting in loco Santaclausis, "Actually, as it gets closer to Christmas Eve, just loco. See, the North Pole is not so much about fabrication anymore, elves have gradually moved out of the workshop and into fulfillment and delivery, where they're busy outsourcing and routing toy requests. Pretty much everything these days is transacted via Santanet."

"Via what?" Ziggy and Otis inquire.

"Hey. Nobody has any trouble believing in the Internet, right, which really is magic. So what's the problem believing in a virtual private network for Santa's business? It results in real toys, real presents, delivered by Christmas morning, what's the difference?"

"The sleigh," Otis promptly. "The reindeer."

"Only cost-efficient in snow-covered areas. As the planet warms up, and Third World markets become more important, North Pole HQ has to start subcontracting delivery out to local companies."

"So this Santanet," Ziggy relentless, "there's passwords?"

"Kids aren't allowed," Horst beyond ready to change the subject, "it's like they don't let you guys watch pirate movies either?"

"What?"

"Pirate movies? Why not?"

"'Cause they're rated Ahrrrh. Look, somebody want to help me program this scoreboard, I get a little confused . . ."

They're happy to oblige, but Maxine understands, with one of those joys-of-the-season twinges, as a reprieve it's all too temporary.

MARCH KELLEHER MEANTIME has become even more problematic to get hold of. None of the doorstaff at the St. Arnold now has ever heard of her, none of her phones is even defaulting to an answering machine anymore, just ringing on and on into enigmatic silence. According to her Weblog, the attention from cops and cop affiliates public and private has reached alarming levels, obliging her to roll up her futon every morning, hop on a bicycle, and relocate someplace new, trying not to sleep in the same place too many nights in a row. She has a network of friends who warbike around town with compact PCs and provide her with a growing list of free Wi-Fi hotspots, which she likewise tries not to use the same one of too often. She carries an iBook clamshell in a shade known as Key Lime and logs in from wherever she can find free Internet access.

"It's getting weird," she admits on one of her Weblog entries. "I'm keeping a step or two ahead so far, but you never know what they've got, how state-of-the-art it might be, who works for them and who doesn't. Don't get me wrong, I love them nerds, in another life I would've been a nerd groupie, but even nerds can be bought and sold, almost as if times of great idealism carry equal chances for great corruptibility."

"After the 11 September attack," March editorializes one morning, "amid all that chaos and confusion, a hole quietly opened up in American history, a vacuum of accountability, into which assets human and financial begin to vanish. Back in the days of hippie simplicity, people liked to blame 'the CIA' or 'a secret rogue operation.' But this is a new enemy, unnamable, locatable on no organization chart or budget line—who knows, maybe even the CIA's scared of them.

"Maybe it's unbeatable, maybe there are ways to fight back. What it may require is a dedicated cadre of warriors willing to sacrifice time, income, personal safety, a brother/sisterhood consecrated to an uncertain struggle that may extend over generations and, despite all, end in total defeat."

She's going crazy, Maxine thinks, this is Jedi talk. Or maybe that graduation speech last summer at Kugelblitz really was prophecy, and now it's coming true. For all Maxine knows, March is sleeping in the park by now, her possessions in Zabar's bags, hair growing out wild and gray, no hot baths anymore, depending for showers on the winter rains. How guilty is Maxine supposed to feel about passing her Reg's video?

VYRVA COMES OVER ONE MORNING after leaving the kids off at school. It isn't that a coolness has grown between her and Maxine, exactly. Among the underlying rules of the fraud-investigation universe is that on any given Saturday night anybody may be playing canasta with anybody, who in particular seldom being as important as what's on the score sheet.

Nose in her coffee cup, Vyrva announces, "It finally happened. He dumped me."

"Why, the li'l rat."

"Well . . . I sort of provoked it?"

"And he didn't . . ."

"Take revenge because DeepArcher went open source? Hell no, he's delighted, means he's got it for free, saves him a purchase price that could have put Fiona, Justin, and me in any twelve-room penthouse in town."

"Oh?" Real estate, now there's a return to mental health. "You guys've been looking?"

"I have. Still got to talk Justin into it, 'course, he's homesick for California."

"You're not."

"Remember a movie called *Lawrence of Arabia* (1962), guy from England goes out in the desert, suddenly realizes he's home?"

"You remember a movie called *The Wizard of Oz* (1939), where—"

"All right, all right. But this is the version where Dorothy gets heavily into Emerald City residential property?"

"After an inappropriate relationship with the Wiz."

"Who's done with me in any case, tossed me aside, a fallen woman but I live with my guilt, yes I'm free, free I tell you."

"So why the face?" Maxine allows herself once a year to do her Howard Cosell impression, and today's the day. "Vyrva, you are wallowing in lachrymosity."

"Oh, Maxi, I feel so totally, like, used?"

"What, you're a decent-looking enough broad, at least when you're not blubbering, what if it wasn't only business intrigue, what if it really was lust he felt," is she really saying this? "true and simple lust, all along."

Which turns the spigot on full blast. "That sweet little guy! I told him to just fuck off, I hurt him, I'm such a bitch . . ."

"Here, a tip." Sliding over a roll of paper towels. "From one who has been there. Absorbs better than tissues, you don't use as many cubic feet, less to clean up later."

DAYTONA, AS IF HAVING MADE some year-end resolution, suspends her comical-Negro shtick for a minute. "Mrs. Loeffler?"

"Uh-oh." Checking the area for vengeance seekers, bill collectors, cops.

"No, it's only about that Ehbler-Cohen ticket? With the weird-ass defined-benefit plan? They were hiding it in the spreadsheets. Look."

Maxine looks. "How did you—"

"It was luck, really, I happened to take my reading glasses off, and suddenly, blurry but there it was, the pattern. Just way too many them damn empty cells."

"Walk me through this idiot style, please, I'm hopeless at spreadsheets, people say Excel, I think they're talking about a T-shirt size."

"Look, you pull down Tools, click on Auditing, and that lets you see everything that's going into the formula cells, and . . . dig it."

"Oh. Wow." Following along, "Sweet." Nodding appreciatively, like it's a cooking show. "Nice going, I would never have caught that."

"Well, you were out working on some other thing, so I took the liberty . . ."

"Where'd you pick this stuff up, if you don't mind my asking?"

"Night school. All this time you thought I was at rehab? Ha, ha. I've been taking CPA classes. Going for my license next month."

"Daytona! This is wonderful, so why keep it such a secret?"

"Didn't want you be thinkin *All About Eve* and shit."

CHRISTMAS COMES AND GOES, and maybe it isn't Maxine's holiday but it is Horst's and the kids', and this year it seems less of an effort for her to be a sport, though she does predictably find herself the night before Christmas screaming desperate in Macy's at midnight, her brain the usual Sno-Kone with convolutions, up on the mezzanine rejecting one gift idea after another, suddenly here's a warm and friendly tap on her shoulder—aaahh! Dr. Itzling! Her dentist! This is what it's come to!

But somewhere in the tinsel dazzle, there are also fragrances from weeklong oven exercises, Horst and his possibly toxic Old-Time Eggnog recipe, the coming and going of friends and relatives including the distant in-law who always ends up telling mohel jokes, *A Beast Wars Family Christmas* at Radio City Music Hall, with Optimus Primal, Rhinox, Cheetor, and the gang helping a middle school with its Christmas pageant by doing singing cameos as manger animals, the boys, overindulged, sitting among an early-morning mountain of unreusable wrapping paper and packaging, out of which have emerged game platforms, action figures, DVDs, sporting equipment, clothes they may or may not ever wear.

During this occur odd moments of slack, reserved for visits more spectral, from those who cannot or would not ever be here—among them, at a typically uneasy distance from the jollification, Nick Windust, from whom there's been not a word, though why should there be. Out somewhere in that nomad's field of indifference, riding the Chinese bus into a futurity of imprecise schedules and reduced options. How long does that go on?

"Nick."

He's silent, wherever he is. By now one more American sheep the shepherds have temporarily lost track of, somewhere in the high country above this ruinous hour, cragfast in the storm.

MONDAY AFTER THE HOLIDAYS, Kugelblitz has resumed, Horst and Jake Pimento are over in New Jersey looking for office space, Maxine should either try to cop another hour of z's or go in to work, but she knows where she ought to be, and as soon as everybody's out of the house, she brews twelve cups of coffee, gets in front of her screen, logs in, and heads for DeepArcher.

Open source has certainly brought some changes. Core is teeming these days with smartasses, yups, tourists, and twits writing code for whatever they think they want and installing it, till some other head-case finds it and deinstalls it. Maxine goes in with no clear idea of what she'll find.

Onto the screen, accordingly, leaps a desert, correction, *the* desert. Empty as the train stations and spaceport terminals of a more innocent time were overpopulated. No middle-class amenities here, beyond arrows to let you scan around the horizon. This is survivalist country. Movements are blurless, every pixel doing its job, the radiation from above triggering colors too unsafe for hex code, a sound track of ground-level desert wind. This is what she's supposed to pick her way across, dowsing a desert which is not only a desert, for links invisible and undefined.

Not yet in despair, off she goes, zooming and swiveling, up and down dunes and wadis of deep purity finely touched with mineral tints, beneath rocks and ridgelines, empty stretches in which Omar Sharif continues not to come riding in out of a mirage. It should be just one more teen-sociopath video game, except it's not a shooter, so far anyway, there's no story line, no details about the destination, no manual to read, no cheat list. Does anybody get extra lives? Does anybody even get this one?

She pauses in the uneasy melismas of desert wind. Suppose it's all about losing, not finding. What has she lost? Maxine? Hello? To put it another way, what's she trying to lose?

Windust, back to Windust. Dowsing through her off-screen day-to-day, did she once in the pre–11 September past somehow click on the exact invisible pixel that brought her to him? Did he do the same and find himself entering her life? How does one of them reverse the process?

Toggling between horizontal and overhead views, she discovers a way to vary the angle in between, so that like an archaeologist at dawn she can now see this desert landscape at a very shallow raking angle, allowing her to pick up relief features that would otherwise be invisible. These prove to be fertile sources of the links she needs to be clicking on. Soon she finds herself getting crossfaded to relay stations, oases, very rarely a traveler coming the other way, back from whatever's out ahead, with very little to tell beyond cryptic allusions to some icy uncanalized river on whose far bank lies a city built of a rare impregnable metal, gray and gleaming in self-contained mystery, entered only after lengthy exchanges of signs and countersigns . . .

Structures begin to emerge ahead, carrion birds appear in the sky. Now and then, far off, human figures, robed and hooded, still, wind-ruffled, taller than the perspective would call for, stand and watch Maxine. No attempts at approach or welcome. Ahead, past the baked-mud district that now rises around her, she can feel a presence. The sky changes, beginning to pick up saturation, edging into SVG Alice Blue, the landscape acquiring a queer luminosity, moving toward her, picking up speed, rushing in to envelop her.

Where should her freakout point be set here, exactly? The town, the casbah, whatever it is, sweeps past, leaving her in what is now a Third World darkness, lit only by isolated episodes of fire. After a while, feeling her way in the dark, she strikes oil. An enormous gusher, sudden, bass-intensive, black on black, goes booming upward, prospectors appear from nowhere with generators and searchlights, in whose glare the top of the thing can't even be seen. Every wildcatter's dream, and for many the point of the journey. Maxine goes wow, takes a virtual snapshot, but continues on her way. Not long after, the blowout bursts into flame and remains visible behind her for miles.

A night whose length can't be selected as a preference. A midwatch whose purpose is to turn whoever's out in it into a blind dowser of the unknown, all but lost in the empty quarter. Never to focus on anything that can be seen.

At virtual daybreak who should Maxine run into but Vip Epperdew, up on a ridgeline gazing at the desert. She's not sure he recognizes her. "How are Shae and Bruno?"

"I think they're in L.A. I'm not, I'm still in Vegas. We seem to be no longer a threesome."

"What happened?"

"We were at the MGM Grand, I was playing one of the Stooges slots, had just got three Larrys, a Moe, and a pie on the payline, turned around to share my good fortune, Shae and Bruno were nowhere in sight. Collected my jackpot, went looking all over for them, they were gone. I always imagined if they ever did run out, I'd be left in some embarrassing public situation, handcuffed to a lamppost or whatever. But there I was, free as any normal citizen, with the room paid up and enough casino credit to last me a couple of days anyway."

"Must've been unsettling."

"At that point I was still too preoccupied with the slots, actually. By the time I understood the kids weren't coming back, I'd won enough to sign a lease on a one-bedroom unit in North Las Vegas. The rest has been coasting on momentum." Nowadays Vip is a professional slots jockey, somehow so far staying a fraction of a percent ahead, a regular, known all around town, from carpet joints to convenience stores. He's picked up an attitude to go with his casino butt. He's found a calling.

"Like my rig?" gesturing downhill at a Citroën Sahara, built back in the sixties, front and rear engines, four-wheel drive for desert terrain, rendered in affectionate detail, looks like a normal 2CV except for the spare tire on the hood. "Only 600 of 'em ever produced, won the real one on a pair of fishhooks nobody believed I had. Cut you for it if you'd like, high card. Case you're wondering, the beauty of this site," looking around the empty desertscape, "is it *ain't* Vegas. No casinos, honest odds. Random numbers here are strictly legit."

"So I was told once. Nowadays, not so sure. You might want to be careful, now—Vip? do you remember me?"

"Darlin, I don't even remember the last deal."

She finds a link that brings her into an oasis, a wraparound garden straight out of the Islamic paradise, more water than has ever flowed in all the broken country she's come in out of, palms, swimming pools with in-pool bars, wine and pipe smoke, melons and dates, a music track heavy on the hijaz scale. This time, as a matter of fact, she has a confirmed Omar Sharif sighting, inside a tent, playing bridge and flashing that killer smile. And then, with no intro,

"Hi, Maxine." Windust's avatar is a younger version of himself, a not-yet-corrupted entry-level wise-ass, brighter than he deserves.

"Never expected to find you in here, Nick."

Oh, really? This isn't what she hoped would happen? That somebody, some all-knowing cyber-yenta her online history has always belonged to, would be logging her every click, every cursor movement? Knowing what she wants before she does?

"Did you get back to D.C. all right?" Which, if it sounds too much like where's my money, tough shit.

"Not all the way back. There are exclusion zones now. Around my house, my family. I haven't been getting much sleep. It looks like they've cut me loose. Loose at last. All gone dark, everybody in my address book, even those with no names, only numbers."

"Where are you now, like physically?"

"Some Wi-Fi hotspot. Starbucks, I think."

He thinks. She has to take an unexpected breath then. This is almost the first thing he's said that she really believes. He doesn't fucking know where he is anymore. Some transparent beam of feeling passes through her, which she won't identify till later. This is how long it's been since she felt pity.

Abruptly, she isn't sure who took the first step, they're back out on the desert again, moving at high speed, not exactly flying because that would mean she's asleep and dreaming, beneath a crescent moon that sheds more illumination than it should, past wind-shaped rock formations that Windust tends to dodge suddenly and violently into the cover of, pulling her somehow with him.

"Somebody's shooting at us?"

"Not yet, but we have to assume something's tracking us, everything we do, holding it short-term. They'll think they see a pattern of run for cover. Then we'll surprise them and stay in the open . . ."

"'We'? I kind of like hide behind the rocks myself. Are these the same people who were shooting AKs at us that time?"

"Don't go sentimental on me."

"Why not? We could've been just like this. Lovers on the run."

"Oh, great call. Your kids, your home, your family, your business and reputation, in exchange for a cheap fatality for all those you can't save. Works for me." The avatar gazes at her, steady, unremorseful, all a deliberate front, granted, but whoever "they" are, she needs to believe they are far worse than anything Windust became later on, working for them. They found his careless gift of boy's cruelty and developed it, deployed and used it, by tiny increments, till one day he was a professional sadist with a GS-1800-series job and no regrets. Nothing could touch him, and he thought that would just go on, deep into his retirement years. Chump. Asshole.

She's furious, she's helpless. "What can I—"

"Nothing."

"I know. But—"

"I didn't come looking for you. You clicked on me."

"Did I."

Long silence, as if he's having an argument with himself and they finally settle it. "I'll be at the place. I can't guarantee an erection."

"Aw. You OK with opening your heart to somebody?"

"I was thinking more like, bring money?"

"I'll see how much I can steal from the children."

37

Due to some likely 007–related mental block about packing it, she has tried to avoid the Walther PPK with the laser in the grip, depending instead on her secondary, the Beretta, which, if handguns had conscious careers, it might consider a promotion. But now she goes, gets the stepladder, roots around up in the back of the closet, and brings out the PPK. At least it isn't the ladies' model where the grip comes in pink pearl. Checks the batteries, cycles the laser on and off. Never know when a gal might need a laser.

Out into one of those oppressive wintry afternoons, the sky over New Jersey a pale battle flag of the ancient nation of winter, divided horizontally, hex thistle above, buttermilk yellow below, over to Broadway to look for a cab, which this time of day is likely heading back off shift to Long Island City and unwilling to pick up fares. So it turns out. By the time she can finally wave one down, city lights are coming on and darkness is falling.

Down at the "safe house," she hits the buzzer, waits, waits, no reply, the door's locked, but she can see light around the edges. She peers in to check out the lock situation and notices that only the latch is on, no bolt. After years of experimenting with different store and credit cards, she's found the ideal combination of strength and flexibility in the plastic game cards the boys keep bringing home from ESPN Zone. Taking one of these now, down briefly on one knee, she has 'loided her way in before she can let herself wonder if it's such a good idea.

Rodent life, quick shadows flickering across her path. Echoing in the stairwells, screamers on other floors, nonhuman noises she can't identify. Corner shadows thick as grease, that can't be seen into no matter how bright your bulb. Hallways lighted fitfully and heat, if any, only through selected radiators, so that there are cold patches, indicating the presence of malevolent spirit forces, according to ex–New Agers of Maxine's acquaintance. Down some corridor a fire alarm with a dying battery repeats a shrill, desolate chirp. She remembers Windust saying that sundown is when the dogs come out.

The door of the apartment is open. She brings out the PPK, hits the laser, flips up the safety, eases inside. The dogs are there, three, four of them surrounding something lying between here and the kitchen. There's a smell you don't have to be a dog to pick up. Maxine slides away from the door in case any of them want to leave in a hurry. Her voice firm enough so far, "All right, Toto—freeze!"

Their heads come up, their muzzles are darker-colored than they need to be. She edges in, along the wall. The object hasn't moved. It announces itself, the center of attention, even if it's dead, it's still trying to manage the story.

One dog goes running out the door, two move up snarling to confront her, another stands by Windust's corpse and waits for the intruder to be dealt with. Gazing at Maxine with—not a canine look really, Shawn if he were here certainly could confirm—the face before the face. "Don't I remember you from Westminster last year, Best in Category?"

The nearest dog is a mix of rottweiler plus you name it, and the little red dot has moved to the center of its forehead, encouragingly not jittering around but steady as a rock. The wingdog pauses, as if to see what will happen.

"Come on," she whispers, "you know what it is, pal, it's drilling right into your third eye . . . come on . . . we don't need to have this happen . . ." The snarling stops, the dogs, attentively, step toward the exit, the alpha in the kitchen backs away finally from the corpse and—is it nodding at her? joins them. They wait out in the hallway.

The dogs have done some damage she tries not to look at, and there's the smell. Reciting to herself a rhyme from long-ago girlhood,

> Dead, said the doc-tuhvr,
> Dead, said the nurse,
> Dead, said da lady wit
> De al-liga-tuh purse . . .

She stumbles to the toilet, hits the exhaust fan, and kneels on the cold tiles beneath the racket of the fan. The contents of the bowl give a slight but unmistakable surge upward, as if trying to communicate. She vomits, seized in a vision of all the exhaust ducts from every dismal office and forgotten transient space of the city, all feeding by way of a gigantic manifold into a single pipe and roaring away in a constant wind of anal gas, bad breath, and decaying tissue, venting as you'd expect someplace over in New Jersey . . . as meantime, inside the gratings over each one of these million vents, grease goes on collecting forever in the slots and louvers, and the dust rising and falling is held there, accumulating over the years in a blackened, browned, secret fur . . . merciless powder-blue light, black-and-white floral wallpaper, her own unstable reflection in the mirror . . . There's vomit on the sleeve of her coat, she tries to wash it out with cold water, nothing works.

She rejoins the silent stiff in the other room. Over in the corner, the Lady with the Alligator Purse watches, silent, no highlights off her eyes, only the curve of a smile faintly visible in the shadows, the purse slung over one shoulder, its contents forever unrevealed because you always wake up before you see them.

"Time's a-wastin," the Lady whispers, not unkindly.

Despite which Maxine takes a minute to observe the former Nick

Windust. He was a torturer, a murderer many times over, his cock has been inside her, and at the moment she's not sure what she feels, all she can focus on are the bespoke chukka boots, in this light a soiled pale brown. What is she doing here? What the blessed fuck, did she run over here thinking she could do to stop this? . . . These poor, stupid shoes . . .

She takes a rapid tour of his pockets—no wallet, no money, folding or otherwise, no keys, no Filofax, no cellular phone, no smokes or matches or lighters, no meds or eyewear, just the collection of empty pockets. Talk about going out clean. At least he's consistent. He was never in this for the money. Neolib mischief must have held some different and now-unknowable appeal for him. All he had at the end, with the other world drawing near, was his rap sheet, and his dispatchers have left him to its mercy. The full length of it, the years, the weight.

So who was she talking to, back there in the DeepArcher oasis? If Windust, judging by the smell, was already long dead by then, it gives her a couple of problematic choices—either he was speaking to her from the other side or it was an impostor and the link could have been embedded by anybody, not necessarily a well-wisher, spooks, Gabriel Ice . . . Some random twelve-year-old in California. Why believe any of it?

The phone rings. She jumps a little. The dogs come to the doorway, curious. Pick up? she thinks not. After five rings an answering machine on the kitchen counter comes on, with the volume set on high so there's no avoiding the incoming. It's no voice she recognizes, a high harsh whisper. "We know you're there. You don't have to pick up. This is just a reminder that it's a school night, and you never know when your kids might need you with them."

Oh, fuck. Oh, fuck.

On the way out, she passes a mirror, takes an automatic look, sees a blurred moving figure, maybe herself, likely something else, the Lady again, all in shadow except for a single highlight off her wedding band, whose color, if you could taste light, which for a moment she imagines she can, you'd have to call faintly bitter.

411

. . .

NO COPS OUTSIDE ANYPLACE, no cabs, early-midwinter darkness. Cold, a wind picking up. The glow of inhabited city streets too far away. She has stepped out into a different night, a different town altogether, one of those first-person-shooter towns that you can drive around in seemingly forever, but never away from. The only humanity visible are virtual extras in the distance, none offering any of the help she needs. She gropes through her bag, finds her cellular phone, and of course can't get a signal this far away from civilization, and even if she could, the batteries are almost dead.

Maybe the phone call was only a warning, maybe that's all, maybe the boys are safe. Maybe this is a fool's assumption she can't make anymore. Vyrva was supposed to be picking up Otis at school, Ziggy should be down at krav maga with Nigel, but so what. Every place in her day she's taken for granted is no longer safe, because the only question it's come down to is, where will Ziggy and Otis be protected from harm? Who of all those on her network really is trustworthy anymore?

It might be useful, she reminds herself, not to panic here. She imagines herself solidifying into not exactly a pillar of salt, something between that and a commemorative statue, iron and gaunt, of all the women in New York who used to annoy her standing by the curbsides "hailing a taxi," though no taxis might be visible for ten miles in any direction—nevertheless holding their hand out toward the empty street and the oncoming traffic that isn't there, not beseechingly but in a strangely entitled way, a secret gesture that will trigger an all-cabbie alert, "Bitch standing at corner with hand up in air! Go! Go!"

Yet here, turning into some version of herself she doesn't recognize, without deliberation she watches her own hand drift out into the wind off the river, and tries from the absence of hope, the failure of redemption, to summon a magical escape. Maybe what she saw in those women wasn't entitlement, maybe all it is really is an act of faith. Which in New York even stepping out onto the street is, technically.

Back in Manhattan meatspace, what she ends up doing is somehow passing through the shadowy copless cross streets to Tenth Avenue and finding headed uptown a curb-to-curb abundance of lighted alphanumerics on cheerful yellow rooftops, traveling the darkening hour as if the pavement like a black river is itself flowing away forever uptown, and all the taxis and trucks and suburbanite cars only being carried along on top of it . . .

HORST ISN'T HOME YET. Otis and Fiona are in the boys' room, having creative differences as usual. Ziggy is in front of the tube, as if nothing much has been happening in his day, watching *Scooby Goes Latin!* (1990). Maxine after a quick visit to the bathroom to reformat, knowing better than to start in with the Q&A, comes in and sits down next to him about the time it breaks for a commercial.

"Hi, Mom." She wants to enfold him forever. Instead lets him recap the plot for her. Shaggy, somehow allowed to drive the van, has become confused and made some navigational errors, landing the adventurous quintet eventually in Medellín, Colombia, home at the time to a notorious cocaine cartel, where they stumble onto a scheme by a rogue DEA agent to gain control of the cartel by pretending to be the ghost—what else—of an assassinated drug kingpin. With the help of a pack of local street urchins, however, Scooby and his pals foil the plan.

The cartoon comes back on, the villain is brought to justice. "And I would've got away with it, too," he complains, "if it hadn't been for those Medellín kids!"

"So," innocent as she can manage, "how was krav maga today?"

"You know, funny you should ask. I begin to see the point."

Right after class Nigel was outside someplace looking for his sitter, and Emma Levin was going around setting the security perimeter, when Ziggy heard a beep from his backpack.

"Uh-oh. Nige." Ziggy fished out his Cybiko, checked the screen, started punching buttons with a little stylus. "He's in the Duane Reade around the corner. There's a van out in front of this place with some creepy guys and the motor idling."

"Hey, cool, a pocket keyboard, you can send, like, e-mails on this?"

"More like instant messaging. You don't think this van is anything to worry about?"

Suddenly there was a huge flash of light and burst of noise. *"Harah!"* muttered Emma, "the tripwire."

They ran out the back exit to find a large paramilitary-looking party in the areaway blinking, staggering, and cursing. Everything smelling like fireworks.

"Something we can do for you?" Emma stepping quickly to the right and motioning Ziggy to the left. The visitor turned toward where she'd spoken from and appeared to be reaching for something. Emma went blurring into action. The ape didn't fly very far through the air but was disorganized enough by the time he hit that it took her only a few economical gestures, with Ziggy as backup, to dispose of him.

"Not only an amateur but stupid too. He doesn't know who he's fooling with?"

"You're awesome, Ms. Levin."

"'Course, but I meant you. You're part of my unit, Zig, nobody messes with any of us, he didn't even get that far with it?"

She searches the intruder and finds a Glock with an oversize magazine. Ziggy's eyes grow distant, as if attending to something internal. "Hmm . . . maybe not a civilian, yet not much of a professional, what else does that leave, I wonder."

"Private contractor?"

"What I was thinking."

"So you're a sleeper cell after all."

Shrug. "I'm on call 24/7. When I'm needed, I'm there. Looks like I'm needed. Just let me set another flashbang here, then we'll check down in the basement, find a dolly, roll this idiot out to someplace his friends in the van can collect him."

They rolled the unconscious gunhand on up the block and dumped him by the curb next to a broken pressboard credenza, swollen and lopsided from rainwater. They discussed whether or not to dial 911, figured what could hurt. "And that was about it. Nigel typically was pissed that he didn't get in on it."

"And . . . this is all something you saw on *Power Rangers* or one of them," Maxine hopefully.

"Bad karma to lie about stuff like that . . . Mom? You all right?"

"Oh Ziggurat . . . I'm just glad you're safe. So proud of you, how you handled yourself . . . Ms. Levin must be, too. OK if I call her later?"

"Tellin ya, she'll confirm."

"Just to say thanks, Ziggy."

Otis and Fiona come blasting out the bedroom door.

"Listenna me, Fi, lose the perpetuity language, you'll regret it."

"It's only boilerplate, Satjeevan says I can walk anytime I want."

"You believe that? He's a recruiter."

"Now you're acting like a jealous boyfriend."

"Real mature, Fiona."

Horst comes blinking into the apartment, has a look at Maxine. "Need a minute with yer ma here, guys," lifts her by one wrist, gently steers her to the bedroom.

"I'm all right," Maxine avoiding eye contact.

"You're shaking, you're whiter than Greenwich, Connecticut on a Thursday. It's nothing to worry about, darlin. I talked to Zig's instructor, just the standard New York creep that krav maga's designed to deal with." She knows what this honest never-to-be-wised-up face can change into, knows she better let this ride unless she wants to collapse under whatever it is, call it guilt, settles for nodding, distant, miserable. Let Horst have the standard-creep story. There are a thousand things in this town to be afraid of, maybe even two thousand, and there's too much else he won't likely ever know. All the silences, all the years, fraud-examiner infidelities without the fucking, plus unexpectedly some real fucking and now the other party is dead. No question of improvising around what happened today, first thing Horst will go, this dead guy, you were seeing him? and she'll flare up, you don't know what you're talking about, then he'll blame her for putting the boys in danger, then she'll go, so where were you when you should've been here for them, and so fuckin on and on, yes and it'll be right back to the olden days. So best to just dummy up here, Maxine, once again, just, dummy, up.

NEXT DAY EMMA LEVIN CALLS with news of an anonymous floral bouquet heavy on the roses delivered to her studio, with a note in Hebrew to the effect that all will be well.

"The BF, maybe?"

"Naftali knows flowers exist, he sees them at the corner market, but he still thinks they're something to eat."

"So maybe . . . ?"

"Maybe. Then again, nobody pays us to be Shirley Temple. Let's wait and see."

Still, maybe, at least, not such a bad sign? Meantime Avi and Brooke having just moved into a co-op near Riverside for a settling price whose obscenity is consistent with Avi's salary at hashslingrz, Maxine now has a halfway-plausible excuse to stash the boys for a little while with their grandparents, whose building enjoys security arrangements rivaling any to be found in our nation's capital. Horst goes for this eagerly, not least because he is rediscovering his quasi-ex-wife as an object of lust. "I can't explain it . . ."

"Good, don't."

"It's like committing adultery, only different?"

Mr. Elegant. Maxine guesses it is mysteriously not unconnected with loose-woman vibrations she is giving off like it or not, plus Horst's insane suspicion of every man, ghost or whatever, who gets within ass-grabbing distance of her, and since it does not take too much shift in her own perversity level to feel flattered here, she lets him think what he'll think, and the hardon situation does not suffer thereby.

Additionally, one day out of nowhere Horst hands her the keys to the Impala.

"Why would I need these?"

"Just in case."

"Of . . ."

"Nothing solid, only a feeling."

"A what, Horst?" She peers. He looks normal enough. "You'd be good with that? Given your ding-intolerance problem?"

"Oh, cost of body work, you'd have to pick that up o' course."

Which doesn't mean he's lounging around the house all the time. One night he and his runningmate Jake Pimento, who has moved out of Battery Park and up to Murray Hill, are out on an all-nighter with a posse of venture capitalists from across the sea newly interested in rare earths, which Horst by ESP has determined is the next hot commodity, and Maxine decides to stay over with her parents and the boys.

She crashes early but keeps waking up. Dream fragments, cycles she can't exit. She looks in a mirror, a face appears behind her, her own face but full of evil intent. All night these vignettes keep sending her each time up into a vibrating hollowness of heart. At some point, enough. She rolls muttering from between the damp sheets. Somebody is blasting up and down upper Broadway in a car whose horn plays the first eight bars of Nino Rota's *Godfather* theme. Over and over. This happens once a year, and tonight, apparently, is the night.

Maxine begins to prowl the apartment. The boys stacked in bunk beds, the door left a little open, she likes to think for her, knowing that someday their doors will be shut and she'll have to knock. Ernie's office, which he shares with a washer and dryer, an antique Apple CRT monitor on a desk, left on, Elaine's dining-room museum of long-operating light-bulbs from this apartment, each in its little foam display holder, labeled with the dates of screw-in and burnout. Sylvania bulbs of a certain era seem to've lasted the longest.

Some kind of classical music coming from the TV room. Mozart. In these desperate stretches of early-morning programming, she finds

Ernie tubeside, his face transfigured in the ancient Trinitron glow, watching an obscure, in fact never-distributed Marx Brothers version of *Don Giovanni*, with Groucho in the title role. She tiptoes in barefoot and sits next to her father on the couch. There's a big plastic bowl of popcorn, too big even for two people, which Ernie after a while nudges in her direction. During a recitative he fills her in. "They cut the Commendatore so there's no Donna Anna, no Don Ottavio, this way, without the murder, it's a comedy." Leporello is being played by both Chico and Harpo, one for lines and one for sight gags, Chico fast-talking his way through the Catalogue Aria for example while Harpo runs around after Donna Elvira (Margaret Dumont, in the role she was born for), pinching, groping, and honking his bicycle horn, as well as later picking harp accompaniment for "Deh, vieni alla finestra." Masetto is a studio baritone who is not Nelson Eddy, Zerlina is a very young, lip-synced and more-than-presentable Beatrice Pearson, later to portray another ingenue with a fatality for scoundrels opposite John Garfield in *Force of Evil* (1948).

When the opera's over, Ernie hits the mute button and spreads his hands along with a half shrug, like a basso taking a bow. "So? First time I ever saw you sit through an opera."

"Don't know, Pop, must be the company."

"I taped it for the boys too, seems like it's up their alley."

"Cultural exchange, I notice they've got you playing Metal Gear Solid these days."

"Better than the TV garbage I used to find you and Brooke staring at."

"Yeah, you really hated all those cop shows. If you caught us watching one, you'd turn it off and ground us."

"It's like they've gotten any better? What happened to private eyes, lovable criminals? lost in all that post-sixties propaganda, Orwell's boot on the face, endless prosecution and enforcement, cop cop cop. Why shouldn't we want to keep you girls away from that, protect your sensitive minds? See how much good it did. Your sister the Likudnik, you chasing down poor schmucks who're only trying to pay the rent."

"Maybe TV back then was brainwashing, but it could never happen today. Nobody's in control of the Internet."

"You serious? Believe that while you still can, Sunshine. You know where it all comes from, this online paradise of yours? It started back during the Cold War, when the think tanks were full of geniuses plotting nuclear scenarios. Attaché cases and horn-rims, every appearance of scholarly sanity, going in to work every day to imagine all the ways the world was going to end. Your Internet, back then the Defense Department called it DARPAnet, the real original purpose was to assure survival of U.S. command and control after a nuclear exchange with the Soviets."

"What."

"Sure, the idea was to set up enough nodes so no matter what got knocked out, they could always reassemble some kind of network by connecting up what was left."

Here in the capital of insomnia, it is hours yet from dawn, and this is what innocent father-daughter conversations can drift into. Beneath these windows they can hear the lawless soundscape of the midnight street, breakage, screaming, vehicle exhaust, New York laughter, too loud, too trivial, brakes applied too late before some gut-wrenching thud. When Maxine was little, she thought of this nightly uproar as trouble too far away to matter, like sirens. Now it's always too close, part of the deal.

"Were you ever in on that Cold War stuff, Pop?"

"For me? Too technical. But people at Bronx Science I ran with . . . Crazy Yale Jacobian, nice kid, we used to go downtown, make a little change playing Ping-Pong. He went off to MIT, got a job with the RAND Corporation, moved to California, We lost touch."

"Maybe he didn't work in the blowing–up–the–world department."

"I know, I'm a judgmental person, sue me. You had to been there, kid. Everybody thinks now the Eisenhower years were so quaint and cute and boring, but all that had a price, just underneath was the pure terror. Midnight forever. If you stopped even for a minute to think, there it was and you could fall into it so easily. Some fell. Some went nuts, some even took their own lives."

"Pop."

"Yep, and your Internet was their invention, this magical convenience that creeps now like a smell through the smallest details of our lives, the shopping, the housework, the homework, the taxes, absorbing our energy, eating up our precious time. And there's no innocence. Anywhere. Never was. It was conceived in sin, the worst possible. As it kept growing, it never stopped carrying in its heart a bitter-cold death wish for the planet, and don't think anything has changed, kid."

Maxine goes sorting among semiexploded kernels for what little popcorn is left. "But history goes on, as you always like to remind us. The Cold War ended, right? the Internet kept evolving, away from military, into civilian—nowadays it's chat rooms, the World Wide Web, shopping online, the worst you can say is it's maybe getting a little commercialized. And look how it's empowering all these billions of people, the promise, the freedom."

Ernie begins channel-surfing, as if in annoyance. "Call it freedom, it's based on control. Everybody connected together, impossible anybody should get lost, ever again. Take the next step, connect it to these cell phones, you've got a total Web of surveillance, inescapable. You remember the comics in the *Daily News*? Dick Tracy's wrist radio? it'll be everywhere, the rubes'll all be begging to wear one, handcuffs of the future. Terrific. What they dream about at the Pentagon, worldwide martial law."

"So this is where I get my paranoia from."

"Ask your kids. Look at Metal Gear Solid—who do the terrorists kidnap? Who's Snake trying to rescue? The head of DARPA. Think about that, huh?"

"Pop."

"Don't believe us, ask your friends in the FBI, you know, those kind policemen with their NCIC database? Fifty, a hundred million files? They'll confirm, I'm sure."

She understands this for the opening it apparently is. "Listen, Pop. I have to tell you . . ." Out it comes. The unrelenting vacuum of Windust's departure. Edited for grandparental anxieties, natch, like no mention of Ziggy's krav maga episode.

Ernie hears her through, "Saw something in the paper. Mysterious death, they described him as a think-tank pundit."

"They would. Hit man, they say anything about that? Assassin?"

"Nope. But I guess FBI, CIA, that wouldn't rule out assassin."

"Pop, the petty-fraud community I get to work with, we have our own losers' code, like loyalty, respect, don't snitch till you have to. But that gang, they're out shopping each other before breakfast, Windust was living on borrowed time."

"You think he was done in by his own? I would've guessed revenge, all the seriously pissed-off Third Worlders this guy must have collected along the way."

"You saw him before I did, you passed me his card, you could've said something."

"More than what I was saying already? When you were little, I always tried to keep you as much as I could from joining in on all the brainless adoration of cops, but after a point you make your own mistakes." Then, tentative as she's ever seen him, "Maxeleh, you didn't . . . ?"

Looking more at her knees than at her father, she pretends to explain, "All these penny-ante con artists, I never once cut slack for any of them, but the first major-league war criminal I run into, I'm starstruck, he tortures and murders people, always gets away with it, am I repelled, shocked? no, I'm thinking, he can turn. He can still turn away, nobody's that bad, he has to have a conscience, there's time, he can make up for it, except now he can't—"

"Sh. Shh. It's all right, kiddo," reaching diffidently for her face. No, this doesn't let her off the hook, she knows she's being less than honest, hoping Ernie, either to protect himself or in true innocence she can't bring herself to break, will only take it literally. Which he does. "You were always like this. I kept waiting for you to give it up, let it go, turn as cold as the rest of us, praying all the time you wouldn't. You'd come back from school, history classes, some new nightmare, the Indians, the Holocaust, crimes I hardened my heart against years ago, taught them but didn't feel them so much anymore, and you'd be so angry, passionately hurting, your little hands in fists, how could anybody do these things, how could they live with themselves? What was I supposed to say? We handed you the tissues and said, it's grown-ups, some act that way, you don't have to be like them, you can be better. Best we could ever come up with, pathetic, but you know what, I never found out what we should have said. Think I'm happy about that?"

"The boys ask me the same things now, I don't want to see them turn into their classmates, cynical smart-mouthed little bastards—but what happens if Ziggy and Otis start caring too much, Pop, this world, it could destroy them, so easily."

"No alternative, you trust them, trust yourself, and the same for Horst, who seems to be back in the picture now . . ."

"For a while now, actually. Maybe never out of it."

"Well, as far as this other guy, better somebody else should deal with the flowers, the eulogies. Like Joe Hill always sez, don't mourn, organize. And a word of fashion advice from your stylish old man here, wear some color, stay away from too much black."

38

So down at Shawn's next morning is of course where she lets herself disorganize all to pieces, not with her parents or husband or dear friend Heidi, no—in front of some idiot-surfant whose worst idea of a bad day is one-foot-high waves.

"So you . . . did have feelings for this guy."

"Have feelings," California gobbledygook, translate please, no, wait, don't. "Shawn? OK you were right, I was wrong, you know what, fuck you, how much do I still owe you, we should settle up because I'm never coming back here again."

"Our first fight."

"Our last." For some reason she doesn't move.

"Maxi, it's time. I reach this point with everybody. What you need to deal with now is The Wisdom."

"Great, I'm at the dentist here."

Shawn darkens the blinds, puts on a tape of Moroccan trance music, lights a joss stick. "Are you ready?"

"No. Shawn—"

"Here it is—The Wisdom. Prepare to copy." She stays on her meditation mat despite herself. Breathing deeply, Shawn announces, "'Is what it is is . . . is it is what it is.'" Allowing a silence to fall, lengthy but maybe not as deep as the breaths he's taking. "Got that?"

"Shawn . . ."

"That's The Wisdom, repeat it back."

Sighing pointedly, she complies, adding, "Depending of course what your definition of the word 'is' is."

RIGHT, SOMETHING A LITTLE DIFFERENT. What has the alternative ever been? Reclaimed by the small-time day-to-day, pretending life is Back To Normal, wrapping herself shivering against contingency's winter in some threadbare blanket of first-quarter expenses, school committees, cable-bill irregularities, a workday jittering with low-life fantasies for which "fraud" is often too elegant a term, upstairs neighbors to whom bathtub caulking is an alien concept, symptoms upper-respiratory and lower-intestinal, all in the quaint belief that change will always be gradual enough to manage, with insurance, with safety equipment, with healthy diets and regular exercise, and that evil never comes roaring out of the sky to explode into anybody's towering delusions about being exempt . . .

Each day she sees Ziggy and Otis get through safely is another thousandth of a point added to her confidence level that maybe nobody's really after them, maybe nobody holds her responsible for whatever Windust did, maybe Lester Traipse's probable murderer, Gabriel Ice, is not projecting evil energy into the heart of her family by way of Avi Deschler, who is looking more and more like the kid in the teen horror movie who turns out to be possessed. "Nah," Brooke blithely, "he's probably experimenting. Some Goth thing maybe." Oddly these days Maxine finds herself zeroing in on her sister, understanding that among all the signs and symptoms of city pathology, Brooke historically has been her best indication, her high-sensitivity toxic detector, and she is intrigued now to notice that into Brooke's demeanor some strange anti-kvetchiness has come lately creeping, some willingness to let go of the old obsessions about people and purchases, some . . . glow? Aahh! No, it couldn't be. Could it?

"All right, so let's have it, when are you due?"

"Hmm? 'What do I do'? You mean like all day or . . . Oh. Oh, Maxi the Taxi, you tumbled already? I only told Avi last night."

"Sisterhood is extrasensory, watch more horror movies, you'll get educated. How is Avi with this?"

"Awesome?"

Not quite how Avi would put it. He's now making a weekly practice of slipping in the delivery gate around the corner and past Daytona's headshaking scrutiny to tell Maxine his sad hashslingrz stories, as if she has an arsenal of superpowers to call on.

His workplace has become a rat's nest of empire building, turf defense, careerism, backstabbing, betrayal, and snitchcraft. What Avi once imagined as simple paranoia about the competition is in fact systemic by now, with more enemies inside than out. He finds himself actually using the word "tribal." Also,

"Mind if I use your toilet a minute?"

Which with Avi has become a Frequently Asked Question. Plus the red eyes with the half-closed eyelids, runny nose, dopey and scattered conversation, buzzers do begin to sound. One day Maxine gives him a short lead, then follows him out down the hall and into the toilet, where she finds her brother-in-law with a computer-duster nozzle up his nose, committing propellant abuse.

"Avi, really."

"It's air in a can, harmless."

"Read the label. Some planet where the atmosphere is fluoroethane gas, 'air,' maybe. Meanwhile, back on earth, you should remember you'll be a patafamiliarass before you know it here."

"Thanks. I should be totally euphoric, right? Guess what, I'm not, I'm anxious, I know I need to find another job, Ice has me by the balls, how do I pay off a mortgage, support a family, without a paycheck?"

"All Ice cares about," there-there as usual, "is the lunchhooks of others in the company tambourine, with nondisclosure a distant second. If you can convince him you're no threat in either area, he'll go out and headhunt you the perfect dream job himself."

BUT SHE CAN'T stay out of DeepArcher. Since it went open source and welcomed in half the planet, none of them who they say they are, acquiring a set of option menus the size of the Internal Revenue Code, anybody is likely to be wandering around the site, herds of tourist-idle, cop-curious, the end of life below the spiders as we've known it, ROM hackers, homebrewers, RPG heretics, continually unwriting and overwriting, disallowing, deprecating, newly defining an ever-growing inventory of contributions to graphics, instructions, encryption, escape . . . the word is out, and it seems they've been waiting years, such is the what's called pent-up demand. Maxine is able to settle in among the throngs, invisible and at ease. Not addicted exactly, though one day she happens to be back out in meatspace for a second, looks at the clock on the wall, does the math, figures three and a half hours she can't account for. Luckily there's nobody but herself to ask what she's down there looking for, because the answer's so pathetically obvious.

Yes, she's aware DeepArcher doesn't do resurrections, thanks for pointing it out. But something odd has been going on with Windust's dossier, the one she copied onto her computer shortly after Marvin brought the thumb drive it was on. She's been sneaking moments away to look at it, not, lately, without twinges of colonorectal fear, because each time she consults it now, there's been *new material* added. As if—a breeze given her generations-old firewalls—somebody has been hacking in whenever they feel like it.

"Consider the recently advanced theory," for example, "that subject, while not a double agent in the classic sense, may have been pursuing a well-defined personal agenda. According to recently downgraded files, this may have begun as early as 1983, when subject allegedly expedited the escape of a Guatemalan national, of interest to the Archivo as an insurgent element and to whom subject was married at the time." And similar updates, all strangely nonnegative when not outright eulogy material. For whose eyes would stuff like this be intended? For Maxine's Only? who would benefit from knowing that twenty years ago Windust was still capable of a good deed, in saving his then-wife Xiomara from the fascist murderers he was technically working for?

The first author to suspect here would be Windust himself, trying to look good, except this is insane because Windust is dead. Either it's Beltway tricksters out on maneuvers or the Internet has become a medium of communication between the worlds. Maxine begins to catch sight of screen presences she knows she ought to be able to name, dim, ephemeral, each receding away into a single anonymous pixel. Maybe not. Much more likely that Windust remains unlit, terribly elsewhere.

Even though its creators claim not to Do Metaphysical, that option in DeepArcher remains open, alongside more secular explanations—so when she runs unexpectedly into Lester Traipse, instead of assuming it's a Lester impersonator with an agenda, or a bot preprogrammed with dialogue for all occasions, she sees no harm in treating him as a departed soul.

Just to get it out of the way, "So! Lester. Who did the deed?"

"Interesting. First thing most people want to know is what's it like being dead."

"OK, what's it—"

"Ha, ha, trick question, I'm not dead, I'm a refugee from my life. As for whodunit, I'm supposed to know? I arranged over the phone to drop a shrink-wrapped cube of cash as a first installment for Ice underneath The Deseret pool at midnight, next thing I know, I'm here wandering around with my spectral thumb in my metaphysical ass."

"Igor Dashkov said you talked about trying to seek some kind of asylum in DeepArcher. Is this who I'm really talking to now, Igor? Misha, Grisha?"

"Don't think so, I say 'the' too much."

"All right, all right. Assuming there's still an edge somewhere. And beyond it a void. If you've been out there—"

"Sorry. Just a mail-room scrambler here, remember? You want prophecy, sure, I can do that, but it'll all be bullshit."

"How about at least letting me bring you back up. Whoever you are."

"What. Up to the surface?"

"Closer anyway."

"Why?"

"I don't know." She doesn't. "If it's really you, Lester, I hate to think of you being lost down here."

"Lost down here is the whole point. Take a good look at the surface Web sometime, tell me it isn't a sorry picture. Big favor you'd be doing me, Maxine."

MIGHT AS WELL BE HOMECOMING weekend down here. Next thing she knows, here's who but her very own Ziggy and Otis. With a whole expanding universe to choose from, among the global torrents somehow the boys have located graphics files for a version of NYC as it was before 11 September 2001, before Ms. Cheung's bleak announcement about real and make-believe, reformatted now as the personal city of Zigotisopolis, rendered in a benevolently lighted palette taken from old-school color processes like the ones you find on picture postcards of another day. Somebody somewhere in the world, enjoying that mysterious exemption from time which produces most Internet content, has been patiently coding together these vehicles and streets, this city that can never be. The old Hayden Planetarium, the pre-Trump Commodore Hotel, upper-Broadway cafeterias that have not existed for years, smorgasbords and bars offering free lunches, where regulars hang around the door to the kitchen so they can get first shot at whatever's being carried in, city-summertime movie theaters with signs in blue display type bordered by frost and icicles promising IT's COOL INSIDE, Madison Square Garden still at Fiftieth and Eighth Avenue and Jack Dempsey's still across the street, and in the old Times Square, before the hookers, before the drugs, arcades like Fascination, pinball machines so classic now that only overly compensated yups can afford to buy them, and recording booths where half a dozen of you can jam inside and cover the latest Eddie Fisher single on acetate. The retro machinery in the streets, though undefined as to makes and years, is plentiful and ever on the move. Ernie and Elaine, as probable sources for all this, would be screaming with recognition.

She sees the boys, but they haven't seen her. There aren't any passwords, still she hesitates to log in without an invitation, it's their city after all. They have different priorities here, the cityscapes of Maxine's DeepArcher are obscurely broken, places of indifference and abuse and unremoved dog shit, and she doesn't want to track any more of that than she can help into their more merciful city, with its antiquated dyes, its acid green shrubbery and indigo pavements and overdesigned traffic flows. Ziggy has his arm over his brother's shoulder, and Otis is looking up at him with unhesitating adoration. They are ambling around in this not-yet-corrupted screenscape, at home in it already, unconcerned for their safety, salvation, destiny . . .

Don't mind me, guys, I'll just lurk here on the visitors' page. She makes a note to bring it up, carefully, gently, when they're all back in meatspace, soy-extenderspace, whatever it is anymore. Because in fact this strange thing has begun to happen. Increasingly she's finding it harder to tell "real" NYC from translations like Zigotisopolis . . . as if she keeps getting caught in a vortex taking her farther each time into the virtual world. Certainly unforeseen in the original business plan, there arises now a possibility that DeepArcher is about to overflow out into the perilous gulf between screen and face.

Out of the ashes and oxidation of this postmagical winter, counterfactual elements have started popping up like li'l goombas. Early one windy morning Maxine's walking down Broadway when here comes a plastic top from a nine-inch aluminum take-out container, rolling down the block in the wind, *on its edge*, an edge thin as a predawn dream, keeps trying to fall over but the airflow or something—unless it's some nerd at a keyboard—keeps it upright for an implausible distance, half a block, a block, *waits for the light*, then half a block more till it finally rolls off the curb under the wheels of a truck that's pulling out and gets flattened. Real? Computer-animated?

Same day, after lunch at a hummus joint where you can't always rule out psychedelic toxins in the tabouli, she happens to be passing the neighborhood Uncle Dizzy's and here's the ol' eponym himself, around the corner with the usual delivery truck thumping it on its side and hollering "Go! Go!" She pauses to stare one eyeblink too long and Dizzy spots her. "Maxi! Just the person I want to see!"

"No Diz, I'm not, really."

"Here. This is for you. In appreciation." Holding out a small hinged box with what seems to be a ring inside.

"What's this, he's proposing?"

"Just in from the jobber, brand-new. It's Chinese. Not even sure what I should be charging."

"Because . . ."

"It's an *invisibility ring*."

"Um, Diz . . ."

"I'm serious, I want you to have it, here, try it on."

"And . . . it'll make me invisible."

"Uncle Dizzy's personal guarantee."

Not sure why she's doing this, she slips on the ring. Dizzy performs a couple of unassisted spins and begins groping in the air. "Where'd she go? Maxi! You there?" so forth. She finds herself skipping around to avoid him.

This is such bullshit. She takes off the ring, hands it back. "Here. Tell you what, you try it."

"You're sure . . ." She's sure. "OK, it was your idea." He puts on the ring and abruptly vanishes. She spends more time than she really has today looking for him, can't find him, passersby begin making with the curious stares. She returns to the office, finds the day somehow blighted by this what-is-reality issue, gives up around four, and is down on 72nd Street, soon to be known as midtown, where she runs into Eric coming out of Gray's Papaya with a teenage accomplice all of whose signifiers scream sublegal.

"Maxi, meet my man Ketone, fake ID portraits a specialty, come on, you can help us look."

"For what?"

A white van, Eric explains, preferably parked, free of dings, dirt, logos, or lettering. They track up and down a number of blocks, over to CPW and back, before finding a van acceptable to Ketone, who has Eric pose against it, takes out a flash camera, and tells him to smile. He gets about half a dozen shots, and they go over to Broadway and into a low-end luggage store, which puts Maxine's sensors on full alert, for stashed inside any of these attractive travel bags and trolley cases out on display is sure to be whatever contraband you, and the boys from the precinct, can imagine. After a brief download interval, Ketone comes back with a selection of Eric ID photos. "Which one you like, Maxi?"

"This one here's nice."

"Five, ten minutes," sez Ketone, heading for the printing and laminating setup in the back room.

"Some exploit," she guesses, "I don't want to know about?"

Eric gets a little shifty. "In case I have to be out of town in a hurry." Pause, as if for thought. "Is, things are getting weird?"

"Tell me." She fills him in on the rolling container top and Uncle Dizzy's disappearing act. "Just seem to be having some of this, don't know, virtuality creep lately."

Eric has noticed it too. "Maybe it's those Montauk Project folks again. Like, traveling back and forth in time, busy interfering with cause and effect, so whenever we see things begin to break up, pixelate and flicker, bad history nobody saw coming, even weather getting funny, it's because the special time-ops folks have been out meddling."

"Sounds good to me. No harder to buy than what's on the news channels. But we'd never have any way to tell. Anybody comes too close to the truth, they disappear."

"Maybe what we've been living through is just a privileged little window, and now it's going back to what it always was."

"You see, ah, trouble down the tracks?"

"Only this strange feeling about the Internet, that it's over, not the tech bubble, or 11 September, just something fatal in its own history. There all along."

"You sound like my father, Eric."

"Look at it, every day more lusers than users, keyboards and screens turning into nothin but portals to Web sites for what the Management wants everybody addicted to, shopping, gaming, jerking off, streaming endless garbage—

"Gee Eric, li'l judgmental. How about some what the Buddha calls compassion here?"

"Meantime hashslingrz and them are all screaming louder and louder about 'Internet freedom,' while they go on handing more and more of it over to the bad guys . . . They get us, all right, we're all lonely, needy, disrespected, desperate to believe in any sorry imitation of belonging they want to sell us . . . We're being played, Maxi, and the game is fixed, and it won't end till the Internet—the real one, the dream, the promise—is destroyed."

"So where's the Undo command?"

Some all but invisible tremor. Maybe he's laughing to himself. "Could be there's enough good hackers around interested in fighting back. Outlaws who'll work for free, show no mercy for anybody who tries to use the Net for evil purposes."

"Civil war."

"OK. Except the slaves don't even know that's what they are."

It isn't till later, in the unpromising wastelands of January, that Maxine understands this was Eric's idea of saying so long. Something like it may've always been in the cards, though she expected more of a slow virtual slideaway, beneath the overlit pondscum of shopping sites and gossip blogging, down through an uncertain light, slipping behind veil after veil of encryption, deeper into the Deep Web. No, instead just one day, pow—no more L train, no more Joie de Beavre, just abruptly dark and silent, another classic skip, leaving only an uneasy faith that he maybe still exists somewhere on the honorable side of the ledger.

Driscoll as it turns out is still in Williamsburg, still answering e-mails.

"Is my heart broken, thanks for asking, I never knew what was going on anyway. Eric all along had this, can I say alternative destiny? Maybe not, but you must have noticed. Right now I have to deal with more immediate shit like too many roommates around here, hot-water issues, shampoo and conditioner theft, I need to focus on getting far enough ahead to afford a place of my own, if it means changing phase, daylight hours in a cube in a shop someplace across the bridge, so be it. Please don't move to the burbs or nothing just yet, OK? I may want to drop by if I get a minute."

Fine, Driscoll, 3-D and out here in "objective reality" would sure be nice if you could manage it, which side of the river being not so important as which side of the screen. Maxine is no happier than she was with the epistemological bug going around, avoiding only Horst, who, typically immune, before long finds himself coming in handy as the calibration standard of last resort. "So, Dad, is this real? Not real?"

"Not real," Horst sparing Otis a brief glance away from, say, Ben Stiller in *The Fred MacMurray Story.*

"It's just the strangest feeling," Maxine confides impulsively to Heidi.

"Sure," Heidi shrugs, "that'd be GAPUQ, the old Granada–Asbury Park Uncertainty Question. Been around forever."

"Inside the closed, inbred world of academia, you mean, or . . ."

"Actually you might enjoy their Web site," just as pissily, "for victims whose struggle to tell the difference is especially vivid, like your own, for example, Maxi—"

"Thank you, Heidi," with a certain upward cadence, "and Frank, I believe, was singing about love."

They're at JFK, in the Lufthansa business-class departure lounge, sipping on some kind of organic mimosa, while everybody else in the room is busy getting hammered as quickly as possible. "Well it's all love isn't it," Heidi scanning the room for Conkling, who has gone off on a nasal tour of the premises.

"This real/virtual situation, it doesn't come up with you, Heidi."

"Guess I'm just a Yahoo! type of gal. Click in, click back out, nothing too far afield, nothing too . . ." the characteristic Heidi pause, "deep."

It's between semesters at City, and Heidi, on her break, is about to fly off with Conkling to Munich, Germany. When Maxine first heard about this, a Wagnerian brass section began to blare rudely down the corridors of short-term memory. "This is about—"

"He"— no longer, Maxine noted, "Conkling" — "has recently purchased a pre-owned bottle of 4711 cologne, liberated by GIs at the end of the war from Hitler's private bathroom at Berchtesgaden . . . and . . ." That old Heidical yes-and-what's-it-to-you look.

"And the only forensic lab in the world equipped for a Hitler's-cooties workup on it happens to be located in Munich. Well, who wouldn't want to be certain, it's like pregnancy, isn't it."

"You've never understood him," nimbly stepping out of the way of the half-eaten sandwich that Maxine reflexively picked up then and launched at her. It's true that she still doesn't get Conkling, who is now returning to the Lufthansa lounge all but skipping. "I'm ready! How about you, Poisongirl, are you ready for this adventure?"

"Rarin to go," Heidi kind of semiabsently, it seems to Maxine.

"This could be it, you know, the lost connection, the first step back along that dark *sillage*, across all that time and chaos, to the living Führer—"

"You never called him that before," it occurs to Heidi.

Conkling's reply, likely to be idiotic, is interrupted by a young lady on the PA announcing the flight to Munich.

There is an extra checkpoint these days, an artifact of 11 September, at which the authorities discover in one of Conkling's inner pockets the possibly historic flask of 4711. Excited colloquial German on the PA. Armed security of two nations converging on the suspects. Oops, Maxine remembers, something about no bringing liquids on board the airplane . . . standing behind a bulletproof plastic barrier she tries to convey this with charade gestures to Heidi, who is glaring back with a don't-stand-there-call-a-lawyer tilt to her eyebrows.

Later, hours later, in the taxi back to Manhattan, "It's probably for the best, Heidi."

"Yes, there may still be lingering in Munich the odd pocket of bad karma," Heidi nodding you could say almost with relief.

"All is not lost," pipes Conkling, "I can send it by bonded courier, and we've only lost a day, my tuberose blossom."

"We'll restrategize," Heidi promises.

"MARVIN, YOU'RE OUT OF UNIFORM. Where's all the kozmo gear?"

"Sold it all on eBay, dahlin, movin with the times."

"For $1.98, come on."

"For more than you would ever dream. Nothing dies anymore, the collectors' market, it's the afterlife, and yups are its angels."

"OK. And this thing you just brought me here . . ."

What else, another disc, though it isn't till after supper, with Horst conclusively tubeside in front of Alec Baldwin in *The Ray Milland Story*, that Maxine, less than eager, gets to have a look. Another traveling shot, this time out the sleet-battered windshield of some kind of big rig. From what's visible through the weather, it's mountain terrain, gray sky, streaks and patches of snow, no horizontal references till an overpass comes swooping in, and then she can see how unnecessarily dutched the frame actually is, so who else can it be behind the camera but Reg Despard.

And it's not only Reg—as if on cue, the shot swivels to the left, and here at the wheel, mesh cap, outlaw cheroot, week's growth of beard and all, is their onetime partner in mischief Eric Outfield again, risen from the deep or wherever.

"Breaker breaker good buddy, so forth," beams Eric, "and a belated happy New Year's to ya, Maxi, you and yours."

"Ditto," adds invisible Reg.

"Karma, see, me and Reg just keep running into each other."

"This time ol' Black Hat here was lurking around the Redmond campus, somehow physically hacked his way in through the gate—"

"Common interest in security patches."

Heh, heh. "Different motives, of course. Meantime this other gig comes up."

"Our exit here."

Off the interstate, after a couple of turns, they pull in to a truck stop. The camera goes around to the back of the trailer, Eric in close-up gets a serious face. "This is all deeply secret right now. This disc you're watching has to be destroyed soon as you're done with it, grind it, shred it, pop it in the microwave, someday it'll all be in a feature-length documentary, but not today."

"Couple guys in a truck?" Maxine interrogates the screen.

Eric unlatching the door and rolling it up, "You never saw this, OK?" She can make out, stuffed inside, racks of electronic gear receding to infinity, LEDs glowing in the dimness. She hears the hum of cooling fans. "Custom shock-mounted, everything mil-spec, these here are all what they call blade servers, warehouses full going as you might expect for rock-bottom prices these days and who," Eric in a cheerful cloud of cigar smoke, "I bet you're wondering, would be springing for a rolling server farm, in fact a fleet of us, out on the move and untrackable 24/7? what kind of data would these units be carrying on their hard drives, so forth."

"Don't ask," Reg cackles, "It's all experimental right now. Could be a big waste of our time and some unknown party's money."

Calm breathing over Maxine's shoulder. For some reason she doesn't jump or scream, or not much, only pauses the disc. "Looks like up around the Bozeman Pass," Horst guesses.

"How's your movie, honey?"

"Just on a commercial break, they're as far as the making of *The Lost Weekend* (1945), nice cameo by Wallace Shawn as Billy Wilder, but listen, don't go by this footage here, OK? it's really nice country out there, you might enjoy it . . . Maybe some summer we could . . ."

"They want me to destroy this disc, Horst, so if you wouldn't mind . . ."

"Never saw it, deaf and dumb, hey, that's 'at there Eric guy, ain't it."

Might be some envy in his voice, but this time no husbandish whine. She sneaks a look at his face and catches him gazing into the stormswept mountains like a man in exile, his wish so blatant, to be schlepping once again through blizzards and relentless wind, out solo on the far northern highways. How is she ever supposed to get used to such wintry nostalgia?

"Think your picture's back on, 18-wheeler. You're looking for a role model, you could do worse than Ray Milland, maybe you should be taking notes?"

"Yep, always been a *The Thing with Two Heads* (1972) man myself."

Maxine resumes the disc. The truck is in motion again. The gray unprophetic miles unrolling. After a while Eric sez, "This ain't the civil war, by the way, case you were wondering. What we talked about last time. Not even Fort Sumter. Just a li'l spin up the interstate's all. Bleeding-edge development phase yet. We could be heading anywhere, Alberta, Northwest Territories, Alaska, we'll see where it takes us. Sorry about no more e-mail, but we're all down where you might not want to be bringing your family computer anymore. Inappropriate content plus crashing the machine in ways you'll be unhappy with. From here on, contact will have to be kind of intermittent. Maybe someday—" The picture goes dark. She fast-forwards looking around for more, but that seems to be it.

39

Sometimes, down in the subway, a train Maxine's riding on will slowly be overtaken by a local or an express on the other track, and in the darkness of the tunnel, as the windows of the other train move slowly past, the lighted panels appear one by one, like a series of fortune-telling cards being dealt and slid in front of her. The Scholar, The Unhoused, The Warrior Thief, The Haunted Woman . . . After a while Maxine has come to understand that the faces framed in these panels are precisely those out of all the city millions she must in the hour be paying most attention to, in particular those whose eyes actually meet her own—they are the day's messengers from whatever the Beyond has for a Third World, where the days are assembled one by one under non-union conditions. Each messenger carrying the props required for their character, shopping bags, books, musical instruments, arrived here out of darkness, bound again into darkness, with only a minute to deliver the intelligence Maxine needs. At some point naturally she begins to wonder if she might not be performing the same role for some face looking back out another window at her.

One day, on the express headed downtown from 72nd, a local happens to leave the station at the same time, and as the tracks at the end of

the platform draw closer together, there's a slow zoom in onto one particular window of the other train, one face in this window, too clearly
meant to invite Maxine's attention. She's tall, darkly exotic, good posture, carrying a shoulder bag she now briefly unlatches her gaze from
Maxine's for long enough to reach inside of and pull out an envelope,
which she holds up to the window, then jerks her head toward the next
express stop, which will be 42nd. Maxine's train meantime accelerating
and carrying her slowly past.

If this is a tarot card with a name, it's The Unwelcome Messenger.

Maxine gets off at Times Square and waits under a flight of exit
stairs. The local rolls and hisses in, the woman approaches. Silently Maxine is beckoned down into the long pedestrian tunnel that runs over to
the Port of Authority, on whose tiled walls are posted the latest word on
movies about to come out, albums, toys for yups, fashion, everything
you need to be a wised-up urban know-it-all is posted on the walls of this
tunnel. It occurs to Maxine that if hell was a bus station in New York,
this is what ALL HOPE ABANDON would look like.

The envelope doesn't have to get closer to her snoot than a foot and
a half before there it is, the unmistakable odor of regret, bad judgment,
unproductive mourning—9:30 Cologne For Men. Maxine is taken by a
chill. Nick Windust has staggered forth again from the grave, hungry,
unappeasable, and she doubts, whatever's in the envelope, that she needs
to see it.

There's writing on the outside,

Here's the money I owe you. Sorry it isn't the earrings.

Adios.

Half glaring at the envelope, expecting only the ghost outline of the
wad that used to be there, Maxine is surprised to find instead the full
amount, in twenties. Plus some modest vig, which is not like him. Was
not. This being New York, how many explanations can there be for why
it hasn't been made off with? Likely it's to do with the messenger . . .

Oh. Seeing the other woman's eyes begin to narrow, enough to
notice, Maxine makes a judgment call. "Xiomara?"

The woman's smile, in this bright noisy flow of city indifference, comes like a beer on the house in a bar where nobody knows you.

"You don' t need to tell me how you were able to contact me."

"Oh. They know how to find people."

Xiomara has been up at Columbia all morning, chairing some kind of seminar on Central American issues. Accounts for her being on the local maybe, but little else. There are always secular backup stories, some comm link in Xiomara's shoulder bag, not yet on the market outside the surveillance community . . . but at the same time there's no shame in going for a magical explanation, so Maxine lets it ride. "And right now, you're headed for . . ."

"Well, actually the Brooklyn Bridge. Do you know how we'd get there from here?"

"Take the shuttle over to the Lex, ride down on the Number 6, and what's with the 'we,'" Maxine wishes to know also.

"Whenever I come to New York, I like to walk across the Brooklyn Bridge. If you have time, I thought you could, too."

Jewish-mother defaults switch in. "You eat breakfast?"

"Hungarian Pastry Shop."

"So we get over in Brooklyn, we'll eat again."

Maxine can't say what she might've been expecting—braids, silver jewelry, long skirts, bare feet—well, surprise, here instead is this polished international beauty in a power suit, not some clueless eighties hand-me-down either, but narrower in the shoulders the way they're supposed to be, longer jacket, serious shoes. Perfect makeup job. Maxine must look like she's been out washing the car.

They start off cautiously enough, politely, before either of them knows it, it's turning into morning talk-show TV. Had Lunch with Ex-Husband's Ex-Girlfriend.

"So the money, you got it from Dotty, the widow in D.C., correct?"

"One of a thousand chores she suddenly finds on her list."

And it's also possible, given the depths of Beltway connivance running parallel to and just behind the visible universe, that Xiomara is up here today at not so much Dotty's behest as that of elements interested in how doggedly Maxine's apt to go after the truth behind Windust's passing.

"You and Dotty are in touch."

"We met a couple of years ago. I was in Washington with a delegation."

"Your— Her husband was there?"

"Not likely. She swore me to secrecy, we met for lunch at the Old Ebbitt, noisy, Clinton people all milling around, both of us picking at salads, trying to ignore Larry Summers at a distant booth, no problem for her, but I felt like I was auditioning for something."

"And the topic under discussion, of course . . ."

"Two different husbands, really. Back when I knew him, he was a person she wouldn't have recognized, an entry-level kid who didn't know how much trouble his soul was in."

"And by the time she got to him . . ."

"Maybe he didn't need quite so much help."

Classic New York conversation, you're having lunch, you talk about having lunch someplace else. "So you ladies had a nice chat."

"Not sure. Toward the end Dotty said something strange. You've heard about the ancient Mayans and this game they played, an early form of basketball?"

"Something about," Maxine dimly, " . . .vertical hoop, high percentage of fouls, some of them flagrant, usually fatal?"

"We were outside trying to hail a cab, and out of nowhere Dotty said something like, 'The enemy most to be feared is as silent as a Mayan basketball game on television.' When I politely pointed out that back in Mayan times there wasn't any TV, she smiled, like a teacher you've just fed the right cue to. 'Then you can imagine how silent that is,' and she slid into a cab I hadn't seen coming, and disappeared."

"You think it was her way of talking about . . ." oh, go ahead, "his soul?"

She gazes into Maxine's eyes and nods. "Day before yesterday, when she asked me to bring you the money, she talked about the last time she saw him, the surveillance, the helicopters, the dead phones and frozen credit cards, and said she'd really come to think of them again as comrades-in-arms. Maybe she was only being a good spook widow. But I kissed her anyway."

Maxine's turn to nod.

"Where I grew up in Huehuetenango, where Windust and I met, it was less than a day's journey to a system of caves everyone there believed was the approach to Xibalba. The early Christian missionaries thought tales of hell would frighten us, but we already had Xibalba, literally, 'the place of fear.' There was a particularly terrible ball court there. The ball had these . . . blades on it, so games were in deadly earnest. Xibalba was—is—a vast city-state below the earth, ruled by twelve Death Lords. Each Lord with his own army of unquiet dead, who wander the surface world bringing terrible afflictions to the living. Ríos Montt and his plague of ethnic killing . . . not too different.

"Windust began hearing Xibalba stories as soon as his unit arrived in country. At first he thought it was another case of having fun with the gringo, but after a while . . . I think he began to believe, more than I ever did, at least to believe in a parallel world, somewhere far beneath his feet where another Windust was doing the things he was pretending not to up here."

"You knew . . ."

"Suspected. Tried not to see too much. I was too young. I knew about the electric cattle prod, 'self-defense' is how he explained it. The name the people gave him was Xooq', which means scorpion in Q'eqchi'. I loved him. I must have thought I could save him. And in the end it was Windust who saved me." Maxine feels a strange buzzing at the edges of her brain, like a foot trying to come back awake. Still inside the perimeter of newlywed bliss, he sneaks out of bed, does what he's in Guatemala to do, slips back, in the worst hours of the morning, nestling his cock against the crack of her ass, how could she not have known? What innocence could she still believe in?

Automatic-rifle fire every night, irregular pulses of flame-colored light above the treelines. Villagers began leaving. One morning Windust found the office he'd been working out of abandoned and cleared of everything sensitive. No sign of any of the neoliberal scum he'd oozed into town with. Perhaps owing to the appearance overnight of ill-disposed country folk carrying machetes. Somebody had written SALSIPUEDES MOTHERFUCKERS in lipstick on a cubicle wall. A 55-gallon oil drum out in back full of ashes and charred paperwork was still seeping smoke. Not a yanqui in sight, let alone the Israeli and Taiwanese mercs they'd been coordinating with, all of them suddenly gathered back into the Invisible. "He gave me about a minute to pack a bag. The blouse I wore at our wedding, some family photographs, a sock with a roll of quetzals in it, a little SIG Sauer .22 handgun he was never comfortable with and insisted I take."

On the map the Mexican border wasn't far, but even though they first headed down to the coast, away from the mountains, the terrain was demanding and there were obstacles—army patrols, blood-drinking Kaibil special ops, *guerrilleros* who would shoot a gringo on sight. At any moment Windust was apt to mutter, "Spot of bother here," and they'd have to hide. It took days, but finally he got them safely into Mexico. They picked up the highway at Tapachula and rode buses north. One morning at the bus station in Oaxaca, they were sitting out under a canopy of poles and palm thatchwork, and Windust suddenly was down on one knee offering Xiomara a ring, with the biggest diamond she'd ever seen.

"What's this?"

"I forgot to give you an engagement ring."

She tried it on, it didn't fit. "It's OK," he said, "When you get to D.F., I want you to sell it," and it wasn't till then, that "you" instead of "we," that she understood he was leaving. He kissed her good-bye, and turning away from maybe the last merciful act in his résumé, moseyed on out of the bus station. By the time she thought to get up and run after him, he'd vanished down the hard roads and into the heavy weather of a northern destiny she'd thought she could protect him from.

"Foolish little girl. His agency took care of the annulment, found me a job in an office out on Insurgentes Sur, after a while I was on my own, there was no more interest or profit in tracking me, I found myself working more and more with exile groups and reconciliation commit-tees, Huehuetenango was still down there, the war was never going to go away, it was like the old Mexican joke, *de Guatemala a Guatepeor.*"

They've walked down to Fulton Landing. Manhattan so close, so clear today, yet back on 11 September the river was an all but metaphysical barrier. Those who witnessed the event from over here watched, from a place of safety they no longer believed in, the horror of the day, watched the legions of traumatized souls coming across the bridge, dust-covered, smelling like demolition and smoke and death, vacant-eyed, in flight, in shock. While the terminal plume ascended.

"Do you mind if we walk back across the bridge, over to Ground Zero?"

Sure. Just another visitor to the Apple here, another one of those obligatory stops. Or was this the idea all along, and Maxine's being played here, like an original-cast vinyl LP? "That 'we' again, Xiomara."

"You've never been there?"

"Not since it happened. Made a point of avoiding it, in fact. You gonna report me to the patriotism police now?"

"It's me. I've gotten obsessed."

They're up on the bridge again, as close to free as the city ever allows you to be, between conditions, an edged wind off the harbor announc-ing something dark now hovering out over Jersey, not the night, not yet, something else, on the way in, being drawn as if by the vacuum in real-estate history where the Trade Center used to stand, bringing optical tricks, a sorrowful light.

They glide like attendants toward the room of a waker from civic nightmare who will not be comforted. Open-top tour buses cruise by carrying visitors in matching plastic ponchos with the tour-company logo. At Church and Fulton, there's a viewing platform, allowing civilians to look in past the chain-link and barricades to where dump trucks and cranes and loaders are busy reducing a pile of wreckage that still reaches ten or twelve stories high, to gaze into what should be the aura surrounding a holy place but isn't. Cops with bullhorns are managing the foot traffic. Buildings nearby, damaged but standing, some draped like mourners in black façade netting, one with a huge American flag attached across the top stories, gather in silent witness, glassless window-sockets dark and staring. There are vendors selling T-shirts, paperweights, key chains, mouse pads, coffee mugs.

Maxine and Xiomara stand for a while looking in. "It was never the Statue of Liberty," sez Maxine, "never a Beloved American Landmark, but it was pure geometry. Points for that. And then they blew it to pixels."

And I know of a place, she's careful not to add, where you dowse across an empty screen, clicking on tiny invisible links, and there's something waiting out there, latent, maybe it's geometric, maybe begging like geometry to be contradicted in some equally terrible way, maybe a sacred city all in pixels waiting to be reassembled, as if disasters could be run in reverse, the towers rise out of black ruin, the bits and pieces and lives, no matter how finely vaporized, become whole again . . .

"Hell doesn't have to be underground," Xiomara looking up at the vanished memory of what had stood there, "Hell can be in the sky."

"And Windust—"

"Dotty said he came here more than once after 11 September, haunting the site. Unfinished business, he told her. But I don't think his spirit is here. I think he's down in Xibalba, reunited with his evil twin."

The condemned ghost structures around them seem to draw together, as if conferring. Some patrolman from the karmic police is saying move along folks, it's over, nothing to see here. Xiomara takes Maxine's arm, and they glide off into a premonitory spritzing of rain, a metropolis swept by twilight.

Later, back in the apartment, in a widowlike observance, Maxine finds a moment alone and switches off the lights, takes the envelope of cash, and snorts the last vestiges of his punk-rock cologne, trying to summon back something as invisible and weightless and inaccountable as his spirit . . .

Which is down in the Mayan underworld now, wandering a deathscape of hungry, infected, shape-shifting, lethally insane Mayan basketball fans. Like Boston Garden, only different.

And later, next to snoring Horst, beneath the pale ceiling, city light diffusing through the blinds, just before drifting downward into REM, good night. Good night, Nick.

40

There is a particular weirdness to be found on weekends in the evening in NYC health and fitness clubs, especially when economic times are sluggish. Unable anymore to bring herself to swim in The Deseret pool, which she believes to be cursed, Maxine has joined her sister Brooke's state-of-the-art health club Megareps around the corner but isn't quite used yet to this nightly spectacle of yups on treadmills, plodding to nowhere while watching CNN or the sports channels, laid-off dotcommers who aren't at strip clubs or absorbed into massively multiplayer online games, all running, rowing, lifting weights, mingling with body-image obsessives, folks recuperating from dating disasters, others desperate enough tonight actually to be looking for company here instead of in bars. Worse, hanging around the snack section, which is where Maxine, coming in out of the strange kind of late-winter rain that you can hear rattling lightly off your umbrella or raincoat but when you look, nothing is getting wet, finds March Kelleher, busy on her laptop, surrounded by muffin debris and a number of paper coffee cups she's using, much to the annoyance of the rest of the room, for ashtrays.

"Didn't know you were a member here, March."

"Walk-in, just using the free Internet, hot spots all over town, haven't been in this one for a while."

"Been following your Weblog."

"I had an interesting tip about your friend Windust. Like he's dead, for example. Should I post it? Should I be offering condolences?"

"Not to me."

March puts the screen to sleep and regards Maxine with a level gaze. "You know I never asked."

"Thanks. You wouldn't have found it entertaining."

"Did you?"

"Not sure."

"Long sad career as a mother-in-law, only thing I ever learned is don't advise. Anybody needs advice these days, it's me."

"Hey, more than happy to, what's up?"

A sour face. "Worried sick about Tallis."

"This is news?"

"It's all getting worse, I can't just stand by anymore, I have to be the one to take the step, try to get to see her somehow. Fuck the consequences. Tell me it's a bad idea."

"It's a bad idea."

"If you mean life is too short, OK, but around Gabriel Ice, as you must know, it can get even shorter."

"What, he's threatening her?"

"They've split. He's kicked her out."

Well. "So good riddance."

"He won't leave it at that. Something I can feel. She's my baby."

All right. The Code of the Mom stipulates you don't argue back at this kind of talk. "So," nodding, "can I help?"

"Lend me your handgun." Beat. "Just kidding."

"Yet another license pulled, would be the thing . . ."

"Only a metaphor."

OK, but if March, already on the fly, living with her own danger levels, sees Tallis in this much trouble . . . "Can I do some recon first, March?"

"She's innocent, Maxine. Ah. She's so fuckin innocent."

Running with Gulf Coast gangsters, party to international money laundering, any number of Title 18 violations, innocent, well . . . "How's that?"

"Everybody thinks they know more than her. The old sad delusion of every insect-free know-it-all in this miserable town. Everybody thinks they live in 'the real world' and she doesn't."

"So?"

"So that's what it is, to be an 'innocent person.'" In the tone of voice you use when you think somebody needs to have it explained.

TALLIS, booted out of the East Side stately home she and Ice were sharing, has found a utility closet converted to residential use in one of the newer high rises on the far Upper West Side. Looks like a machine more than a building. Pale, metallic, highly reflective, someplace up in the mid–two figures with respect to floors high, wraparound balconies that look like cooling fins, no name, only a number hidden so discreetly not one in a hundred locals you ask can even tell you it. Keeping Tallis company this evening are enough bottles to stock an average Chinese-restaurant bar, from one of which she is drinking directly something turquoise called Hypnotiq. Neglecting to offer any to Maxine.

Out here at the far ancient edge of the island, this all used to be trainyard. Deep below, trains still move through tunnels in and out of Penn Station, horns chiming in B-major sixths, deep as dreams, while ghosts of tunnel-wall artists and squatters the civil authorities have no clue what to do about—evict, ignore, re-evict—go drifting past the train-car windows in the semidark, whispering messages of transience, and overhead in this cheaply built apartment complex tenants come and go, relentlessly ephemeral as travelers in a nineteenth-century railroad hotel.

"First thing I noticed," not complaining to Maxine so much as to anybody who'll listen, "is I was getting systematically cut off from the Web sites I usually visit. Couldn't shop online, or chat in chat rooms, or after a while even do normal company business. Finally, wherever I tried to go, I ran into some kind of wall. Dialogue boxes, pop-up messages, mostly threatening, some apologizing. Click by click, forcing me away into exile."

"You discussed this with CEO-and-hubby?"

"Sure, while he was screaming, throwing my stuff out the window, reminding me how badly I'm expected to come out of this. A nice adult discussion."

Matrimonials. What is there ever to say? "Just don't forget about the loss carry-forwards and all that, OK?" Running a quick EHA or Eyeball-Humidity Assessment, Maxine thinks for a minute Tallis is about to go all mushy, but instead she's relieved to see, as if jump-cut to, the reliably annoying Fingernail, cycling toward and away from her lips,

"You've been discovering secrets about my husband . . . any you'd like to share?"

"There's no proof of anything yet."

An unsurprised nod. "But he is, I don't know, a suspect in some-thing?" Gazing toward a neutral corner, voice softening to edgelessness, *The Geek That Couldn't Sleep*. A make-believe horror movie we used to pretend we were in. Gabe was really such a sweet kid, a long time ago."

Off she goes goes on the time machine, while Maxine investigates the liquor inventory. Presently Tallis is recalling one of several memorial services after 11 September she was at representing hashslingrz, standing there among a delegation of dry-eyed wisefolk who looked like they were waiting for it to be over so they could get back to which stock to short next, when she observed one of the bagpipe players, improvising grace notes on "Candle in the Wind," who seemed to her dimly familiar. It turned out to be Gabriel's old college roommate Dieter, now in busi-ness as a professional bagpiper. There were catered eats afterward, over which she and Dieter got into conversation, trying to avoid kilt jokes, though whatever he'd grown into, it wasn't Sean Connery.

Demand for bagpipers was brisk. Dieter, filing as an S-corporation these days, teamed up with a couple of other classmates from CMU, had been swamped since 11 September with more gigs than he knew what to do with, weddings, bar mitzvahs, furniture-store openings . . .

"Weddings?" sez Maxine.

"He sez you'd be surprised, a funeral lament at a wedding, gets a laugh every time."

"I can imagine."

"They don't do cop funerals so much, the cops apparently have their own resources, most of it's private functions like this one we were at. Dieter grew philosophical, said it got stressful from time to time, he felt like a branch of emergency services, being held in readiness, waiting for the call to come in."

"Waiting for the next . . ."

"Yeah."

"You think he might be some kind of a leading indicator?"

"Dieter? Like bagpipe players would get a heads-up before the next one happens? That would be so weird?"

"Well, after that—did you and your husband get together socially with Dieter?"

"Uh-huh? He and Gabe might have even done some business."

"Natch. What are ex-roomies for?"

"It looked like they were planning some project together, but they never shared it with me, and whatever it was, it didn't show up on the books."

A joint project, Gabriel Ice and somebody whose career depends on widespread public bereavement. Hmmm. "Did you ever invite him out to Montauk?"

"As a matter of fact . . ."

Cue the theremin music, and you, Maxine, get a grip. "This split could all turn out to be a blessing in disguise for you, Tallis, and meantime, you . . . have called your mother."

"Do you think I should?"

"I think you're overdue." Plus a related thought, "Listen, it's none of my business, but . . ."

"Is there a fella. Of course. Can he help, good question." Reaching for the Hypnotiq bottle.

"Tallis," trying to keep as much weariness as she can out of it, "I know there's a boyfriend, and he's nobody's 'fella' except maybe your husband's, and frankly none of this is as cute as you're hoping . . ." Giving her the abridged version of Chazz Larday's rap sheet including his wife-sitting arrangements with Ice. "It's a setup. So far you're doing exactly everything hubby wants you to."

"No. Chazz . . ." Is the next part of this going to be ". . . loves me?" Maxine's thoughts wander to the Beretta in her purse, but Tallis surprises her. "Chazz is a dick with an East Texan attached to it, one being the price of the other, you could say."

"Wait a minute." Out at the edge of Maxine's visual field, something's been blinking for a while. It turns out to be an indicator light on a little CCTV camera up in one dim corner of the ceiling. "This is a motel, Tallis? Who put this thing in here?"

"It wasn't in here before."

"Do you think . . . ?"

"It would figure."

"You got a stepladder?" No. "A broom?" A sponge mop. They take turns banging at it, like an evil high-tech piñata, till it comes crashing to the floor.

"You know what, you should be someplace safer."

"Where? With my mom? One step away from a bag lady, never mind me, she can't help herself."

"We'll figure out where, but they just lost their picture, they'll be coming here, we need to be gone."

Tallis throws a couple of things in an oversize shoulder bag and they proceed to the elevator, down twenty floors, out through the gold-accented Grand Central–size lobby, with its four-figures-per-day floral arrangements—

"Mrs. Ice?" The doorman, regarding Tallis with something between apprehension and respect.

"Not for long," Tallis sez. "Dragoslav. What."

"These two guys showed up, said they'll 'be seeing you soon.'"

"That's it?" A puzzled frown.

Maxine gets a brain wave. "Doing Russian rap lyrics, by any chance?"

"That's them. Please be sure and tell them I gave you the message? Like, I promised?"

"They're nice guys," sez Maxine, "really, no need to worry."

"Worry, excuse me, does not begin to describe."

"Tallis, you haven't been . . ."

"I don't know these guys. You however seem to. Anything you'd like to share?"

They have wandered out onto the sidewalk. Light draining away over Jersey, no cabs around and miles to the subway. Next thing they know, around the corner on apparently new hydraulics and up the block comes, yes, it's Igor's ZiL-41047, gussied up tonight into a full-scale *shmaravozka,* gold custom spinner rims with blinking red LEDs, high-tech antennas and lowrider striping—screeches to a pause next to Tallis and Maxine and out leap Misha and Grisha, wearing matching Oakley OvertheTop shades and packing PP-19 Bizons, with which they gesture Tallis and Maxine into the back of the limo. Maxine gets a professional if not exactly courtly patdown, and the Tomcat in her purse goes on the unavailable list.

"Misha! Grisha! And here I thought you were such gentlemen!"

"You'll get your *pushka* back," Misha with a friendly stainless grin, sliding behind the wheel and pimpmobiling away from the curb.

"Reducing complications," Grisha adds. "Remember *Good, Bad and Ugly*, three-way standoff? Remember how much trouble even to watch?"

"You don't mind my asking, guys, what's going on?"

"Up till five minutes ago," sez Grisha, "simple plan, put snatch and grab on cute Pamela Anderson here."

"Who," inquires Tallis, "me?"

"Tallis, please, just— And now the plan's not so simple?"

"We weren't expecting you too," Misha sez.

"Aw. You were gonna kidnap her and ask Gabriel Ice for ransom money? Let me just roll on the floor here a minute, you guys. You want to tell them, Tallis, or should I?"

"Uh-oh," go the gorillas in unison.

"You didn't hear, I guess. Gabe and I are about to get into a really horrible divorce. At the moment my ex-to-be is trying to delete me, my existence, from the Internet. I don't think he'll even spring for gas money, guys, sorry."

"*Govno,*" in harmony.

"Unless he's really the one who hired you, to get me out of the way."

"Fucking Gabriel Ice," Grisha indignant, "is oligarch scum, thief, murderer."

"So far, *nichego,*" Misha cheerfully, "but he's also working for U.S. secret police, which makes us sworn enemies forever—we have oath, older than *vory,* older than gulag, never help cops."

"Penalty for violation," Misha adds, "is death. Not just what they'll do to you. Death in spirit, you understand."

"She's nervous," Maxine hastily, "she means no disrespect."

"How much did you think he was gonna pay?" Tallis still wants to know.

An amused exchange in Russian that Maxine imagines going something like "Fucking American women only care about price they bring on market? Nation of whores."

"More like Austin Powers," Misha explains— "telling Ice, 'Oh, behave!'"

"'Shagadelic!'" cries Grisha. They high-five.

"We have something to do tonight," Misha continues, "and holding Mrs. Ice was only supposed to be for insurance, in case somebody gets cute."

"Looks like it ain't gonna work," sez Maxine.

"Sorry," sez Tallis. "Can we get out now?"

By this point they are off the Cross County and onto the Thruway, just passing the fake barn and silo of Stew Leonard, a legendary figure in the history of point-of-sale fraud, heading for what Otis used to call the Chimpan Zee Bridge.

"What's the hurry? Pleasant social evening. Some conversation. Chillax, ladies." There's champagne in the fridge. Grisha breaks out El Productos stuffed with weed and lights up, and soon secondhand effects begin to occur. On the sound system, the boys have arranged a hip-hop-plus-Russian eighties nostalgia mix, including DDT's road anthem "Ty Nye Odin" (You Are Not Alone) and the soulful ballad "Veter."

"Where are we going, then?" Tallis sullenly flirtatious, as if hoping this will develop into an orgy.

"Upstate. Hashslingrz has secret server farm up in mountains, right?"

"Adirondack Mountains, Lake Heatsink—are you really planning to take us all the way up there?"

"Yeah," sez Maxine, "something of a drive, ain't it?"

"Maybe you won't have to go all the way there," Grisha fondling his Bizon menacingly.

"He's being dickhead," Misha explains. "Years in Vladimirski Tsentral, learned nothing. We have to meet this guy Yuri in Poughkeepsie, we can let you off there at train station."

"You want to get to the server," Tallis bringing out her Filofax and finding a blank page, "I can draw you boys a map."

Grisha narrowing his eyes, "We don't need to shoot you or nothing?"

"Oh you wouldn't really shoot me with that big, mean gun?" Withholding eye contact till around "big."

"Map would be nice," Misha trying to sound like the good torpedo.

"Gabe took me up there once. Deep underground caves near the lake. Very like vertical, many levels, floor numbers on the elevator all had minus signs. The property itself used to be a summer camp, Camp . . . some Indian name, Ten Watts, Iroquois, something . . ."

"Camp Tewattsirokwas," Maxine just refrains from screaming in recognition.

"That's it."

"Mohawk for 'firefly.' At least that's what they told us."

"You went to camp there, oh my God?"

"Oh your God what, Tallis, somebody had to." Camp Tewatt-sirokwas was the brainchild of a Trotskyite couple, the Gimelmans from Cedarhurst, begun back at the time of the Schachtman unpleasantness amid epical all-night screaming matches and not much quieter by the time Maxine got there, the standard poison-ivy facility you found back then all through the mountains of New York State. Cafeteria food, color wars, canoes on the lake, singing "Marching to Astoria," "Zum Gali Gali," dance parties—aaahhh! Wesley Epstein!

Counselors at Camp Tewattsirokwas delighted in creeeping kids out with local legends about Lake Heatsink—how from ancient times the Indians avoided the place, in terror of what lived in its depths, cloak-shaped rays of glowing ultraviolet, giant albino eels that could get around on land as well as through water, with demonic faces that spoke to you in Iroquois of the horrors that awaited you should you dip so much as a toe . . .

"Make her stop," Grisha shivering, "she's scaring me."

"No wonder Gabe seemed to fit right in," figures Tallis. Ice apparently chose Lake Heatsink because it's deeper and colder than anything else in the Adirondacks. Maxine flashes back to his spiel at the Geeks' Cotillion, northward migration to fjordsides, to subarctic lakes, where the unnatural flows of heat generated by server equipment can begin to corrupt the last patches of innocence on the planet.

Onto the sound system comes Nelly singing "Ride Wit Me." As the Thruway unreels toward and around the speeding ZiL a sorrowful winterscape of little farms, frozen fields, trees that look like they'll never bear leaves again, Misha and Grisha start bouncing up and down and chiming in on "Hey! Must be the money!"

"Don't mean to seem nosy," of course not Maxine, "but I gather you're not going up there just to drop in and hang out by the snack machine."

Another exchange in jailhouse Russian. Suspicious glances. In some neglected area of her brain, Maxine understands how easily yenta activities can turn dangerous, but this doesn't keep her from a little lobe probe here. "Is it true what I hear," adopting Elaine's murderous perkiness, "that server farms, no matter how carefully hidden, are all sitting ducks, because they put out an infrared signature that a heat-seeking missile can read?"

"Missiles? Sorry."

"No missiles tonight. Small-scale experiment only."

They stop for gas, Misha and Grisha take Maxine around to the back of the ZiL, open the trunk. Something long, cylindrical, flanges with bolts, projections that look electrical . . . "Nice, which end are you supposed to inhale out of— Oh, shit, wait, I know what this is! I saw this in Reg's movie! it's one of those vircators, isn't it, what are you guys—let me guess, you're gonna hit that server farm with an EM pulse?"

"Shh-*shh*," cautions Misha.

"Only ten-percent power," Grisha assures her.

"Twenty maybe."

"Experiment."

"You shouldn't be showing me this," Maxine thinking, on the one hand nonnuclear means minor league, while on the other, don't rule out that they're insane also.

"Igor says trust you."

"Anybody asks, I didn't see this, good with whatever fellas, *nichego,* hashslingrz in my opinion, they're way overdue for a little inconvenience."

"*Po khuy,*" Grisha beams, "Ice's server is toast."

Of course Maxine sees attitude like this all the time, blind confidence, sure disaster for the other guy, somehow it never works out. Oh, this trip does not bode well. No orgies tonight, no hostage situation, God help them all, it's a nerd exploit, a journey far from the comforts of screenside, out into the middle of an increasingly arctic night right up in the enemy's face.

Back on the Thruway, Grisha replacing Misha behind the wheel now, "They've got to have pretty tight security up there," Maxine as if it's just occurred to her, "how are you planning to get past it?"

"Yeah," Tallis shifting into a cheery tough-moppet voice, "are you gonna go crashing in the gate?"

Misha pushes up a sleeve, revealing one of his prison tats, Ever-Virgin Mary Mother of God holding her baby, Jesus, on whose forehead at about third-eye position Maxine now can just detect a little bump about the size of a zit, which babies aren't supposed to have. "Transponder implant," Misha explains. "We found out from social-engineering cute *nyashetchka* we met in bar."

"Tiffany," Grisha recalls.

"Everybody who works for hashslingrz gets one of these, so Security can track them wherever they go."

Wait a minute. "My sister's husband has been walking around with a tracking implant? Since—"

Shrug, "Couple months. Even Ice Man himself has one. You didn't know that?"

"You, Tallis?"

"Only till I could get my dermatologist back from St. Maarten's to take it out."

"And when you went dark, Hubby never said anything?"

The cute fingernail. "I guess I wasn't thinking past Chazz and me, and how to keep it from Gabe."

"Once again, Tallis," Maxine doesn't want to be the bully here, but the news isn't penetrating. "Gabe knew, he planned the whole thing, of course he didn't make an issue." Stubborn kid. She wonders how March ever dealt with this.

The interior of the limo has picked up a Gaussian blur from the smoke of inexpensive cigar tobacco and high-priced weed. Things grow merry. Not to mention less cautious. The boys admit, for one thing, that their tattoos aren't quite legit. Seems that back in Russia, having been popped actually for minor hacker beefs under Article 272, illegal access, they were never inside for long enough to rate real prison tattoos, so later on had to settle drunkenly instead for a Brooklyn ink parlour that does knockoffs for those who wish to appear more dangerous than they are. In a passage of lighthearted back-and-forth, Misha and Grisha discuss who is more of a wannabe badass than whom, during which the Bizons get waved around, Maxine has to hope rhetorically.

"According to Igor last time we talked," Maxine schnozzing right ahead, "this beef between you people and Ice isn't KGB business—"

"Igor doesn't know about this thing tonight."

"Of course not, Misha. Let's say he has deniability and you guys are strictly on your own here. I'm still wondering why you aren't doing it from a little further away, like on the Internet. Overflow exploit, denial of service, whatever."

"Too institutional. Hacker-school approach. Grisha and I are close-up type of scumbags. You didn't notice? More personal this way."

"So if it's personal . . ." She doesn't quite mention Lester Traipse, but a crinkled, almost-kind look, the sort of expression Stalin liked to beam at you in his publicity shots, has crept into Misha's eyes.

"Isn't only Lester. Please. Ice has this coming, you know it, we all know it. But better you don't have full history."

Deimos-and-Phobos gamer machismo, legitimate avenging angels, what? Maybe it is about more than Lester tonight, but isn't Lester enough? whatever he saw that he shouldn't've, the visitation that meant his end rising spooky and vaporous above the spreadsheets of secret cash flow, was something that couldn't be allowed out among civilians. . . .

"OK, but how about a *little* history?"

The fellows exchange a mischievous look. Anasha can do funny things to a man. Even to two men.

"You heard about HALO jump." Misha sez. "Igor tells story to everybody."

"Especially cute women." sez Grisha.

"Was not HALO jump, however. Was HAHO jump."

"That's . . . laughing all the way down, no wait, High Altitude . . ."

"High Opening. Chutes open, maybe 27,000 feet, you and your unit can fly 30, 40 miles, all stacked up in sky, lowest guy carries GLONASS receiver—"

"Like Russian GPS. One night Igor is on insertion job, everything gets fucked up, *praporschik* freaks out from no oxygen, wind spreads everybody over half Caucasus, GLONASS quits working. Igor gets down OK, but now he's all by himself. No idea where or if base camp is set up. Uses compass and map to try and find rest of his unit. Days later, smells something. Little village, totally like massacred. Young, old, dogs, everybody."

"Torched. That's when Igor has soul crisis."

"He doesn't only get out of Spetsnaz—when he has enough money, he sets up his own private reparation plan."

"Sending money to the Chechens?" wonders Maxine, "this isn't considered treason?"

"It's a lot of money, and by then Igor is well protected. He even thinks abut converting to Islam, but there's too many problems. War ends, second war starts, some of people he's been helping are now guerrillas. Situation has grown complicated. There are Chechens and there are Chechens."

"Some good guys, some not so good."

Names of resistance organizations that Maxine can't keep straight. But now, well, not exactly a lightbulb—more like the glowing end of an El Producto—goes on over her head.

"So the money Lester was diverting from Ice—"

"Was going to bad guys, by way of Wahhabist bullshit front. Igor knew how to reach money before it would get all mixed up in Emirates account. He expedites matters for Lester, takes little commission. Everything *dzhef*, till somebody finds out."

"Ice?"

"Whoever is running Ice? You tell us."

"And Lester . . ." Maxine realizes she has blurted.

"Lester was like little hedgehog in fog. Only trying to find his friends."

"Poor Lester."

What, now it's all gonna go saline, here?

"Exit 18," Misha announces instead, exhaling smoke, eyes gleaming, "Poughkeepsie." And not a moment too soon.

The train station's just over the bridge. Waiting in the parking lot is Yuri, a cheerful athletic type leaning against a Hummer bearing stigmata from a long history of hard road, behind it a sizable trailer with a generator for the pulse weapon. From RV generators she's seen, Maxine estimates 10, 15,000 watts. "Ten-percent power" may be a figure of speech.

They're in time to catch the 10:59 to New York. "So long, boys," Maxine waves, "go safe, can't say I really approve, I know if my own kids ever got hold of a vircator . . ."

"Here, don't forget this," discreetly handing her back the Beretta.

"You realize you've just made Tallis and me accessories to some criminal, probably even terrorist, act."

The *padonki* exchange a hopeful glance. "You think so?"

"First of all, it's federal, hashslingrz is an arm of U.S. security—"

"They don't want to hear about this right now," Tallis dragging her down the platform. "Fuckin dweebs."

The boys wave out the windows as they pull away. *"Do svidanya Maksi! Poka, byelokurva!"*

41

In the train on the way back, Maxine must've fallen asleep. She dreams she's still in the ZiL. The landscape out the windows has frozen to deep Russian midwinter, snowfields under a piece of moon, illumination from the olden days of sleigh travel. A snow-inundated village, a church spire, a gas station shut for the night. Crossfade to Brothers Karamazov, Doctor Zhivago and others, covering their winter distances like this, frictionless, faster than anything else, suddenly you can get more than one errand done per trip, a breakthrough in romantic technology. Somewhere between Lake Heatsink and Albany, across the dark wilderness, a fleet of black SUVs now with only their fog lights lit, on the way to intercept. Maxine falls into an exitless loop, the dream as she surfaces turning into a spreadsheet she can't follow. She wakes up around Spuyten Duyvil to Tallis's sleeping face, closer to her own than you'd expect, as if sometime in sleep their faces had been even closer.

They roll into Grand Central about 1:00 A.M., hungry. "Guess the Oyster Bar is closed."

"Maybe the apartment is safe by now," Tallis offers, not believing it herself, "come on back, we'll find something."

What they find, actually, is a good reason to leave again. Soon as they step out of the elevator they can hear Elvis-movie music. "Uh-oh," Tallis looking for her keys. Before she can find them, the door is flung open and a less-than-towering presence starts in with the emotions. Behind him on a screen Shelley Fabares is dancing around holding a sign announcing I'M EVIL.

"What's this?" Maxine knows what it is, she chased him across half Manhattan not so long ago.

"This is Chazz, who isn't even supposed to know about this place."

"Love will find a way," Chazz replies, jive-assingly.

"You're here because we broke the spy camera."

"You kiddin, I hate them things, darlin, if I'd known, I would've broke it myself."

"Go back, Chazz, tell your pimp it's no sale."

"Please just give me a minute, Sugar, I confess at first it was all strictly business, but—"

"Don't call me 'Sugar'."

"Nutrasweet! I'm pleading here."

Ah, the big, or actually midsize, lug. Tallis stalks on headshaking into the kitchen.

"Chazz, hi," Maxine waving as if from a distance, "nice to meet you finally, read your rap sheet, fascinating stuff, tell me, how'd a Title 18 Hall of Famer end up in the fiber business?"

"All 'at old misbehavior, ma'am? try and rise above it 'stead of judgin me, maybe you'll notice a pattern?"

"Let's see, strong background in sales."

Nodding amiably, "You try and hit 'em when they're too disoriented to think. Last year when the tech bubble popped? Darklinear started hirin big time. Made a man feel like some kind of a draft pick."

"At the same time, Chazz," Tallis, switched briefly to her Doormat setting, fetching beers, dips, snacks in bags, "my ex-husband-to-be wasn't paying your employer that much just to keep little me busy."

"He really is just buyin fiber's all it is, totally a fatpipe person, payin top dollar, tryin to nail down as many miles of cable as he can get, outside plant, premises, first it was just in the Northeast, now it's anywhere out in the U.S.—"

"Tidy consultation fees," Maxine imagines.

"There you go. And it's legal too, maybe even more than some of the stuff . . ." pausing to downshift.

"Oh, go ahead, Chazz, you were never shy about the contempt you felt for me, Gabe, the business we're in."

"Real and make-believe's all I ever meant, my artificial sweetener, I'm just a logistics- and infrastructure-type fella. Fiber's real, you pull it through conduit, you hang it, you bury it and splice it. It weighs somethin. Your husband's rich, maybe even smart, but he's like all you people, livin in this dream, up in the clouds, floatin in the bubble, think 'at's real, think again. It's only gonna be there long as the power's on. What happens when the grid goes dark? Generator fuel runs out and they shoot down the satellites, bomb the operation centers, and you're all back down on planet Earth again. All that jabberin about nothin, all 'at shit music, all 'em links, down, down and gone."

Maxine has a moment's image of Misha and Grisha, surfers from some strange Atlantic coast, waiting with their boards far out on the winter ocean, in the dark, waiting for the wave no one else besides Chazz and maybe a couple others will see coming.

Chazz reaches again for the jalapeño chips, and Tallis snatches the bag away. "No more for you. Just good night already, and go tell Gabe whatever you're going to tell him."

"Can't, 'cause I quit working for him. Ain't about to be the clown in his rodeo no more."

"Sounds good, Chazz. You're here on your own, then, all because of me, how sweet is that?"

"Because of you, and because of what it was doing to me. Guy was beginnin to feel like a drain on my spirits."

"Funny, that's what my mother always said about him."

"I know you and your mama have been on the outs, but you should really find some way to fix 'at, Tallis."

"Excuse me, it's two A.M. here, daytime TV doesn't start for a while yet."

"Your mama is the most important person in your life. The only one who can get the potatoes mashed exactly the way you need 'em to be. Only one who understood when you started hangin with people she couldn't stand. Lied about your age down to the multiplex so's you could go watch 'em teen slasher movies together. She'll be gone soon enough, appreciate her while you can."

And he's out the door. Maxine and Tallis stand looking at each other. The King croons on. "I was going to advise 'Dump him,'" Maxine pensive, "while shaking you back and forth . . . but now I think I'll just settle for the shaking part."

HORST IS NODDED OUT on the couch in front of *The Anton Chekhov Story*, starring Edward Norton, with Peter Sarsgaard as Stanislavski. Maxine tries to tiptoe on into the kitchen, but Horst, not being domestic, tuned to motel rhythms even in his sleep, flounders awake. "Maxi, what the heck."

"Sorry, didn't mean to—"

"Where've you been all night?"

Not yet having slid far enough into delusion to answer this literally, "I was hanging out with Tallis, she and the schmuck just parted ways, she's got a new place, she was happy to have some company."

"Right. And she hasn't had a telephone put in yet. So what about your mobile? Oh—the battery ran down, I bet."

"Horst, what's the matter?"

"Who is it, Maxi, I'd rather hear now than later."

Aahhh! Maybe last night the vircator in the trunk of the ZiL came on by accident? and she got zapped around by some secondary lobe from it, which hasn't worn off yet? Because she finds herself now declaring, with every reason to believe it's true, "There is nobody but you, Horst. Emotionally challenged fuckin ox. Never will be."

One tiny unblocked Horstical receptor is able to pick up this message for what it is, so he doesn't lapse totally into Midwest Ricky Ricardo after all, only grabs his head in that familiar free-throw way and begins to unfocus the complaining a little. "Well, I called hospitals. I called cops, TV news stations, bail-bond companies, then I started in on your Rolodex. What are you doing with Uncle Dizzy's home number?"

"We check in from time to time, he thinks I'm his parole officer."

"A-and what about that Italian guy you go to karaoke joints with?"

"One time, Horst, one group booking, nothing I'm about to repeat anytime soon."

"Hah! Not 'soon,' but sometime, right? I'll be sitting at home, overeating to compensate, you'll be out on that happy scene, red dress, 'Can't Smile Without You,' showcase duets, gym instructors from the other side of some bridge or tunnel—"

Maxine takes off her coat and scarf and decides to stay a couple of minutes. "Horst. Baby. We'll go down to K-Town some night and do that, OK? I'll find a red dress someplace. Can you sing harmony?"

"Huh?" Puzzled, as if everybody knows. "Sure. Since I was a kid. They wouldn't let me in the church till I learned." Prompt to Maxine—add one more item to list of things you don't know about this guy . . .

They may have dozed off on the couch for a second. Suddenly it's daybreak. The Newspaper of Record splats on the floor outside the back door. The Newfoundland puppy up on 12 starts in with the separation-anxiety blues. The boys commence their daily excursions in and out of the fridge. Catching sight of their parents on the couch, they start in with some hip-hop version of the Peaches & Herb oldie "Reunited and It Feels So Good," Ziggy declaiming the lovey-dovey lyrics in the angriest black voice he can locate at this hour, while Otis does the beatboxing.

· · ·

THE LESTER TRAIPSE MEMORIAL PULSE, as Maxine will come to think of it, barely gets onto the local news upstate, forget Canadian coverage or the national wire, before being dropped into media oblivion. No tapes will survive, no logs. Misha and Grisha are likewise edited from the record of current events. Igor tosses hints that they might've been reassigned back home, even once again inside the *zona*, some numbered facility out in the Far East. Like UFO sightings, the night's events enter the realm of faith. Hill-country tavern regulars will testify that out to some unknown radius into the Adirondacks that night, all television screens went apocalyptically dark—third-act movie crises, semifamous girls in tiny outfits and spike heels schlepping somebody's latest showbiz project, sports highlights, infomercials for miracle appliances and herbal restorers of youth, sitcom reruns from more hopeful days, all forms of reality in which the basic unit is the pixel, all of it gone down without a sigh into the frozen midwatch hour. Maybe it was only the failure of one repeater up on a ridgeline, but it might as well have been the world that got reset, for that brief cycle, to the slow drumbeat of Iroquois prehistory.

AVI DESCHLER IS COMING HOME from work in a cheerier frame of mind. "The upstate server? No worries, we switched over to the one in Lapland. But the even better news," hopefully, "is I think I'm gonna get bounced."

Brooke gazes at her stomach like a geographer with a globe of the world. "But . . ."

"Nah—wait'll you hear about the compensation package."

"Look out for 'enhanced severance' language," Maxine advises, "it means you can't sue."

Gabriel Ice, not too mysteriously, has gone silent. Distracted at least, Maxine hopes.

"Tallis ought to be a little safer," she tries to reassure March. "She's a good kid, your daughter, not the nitwit she initially comes across as."

"Better than I ever gave her credit for," which does come as a surprise, Maxine having assumed that March doesn't even know how to do remorseful. "Too good for the shitty parent I've been. Remember when they were little and still held your hand in the street? I used to pull them along at my speed so they had to skip to keep up, where was I going in such a hurry I couldn't even walk with my kids?" About to go off into some act of contrition.

"Someday shitty-parent skills will be an Olympic event, the Mishpochathon, we'll see if you even qualify, meantime lose the holy face, you know you've done worse."

"Much worse. Then I refused to think about it for years. Now it's like, how can I even—"

"You want to see her more than anything. Look, you're just nervous, March, why don't you both come over to my place, it's a neutral corner, we'll have coffee, order in lunch," as it turns out from Zippy's Appetizing down on 72nd, where a person can still find for example a gigantically overstuffed rolled-beef and chicken-liver sandwich with Russian dressing on an onion roll, a rarity in this town since deep in the last century, in on the paragraph allotted it by the take-out menu Tallis instantly zooms.

"You would actually eat something like that?" March despite a warning glance from Maxine.

"Well, no Mother, I thought I'd just sit and gaze at it for a while, would that be all right?"

March thinking fast, "Only that if you do get one . . . maybe I could try just a small piece of it? Only if you could spare?"

"How long you been Jewish?" Maxine out the side of her mouth.

"Where do you think I got my eating profile?" Tallis passive-aggressively making with the fingernail. "The meals you would order in, I'd go to the door and find a *small crew* of delivery kids holding sacks—"

"Two. Maybe. And only that one time."

"Obesity, cardiac issues, tra-la-la who cares, as long as the quantity's right, eh Mother?"

This may call for some subtle intervention. "Guys," Maxine announces, "the check, we're gonna split it, OK? Maybe before it gets here, we could . . . March, you ordered the Sunrise Special with double beef bacon and sausage, plus the latkes and applesauce, plus the extra *side* of latkes and—"

"That's mine," sez Tallis.

"OK, and you have the rolled beef . . . the potato salad on the sandwich is another 50¢ . . ."

"But you ordered that extra pickle, so call that an offset . . ." Degenerating, as Maxine hoped it might, into the old bookkeepers-at-lunch exercise, God forbid there should be real cash on a real table, which, while consuming energy useful elsewhere, is still worth it if it keeps everybody grounded, somehow, in reality. The downside, she admits, is that neither of these two is above playing this lunch strategically, trying to create anxiety enough to dampen or destroy somebody's appetite, which better not be Maxine's is all, as she herself is expecting the Turkey Pastrami Health Combo, whose menu copy promises alfalfa sprouts, portobello mushrooms, avocados, low-fat mayo, and more, in the way of redemptive add-ons. This has drawn looks of distaste from the other two, so good, good, they agree on something at least, it's a start.

Competitive math, mistakes real and tactical, figuring out the tip and how to divide up the sales tax, go on till Rigoberto buzzes up. It turns out to be only one delivery kid, but he does seem to be wheeling the food down the hall on a dolly of some kind.

Presently the entire surface of the table in the dining room is covered with containers, soda cans, waxed paper, plastic wrap, and sandwiches and side orders, and everybody is intensely fressing without regard to where, besides into mouths, it's all going. Maxine takes a short break to observe March. "What happened to 'corrupt artifact of . . .' whatever it was?"

"Yaycchhh gwaahhihucchihnggg," March nods, removing the lid from another container of coleslaw.

When face-stuffing activities slow down a bit, Maxine is thinking of how to bring up the topic of young Kennedy Ice, when the mother and grandma beat her to it. According to Tallis, her husband is now looking for custody.

"OH, no," March detonates. "No way, who's your lawyer?"

"Glick Mountainson?"

"They got me off from a libel beef once. Good saloon fighters basically. How's it looking so far?"

"They say the one bright spot is I'm not contesting the money."

"It doesn't, uh, interest you, the money?" Maxine curious more than shocked.

"Not as much as it does them—they're working on contingency. Sorry, but all I can think about is Kennedy."

"Don't apologize to me," sez March.

"Actually I should, Mom . . . keeping you guys apart all that time . . ."

"Well, full disclosure, actually we've been sneaking a couple minutes together when we can."

"Oh, he told me about that. Afraid I'd be angry."

"You weren't?"

"Gabe's problem, not mine. So we kept quiet about it."

"Sure. Wouldn't do to provoke any patriarchal anger." Maxine, seeing the further but not always useful phrase "fucking doormat" taking shape, preemptively grabs a somehow overlooked pickle and inserts it into March's mouth.

On through lunch and the fall of the afternoon, through a daylight-saving's evening too bright for the winter most NYers still think they're in. Maxine, Tallis, and March move into the kitchen, then out of the house, out onto the street, through slowly deepening streetlight over to March's place.

At some point Maxine remembers to call Horst. "This is all girls tonight, by the way."

"Did I ask?"

"OK, you're improving. I might need the Impala also."

"Will you be taking it out of state, by any chance?"

"There's some, what, federal situation?"

"Li'l risk assessment is all."

"May not come to that, just asking."

TALLIS HAPPENS TO look out the window into the street. "Shit. It's Gabe."

Maxine sees a snow-white stretch limo pulling up in front. "Looks familiar, but how do you know it's—" then she spots the well-known iterated diagonals of the hashslingrz logo, painted on the roof.

"His own personal satellite link," Tallis explains.

"The staff here are all related, sort of emeritus members of the Mara Salvatrucha," March sez, "so there shouldn't be any problem."

"If they're acquainted with the appearance of $100 bills in quantity," Tallis mutters, "Gabe will be up here before you know it."

Maxine grabs her purse, which she's happy to feel is as heavy today as it should be. "There's another way out, March?"

Service elevator to the basement, fire door out into the courtyard in back. "You guys wait down here," sez Maxine, "I'll be back with the car soon as I can."

Her local, Warpspeed Parking, is just around the corner. While they're bringing up the Impala, she runs a quick Roth IRA tutorial for Hector, the guy on the gate, whom somebody has misinformed about the virtues of converting from traditional.

"Without a penalty? Not right away, they make you wait five years, Hector, sorry."

She gets back to March's building to find everybody somehow out on the sidewalk in front, in the middle of a screaming match. Ice's chauffeur, Gunther, is waiting at the wheel of the idling limo. Far from the massive Nazi ape that Maxine was expecting, he turns out to be a per-haps overgroomed Rikers alumnus who's wearing his shades down on his nose to accommodate the extra eyelash length.

Grumbling, Maxine double-parks and joins the merriment. "March, come here."

"Soon as I kill this motherfucker."

"Don't put in," Maxine advises, "her life is her business."

Reluctantly March gets in the car while Tallis, surprisingly calm, continues her adult discussion with Ice.

"It isn't a lawyer you need, Gabe, it's a doctor."

She means mentally, but at this point Gabe isn't looking too fit ei-ther, his face all red and swollen, some trembling he can't control. "Lis-ten to me, bitch, I'll buy as many judges as I need to, but you'll never see my son again. Fuckin never."

OK, Maxine thinks, he raises a hand, time for the Beretta.

He raises a hand. Tallis avoids it easily, but the Tomcat is now in the equation.

"It doesn't happen," Ice carefully watching the muzzle.

"How's that, Gabe."

"I don't die. There's no scenario where I die."

"Batshit fuckin insane," March out the car window.

"Better hop on in there with your mom, Tallis. Gabe, that's good to hear," Maxine calm and upbeat, "and the reason you don't die? is that you come to your senses. Start thinking about this on a longer time scale and, most important, walk away."

"That's—"

"That's the scenario."

The odd thing about March's street is that it would be rejected by any movie-location scout, regardless of genre, as too well behaved. In this fold of space-time, women accessorized like Maxine do not point sidearms at people. It must be something else in her hand. She's offering him something, something of value he doesn't want to take, wants to pay him back a debt maybe, which he's pretending to forgive and will eventually accept.

"She forgot the part," March can't help hollering out the window, "where you don't get to be master of the universe, you go on being a schmuck, all kinds of competition starts coming out of the woodwork and you have to scramble to not lose market share, and your life stops being your own and belongs to the overlords you always worshipped."

Poor Gabe, he has to stand here at gunpoint and be lectured by his ex-mother-in-law-to-be, a forever-unreconstructed lefty yet.

"You guys gonna be all right?" calls Gunther. "I had tickets to *Mamma Mia*, it's nearly curtain time, I can't even scalp em now."

"Try calling it a travel and entertainment deduction anyway, Gunther. And you be nice to him too," Maxine warns Ice as he carefully backs away and gets in his limo. She waits till the elongated vehicle has made it to the corner and turned, slides behind the wheel of the Impala, cranks up the radio, which is in the middle of a Tammy Wynette set from someplace across the river, and proceeds cautiously crosstown.

"We better assume he saw your plates," sez March.

"Means an all-points bulletin."

"Killer drones, more likely."

"Precisely why," Maxine wrestling the power-steering-challenged monster up and down a number of underlit streets, "we're going to keep off bridges, out of tunnels, stay right here in town, and go hide in plain sight."

Which after a scenic spin against a deep panorama of lights down and up the West Side Highway, turns out to be Warpspeed Parking again. Glancing up in the mirror, still empty of anything but the night street, "OK if I take it down myself, Hector? You didn't see us, right?"

"D and D, *mami*."

Winding forever down into regions of older and more dilapidated brickwork, corroded from generations of car emissions. The Impala's exhaust comes into its own, like a teen vocalist in a high-school boys' room.

March lights a joint and after a while, paraphrasing Cheech & Chong, drawls, "I woulda shot him, man."

"You heard what he said. I think this is in his contract with the Death Lords he works for. He's protected. He walked away from a loaded handgun, that's all. He'll be back. Nothing's over."

"You think he meant all that about getting Kennedy away from me?" Tallis quavers.

"Might not be that easy. He'll keep running cost-benefit workups and find that there's too many people coming at him from too many different directions, the SEC, the IRS, the Justice Department, he can't buy them all off. Plus competitors friendly and otherwise, hacker guerrillas, sooner or later those billions will start to dwindle, and if he has any sense, he'll pack up and split for someplace like Antarctica."

"I hope not," sez March, "global warming's not bad enough? The penguins—"

Maybe it's this Luxury Lounge interior—forty years down the road with the not-yet-damped vibrations of Midwest teen fantasies that've worked their way into the grain of the metallic turquoise vinyl, the loop-carpet floor mats, the ashtrays overflowing with ancient cigarette butts, some with lipstick shades not sold for years, each with a history of some romantic vigil, some high-speed pursuit, whatever Horst saw in this rolling museum of desire when he answered the ad in the *Pennysaver* back whenever it was, set and setting, as Dr. Tim always liked to say, now, presently, has wrapped them, brought them in from the unprofitable drill-fields of worry about the future, here inside, to repose, to un-furrowing, each eventually to her own dreams.

Next thing anybody knows, it's morning. Maxine is slouched across the front seat, and March and Tallis are waking up in back, and everybody feels creaky.

They ascend to the street, where once again, overnight, all together, pear trees have exploded into bloom. Even this time of year, there could still be snow, it's New York, but for now the brightness in the street is from flowers on trees whose shadows are texturing the sidewalks. It's their moment, the year's great pivot, it'll last for a few days, then all collect in the gutters.

The Piraeus Diner is coming off another overnight of dope-scourged hipsters, funseekers who have failed to hook up, night owls who've missed the last trains back to the suburbs. Refugees from the sunless half of the cycle. Whatever it was they thought they needed, coffee, a cheeseburger, a kind word, the light of dawn, they've kept watch, stayed awake and caught sight of it at least, or nodded off and missed it once again.

Maxine has a quick cup of coffee and leaves March and Tallis with a tableful of breakfast to revisit their food issues. Heading back to the apartment to pick up the boys and see them to school, she notices a reflection in a top-floor window of the gray dawn sky, clouds moving across a blear of light, unnaturally bright, maybe the sun, maybe something else. She looks east to see what it might be, but whatever it is shining there is still, from this angle, behind the buildings, causing them to inhabit their own shadows. She turns the corner onto her block and leaves the question behind. It isn't till she's in the elevator of her building that she begins to wonder, actually, whose turn it is to take the kids to school. She's lost track.

Horst is semiconscious in front of Leonardo DiCaprio in "The Fatty Arbuckle Story," and does not look street-ready. The boys have been waiting for her, and of course that's when she flashes back to not so long ago down in DeepArcher, down in their virtual hometown of Zigotisopolis, both of them standing just like this, folded in just this precarious light, ready to step out into their peaceable city, still safe from the spiders and bots that one day too soon will be coming for it, to claim-jump it in the name of the indexed world.

"Guess I'm running a little late, guys."

"Go to your room," Otis shrugging into his backpack and out the door, "you are, like, so grounded."

Ziggy surprising her with an unsolicited air kiss, "See you later at pickup, OK?"

"Give me a second, I'll be right with you."

"It's all right, Mom. We're good."

"I know you are, Zig, that's the trouble." But she waits in the doorway as they go on down the hall. Neither looks back. She can watch them into the elevator at least.

ABOUT THE AUTHOR

THOMAS PYNCHON is the author of *V.*, *The Crying of Lot 49*, *Gravity's Rainbow*, *Slow Learner*, a collection of short stories, *Vineland*, *Mason & Dixon*, *Against the Day*, and, most recently, *Inherent Vice*. He received the National Book Award for *Gravity's Rainbow* in 1974.

A NOTE ABOUT THE TYPE

This text of this book
is set in Dante MT Std.
The display is set
in Knockout.